About the A

New Zealander **Alison Roberts** has written more than eighty romance novels for Mills & Boon. She has also worked as a primary school teacher, a cardiology research technician, and a paramedic. Currently, she is living her dream of living – and writing – in a gorgeous village in the south of France.

Born and raised just outside of Toronto, Ontario, **Amy Ruttan** fled the big city to settle down with the country boy of her dreams. After the birth of her second child, Amy was lucky enough to realise her lifelong dream of becoming a romance author. When she's not furiously typing away at her computer, she's a mum to three wonderful children who use her as a personal taxi and chef.

Teresa Southwick lives with her husband in Las Vegas, the city that reinvents itself every day. An avid fan of romance novels, she is delighted to be living out her dream of writing for Mills & Boon.

Fake Dating

Fake Dating:

Doctor's Orders

ALISON ROBERTS

AMY RUTTAN

TERESA SOUTHWICK

MILLS & BOON

First Published in Great Britain 2024
by Mills & Boon, an imprint of HarperCollins*Publishers* Ltd,
1 London Bridge Street, London, SE1 9GF

www.harpercollins.co.uk

HarperCollins*Publishers*
Macken House, 39/40 Mayor Street Upper,
Dublin 1, D01 C9W8, Ireland

Fake Dating: Doctor's Orders © 2024 Harlequin Enterprises ULC.

From Venice with Love © 2013 Alison Roberts
Perfect Rivals... © 2016 Harlequin Enterprises ULC.
The Doctor's Dating Bargain © 2013 Teresa Southwick

Special thanks and acknowledgement are given to Amy Ruttan for her contribution to *The Hollywood Hills Clinic* series.

ISBN: 978-0-263-32301-6

FROM VENICE WITH LOVE

ALISON ROBERTS

To Fi, with lots of love.
Here's to friendship. And memories xxx

CHAPTER ONE

THE SOUND OF more than one person shouting got steadily louder as Nico Moretti turned into the narrow Venetian alleyway that would get him to his destination a little faster.

He tried to ignore the sound. He was in a hurry and it wasn't as if the sound of shouting was anything unusual for a large Italian city but he could feel his frown deepening. It was a disturbing echo of what was already occupying too much of his head.

The noise was loud enough to have people stopping in the street now. Turning their heads and asking each other what they thought it might be about. The slowing pace and knots of people forming made it harder to move forward and Nico heard a growl of frustration escape his own throat.

He could tell them what it was about if he had either the time or the inclination. It was about people who wanted different things. People who were passionate about what they believed in. People who weren't prepared to even try and understand each other and left broken lives in their wakes. But he didn't have the inclination. Not when he felt so out of place in this city of his birth and with the sound of his childhood lan-

guage surrounding him and reinforcing that exclusion. And he certainly didn't have the time. Not when the real reason for his return to Venice was due to start in less than thirty minutes.

At least he had the advantage of his height. And plenty of practice in cutting through obstructions to get to the heart of an emergency. All he needed to do was take on the mantle of an expert consultant en route to an urgent call in an emergency department or at an accident scene.

'Scusi.' The word was a command, not a request, and, as always, it had the desired effect. A path appeared through the gathering crowd. Those closest to him actually stopped talking to stare at him but that only made the sound of whatever was happening ahead clearer.

Whatever it was about, it wasn't simply a misunderstanding or disagreement. There was a language barrier as well. He could hear English being spoken by a forceful, female voice.

'Stand back. Don't move him yet. Call an ambulance. *Ambulanza.'*

More shouting. In Italian. Had someone called an ambulance? Where was it? Why wasn't it here yet? They were right beside the Grand Canal, for heaven's sake. Practically a highway in Venice. Where were the police? Where was a doctor when you needed one?'

'Sì.' The English woman had understood something in the furore. *'Dottoressa.* I'm a doctor. Let me get close. I have to find out if he's breathing.'

'He's not,' someone close to Nico muttered. 'He's dead. He has to be, falling off the roof like that. He must have broken his sorry neck. Who does that En-

glish woman think she is? An angel who can work some kind of miracle?'

'It's almost Christmas,' a black-clad Italian grandmother said sagely. 'A good time for a miracle to happen.'

'*Scusi.*' Nico schooled himself not to show any personal frustration as he recognised the inevitability of what he had to do. He raised his voice and spoke in Italian. 'I'm a doctor. Let me through. What's going on?'

Charlotte Highton heard the commanding male voice that overrode the almost hysterical barrage of Italian around her. She could also hear the faint sound of a siren. Please, God, she breathed. Let that be an ambulance.

Getting caught up in an accident scene had been the last thing she'd needed after getting lost in the back alleys of Venice, trying to take a shortcut to her destination near St Mark's Square, but what could she have done? She'd seen the man fall from the scaffolding. More than that. She'd been caught by the way he had been doubled over and clutching at his chest seconds before he'd fallen. There was no chance of him surviving any injuries the fall might have caused if he'd already been in cardiac arrest before it had happened.

But they wouldn't let her near and precious seconds were being lost. One of the man's workmates was probably the first-aid officer for the building company and he'd decided that the fall had caused a spinal injury. He was holding the victim's head still and shouting at anybody who so much as bumped the unconscious body.

Now he was shouting in response to a query from the newcomer, who Charlotte couldn't see because

other people were also trying to tell him the story and some were gesticulating madly—pointing to the roof of the house and circling their arms in the air to represent the fall. For a crazy moment Charlotte almost smiled.

Here she was in this beautiful, ancient city with the water of a canal lapping almost at her feet. Surrounded by the sounds of a language she loved but had never had the time to learn. Caught by the passionate involvement of people who were, for the most part, probably complete strangers to the unfortunate man who had fallen. This would never happen in England. It was *so* Italian.

Then a single, curt word from the newcomer and everybody fell silent. And shifted enough to make an opening. The man who stepped in to fill the gap was as Italian as everything else. Tall and dark. Strong featured and exuding a masculinity that was supremely confident. Such a stereotype that, for another crazy moment, Charlotte was sure she'd met him before.

Or maybe she just recognised that kind of confidence. It didn't come from any awareness of his effect on women. This kind of quiet power came from being in a situation where he knew exactly what needed to be done.

'You're a doctor?'

'Yes.'

'And you speak English?'

'Yes. I'm a specialist in emergency neurology.' He was bending over the unconscious man now. 'Did you see the fall? Has he been moved at all?'

'Yes, I saw the fall.' Charlotte was right behind the man and she was reaching for the victim's neck. The newcomer caught her wrist in a grip that was as power-

ful as everything else about this man. His confidence. His voice. The eyes that were locked on hers right now.

'What do you think you're doing?'

'I *saw* him fall.' Charlotte spoke the way she would to anyone who was preventing her doing her job. Or some unfortunate junior doctor who was getting the basics dangerously wrong. 'I saw him *before* he fell. He clearly had severe chest pain. He didn't trip. He *collapsed*. I need to see whether he's got a pulse.'

For a stunned heartbeat the dark eyes continued to hold hers. Charlotte could see how swift his comprehension was. She actually felt the moment when he stepped back from confronting her action and they became a team. He let go of her wrist.

Rapid instructions in Italian followed. The Italian specialist took over holding the man's head and guided a log roll that had the patient on his back with his airway opened in an admirably short space of time. The nearby siren was getting louder but it wasn't yet close enough. Charlotte was crouched with her cheek against the patient's mouth, one hand on his neck with her fingers searching for a pulse and the other resting gently on his diaphragm seeking the movement that would indicate breathing.

'Nothing,' she snapped. She wasn't exactly dressed for performing CPR. She had to hoist up her slim-fitting skirt so that she could kneel on the rough cobblestones of the alleyway. Her equally neat-fitting blouse beneath the skirt's matching blazer hadn't been designed for vigorous movement either. Charlotte felt a seam ripping within the first seconds of pushing her body weight down hard enough to depress the chest of the large man.

Her unexpected medical colleague was still com-
municating in Italian to those around him. Explaining
what was going on perhaps. And then he was showing
the person who'd been guarding his patient so effec-
tively from Charlotte how to support the man's cervical
spine but do a jaw thrust at the same time.

As she stayed in position, with her body weight di-
rectly over her straight arms, Charlotte could look side-
ways. She saw the way he demonstrated the required
position, with his large hands splayed, the palms push-
ing against the angle of the man's jaw and his thumbs
resting on his cheeks. She knew the pressure required
to keep that kind of hold and yet he made it look like
he was being gentle with the critically ill patient.

And then he let the first-aider take over the hold and
shifted so that he was kneeling right beside Charlotte.
The shafts of pain from the movement of her knees on
the cobblestones seemed to fade as his body lined up
so close beside hers their arms were touching.

That eye contact was extraordinary. Reassuring and
encouraging at the same time. The almost invisible
movement of his head told Charlotte that he was in sync
with what she was doing. That he was ready for her to
pause so that he could deliver a breath. With an equally
subtle nod, Charlotte began counting aloud. She had
no idea how many compressions she'd done already
but it was standard international protocol to deliver
two breaths for every thirty compressions and a lead-
in was given so that minimum pumping time was lost.

'Twenty-eight, twenty-nine…thirty.' Charlotte raised
her hands and sat back on her heels as her CPR partner
bent down, pinching the man's nose and covering his
mouth with his own. She watched the man's chest rise

and fall. Twice. And then she was back in position and the compressions continued smoothly.

Wow. Not only could this guy get air into someone without disturbing the protected position of a C spine, he was prepared to do mouth-to-mouth resuscitation on a stranger. A risk very few medical people would be prepared to take these days. And compressions were deemed the more important component of CPR now. If an ambulance was on its way and the compressions were effective, you had a window of ten minutes or so before the lack of extra oxygen would cause irreversible brain damage.

Charlotte was impressed. She was also sweating despite the deep chill of Venice in December, and her knees felt as if someone had attacked them with a baseball bat. She'd never been more grateful to hear the sound of a siren so close. Looking up, as she paused to let another two breaths be delivered, she was astonished to see that it was a jet boat, arriving on the canal, complete with flashing beacons and a uniformed paramedic, with a defibrillator in his hand, waiting to jump ashore.

She knew better than to stop what she was doing and wait for these emergency medics to take over the scene. Automatically, she rocked forward, her hands back in position on the centre of the man's chest with one flat and the other locked around the wrist to give her extra strength as she pushed down and began the count that would remain silent until the warning of breaths needed.

One...two...three...

Nico could hear the shouts of the paramedics arriving and securing the ambulance. Thank goodness! The dis-

comfort of kneeling on cold, hard cobbles to perform CPR was truly unbearable.

Not that the English woman was showing any signs of discomfort. Nico had been watching her, waiting for the signal to deliver another couple of breaths but also because she was so…so *in control*. So very British.

She had that English peaches and cream type of complexion and the kind of reserve that always felt so foreign to Nico, but he had spent so many years away from Italy it was very familiar. So familiar, in fact, that he could imagine he'd met this woman before. He'd certainly met the type.

Virtually the exact opposite of the type of women he preferred.

It was perhaps unfortunate that he'd inherited his father's taste in women. He liked them small and dark, curvy and vivacious. With an appetite for life and fun that could negate any tendency to take life too seriously out of working hours. But as long as he didn't make his father's mistake of marrying a woman like this, he wouldn't end up abandoned and broken-hearted when someone on another continent offered something more exciting. Like when his father's beloved Irish wife had simply taken their only child and made off for greener pastures.

Nico shook off the thought. Normally, snippets of family history would never distract him from a situation like this but his mind had been full of it until the moment he'd intervened in this rescue scene. Even now, he was aware of the small object in his pocket that the solicitor had insisted he take with him. It should be small enough to dismiss out of hand but unfortunately it carried a significance that could never be dismissed.

He had to push it firmly to one side right now, however. After a second glance to reassure himself that the paramedics were coming in the right direction, Nico took another look at the woman who hadn't missed a beat in performing the chest compressions.

Strands of her blonde hair had worked themselves loose thanks to her current physical exertion but the rest of it was still tightly bound into an intricate kind of knot that removed the feminine allure of long tresses. She had grey eyes that could have looked attractively smoky but she was so focused on the clinical aspects of this situation that they were devoid of an identifiable emotion.

Even now, as the paramedics set up the defibrillator and prepared to take over the management of this patient, he couldn't detect any sign of relief or distress, perhaps, that she'd been caught up in this traumatic event. She was watching what the paramedics were doing with hawk-like intensity. She might not speak Italian but Nico had the distinct impression that she wouldn't hesitate to correct these medics if she felt things were not being done to an expected standard.

He filled them in as they attached the patches to the man's chest. He provided the cervical spine support as preparations were made to secure the airway and the first shock was delivered, but then a second crew arrived, along with the police, and Nico found himself stepping back and merely watching, along with the crowd of people the police couldn't manage to disperse.

The English doctor was in the same position. Nico saw her tucking the hem of her blouse back into the tight waistband of her skirt. He noticed the holes in her tights and the red, grazed skin of her knees. He could

feel the ache in his own joints and it gave him an oddly powerful feeling of connection with this stranger. He tried to catch her eye and smile but she was looking at her watch and frowning, as though she was running late for something.

And then she looked over her shoulder and her frown deepened. Whatever she was looking for was obscured by the crowd of people who were watching in fascination as the resuscitation scene reached fever pitch.

The man's airway was secured and a paramedic was delivering oxygen via a bag mask unit. An IV line was in place and drugs had been administered. And then the shout was given to stand clear and another shock was delivered.

There was a collective gasp from the onlookers as the man's body jerked in response to the shock and then silence fell as everybody held their breath. Only those closest could see the blip on the screen of the life pack and then another and another as the rhythm picked up. One of the paramedics felt the neck of the patient and grinned at his colleague.

'We have a pulse.'

A cheer went up from the crowd and the atmosphere only became more excited as the emergency services prepared to transport the man to hospital as quickly as possible. People were moving away in response to the shouted instructions of the police officer and Nico saw the English woman disappearing behind others.

He couldn't let her vanish. Somebody had to thank her for her contribution to saving the man's life.

'*Scusi.*' Again, Nico pushed his way through the human obstruction. He was going against the flow to-

wards the canal and where they were trying to manoeuvre the stretcher that now carried the still-unconscious man into the ambulance, but that was also the direction in which the woman was going. She was still looking for something, her head bent as she peered around people, and suddenly Nico spotted what she was after. A black laptop case, propped against the wooden piling the ambulance launch had been tied up to.

He could get to it first. She'd have to stop and talk to him then and he could thank her. Get her address, maybe, and then follow up on the patient and let her know the outcome. With a determined effort Nico stepped in front of a man and reached for the case. He had it in his hand when someone bumped into him from behind with such force that his hand simply opened. The case fell, bounced on the cobbles and fell again, in a graceful arc, to land in the canal. For a second or two it floated on the surface. And then it sank.

Charlotte watched the laptop case disappear under the murky water of the canal, its disappearance hastened by the wash of the ambulance as it took off with its beacons flashing and siren sounding.

If she took her shoes and jacket off...

Good grief...was she actually considering diving in to try and retrieve it before it sank too far?

The downward glance towards her shoes had hammered home the reality of what was happening. Straightening and dusting off her skirt after she'd got to her feet hadn't cured the creases and streaks of grime. Her tights were shredded and one knee was grazed enough for a trickle of blood to be obvious.

Her armour had been dented.

But worse than that—far, far worse than that—her shield had been ripped away from her and destroyed.

'Oh…my…God…' Charlotte had about a heartbeat before she knew the fear would try and kick in.

The man was turning towards her, clearly appalled at what had just happened.

She couldn't let him see her fear. Couldn't let anybody see it because if they did it would become real. It would take over and she would be sucked back into that place where she was utterly powerless. Where she became nobody.

It wasn't going to happen. Charlotte fought back, gathering fury as if it could repair the amour. Replace the shield.

'You *idiot*,' she snapped. 'Have you *any* idea what you've just done?'

The dark eyes widened, startled by her ferocity.

'I'm so sorry,' he said. But the apology in his eyes was being replaced by something more like astonishment. Anger, even, at being attacked for something that had clearly been an accident.

Charlotte knew that. She'd seen the person behind being pushed and stumbling, only prevented from falling by the safety barrier this man's back had provided. It didn't help, though, knowing that the action had not been deliberate. How could it, when the effect was the same?

'That laptop has my presentation on it,' Charlotte snapped. 'The presentation I'm supposed to be delivering to an international symposium in…' She jerked her gaze to her wrist. 'In exactly *ten* minutes.'

His face was changing again, along with the expression in his eyes. He was putting pieces of a puz-

zle together with the same kind of swiftness that had been obvious when they had become a team, working in sync to try and save the life of the unfortunate man who'd fallen from the scaffolding in the wake of his cardiac arrest.

They weren't a team now. They were on different sides of a battle and Charlotte felt as if she was fighting for her life. He couldn't possibly understand how important this was to her but he obviously knew more than she would have expected.

'Not by any chance the symposium on critical interventions in the emergency department? Being held at the Bonvecchiata hotel?'

'Yes. I'm Dr Charlotte Highton. Due to open the symposium in…' Charlotte had to swallow hard '…*eight* minutes.'

'*You're* Charlotte Highton?'

'Yes.' Charlotte glared at the stranger, who was looking at her as if he'd seen a ghost. As if he couldn't believe she was who she'd said she was.

He gave his head a sharp shake. And then he held out his hand. 'Dr Nicholas Moretti,' he told her. 'Nico. We've met before. Twice, in fact. At St Margaret's Hospital in London. And that night at The Cosmopolitan Club. It was a few years ago now…' His voice trailed off. He was frowning and still staring as if he could barely recognise her. As if he couldn't make sense of what he was seeing.

Well…no surprises there. He was talking about a lifetime ago. She'd been a different person then.

A person she couldn't afford to be reminded of because it would only make this situation even worse. How incredibly unfortunate was this? To not only lose

the protection she depended on but to meet someone who had known her back then? Before...

Before her life had turned so sharply it had virtually doubled back on itself to take the path she was now on.

For just a moment Charlotte could remember what it had been like at that crossroad.

She could feel the fear.

She didn't remember meeting him. Oh...she'd felt the beat of familiarity when she'd seen him. She probably *would* remember him if she allowed her mind to go back to that time. To when she'd been the rising star of a prestigious London hospital and her academic brilliance had been enough to erase the shadows of a painfully shy youth. To when she'd had the world at her feet and she had been courted by albeit distant royalty and wined and dined at places like The Cosmopolitan Club.

A time that it hadn't even occurred to her that she might be reminded of today.

Not only reminded of but stripped of any protection she would normally have to ward it off. How long had it been since she'd felt this vulnerable?

To Charlotte's *absolute* horror, she could actually feel the prickle of tears at the back of her eyes. Tears that could unleash weakness that might undo her completely. She blinked. Hard. She dragged her gaze away from yet another expression she could read in this man's eyes. He had such an open face. He was probably a very nice person but she didn't need anyone to be *concerned* about her.

She could look after herself. And succeed. She'd learned that long ago.

A police officer had come to stand beside them. This man who had an Italian name that matched his

looks but who, curiously, spoke perfect English with an Irish accent, translated his query.

'He wants to know if you need assistance of any kind.'

A snort of something akin to laughter escaped Charlotte. She alone was the only person who could provide the kind of assistance she needed right now. Unless by some miracle a police diving team could be available within seconds and an even more impressive miracle would reveal a laptop that could survive total submersion.

But a rapid conversation in Italian led to the police officer nodding and indicating, with a wave of his arm, that Charlotte should follow him.

Nick was also following. 'He's going to take us to the symposium venue,' he said briskly. 'In the police launch. It will only take a few minutes.'

Charlotte looked down at her ruined clothes. She couldn't appear anywhere looking like this.

'We will explain what's happened.' His hand was on her arm, guiding her through the crowd that was only now dispersing properly. 'Please let me help if I can. I feel responsible for this unfortunate turn of events and I will do anything I can to put things right. Perhaps they can rearrange the order of the presentations. And do you have a back-up of your material?'

Having a man step in and try and solve this problem was the last thing Charlotte needed.

'Of course I do. It's on a flash drive.'

'Which is where?'

Charlotte focused as the police officer offered her a hand to step into the speed boat. She ignored the hand, climbed aboard unaided and then turned back.

She had to speak through gritted teeth. 'It's in the side pocket of the laptop case that you *threw* into the canal.'

It was a totally unjustified accusation in the wake of an obvious accident. It was also an undeserved slap in the face given that he was trying so hard to help.

But Charlotte didn't care. She couldn't afford to.

'Please don't concern yourself any further.' She turned away and nodded to the pilot of the boat, who revved the engine. Waved at him imperiously enough to indicate that speed was of the essence and it was time to leave. 'This is my problem and I will deal with it.'

Nico watched the police launch speed away down the canal.

He could walk to the venue in only a few minutes longer than the boat trip would take. He hadn't actually told her that he was booked to attend the symposium himself so he couldn't really take offence that he hadn't been invited to share the ride.

Besides…he needed a few minutes to try and get his head around this extraordinary development.

She might not remember him but he remembered Charlotte Highton very well indeed. He'd been looking forward to seeing what that dynamic young doctor was like further down the track of her brilliant career.

Not that she'd been his type when he'd met her all those years ago but he'd been able to appreciate her attributes. The soft femininity that had been such a delightful contrast to the skill and intelligence she'd radiated as a young clinician. The sparkle of a woman who'd had the world and most of its men at her feet.

Now she was a female clinician who exuded power and control. There wasn't even the slightest hint of softness.

Or emotion, other than anger.

Except…just for a moment there, when he'd told her that he'd met her before, Nico could swear he had seen real fear in her eyes. A vulnerability that had been so out of place with the external appearance of this woman that he'd thought he'd been imagining things.

What he certainly wasn't imagining was the stark contrast between the woman he remembered admiring in the past and the one he'd just encountered.

What the hell had happened to Charlotte Highton?

And what was she trying to hide?

CHAPTER TWO

'CHARLOTTE...THERE YOU ARE! Thank goodness...I've been seriously worried about what might have happened to you.' The tall, grey-haired man was hurrying towards her. As he got closer, however, his step faltered and his eyes widened. 'Oh, my goodness. What *has* happened to you?'

The hotel Bonvecchiata had a water landing for gondolas and motorboats so Charlotte had entered the foyer moments after leaping out of the police launch. She knew she looked a fright but there'd been no chance to duck into a restroom and at least tidy her hair and sponge some of the mud from her clothing. Richard Campbell, the co-ordinator of this select symposium and the man who'd invited her to open it, must have been pacing the foyer as he'd waited anxiously for her to arrive.

'Long story, Richard. I'm very sorry, but I got caught up in an emergency. A man went into cardiac arrest and fell off some scaffolding right in front of me. I had to keep up the CPR until the ambulance got there.'

Charlotte was speaking quickly but her mind was working even faster. There were about fifty people who'd been invited to attend this symposium. Where

were they? Sitting in the conference room already, drumming their fingers on the tabletops and muttering about the substandard organisation of this gathering?

Richard was an old friend. Charlotte felt terrible about letting him down like this by being late and he didn't even know the worst of it yet. How was she going to tell him that she'd lost her presentation material?

He'd noticed her gaze sweep the foyer.

'They're serving coffee and cake in the restaurant for everybody. As soon as I knew you were running late I put back the start time for half an hour. There's a couple of attendees that aren't here yet as well.'

'Oh…' Charlotte nodded. She had been given a small breathing space. Now she had to decide if there was any way in the world she could rescue the situation. 'Richard…about my opening address…'

The older man smiled. 'Catchy title. "Miracles or Mutilation?" It's caught everybody's attention already, I have to say. But, Charlotte…' Richard was frowning now, looking down at her shredded tights and grazed knees. 'Are you going to be able to deliver it?'

Richard Campbell's reputation was on the line here. There were people from all over the world who'd chosen to come to this satellite symposium—a breakaway group from the much larger conference that had finished in Rome yesterday—plus others who had chosen to come to this forum without attending the main conference. They were all leaders in the field of emergency medicine. Exceptionally busy people who would not be happy to have their precious time wasted.

Charlotte's presentation had been researched meticulously. The medical illustrations department of her university hospital had spent hours preparing the

graphics that represented the facts and figures, the trends and the controversies about cost-effectiveness. It didn't matter how phenomenal her memory was, there was no way she could do justice to her presentation.

If she could get hold of someone at St Margaret's they could find the presentation on her desk computer and email it to her, but that would take too much time. They only had a matter of hours to fit in the other presentations and discussions before the symposium dinner this evening. And someone needed to open the day's programme.

How would it look it she backed out? Even with the best excuse in the world it would still dent her reputation as a young leader in this field, and Charlotte *needed* that reputation. It was who she was. The professional Charlotte Highton was strong enough to hide the *real* Charlotte. The inadequate, shameful one who wasn't a real woman at all.

She was caught between a rock and a hard place here. If she explained that there was no way she could do this, she would tarnish her reputation with the taint of failure and that chink in her armour might never be mended. It might grow, in fact, and eventually split open and the whole world would know what she was hiding.

They might look at her the way Nico Moretti had. As if they knew she was a fraud.

Charlotte could feel her heart thumping rapidly and there was a sinking sensation in her stomach that threatened to spiral into nausea.

'I've got a small problem,' she confessed to Richard. 'I've lost my presentation. My laptop ended up in the canal.'

'Oh...Lord...' Richard shaded his eyes with his hand. 'Can you manage without it?'

Charlotte opened her mouth to tell him how unlikely that was, but before she could force the words out she was distracted by the sound of her name being called from somewhere near the reception desk.

'*Charlotte Jane Highton...*'

The voice was as familiar to her as her own but Charlotte didn't want to believe that there was yet another problem she had to deal with. She kept her gaze on Richard, who gave her a rueful smile.

'Sorry. I hadn't got around to telling you. Your grandmother's here.'

Charlotte shook her head sharply. 'No. She's not supposed to arrive until tonight. After the symposium. We're travelling back to London together tomorrow.'

But the voice was much closer now. It couldn't be ignored.

'Charlotte Jane... What on *earth* have you done to yourself, child? You look like you've been run over by a gondola.'

Charlotte closed her eyes. She might be thirty-one years old but her grandmother could make her feel like a child again in a heartbeat. Flame-haired and larger than life, Lady Geraldine Highton was never one to stand on ceremony.

'Gran...what are you doing here?'

'I'm supposed to be here. I booked a room for us tonight.'

'Yes, but you were flying in this evening.'

'I changed my flight and arrived first thing this morning. I decided I wanted to hear you speak and this

lovely man has told me I can sit in with all the translators and hear you on some headphones.'

Richard was nodding now and his smile was intended to reassure Charlotte that this problem, at least, had been dealt with. Clearly, he had been charmed by Lady Geraldine. Or intimidated. Either way, she had made arrangements that she now deemed satisfactory.

'But, Gran, you hate hearing anything about medical procedures. You've never wanted to hear me talk about my work.'

'Today's different.'

Something *was* different. With the kind of skill Charlotte found invaluable in her dealings with people in traumatic situations, she could sense that there was something important her grandmother was keeping to herself.

'I might not like hearing it,' Lady Geraldine continued, 'and I might not understand it, but it won't stop me wanting the chance to be proud of my granddaughter. Who knows? It might be the only chance I ever get.'

Yes. There was a shadow there in her grandmother's eyes. Eyes that usually sparkled with the determination to squeeze the best that life had to offer out of every opportunity. What was going on?

Charlotte knew she was staring. She also knew that her grandmother could read her like a book.

'We'll talk later,' Lady Geraldine said crisply. 'What we have to do now is get you tidied up. Thankfully, I have spare hosiery in my bag. And a hairbrush. Come on, Charlotte. Where's the nearest bathroom? There's no time to waste. You don't want to keep all these important people waiting, do you?'

'But…'

There was a plea on Richard's face now. 'You don't have to give the presentation you prepared,' he said quietly. 'I have every confidence that you can think of something to say that would be an appropriate way to open this symposium. Could you do that, Charlotte? Please?'

The space between that rock and hard place suddenly got so small that it squeezed the breath out of Charlotte's lungs. She couldn't think. Maybe because she had no choice.

'I'll do my best.'

So it was that Charlotte found herself looking almost presentable again fifteen minutes later, standing in front of a room full of people who sat at a huge, U-shaped table. Some wore headphones to receive the translation service. Most had laptops or tablets on the table in front of them, along with pads of paper, pens, pitchers of iced water and even bowls of mints.

Charlotte had nothing other than a microphone clipped to the lapel of her jacket. From the way her heart was pounding and how exposed she felt, she could have been standing here stark naked.

She tried to smile at the group but failed. She did, however, manage to introduce herself and apologise for the delay in starting.

'I'm sure you've all heard by now of the reason why I was delayed and you, more than most, will understand that emergencies happen.'

Oh, help. Charlotte could hear the sound of her own voice, magnified by the loudspeaker system. Where was the calm, professional tone she always used in public?

What would her grandmother think of this? The niggling worry that there was something wrong that her grandmother wasn't telling her couldn't be allowed to surface until this was all over but it was impossible not to have a flash of shame that the pride her only living relative had taken in her achievements was going to be dented.

'Ah…' Charlotte stared at the group, totally at a loss for what she could say next. Please, God, let the ground open and swallow me up, she thought.

The ground didn't open but the door of the conference room did, to admit a latecomer. Everybody's head turned at the interruption but Charlotte's gaze had got there first and now it was stuck.

The worst moment of her life had just taken a dive to a new low.

How on earth could Nicholas Moretti have the nerve to show up here, knowing he'd ruined her preparation for this talk? He'd already revealed his disbelief that she was who she said she was. Did he now want to see if she was going to make a fool of herself and confirm that disbelief?

He was about to get what he came for, then, wasn't he?

Nico gave a very European hand gesture, apologising for his interruption as he took the empty space at the table. His body language conveyed complete confidence that he had the right to be here, though. That he was, in fact, eager to take part in the proceedings. And then his gaze locked with Charlotte's and that weird spinning sensation in her gut seemed to catch fire.

Anger?

Quite possibly.

Charlotte Highton wasn't about to let the actions of a man even threaten to destroy her.

Not again.

She took a deep breath, jerking her gaze away from Nico and vowing not to let it return to that section of the table until she was finished. In a way, he'd done her a favour. His entrance had covered her stumble and now she was fired up. Whether it was from anger or desperation was immaterial.

'Some of you might be asking whether I should have let myself become involved in that emergency situation, especially when the result has deprived you of the audiovisual accompaniment you were supposed to have this morning.'

A ripple of sympathy went through the gathering.

'It's a fair question,' Charlotte continued. 'How far should any of us go in getting involved? How far should we go as emergency medicine specialists? Out in the field or in our own departments?'

Her words were clear and her tone as professional as ever now. Everybody was listening. Looking at her. She could feel one gaze in particular so strongly that she knew exactly who it was coming from. Good. Let him watch and listen. Let him see who Charlotte Highton was now.

'We can do so many things that can be done in an operating theatre in our emergency departments or out in the field. Burr-holes, tracheotomies, amputations, thoracotamies, Caesareans.' Charlotte paused for effect. 'Extreme measures in desperate circumstances. How many are justified? Does the weight of evidence

suggest we're performing miracles? Or guilty of performing mutilations?'

Another pause. This was the moment that would make or break this talk.

'I had a presentation that was full of statistics about these kinds of extreme procedures and graphics to show you the controversial relationship between patient outcomes and cost-effectiveness. Obviously it's not possible to do those facts and figures justice from memory, so instead…' The solution to this problem came to her in a flash of inspiration. 'I'm going to present a case history.'

Nico sat back in his chair.

He could feel the surprise of the people around him. What was this? They were all intelligent people who were hungry for new knowledge. They wanted to be presented with the results of cutting-edge research that they could use to improve what they did for a career. But they were going to be told a *story*?

'The man I'll call Bernie was forty-three years old,' Charlotte was saying. 'He went to the corner shop very late one night, because his pregnant wife had a craving for chocolate ripple ice cream. The timing was unfortunate. The shop was held up and Bernie got stabbed. A small knife with a short blade was buried to its hilt in his chest, deflected by the sixth rib, maybe five or six inches to the left from the midline.'

Nico could sense the interest picking up around him. The injury had been dangerously close to the man's heart.

'The ambulance crew knew not to remove an impaled object. Bernie's still conscious when they arrive

but his blood pressure's dropping. Fortunately, this corner shop is only about two minutes' drive from St Margaret's hospital. They put a doughnut dressing around the knife to stabilise it, give Bernie some oxygen and load and go. They establish IV access en route.'

The way Charlotte had changed to the present tense drew them all into the urgency of this case. Clever. Or were they all drawn in, as he was, by the sound of her voice? Soft, but as clear as a bell. As under control as her hair was again, all scraped back into that complicated knot thing.

Nico had preferred it the way he'd seen it after that resuscitation scene, with enough loose wisps to suggest that the whole knot could be released if you buried your fingers in it, wiggled them and then dragged them gently through the length of the hair. How long was it when it was loose? he wondered. And then he sharply dismissed the errant speculation and concentrated again on what she was saying.

'By the time Bernie comes through our doors, he's lost consciousness. His BP's unrecordable. His cardiac rhythm goes from SVT to VF to asystole within thirty seconds of my team getting him hooked up to the monitors.'

Nico was really listening now. So this was a case that Charlotte herself had managed? He could imagine her there, in the emergency department of St Margaret's. Wearing scrubs, probably, with a white coat over them. No…she'd been expecting a major trauma. She'd have a plastic apron on. And gloves. And a head covering that probably had a plastic face shield to protect her from blood spatter. She would have been in

charge. In control. Her voice might have been louder than it was right now but just as clear.

'We know our protocols inside out but how do we start CPR? This man's got a knife in his chest that's probably punctured his left ventricle. He's bleeding out. We can pull the knife out and push fluids but there's a hole in his heart so that would be futile.'

Nico was holding his breath without realising it. Everybody here knew that the only option was to do one of the most invasive procedures that could ever be done out of an operating theatre. Cracking open this man's chest and getting to the heart of the problem, so to speak.

'He's dead already unless we do something major and do it fast.' Charlotte's tone told them she agreed with the conclusion they'd all reached. 'A thoracotomy is the only option but I know as well as everybody else in the team what the odds are for a successful result. Virtually nil. But, hey…we have to try, don't we? This man is about to become a father. Right now, his pregnant wife is probably wondering why it's taking him so long to get back with her ice cream.'

Charlotte seemed to straighten her back. 'I'm the one who has to make the call and, as far as I'm concerned, it's a no-brainer. We take out the knife and I do a clam-shell thoracotomy. There's a gaping hole in the left ventricle and I suture it shut while we deal with more blood in a thorax than I've ever seen before.'

Nico closed his eyes for a heartbeat. He could picture it. A nightmare scene. The tissue of the myocardium would have been slippery. The visual field would have been impossible to keep clear with all that blood so you'd have to work almost blind.

'We start pushing fluids and begin CPR. I'm riding that stretcher to Theatre with my hand inside Bernie's chest, doing internal compressions and praying that my rough suturing is going to hold.'

Oh, Nico could imagine that scene too. Charlotte would have had to have been astride the man's legs, with one hand on the side rail to steady herself. Amongst the bank of monitoring and ventilation equipment that would have been in place. Speeding along with her team running to get them to Theatre as fast as possible.

It felt like he was standing in one of the wide corridors of St Margaret's right now, watching the dramatic spectacle rush past him. Opening his eyes again, he knew that he was looking at Charlotte with growing admiration. This was some woman.

'The cardiac surgical team is waiting for us. They do a much better job than me in repairing the damage. They replace the blood volume and get Bernie's heart started again. By this time his wife is at the hospital. Bernie's taken to the intensive care unit. He's still alive but what none of us know is whether we've done the right thing in saving him. Will he wake up? And, if he does, how much brain damage has been caused by the lack of oxygen? His wife is distraught and, just to add to the tension, she goes into labour three weeks before her due date.'

A soft groan came from her audience. This might be nothing like what they'd expected as an opening talk but they were all invested in the story now. They had to know the outcome.

'I've told you this story because it does, unlike so many, many others, have a happy ending. Bernie did

have a degree of neurological compromise. His cognition and speech were affected and he had a unilateral weakness on his right side.'

It was the first time Nico had seen Charlotte smile. He felt his own lips curve in an unconscious response.

'But his weak arm didn't stop him being able to cradle his newborn daughter a couple of days later. His difficulty in finding words didn't dim the way he could communicate his joy to his wife.'

Dammit. Was that a *lump* Nico could feel in his throat? He swallowed it away. His own career was full of success stories like this, wasn't it?

'The bottom line,' Charlotte continued quietly, 'is that our job is about the people who come under our care. Bernie was a miracle. But if he hadn't made it, that resus scene in my ED could have been denounced as unnecessary mutilation. We couldn't know how it would go before we started but is it just a coin toss?'

Charlotte was looking around the room. Nico was waiting for her gaze to cross his. He was oddly disappointed when it didn't.

'No.' She answered her own question. 'That's what our chosen specialty is all about. Working towards being the best we can be in our field of expertise. Knowing when there's a choice that pulling out the big guns is going to make the difference between life and death.'

Nico saw Charlotte take a deep breath. She was wrapping up now and the unusual introduction had clearly been a huge success. Everybody was leaning forward, totally engrossed and eager to participate in the programme that was about to start.

He felt the same way so how on earth could he be

distracted by the way that deep breath pushed Charlotte's breasts against the material of the plain blouse she wore under that tailored jacket? The way a hint of cleavage struggled to appear over the top button. Good grief. She was so buttoned up with that hairstyle and the fitted clothes she wore, it was almost as if she was trying not to look remotely feminine.

Maybe she was batting for the other team. Nico tucked the thought away with satisfaction. That would explain a lot. Maybe she had been trying to deny her true preference when he'd seen her out with that man in The Cosmopolitan Club all those years ago. And even if she was now comfortable with who she was, in her position Charlotte probably wouldn't want to come out of the closet and travel in the company of her girlfriend. Or wife, perhaps. It was none of his business and it didn't bother him.

So why did that curious feeling of disappointment in not making eye contact with her a second ago suddenly deepen several notches?

'The papers you are going to be privileged to hear today are from invited speakers who are leading their particular fields. I'm looking forward to hearing the discussions that will follow the presentations. Again, I must apologise for my unorthodox keynote speech but, on behalf of Dr Richard Campbell, our chairman for today, and the others involved in organising this satellite session, let me welcome you to our symposium on critical interventions.'

Nico joined the round of applause. His neighbour leaned sideways to say something about how moving the story had been and how good it was to be reminded of the human aspects of their science. But Nico merely

murmured agreement. He couldn't take his eyes off Charlotte. As if she felt his intense gaze, she looked up from her position at the front of the room.

So there, her gaze seemed to say. *I did it—even if you did do your best to stop me.*

After the awkward start to the day things were running smoothly. Richard was delighted. He smiled at Charlotte as they were preparing to follow the others out of the conference room for the lunch break.

'Do you know, I think your introduction has allowed for some very interesting questions to be raised that people might not have considered appropriate otherwise. You've given this whole forum an informality that has brought people closer together. It was a stroke of brilliance.'

'Thanks.' Charlotte rubbed the back of her neck, trying to ease the tension that still hadn't gone away completely. 'It could have taken things in the opposite direction. I was lucky.'

'I think everyone was impressed.'

Had Nicholas Moretti been impressed? And why did it matter so much that he had been?

'I'm sure they'll want to tell you that themselves, over lunch.'

Charlotte wasn't at all sure she wanted that to happen. She might be used to talking to colleagues while balancing a plate of food and eating but the idea of doing that in Nico's company seemed disturbingly... intimate?

Whatever. She had the perfect excuse.

'I'm going to skip lunch, if you don't mind, Richard. I'll grab a sandwich or something but I really need to

check on my grandmother and make sure she's being taken care of. And that she has something to do for the afternoon. Goodness knows what kind of mischief she could get up to otherwise.'

Richard was grinning now. 'She's quite something, your grandmother. How old is she?'

'Eighty-two. Going on about sixteen, I think. I often feel as if I'm in the company of a wayward teenager.' Charlotte's smile was fond. 'And then, at other times, she comes out with the kind of wisdom and advice that only someone who's experienced life to the full could have. She's amazing.'

Richard patted her arm. 'Go and catch up. I'll give your excuses to anyone who asks.'

'Thanks.' Charlotte hurried out to the reception area, away from the dining room, and asked whether her grandmother had left a message for her.

'No. But she's had lunch delivered to your room. Would you like your key now?'

The room was massive and decorated in Venetian style with sumptuous drapes, bed coverings and deep armchairs all in tones of silver and soft bronze. There was a Persian rug on the floor beneath the chandelier hanging from an astonishingly high ceiling. A small table with spindly legs supported a silver tray that had plates of delicate-looking sandwiches and cakes, a pot of tea and cups.

The first thing that struck Charlotte was that the tray hadn't been touched.

Almost at the same time she noted how tidy the room was. Where were the clothes strewn about that always happened when Geraldine was choosing her

next outfit? The open guidebooks as she chose her next adventure?

And why on earth was her grandmother lying on a bed in the middle of the day? Lady Geraldine Highton might be eighty-two but she didn't *do* naps. 'Life's too short,' she always said. 'And it's getting shorter for me by the day. Why waste it by sleeping? I can sleep when I'm dead.'

'Gran...' Charlotte moved towards the bed. 'What's wrong?'

'Oh...' Geraldine clearly hadn't been expecting a visitor. She sat up swiftly, looking...embarrassed. No, make that *guilty*. 'Charlie...I didn't think I'd see you until this evening.' The odd expression vanished, to be replaced by a beaming smile. 'That was a wonderful talk you gave, darling. I can't tell you how proud I was. And I understood every word. Well, almost every word. The next speaker was terribly dull in comparison. I went for a walk and watched the gondolas for a while. I might go for a ride in one after lunch. It's been years...'

Charlotte sank down onto the edge of the second bed, facing her grandmother. Something here was off-key. Terribly off-key.

'Gran...' She reached out and took hold of a soft hand decorated with several diamond rings. 'What's going on?'

'Whatever do you mean? Nothing's going on, Charlotte. Come and have lunch with me.' Lady Geraldine got to her feet but then her face changed. She couldn't hide a grimace of pain and her hand went to her stomach.

'You're not well,' Charlotte gasped. 'That's why you haven't touched your lunch. Why didn't you *tell* me?'

'I'm fine. There's nothing wrong with me.'

'Lie down,' Charlotte ordered. 'I want to have a look at you.'

For a long, long moment Geraldine looked undecided. But then she quietly lay down and answered the barrage of questions. Yes, she had abdominal pain. No, it wasn't the first time. Yes, she'd been to see a doctor about it. She'd had a scan. She was booked to have a biopsy between Christmas and New Year.

A *biopsy?*

With absolute dread giving her a chill that almost made her shiver visibly, Charlotte quietly asked if she could feel her grandmother's tummy and when she did, the hard edges of the mass she could feel confirmed her worst fear.

'Did…did your doctor tell you what he thought it was after the scan?'

'Oh, yes…' Lady Geraldine took hold of Charlotte's hand with both of hers. 'He's sure it's some form of bowel cancer.' Her voice wobbled. 'I didn't want you to find out, darling. Not yet.'

Charlotte's voice was thick with tears. 'Why not? You should have told me. I should have been there with you when you had your appointments.'

'We've been planning this trip for so long. Going on the Orient Express has been on my bucket list for far too long.' Unbelievably, Geraldine was smiling mischievously. 'And what better time to fulfil a bucket list item than when you've been told the end probably isn't that far off?'

'Gran… We can't spend thirty hours on a train. We have to fly back to London tonight. I'll talk to people.

We'll find a way to bring that procedure forward so we can start treatment earlier.'

'No way, Jose.' The way Lady Geraldine's eyes narrowed was a warning that she was not about to be contradicted. 'I've taken some painkillers. I'll be as right as rain after a little rest. You're not going to spoil this for me, Charlotte. Are you?'

It wasn't really a question. And the look coming from those faded blue eyes wasn't disapproving. It was full of absolute love. The kind of love Charlotte had received from this remarkable woman ever since she'd been orphaned as a small, terrified child.

This was why her grandmother had wanted to hear her speak today. Why she'd wanted to tell her how proud she was of her. Well, that cut both ways, didn't it?

'Let's enjoy this time together,' Lady Geraldine added softly. 'Before we know anything for sure. Let's pretend you didn't find me like this. The way I wanted it to be. Go back to your conference, darling. I need a little rest and then I'm going to choose my outfit for the dinner tonight.'

Those words stayed with Charlotte during the afternoon's symposium proceedings and it was the hardest thing she'd ever done, to keep up her professional image. The papers being presented were fascinating and the discussions lively, and Charlotte had learned long ago to firmly shut the door between her professional and personal lives, but today it was impossible.

Today had started badly. She thought she'd made the best of a bad situation and survived but now it felt as if the world had tilted far too sharply on its axis. What did her brilliant career matter if she was about to lose

the person she loved most? The only person she truly loved, come to that.

The conference attendees were invited to a cocktail session before a break to get ready for the dinner but Charlotte quietly slipped away from the group. She had to pull herself together. Had to find the strength to deal with what was undoubtedly coming. Did she really want to deprive her grandmother of the long-awaited pleasure of the train trip tomorrow and whisk her back to London and into hospital? Did she have that right?

The balcony leading off the now deserted dining room offered a private space with the bonus of an idyllic canal view where more than one ornate gondola could be seen floating past.

One of the gondolas held a pair of young lovers who were locked in a passionate embrace, oblivious to their surroundings for the moment. Maybe they were practising. Wasn't there a bridge here in Venice and if you kissed while going beneath it, it meant that your love would last for ever?

If her grandmother was here on this balcony with her, she'd be poking Charlotte with a bony finger right about now. Clicking her tongue.

That should be you in that gondola, Charlotte Jane, she'd be saying. *Kissing some gorgeous young man whose baby you can't wait to have. You don't know what you're missing, child, and it's the most important thing in life.*

But Charlotte knew all too well what she'd be missing far too soon and hearing her grandmother's voice so clearly in her mind was the final straw.

Tears rolled down her cheeks. Hot, burning tears that felt like acid. No surprise there. They were pretty

concentrated given that she hadn't shed a tear for six years now. They were such a sign of weakness. Feminine weakness.

She knew there was no point in trying to stop them.

Thank God nobody could see her.

The room Nico had been given at the hotel Bonvecchiata was luxurious. He eyed the huge bed, pulled at his tie to loosen it, and looked forward to putting his feet up for a while before heading off to the symposium dinner.

What a day!

Shedding his jacket, Nico walked to the tall windows of his room and looked through the ornate iron grille to find he had the bonus of a canal view. A gondola floated past with a young couple locked in each other's arms.

Nico smiled. Nice. His gaze drifted lazily and then it caught.

His smile faded.

There was a balcony on the floor beneath his. Charlotte Highton was standing there, her shoulders bowed as if she carried the weight of the entire world on them.

And she was *crying*?

Dio, but this woman was so full of contradictions. For a moment Nico stared in fascination. He would never have believed that she was capable of showing such a depth of emotion. But why was she so upset?

Did it have anything to do with being unable to present what she'd intended to present this morning?

Because of the trouble he'd unwittingly caused for her?

For another, long moment Nico kept staring, un-

sure of how to unravel the conflicting emotions being stirred in his own gut. Why did he feel such a strong urge to try and help this prickly, complicated woman? It was more than having contributed to a bad start to her day. More, even, than being curious about how someone's personality could have changed so much in just a few short years.

Being aware that there was some indefinable extra motivation should be enough of a warning to stop him getting involved any further, but did he want to listen to that warning?

He turned away. Stared at the huge, inviting bed for a moment. And then, with a soft growl, he turned on his heel and headed for the door.

CHAPTER THREE

OH...NO.

As if she could cope with her day getting even worse!

Of all the people to discover her at her lowest point in so many years, it had to be Nico Moretti.

Charlotte did her utmost to stem the tide of her tears. She turned her back on Nico and leant on the balustrade of the balcony, gripping the roughened concrete so hard she could feel tendrils of pain in her fingers that flickered into her arms. She fixed her gaze on the canal beneath and blinked again and again, trying to clear the wetness that didn't want to stop. Why couldn't it go back where it had come from, instead of continuing to roll down her face in these humiliating tears?

He didn't say anything. He just came to stand beside her. He, too, seemed to be gazing at the view and he spread his hands on the balustrade as if the only reason he was there was to admire their surroundings.

Charlotte's panic ebbed a little as he just stood there, a silent presence.

She'd never had company during the most unhappy periods in her life. Her first instinct, even as a young child so bereft at the loss of her parents, had been to

hide. To cry alone. And feel alone. To accept that life was a terribly lonely business and you just had to deal with that.

There *was* comfort to be found in simply being close to another person. To feel the presence of another living, breathing human.

The fact that Nico wasn't saying anything made it easy to accept his presence. She didn't have to try and find excuses or explain anything, and to have someone there who was clearly prepared to accept the state she was in made it feel as if it was okay not to be coping. As if she had support.

Strong support. Bit by bit, Charlotte found her thoughts creeping out from the dark knot in her head. She was aware of how big Nico was. Well over six feet in height and broad with it. His hands against the ancient concrete looked huge and powerful but his fingers were long and artistic looking. Clever hands, no doubt capable of performing the careful, intricate movements that were needed when you were dealing with something as precious as brain tissue.

Charlotte blinked again and, amazingly, her vision wasn't blurred any more. Without raising her head from its bowed position, she could study his neatly trimmed nails and olive-brown skin and the smattering of dark hair on the backs of his hands that disappeared under the turned-back cuffs of his white shirt.

Her head turned, as if her gaze was being pulled up by an external force. Up his arms, across his chest, where a loosened tie hung like a necklace and the top buttons of his shirt were undone. It was impossible not to flick her gaze up to his face now, but it was safe. He was still staring down at the canal so Charlotte let

her gaze linger for a moment on the strong profile. Unfairly luxurious eyelashes that brushed his cheeks when he blinked. A nose that made no apology for the space it took and deep creases on each side that ran down to meet a mouth that looked as if it smiled often and easily.

A jaw that looked like it hadn't seen a razor in a fair few hours. And a firmness to it that suggested tension. Was he gritting his teeth? Was he standing there not knowing what to say? Wishing he was somewhere else?

'I'm sorry.' The words came out as a whisper. 'I've had… It's been…' she had to take a tiny gulp of air '…a weird kind of day.'

'I understand.' Nico moved finally, but only his head. He angled it a little towards Charlotte. And then he smiled at her.

And…dear Lord…*what* a smile. Slow and so full of warmth. The most genuine smile she had ever seen. And it was for *her*. She had to catch her breath again.

'And I have a horrible feeling I might have contributed to your day not being the one you hoped for,' Nico continued. 'I really must apologise again.'

His voice was as warm as that smile. The Irish lilt was unmistakeable but, if he had been in Ireland, they would hear something else. An Italian inflection that made it unique. An astonishing accent colouring a depth that was as masculine as his size and aura of power.

How many women had fallen in love with that voice already?

Not that she was about to join the ranks. Charlotte cleared her throat.

'No…really. Losing my laptop was nothing com-

pared to...' Oh, help. Had she really been about to break one of her most ironclad rules and share personal information with a professional colleague?

'Compared to what, *cara*?'

It was the endearment that did her in. An endearment in a foreign language that somehow made it inoffensive and genuinely caring.

'My...grandmother is here. She's not well and... and it's possible she might not have...' Charlotte's intake of breath was a small sob. 'Might not have much time left.'

'Ohhh...' The sound was a drawn-out note of understanding. Empathy.

This man was a stranger even if they *had* met before. She would probably never see him again after today. So it didn't really count as sharing personal information, did it? Nobody would be giving her meaningful glances at work or gossiping about her in the cafeteria at St Margaret's. As if it would help with the anonymity, Charlotte fixed her gaze on the canal again. She could be simply talking aloud to herself.

'She's the most important person in the world to me,' she said softly. 'My parents both got killed in a horrible accident when I was eight years old. I was in the accident too and came out as a terrified shell of a child who wouldn't even speak to anyone for months. Gran never cared how tough it got, she was always so patient and so loving. So proud of any achievements I managed.'

'She would have had a lot to be proud of.'

Charlotte's breath came out in a huff of incredulity as she twisted sharply to glare at Nico. He was so used to giving women compliments, wasn't he? Meaning-

less compliments that demeaned what she was trying to tell him about her wonderful grandmother.

'What makes you think you know anything about me?' The words came out tight and accusing. And then Charlotte shook her head and swallowed fresh tears. 'You know *nothing*.'

There was a flash in his eyes but, while he might be startled by the verbal attack, he didn't look away.

'I know that a few years ago I met a woman who would have made anybody who loved her immensely proud,' he said calmly. 'But you're correct...I know nothing about you on a personal level.'

His gaze still held hers and there was something else in his eyes now. Respect? Curiosity?

'So tell me,' he invited. And then he smiled again. 'I'm listening.'

She was about to walk away.

Nico could sense the internal struggle but, dammit, he *wanted* to hear more. He knew perfectly well he was taking advantage of finding Charlotte in a state that made her vulnerable but he wasn't about to use the situation to his own advantage. Quite the opposite! His only motivation for coming out to this balcony and interrupting an obviously private moment had been to offer assistance.

He owed her that, surely?

Even though she had dismissed any contribution he'd made to her having such a bad day, he knew he hadn't helped it get off to a good start. And it was frustrating not to be able to think of a way to make up for that. Nico Moretti was an expert in making other people's lives better, even in the most dire of circum-

stances. He firmly believed that you could find at least a little patch of joy anywhere if you didn't take life too seriously.

Maybe that was why he knew he had the reputation of being a playboy. But play was the key, wasn't it? Like when he took the time to actually play with one of his smaller patients or do something silly enough to make them smile. And…good grief…he'd never encountered a woman who couldn't accept a compliment, even if it had been an automatic and possibly less than genuine response.

Nico had a strong sense that anything Charlotte told him would be completely honest, no matter how badly it reflected on herself. In his experience, this was an unusual trait, particularly for a woman on first acquaintance.

What really surprised him, however, was how much he wanted to hear more about her. His curiosity about Charlotte Highton was increasing rapidly. He remembered the brilliant young doctor. He'd seen the icy-cool clinician in action. He'd seen a speaker not only cope with facing an international audience having been deprived of her resources but engage them to the point where she'd had them in the palm of her hand.

And now he'd seen a glimpse of a loving granddaughter. Beneath all the layers he could detect there was an orphan who'd been a desperately unhappy child. A woman who currently looked alone. And lonely.

Just who was the real Charlotte?

He tried to send a silent message with his smile. And his eyes.

Talk to me. Please. You never know, I might be able to help. I'm good at helping.

It wasn't working, though. It was as though he was trying to hold a wild creature in his hands and it was struggling to be free. An injured wild creature that wanted to crawl away and lick its wounds somewhere it felt safe.

He needed something more to keep her here. He needed to tap into something that would give them a bond, however tenuous.

'I've met many people at many conferences over the years,' he told her. 'They are often accompanied by their husbands or wives. Or their lovers. Sometimes by their children. You are the very first I've met who is accompanied by a grandparent. That's…intriguing. Special.'

He watched Charlotte take a ragged breath. He heard her sniff and had to hide a smile because it sounded so…unprofessional. Childlike, even. It wasn't as if he'd never witnessed a grown woman crying, of course. They usually did, when he told them things were over, but this was different. The tears had nothing to do with him and they touched a spot in his heart usually reserved for those younger patients or their families. Something poignant.

'Gran *is* special,' Charlotte said, her words a whisper. Then she cleared her throat. 'But she doesn't usually accompany me. In fact, I'm not allowed to talk about anything remotely gruesome or medical when I'm around her. She says that you can always find something uplifting to talk about if you try hard enough.'

'A woman after my own heart,' Nico smiled. 'A finder of joy who can make people around her feel better.'

He let out a quiet breath as he sensed Charlotte re-

laxing. He knew she was almost smiling herself because he was watching so carefully and he could see the softening of her lips. The imperceptible curling at their corners.

'She always has something to look forward to. A new adventure planned. That's why she's here. As soon as she knew I was going to be speaking in Venice she looked up the timetable for the Orient Express going from Venice back to London and when the dates were perfect she said it was meant to be and I couldn't say no because it was well up the bucket list.'

'The bucket list?'

'You know...' Charlotte really smiled this time, as she looked up and caught his gaze. 'The list of things you really, really want to do before you kick the bucket?'

'Kick the...? Oh...' Just occasionally, the fact that English was a second language tripped him up. '*Sì*...' The Italian word slipped out unconsciously as he contemplated the euphemism for dying. 'I understand.'

Her eyes were grey. A dark, stormy sort of grey at the moment. He always expected blonde women to have blue eyes so the colour struck him as different. As unusual as this woman was herself, perhaps?

'But it's a crazy idea. How can we take a slow train trip across Europe when she's so sick? We should fly back to London tonight. I could have her in a hospital by tomorrow, getting the kind of investigations she needs to plan treatment.'

'Is that what she wants? Your grandmother?' It was a relief to be given a problem to solve at last and Nico was more than ready to focus on it, but he needed more information. 'What is her name?'

'Geraldine. Her friends call her Jendi.'

'And what are the symptoms of her illness?'

'I don't really know. She's kept this from me. I wouldn't have known about it at all yet except I found her resting and could see she had abdominal pain. And…I could feel a mass…'

'She has medication for the pain?'

'Yes. She seems fine now. She totally refused to consider cancelling the train trip and getting a flight to London. She told me to go away so she could have a bath in peace and get ready for the dinner tonight. She wants to dress up.'

'If there are no obvious signs that it would be detrimental to her condition, then maybe that's exactly what she *should* do.'

Charlotte's jaw dropped. 'And the train trip? You think that's a good idea, too?'

'Another day or two will not make any difference to the course of her illness,' Nico said. 'And look at it from her point of view. What would be better? To be lying in a hospital bed waiting for possibly a painful procedure or being able to forget about what lies ahead for a brief time and enjoying a wonderful experience in the company of someone you love?'

'But…' Charlotte caught her bottom lip between her teeth and tugged on it. It was another childish gesture that caught Nico in that soft spot in his heart. But then she let go with her teeth and soothed her lip with her tongue and suddenly it was quite another, very unexpected spot that Nico could feel waking up. 'How could *I* forget enough to help her enjoy it?'

'Because you have that kind of strength.' This time the compliment was completely sincere. Nico already

knew enough about Charlotte to be convinced of it. 'You can choose the part of you that you want other people to see and the rest you can keep hidden.'

Something very odd flickered across Charlotte's face. The kind of expression that suggested…guilt? As though she'd been caught out trying to hide something huge and important?

No. The expression was gone as fast as it had appeared. And now Charlotte was turning away. Nico wasn't ready to let her go. Not just yet.

'I think you should make the most of any time you can have together. Be proud that you can help her achieve this bucket-list thing. Maybe you can find out what the other things on her list are too and tick another one off soon.'

A rueful laugh escaped Charlotte. 'Oh, I know what's on the top of that list and it's not something that's ever going to be ticked off.'

'Oh?' Nico tilted his head encouragingly. 'They say that nothing is impossible.'

'*This* is.' Charlotte was looking up at the sky now. Assessing the clouds to see if the forecasted snow might arrive or was she seeking divine inspiration? She flicked Nico the briefest glance. 'Gran's greatest wish is to see me get married. Settled down and ready to present her with her first great-grandchild.'

'Ohhh…' Nico nodded slowly. 'That could be tricky.'

'Impossible.' The word was final.

'Hmm.' He had solved the problem of the train trip. Surely there was a way of at least getting around this one? 'Would there be any harm in letting her *think* it might be possible?'

'Gran's not stupid. She knows perfectly well that I'm not in a relationship. I haven't been for years. I'm hardly likely to get away with pretending I've met "Mr Right" within the next few months, am I?' She took a step away from him, raising her hand to smooth her already perfect hairstyle. 'And I really can't believe I'm having such an astonishingly ridiculous conversation.'

Nico had been distracted for a split second, wondering again what Charlotte's hair would look like if it wasn't so tightly coiled and clipped into place. He wanted to pull out some of those pins. To force her to loosen up a little.

'Because it's not so ridiculous,' he said. 'What if you attended this dinner tonight with...with your new boyfriend? How happy would that make your grandmother?'

This time it was real laughter that escaped. A delicious, totally unexpected chuckle of real mirth. 'Is there a "hire a boyfriend" agency in Venice that you know about?'

'There's no need to hire anybody.' Nico's grin stretched his mouth. 'It's the least I could do to make up for this morning's unfortunate happenstance.'

It was perfect. Here it was on a plate. The opportunity to not only make up for contributing to any distress caused by this morning's incident but to do it in a manner that would be *fun*.

Except that Charlotte was looking at him as if he was totally crazy.

This was surreal.

Just having a personal conversation with a profes-

sional acquaintance would have been weird enough but this incredibly good-looking stranger seemed to be offering to pretend to be her *boyfriend* for an evening.

Imagine that!

Unfortunately, Charlotte *could* imagine it. She could imagine herself introducing him to her grandmother as a…as a *friend*…and Nico turning on his most charming smile and Gran putting two and two together and letting wishful thinking make the impossible a reality.

Oh…God…how happy would she be?

The distraction of a train trip to take her mind off what was coming was nothing compared to the joy she would have if she thought Charlotte had finally found 'the one'.

It was crazy. Wasn't it?

'That's crazy,' she said aloud, hoping the spoken words would confirm it.

'It's only for an evening.' Nico shrugged as if it was no big deal. 'We could tell her we've met before, which is perfectly true. We could say that there's something about Venice being such a romantic city and we've realised we can't fight the attraction any longer. It was meant to be.'

Oh…my… If the look he was giving her right now was any indication of the performance he could put on for her grandmother, she would be totally convinced.

For a skipped heartbeat kind of moment, Charlotte almost believed it herself. She could feel it right down to her bones. How could anyone be so good at looking as if they had just fallen madly in love with someone? It was doing very strange things to something deep inside her. A process that had to be stopped immediately.

He's acting, she reminded herself. And he's only this good at it because he's clearly had a lot of practice.

'You may be an expert in pretending,' she snapped, 'but it's not something I could carry off. I wouldn't even want to try.'

He was still giving her *that* look.

'I watched you this morning,' he said softly. 'I think you can carry off anything that's important enough to you.'

There was a glint of mischief in those dark eyes. Good heavens, he was actually *enjoying* this, wasn't he? He *wanted* to do it?

'You might be surprised at how easy it is,' he continued. 'You might enjoy it.'

Charlotte snorted. 'I don't think so.'

'And wouldn't you even want to try? For your grandmother's sake?'

'No. It would be completely dishonest.'

'Completely?' Nico injected a hurt tone into the word. 'Could you not summon even a tiny bit of attraction to me to work with?'

He tilted his head, moving it closer to her own, his gaze dropping from her eyes to her lips.

And, heaven help her, but Charlotte could actually feel a curl of desire unfolding deep in her belly. It escaped from that place that was locked away. A place she could never enter because, if she did, she would have to remember... Have to face up to what was so wrong with her...

'*No.*' The word came out like the slamming of a door. It was time to get away from there.

Away from this man who was making her think about ridiculous things.

Feel things she had no desire to feel.

'At least think about it.' His words followed her as she almost ran to get off the balcony. 'I'll see you at dinner.'

CHAPTER FOUR

'OH, MY...'

'What's wrong, Gran? Are you all right?' The lighting wasn't so great in this dinner venue. A restaurant within easy walking distance of the conference venue, this ancient stone vault of a room had been transformed into a winter wonderland in honour of the season.

White church candles with multiple wicks, in a nest of holly leaves and poinsettia flowers, made a centrepiece for each of the small tables set for four. Sheets of fairy lights in icicle form hung from the high ceiling and, on one roughened stone wall, a slide show of Christmassy scenes was softly fading in and out as the scenes changed.

It was a beautiful setting for a dinner but the flickering light levels made it impossible to see things as clearly as Charlotte would have liked. She was convinced her grandmother had suddenly gone pale.

'Stop fussing, Charlotte, for goodness' sake.' Lady Geraldine gave her a surprisingly sharp poke with her finger. 'If you weren't half-blind, you would have noticed what I just noticed.' Her smile was almost gleeful as she lowered her voice. 'Eye candy...'

'*Gran*. Wherever did you learn an expression like that?'

'I blame television,' Lady Geraldine sighed. But she was still smiling. Still watching a point well beyond Charlotte's shoulder. The entranceway, most likely, because Charlotte had deliberately chosen a table as far away from the door as possible. A nice, dark corner. With a bit of luck, Nico Moretti would be late and either he wouldn't be able to spot her or the two unoccupied settings at their table would have been taken by another conference attendee and his or her partner.

But no. With a sinking heart Charlotte realised that to have grabbed her grandmother's keen interest, this 'eye candy' would have to be spectacularly good looking. And judging by the way her elderly relative was practically fanning herself with her hand now, he was coming in their direction. Slowly, she turned her head.

Oh, my…was an understatement. Dr Moretti was wearing a beautifully fitting dinner suit, which always made men look good, but so were most of the other male guests here. Maybe the soft lighting had something to do with the way he stood out. Or more likely, it was the man's sheer presence as he wound his way through the tables, pausing to smile at people he knew or share a few words in greeting.

He seemed to have a spotlight on him, in any case, and Charlotte knew her gaze was as transfixed as her grandmother's. As focused as every other woman in this room.

If Nico was scanning the room, looking for her as he kept moving, he certainly gave no indication of it. Anyone watching would assume he knew exactly what table he was expected at. Charlotte could feel

her grandmother's interest sharpen into astonishment as he finally made a beeline for their corner, his face lighting up in a smile of sheer joy.

'Carlotta. *Cara*...' With his gaze locked on hers, Nico reached out and cupped one side of her face with his hand. It was an exquisitely tender touch. Overwhelmingly so. Charlotte had no hope of collecting her thoughts, let alone expressing them. His gaze suggested that if she didn't want him to play this game she only had to say the word, but how could she when she couldn't even draw a breath?

And she saw the moment the question in his gaze turned to delight.

Game on.

With a smoothness that suggested Nico was far too good at acting, he turned his charm onto the unsuspecting Lady Geraldine. He gently picked up the hand with its diamond rings flashing in the candlelight. He pressed his lips to it.

'And you have to be Carlotta's *nonna*. I've heard so much about you. This is...*such* a pleasure.'

And then Nico took hold of one of the two spare chairs and moved it so that it was as close to Charlotte's as possible. He sat down and adjusted the silverware and then nodded at a nearby waiter, who instantly came to fill his champagne glass.

Lady Geraldine was watching this little show with rapt attention and she seemed as lost for words as Charlotte. Until Nico raised his glass, tilted his head in a silent toast to the women, took a long sip and then... smiled.

'Um...Charlotte?'

'Yes, Gran?'

'Is there something you haven't told me?'

This was her chance to pull the plug on this crazy plan that Nico seemed perfectly happy to put into action. To pretend—in public—that they were a couple in love.

Trouble was, even for the short time it had been happening, it was casting a spell that was unbelievably powerful.

They said that falling in love was magical. Maybe even pretending to be tapped into some of that incomprehensible power.

Whatever. Charlotte could feel the waves of envy coming from the other women in this space. She could see the gleam of joyous disbelief in her grandmother's eyes. Worst of all, she could almost feel what it *would* be like having someone like Nico head over heels in love with her.

And, God help her, she wanted more.

Just for an hour or two.

Just enough to give her a bubble of whatever this magic was so that she could remember it when times were bleak.

And there *were* going to be bleak times ahead.

Could there possibly be a greater gift she could give her beloved grandmother than to let her die with the peace of believing that the child she had raised was happy at last? That she would be loved and cared for in her absence?

It was a very strange feeling, this…giving in. Living in the moment without trying to weigh up any consequences or complications. It was incredibly liberating. *Fun*—like Nico had suggested it could be? Something was certainly lifting the corners of Charlotte's mouth.

'Gran…this is…Nico.' Her words sounded hesitant. Breathless. The way they would if someone was about to reveal something secret. Something personal and precious.

'Nico Moretti,' he expanded. He laid his hand over Charlotte's on the crisp, white linen tablecloth as he smiled at Lady Geraldine. 'I am Charlotte's…' He hesitated, clearly at a loss for the right word to describe his relationship to her, and she held her breath. Could he really pull this off?

Nico turned his head and she could swear his sigh was one of pure happiness. 'I am whatever Carlotta will give me the honour of being,' he murmured.

'Charlotte?' The gentle word belied the 'please explain' undertone.

'It's been s-sudden,' Charlotte stammered. 'I was going to tell you today, Gran, but…'

'But then you started worrying about me.' Lady Geraldine clicked her tongue. 'For heaven's sake, child. This is *far* more important. I want to know everything.'

Oh, help… Charlotte tried to buy some thinking time by picking up her champagne glass. The Italian prosecco being served was astonishingly light. Delicious. She took another long sip.

'We actually met years ago,' Nico said into the expectant silence. 'At St Margaret's in London. It was my bad luck that Carlotta was unavailable at that time.'

Uh-oh… It took Lady Geraldine less than a split second to work out exactly what time Nico was referring to and that earned Charlotte a glance she would rather have avoided.

Gran knew there had been far more to the break-up of that relationship—the only one she'd ever known

Charlotte to have—than she'd ever been privy to. It was the only aspect of Charlotte's life she'd ever been shut out of and it was a cloud that had hung over them ever since. Something that was never mentioned but always there.

Charlotte drank the last of her wine and barely noticed the waiter refilling her glass as she listened to Nico continuing to talk.

Why hadn't she thought that this pretence could open that particular can of worms?

And it was too late to stop it now. She was already in too deep.

About to drown?

He knew he'd said the wrong thing.

Nobody could have missed that electric glance that Lady Geraldine had speared her granddaughter with when he'd said that she had been otherwise attached when he'd first met her.

What the hell was that about?

Never mind. He knew he could redeem himself. He'd been quite confident of pulling this off from the moment he'd walked into this exclusive restaurant and spotted the table he needed to aim for.

The table where the two most beautiful women in the room were sitting.

Maybe Charlotte often wore an elegant silver dress to such a formal occasion but Nico had a strong sense that it was not usual practice for her to leave her hair loose like that—a tumble of soft waves that gleamed an ash blonde in the candlelight. Had she be thinking of him when she'd brushed it out and chosen not to wind it back into its prison of pins?

And the grandmother! Nico had expected an English dowager of some kind. Tall and forbiddingly aloof. He had smiled the moment he'd set eyes on the old lady sitting beside Charlotte. Even from a distance he had caught the flash of her bejewelled hands and even a small tiara nestled in fiery red hair. He could sense her interest in the people around her and an ability to see beneath the surface of social niceties. This was going to be a much more entertaining evening than he could have hoped for.

'I can't tell you how often I've thought about her since then,' he told Lady Geraldine with palpable honesty. 'And then fate brings us together in the most romantic city in the world.' He shrugged, his smile suggesting he hadn't made much of an effort to stand firm against the winds of fate.

Was he overdoing things? Judging by the mistiness in Lady Geraldine's eyes, she was swallowing this very happily, but from the corner of his eye he could see that Charlotte was simply sitting there, staring at him, her lips slightly parted and her expression dazed.

He still had his hand covering hers, so he picked it up. Such a soft hand. Such elegant, long fingers and neat nails that were not disguised by any unnatural colours. He touched his lips to her hand and then leaned forward as though drawn irresistibly to kiss her lips next. They looked soft, too, and when Charlotte unconsciously dampened them with the tip of her tongue, Nico realised that he actually *did* want to kiss her.

Dio… That wasn't meant to happen. He closed his eyes for a heartbeat to take control of the unexpected shaft of desire but then he let his breath out in a soft sigh. Did it matter? Charlotte wouldn't need to know

it was anything other than good acting and it would certainly make his performance more believable. He opened his eyes and focused on the owner of the hand he still had imprisoned in his.

'It was meant to be,' he said softly. 'I'm lucky enough to have been given a second chance and even luckier that this beautiful woman seems to feel the same way.' He added a few words in Italian, knowing how limited Charlotte's grasp on the language was, and hoping that it would add to the impression of sincerity.

It had more of an effect than he had anticipated. Lady Geraldine sniffed delicately and picked up her linen serviette to dab at the corner of her eye.

'*Bella*,' she said, her Italian accent flawless. '*Carlotta è una ragazza fortunate.*'

Beneath his fingers, Charlotte's hand stiffened with tension. 'What?'

'She said you are a lucky girl,' Nico murmured. 'That the story of how we met is beautiful.'

'At last…' Lady Geraldine smiled mistily at her granddaughter. 'Oh, darling. I can't begin to tell you how happy this makes me. This…this is the best night of my *life.*'

Charlotte's lips trembled but she managed to smile. In the instant before she turned to look at her grandmother Nico caught the flash of emotion in her eyes that told him how huge this gift of happiness was.

And she couldn't have given her grandmother this if it hadn't been for him. It made him proud.

It made him want to give *more*.

The interruption of the first course of their dinner arriving was a welcome distraction that gave Charlotte

time to try and collect herself. Not that she had the slightest appetite and she couldn't help her gaze straying sideways to look at Nico at noticeably frequent intervals as she wondered how he could be so incredibly good at this pretence, but that was just the sort of behaviour a woman who'd just fallen head over heels in love would display, wasn't it?

No wonder Gran believed it all. Charlotte had been sucked in herself. She'd totally forgotten the fear of the conversation touching on that no-go period in her life. And the way she'd felt when he'd picked up her hand and kissed it... No. What had been utterly shocking had been the way she'd felt when he'd leaned closer and looked as though he was about to kiss her on the lips.

The hum of conversation around them and the elegant strains of the Christmas carols being played by a quartet in the restaurant foyer had faded into nothing more than background static. The flickering light of the candles seemed to mirror the tiny flames licking her skin. Heating her blood and pooling somewhere deep in her belly.

A moment's madness, fuelled by what she could swear was an equal level of attraction in Nico's eyes. But they were dark eyes and the light was low. She couldn't possibly have seen his pupils expand and she must have imagined the electric charge that came through her fingers where his skin was still in contact.

The shock of hearing her grandmother respond to Nico in Italian had been enough to break the extraordinary spell being cast, which was just as well. Nico was enjoying himself quite enough. How appalling would it be if he knew he was having a genuine effect on her?

Lady Geraldine wasn't eating much either, and that

was enough to send Charlotte's thoughts in a darker direction. Her grandmother might be in her eighties but she had always been a woman of amazing energy who lived life to the full. Nobody would deny her the maximum extent of whatever modern medicine could do to prolong that colourful life, but you had to balance additional time earned by what the quality of that life would be. Major surgery and chemotherapy would be a miserable time and it was possible that the end would not justify the means.

Something like despair gathered in a cloud over Charlotte as she toyed with her entrée. Thank goodness Nico and her grandmother were so engaged in conversation. Nobody would thank her for destroying the joyous atmosphere that had been created at this particular table.

'So your mother is still living in Ireland?'

'Yes. With husband number four.'

'Good gracious! What was wrong with the first three?'

'My mother has trouble resisting offers that seem to give her a better opportunity to experience the best that life can give. She is a free spirit, Lady Geraldine, who is not bothered by what others think. A bit like yourself, I'm guessing?'

Gran actually laughed with delight. If she'd had a fan in her hand, Charlotte thought, she might have smacked Nico's hand with it. Instead, the old lady gave him an almost shy smile.

'You can call me Jendi, dear,' she told him. 'As my friends do.'

'I'm honoured…Jendi.'

'And your father? Is he still living, too?'

'No.' Charlotte saw the way Nico laid down his fork as though he had caught the lack of appetite around him. 'He died some years ago now.'

'Oh…' The sound was one of sympathy. 'Too young. Was it an accident?'

'A broken heart.' Nico's voice was expressionless. He was stating a fact.

Charlotte couldn't help her eyebrows rising at such a non-medical notion from a man with his training. She didn't say anything but maybe her breath had escaped with a disparaging sound because Nico flicked a glance in her direction. His words, however, were directed at Lady Geraldine. His new *friend*.

'They called it a heart attack, of course,' he said. 'But his heart broke when my mother left him and on every visit I made back here, I could see his slow decline.'

'That's terrible,' Lady Geraldine declared. She was frowning now. 'But at least it hasn't put you off marriage, Nico.'

'M-marriage?'

The word was so shocked that Charlotte knew the game might be up. Had it not occurred to him that it was a natural direction for someone's thoughts to go in when faced by two people who were 'meant to be together' and had made the connection at last?

'Early days, Gran,' she said in a stage whisper across the table. 'Don't frighten the poor man.'

'Frightened? Me?' To give him credit, Nico recovered fast. He actually winked at Lady Geraldine. 'We men like to pick our own time, that's all. The element of surprise, you understand?'

'Oh, of course.' Lady Geraldine beamed at him. 'I promise I'll be surprised.'

She wouldn't be the only one. Nico was only supposed to be posing as her new boyfriend, that's all. Something that would make Gran happy because it offered hope for her not having a lonely future. This was getting out of hand. He was sharing family secrets as though he was already a prospective grandson-in-law.

How on earth was she going to explain what had happened here tonight if, by some miracle, her grandmother's treatment was effective and she lived for years after this?

The interruption of formal speeches in praise of the symposium and its organisers filled in the time between courses and prevented any further bonding between her gran and Nico, but it didn't lessen the increasing tension Charlotte was experiencing. It only got worse as people began to mingle between the tables and Richard Campbell came to say hello.

'Did you enjoy listening to Charlotte this morning, Lady Geraldine?'

'Oh, I did. So much. Thank you for arranging things, Dr Campbell. I am the happiest woman in the world tonight.'

'So I see.' It was impossible not to respond to the glow her grandmother was exuding. No one would believe that she could be facing confirmation of a terminal disease within days. And the misty look she was giving the young couple at her table was just as easy to read. Richard's jaw sagged visibly as he followed her gaze.

'Charlotte? You and...?'

* * *

'Nico Moretti,' Nico said, extending his hand.

A new challenge, then. Could he pull off this pretence with the people who worked with Charlotte?

'Delighted to meet you, Richard. Although I think we met some years ago. At St Margaret's?'

'That was where he first met Charlotte,' Lady Geraldine put in.

'Mmm.' Richard was giving Charlotte a strange look and Nico's heart sank. He remembered that impression he'd had when he'd been listening to her speak this morning. That her playing down her femininity might reveal a sexual preference that didn't include men. Maybe her closest colleagues were aware of something that was kept strictly private. Something she didn't want her grandmother to know, either.

Was that what had been hidden beneath that absolute conviction that she would never be fulfilling her grandmother's dearest wish of settling down and having babies? Suspicion on Jendi's part might also explain that charged glance directed at her granddaughter, which he'd inadvertently provoked.

Charlotte certainly seemed bothered by something. As soon as possible after Richard moved on to another table, she excused herself, muttering about needing a bathroom. He saw her ask a waiter for directions and then head out a door that led to a long balcony. Presumably the bathrooms opened off the balcony to one side of the restaurant.

Which meant that Nico could also excuse himself and head in that direction. He could catch Charlotte before she came back into the dining room and just check that he wasn't causing even more trouble for

her, although exactly how to broach the subject of her sexuality in a sensitive manner was entirely beyond him at the moment.

The balcony ran right along the canal side of the restaurant. It was quiet out here with the added darkness that came from the still water of the canal. Nico didn't need to use the facilities so he paced back and forth, waiting what seemed an interminably long time for Charlotte to reappear. What was she doing in there? Twisting her hair back into some impossibly tight 'hairdo'? He hoped not.

A gondola drifted past below with just a single light making the ornate brass ornament on the prow of the boat gleam. A couple sat, wrapped in blankets against the cold and silent as they gazed in wonder at the magic of touring this city at night with only the ripple of the boat to disturb the serenity.

The tap of high heels on stone disturbed the moment for Nico. He turned and Charlotte's step faltered.

'What are you doing out here?'

'Waiting for you.'

The only light now that the gondola had passed came from the fairy lights of the restaurant and a small Christmas tree that was being used to reveal where the door to the bathrooms was. Silver light that made Charlotte's dress shine and cast a spotlight on the way the fabric clung to her body and revealed noticeable curves. It also caught matching strands in her hair. It would look golden in the sunshine, Nico thought. Chameleon hair. He could imagine her eyes could create that illusion too. Maybe they would take on a blue hue under a summer sky. Or when she was happy?

Right now they were a stormy, slate grey.

'Why?'

She sounded nervous and added to that impression by pushing her fingers through her hair. The gesture ruffled the loose waves. It was a supremely feminine movement. Confusing, given what Nico was there intending to find out. The reminder made him shake off his focus on how unexpectedly attractive Charlotte was looking. He cleared his throat.

'I...um... It seems to be going well. Your *nonna* is happy.'

'Mmm.' He could see Charlotte swallow. A ripple that ran the length of her elegant neck. 'Too happy, maybe.'

'Is there such a thing? Especially at a time like this?'

Charlotte sighed. 'She *is* happy. I don't think I've ever seen her look so...so contented.'

'There you go, then. It's been a good thing to do. A reprieve from thinking about less happy things. One that you may be able to use for some time.'

Charlotte looked away, watching the tail end of the gondola as it turned a corner. 'But I didn't think things through. I thought other people would just think you were sharing our table for dinner.' Her voice rose and the words sped up a little, revealing how unsettled she was. 'I didn't expect to start a rumour that will follow me back to St Margaret's. I have no idea what I'm going to do about that.'

'You don't have to do anything.' Nico paused, trying to select his words carefully. 'Unless it's going to cause personal distress?'

She frowned at him. 'What kind of personal distress?'

'Well...you might have someone in your life that

wouldn't be happy to know about this…this illusion you're creating.'

'I don't…' She was trying to process his meaning. Then she made an impatient sound. 'I told you I wasn't in a relationship.'

'Not with *Mr* Right,' he murmured.

There was a moment's dead silence and then Charlotte's eyes widened. 'Oh, my God…you think I'm a—' An incredulous huff broke her words. 'Are you *serious*?' And then she turned away but not before Nico had seen a fierce sparkle in her eyes.

Oh…*Dio*… He'd really put his foot in it now, hadn't he? Was she about to start crying again?

No matter. He had come prepared. He reached for the neatly pressed handkerchief he'd pushed into his jacket pocket just before he'd left his room. He pulled it out and, as he did so, something glinted in the light and bounced on the stones with an audible *ping*.

Charlotte turned her head. 'What was that?'

'Nothing important.' Nico knew what it was. It had been weighing his pocket down earlier today. But then he'd forgotten all about it after he'd arrived at the symposium. After he'd been swept along by listening to the story Charlotte had told them. Weirdly, it hadn't occurred to him to think about it again all day. Or remember to take it out of his pocket.

His grandmother's ring. The one his father had given his mother. The one she'd left behind when she'd broken the marriage and Nico's true family. Maybe it was better if it got left behind at the bottom of a Venetian canal. Drowned and lost. Like his belief in true love and marriage and happy families for ever had been lost so many years ago.

But no. This ring was the only thing his father had left him as his inheritance. The only link he could touch that went back to his early childhood. It was important. Nico ignored Charlotte and his gaze raked the rough stones as he searched for what he'd dropped. It must have come out of his pocket at speed, propelled by being caught in the folds of the handkerchief. Had it already bounced irretrievably into the waters of the canal?

Like Charlotte's laptop?

No. There it was, precariously balanced right beside a stone balustrade on the very edge of the balcony. He would have to be careful not to nudge it over the edge, he realised as he stooped. Trying to slow his movement, Nico dropped to one knee and reached for the ring.

'What on *earth* are you doing?' Nico could see the ripple of the long, silver dress as Charlotte stepped closer. He sighed and held the object up to show her.

'It's my grandmother's ring,' he said heavily. 'It's a long story...'

He wasn't going to get a chance to tell her any of it, however. A startling shriek cut through the night air.

'Charlotte! Nico! Oh, my goodness...' Lady Geraldine had come out through the restaurant doors and was standing there, her hands clasped in front of her as though in prayer. 'Is this...? Are you...? Oh...how *romantic*. A proposal. In Venice, of all places...'

It took a long moment for the full horror to sink in but, yes...here he was, on one knee. Kneeling in front of a beautiful woman with a backdrop of a Venetian canal, holding up what was obviously an engagement ring in his hand.

He bought a fraction of time by getting to his feet

somewhat awkwardly. He caught the panicked look in Charlotte's eyes. They were going to have to confess now, weren't they? Ruin the happiest night of this sick old lady's life.

No. He could fix this.

With the ghost of a wink to let Charlotte know he had things in hand, Nico grabbed her hand and shoved the ring onto her finger. It was a tight fit but he gave it an extra push to get it over her knuckle. Was it pain that made Charlotte gasp? Maybe it was the shock of how fast he'd moved or this unexpected twist in the show they were putting on. That didn't matter either. Maybe people would think she was simply shocked at how quickly he had managed to sweep her off her feet.

He kept hold of Charlotte's hand and gave it a squeeze. She dragged her gaze up from the ring and met his eyes and he tried very hard to give her a silent message.

Trust me. We can get through this without hurting anybody.

And then he turned and pasted a smile onto his face.

'Jendi… What wonderful timing. We wanted *you* to be the first to know.'

CHAPTER FIVE

'I KNEW ALREADY.' Lady Geraldine was coming towards them with surprising sprightliness given her age and state of health. 'Nobody can hide the glow of true love...' Tears were running down her wrinkled cheeks as she got close enough to embrace Charlotte. 'Oh, my dear...I'm *so* happy for you.'

She must feel like she was hugging a tree, Charlotte realised, but she couldn't make her body soften. Or even raise the arms now hanging by her sides like dead branches. One of them was even weighed down with an enormous rock. No... She had to be dreaming. He couldn't *really* have shoved that ring on her finger, could he?

Still dazed, Charlotte lifted her left arm. It looked like she was returning her grandmother's effusive hug but, in reality, she was getting her hand to a position where she could see it.

Yep. There it was. On her third finger. A quite respectably sized solitaire diamond in an antique gold setting. Definitely an engagement ring. What on earth did Nico Moretti think he was playing at, walking around with an engagement ring in his pocket?

Words floated into through the sludge in her head. His grandmother's ring. *A long story.*

No story could be long enough to rescue her from this escalating nightmare. What was that saying Gran used to deliver with a wagging finger? Something about the complicated web you weave when first you practise to deceive. Charlotte shook her head to clear the mist. This had to end. Now.

'This isn't what is seems, Gran. I'm not engaged. This is…ridiculous.'

'Oh, I know, darling.' The grip Lady Geraldine still had on her increased a notch. 'You weren't expecting this, were you?'

'Of course I wasn't.' A snort of something like laughter escaped her throat. 'Nico and I have only just met. We're not even…' Charlotte raised her gaze as she searched for the right word to explain the total lack of a genuine relationship between them. It brought her line of vision directly over her grandmother's shoulder. And it locked with Nico's gaze.

He had one eyebrow raised and a curiously disappointed stillness to the rest of his face . What dismissive word was she going to come up with here?

That they weren't even *friends*?

That they weren't connected in any way, shape or form?

Except they were, weren't they?

They'd become connected totally by chance when they'd formed a united medical team to help the man who'd had the cardiac arrest and fallen from the scaffolding. Having him present when she had been floundering in front of so many distinguished symposium attendees this morning had been what had given her

the strength to give any kind of presentation at all. The thought that he might have been impressed had made her feel like she hadn't failed.

Having him right there when she had been already starting to grieve for Gran had been what had given her the strength to try and make whatever time her beloved grandmother had left as happy as possible.

And the way she'd felt when he'd looked at her like that at the table. As if he was in love with her. As if he'd wanted to kiss her.

Oh, yes…she couldn't deny a physical *and* emotional connection to him even if she didn't want it to be there. Somehow Nico had broken through her safety barriers. Despite the short time they had known each other—less than a day, for heaven's sake—he was already enmeshed in her personal life in a way that no man had ever been.

'I know, darling.' Lady Geraldine's soothing words took her back. Way back to when it had seemed that nobody could ever understand. Or put things right. And yet the words had always been sincere. And Gran had always put things right, no matter how long it had taken. 'People will think it's too soon. *You* think it's too soon.'

'Of course I do. It's…it's…' *Ridiculous*. But Charlotte's gaze was still holding Nico's as she tried to read the silent message he was sending. It was a reassuring message, whatever it was. How was she supposed to interpret that? Or believe that this was somehow okay.

'It's love at first sight, that's what it is,' Lady Geraldine said happily. 'The best sort. Wearing Nico's ring doesn't mean you have to get married next week, dar-

ling. It's just a promise of commitment. You can take all the time you need to make sure that it's perfect.'

All the time they needed to keep Gran happy for as long as she lived?

Time.

That's what Charlotte needed.

'It will take time.' Nico's voice was strong. Amazingly calm, considering. 'And you're right, Jendi. I have…what's that expression? Jumped the gun.'

Something about the way he recited the phrase made Charlotte think his choice of words was deliberate. He was reminding her of the euphemism she'd used about kicking the bucket. Reminding her of what was important here. And maybe it was a warning, too.

If she destroyed this illusion she would be ruining not one but two of the items on Gran's bucket list. There was no way the train trip could provide the slightest pleasure if the number-one item on the list was revealed as a deception.

Geraldine let Charlotte go with a final pat. She turned and looked up at Nico, who smiled at her.

'We will have to be apart a lot in the coming weeks,' he said sadly. 'I have commitments in the United States and Europe. In Australia, even. But I had to do something to make my intentions as clear as possible. To achieve what I know will make us *both* happy.' Make us *all* happy, his glance reminded Charlotte.

'Of course you did.' Lady Geraldine beamed.

Charlotte's mind was clearing rapidly. Nico was presenting an easy way out here. He could be her fiancé but he would be absent. She could keep her grandmother happily believing that a wedding was on the cards without any further awkwardness of them hav-

ing to keep up the pretence for real. Or, if she couldn't bear to be less than honest, she could say that things had fizzled out in a few weeks and use the excuse that it would never have worked. They would never have enough time together to keep the relationship alive.

'Mmm.' The sound came out in a strangled fashion. 'I'm still not sure—'

'Of course you're not.' Lady Geraldine slipped her arm through Charlotte's and began to lead her back to the restaurant. 'You like to be in control, child, and you've been swept off your feet.' She slipped her other arm through Nico's. 'Come on. We'll all go and have another glass of that lovely champagne and give Charlotte time to get used to this delightfully unexpected state of being an *engaged* woman.'

Dio mio…

What, exactly, had happened there?

It wasn't the unexpected twist of events that had led to Charlotte now wearing his grandmother's ring that was disturbing Nico most as he followed the women back to the restaurant.

No. It went far deeper than a pretence that was now a little more complicated than intended. Something had happened when Charlotte had been caught in that loving embrace and had looked at him over her grandmother's shoulder. When she'd been searching for a way of trying to explain that this was all a lie. That there was nothing of any significance between them.

She hadn't been able to, had she? Because she'd felt the same thing he had when their gazes had touched and locked. Somehow, over the course of this crazy day, they *had* connected. And on a level that was to-

tally alien to Nico. Inexplicable and deeply disturbing but, at that moment, he would have overturned heaven and earth to protect Charlotte. To extricate her in a dignified fashion from this mess he had created.

He had no idea what had triggered such a strong urge. Guilt from knowing he'd pushed her into this? Or maybe he'd caught another glimpse of that lost and frightened child in her eyes. He'd certainly seen desperation that had been coming from not wanting to hurt somebody she loved so much. Maybe that explained why he was feeling as though the ground was shifting beneath his feet and that the rules he lived by were no longer relevant.

Knowing that Charlotte was capable of that kind of love when, to outward appearances, she was incapable of that much emotion. Knowing that she was such a different woman from the one he'd met years ago. Curiosity was a powerful motivating force and Nico wanted to put as many pieces of this puzzle together as he could before he moved on.

Maybe when he had the full picture he would be able to understand why he was feeling as if he was caught in some invisible web. And then he would be able to avoid it happening again. He liked his life exactly the way it was, thanks very much. He did not like this feeling of long-held beliefs wobbling and his footing being less than secure in his world.

Back at the table, Lady Geraldine waved a bejewelled hand and waiters willingly rushed to refill glasses and serve exquisite-looking desserts. Charlotte was sitting very still, staring at the chocolate creation on the small plate in front of her as though unsure whether it was, in fact, edible.

Or maybe she was unsure whether anything was real. Perhaps she was hoping to wake up and find that this whole evening had simply been a bad dream. Her grandmother was also watching her and then she turned to Nico and smiled. It was an expression of understanding. And reassurance. Charlotte just needed a little more time, the glance suggested. And then she would be able to embrace the joy of this new event in her life.

She certainly needed something. A gentle reminder of why they'd started this charade in the first place?

Nico smiled back at Lady Geraldine. 'Tell me about tomorrow,' he invited. 'I hear you have an adventure planned. On the Orient Express?'

Lady Geraldine beamed at him. 'It's been a long-held dream of mine. One of them, anyway.' She slid another glance at Charlotte and there was a moment's pause as she sighed happily. Then she collected herself and focused on Nico. 'Have you ever travelled on the Orient Express yourself?'

'No. I've heard of it, of course. It has a wonderful history, doesn't it?'

'Right back to 1883.' Lady Geraldine nodded. 'It's the world's most famous train and it's been totally restored to its original glory. You step back in time and travel in the kind of elegant luxury that only the very privileged could afford a hundred years ago. It's an experience everybody should have at least once in their lifetime, don't you think?'

'Absolutely.' Nico was happy to agree. This was what this evening was about after all. To make Charlotte's grandmother happy. To encourage her to make the most of whatever time she had left in her own life-

time. To tick off those 'bucket-list' items. 'I hear that the food is amazing and isn't there someone that plays a grand piano in the bar?'

'Oh, yes.' Lady Geraldine's smile was misty now. 'Everybody dresses in their best and is on their best behaviour. We'll all be thoroughly spoiled as we glide through Italy, Austria, Switzerland and France and back to London just in time for Christmas.'

She eyed Nico over a spoon containing a tiny portion of chocolate mousse. 'I expect you'll be visiting your mother for Christmas Day, Nico?'

'Ah…no.' Nico shook his head. 'I believe her new husband has whisked her off to New Zealand to have Christmas in the sun.'

'But you have other family?'

Uh-oh… Any moment now he was going to be invited to have Christmas dinner with Charlotte and her grandmother. He needed to head this one off at the pass.

'Sadly, I have work commitments in London I can't break. That's partly why I'm taking a day or two at my leisure in Venice now.' This was true enough, wasn't it? He was always happy to work over family-oriented holidays to give his colleagues time off. He didn't have a family to spend time with. And he didn't want one. Nico shifted in his seat, which brought his knee into contact with Charlotte's. He heard her sudden intake of breath and she finally seemed to become aware of her surroundings again.

Good. He needed some help here to avoid being pressured into joining the Highton clan for Christmas dinner. Who knew how many other distant but for-

midable relatives Charlotte might have waiting in the wings?

Lady Geraldine had a very benign smile on her face right now as she apparently enjoyed her taste of the dessert but Nico had the distinct feeling that the impression of a sweet old lady was probably deceptive. There was an ironclad will beneath that perfectly groomed exterior and that improbable red hair. What Lady Geraldine wanted, she would no doubt get. Except, maybe, the chance to live to an even riper old age.

He reached for his glass of wine. He increased the pressure on Charlotte's knee a little to encourage her to say something but she was watching her grandmother, who was shaking her head as she put down her spoon.

'Absolutely delicious,' she said sadly. 'But I can't eat it.'

Nico could feel the tension in Charlotte's focus. 'You've hardly eaten anything, Gran.'

'I'm too excited,' Lady Geraldine said.

'About the Orient Express?' This was a good direction to steer the conversation back to. A safe one. 'I'm not surprised. It's probably a good idea to save your appetite for all that wonderful food.'

'Mmm...' Lady Geraldine nodded thoughtfully. 'I *am* excited about the train trip but not nearly as excited as I am about this engagement.' She reached over and took hold of Charlotte's hand, bending the fingers so that the diamond ring took centre stage. 'I don't think I've ever been so happy.' She was locked in eye contact with her granddaughter. 'You will be, too, Charlotte Jane. I just know you will.'

Charlotte's indrawn breath was ragged. 'But...'

'I know, darling.' Nico could see the way Charlotte's

fingers were being squeezed. Lady Geraldine's voice was soft. 'And it doesn't matter if I don't live to see the wedding. This is enough. To know that you've met such a wonderful man and the attraction is strong enough to be totally irresistible. It's a promise of a happy future for you…and I intend to enjoy every single moment of it.'

She straightened in her chair and turned her gaze to Nico. 'I have two cabin suites booked on the Orient Express,' she said unexpectedly. 'I wanted both Charlotte and myself to enjoy this trip as much as possible, without being cramped.'

'Good thinking.' Nico nodded. Thank goodness the topic of conversation was getting back onto safe territory. 'I'm sure you'll enjoy every moment.'

'Oh, I will. Especially now.'

There was something in the gaze from those faded blue eyes that made Nico feel like a small child again. A small child confronted by someone in ultimate authority.

'Because of the engagement?' Nico's smile was a little forced. He should be pleased because this represented exactly what he'd set out to achieve but he had a sinking feeling that he wasn't going to get off quite this easily.

'Exactly,' Lady Geraldine purred.

Maybe he was. Nico's smile widened.

'I can't think of a better way to celebrate,' Lady Geraldine continued, 'Can you?'

'No. What could possibly be a better way to celebrate than the very best of food and wine while you travel in ultimate luxury?'

'I'm so pleased you agree. I'll let the train manager know that you'll be joining us.'

'What?' Both Nico and Charlotte uttered the horrified exclamation simultaneously.

'It's perfect,' Lady Geraldine said calmly. 'You don't have commitments until Christmas Day, Nico, and we'll be back in London by Christmas Eve. As you said yourself, what better way could there be to celebrate? It sounds as though you and Charlotte are going to have a lot of time apart in the near future and I'm sure we all agree that we should all make the most of every moment we can have together. Who knows how many of them there will be?'

Her voice wobbled just a little as she finished speaking. Charlotte's jaw had been dropping but now it snapped shut.

'You can't do this, Gran,' she said slowly. 'You can't use something like your illness to make people do what you want them to do. It's…it's emotional blackmail.'

'Nonsense.' Any hint of frailty vanished from Lady Geraldine's demeanour. 'It's common sense, that's what it is. You're both important, busy people. You'd never make the time for something like this unless someone pushed you into it. And this is a once-in-a-lifetime opportunity. Do you have any idea how hard it was for me to get a booking on this train? And *two* cabins. If it had only been one, I would have given up my place so that you and Nico could have done the trip together.'

'But this is *your* dream, Gran.' Charlotte was shaking her head now, looking bewildered. 'Why would Nico and I want to do it?'

'Because it's the most romantic journey on earth,' Lady Geraldine said. 'You've found each other in the

most romantic city and by astonishing good fortune you now have the chance to build on that by travelling together to the destination you were both heading for anyway. I'm not going to take you away from Nico the day after you've just become engaged, Charlotte. This is my engagement gift to you both—some more time together. If he won't come with us on the train, then you can stay here and I'll go by myself.'

'No…you can't do that. I won't let you. You're not well enough.'

It was a stand-off. Nico didn't need the combined effect of both women looking at him to know he was expected to say something to defuse the tension but, for the life of him, he couldn't think of anything to say. For heaven's sake, all he needed was an excuse that would keep him at least somewhere in Europe for the next twenty four hours but his mind was blank. Stunned at the way this…diversion had taken on a life of its own. Moving at a pace that appeared as unstoppable as the train he was now expected to board tomorrow.

Tables were being cleared around them and any moment now the waiters would come and interrupt this awkward silence, but clearly it wouldn't be soon enough for Charlotte. She made an exasperated sound as she pushed back her chair and got to her feet.

'I need some air,' she announced. 'I'll leave *you* to talk to Gran, Nico.'

Her tone suggested that he was unlikely to get anywhere but that it was his problem. He'd got himself into this mess and now he could get himself out of it. Her body language as she headed towards the balcony suggested that she was washing her hands of the whole situation because it was clearly uncontrollable. The

slump of her shoulders said that she didn't believe he could do it without causing harm.

And maybe she was right. Maybe now he was going have to confess his part in this deception. Was there a way he could do that and convince Lady Geraldine at the same time that it had been done with the very best of intentions and that Charlotte had only gone along with his stupid idea because she loved her grandmother so much?

Nico took a deep breath and opened his mouth but Lady Geraldine got there first to fill the silence.

'Oh, dear…' she murmured. 'And there I was, hoping that she'd finally got over it all…'

Nico couldn't help himself. 'Over what, Jendi?'

Lady Geraldine looked uncomfortable. 'That's the problem, Nico. I've never been able to find out.' She raised her eyebrows. 'I was hoping you might be able to tell *me*.'

'Scusi?' The Italian word popped out, as they often did in moments of great stress or surprise.

'There's only been one other occasion when I've thought that Charlotte might have found the right man for her. The person she was going to spend the rest of her life with. To raise her own family with. And it was *years* ago. Back when she was just a baby doctor and everybody could see how brilliant she was. *Is*,' Lady Geraldine corrected herself but she was frowning. 'I don't know what went wrong,' she continued softly, almost as if she was talking aloud to herself, 'but Charlotte…changed.'

Yes. He was getting to the heart of the mystery now.

'That was the time I first met her,' he confided to Jendi. 'When she was the star of the emergency depart-

ment and nobody could sing her praises highly enough. And she was so happy. There was a sparkle about her that lit up a room. A smile that advertised such confidence...' His voice trailed off as he realised the extent of how radically Charlotte had changed.

The confidence was still there but it was only professional. Cold. That's what had hit him this morning—that lack of sparkle for want of a better word. It was only when he had pushed himself beyond any acceptably professional boundaries that he'd seen a hint of a woman capable of *real* emotion. That buttoned-up outward appearance was like a suit of armour around the old Charlotte.

Whatever had happened had killed her personal confidence. Her hopes for a future outside her work ambitions. Had she been brutally dismissed by a man she'd been deeply in love with?

How could the man have been such an idiot to pass up a woman like Charlotte?

And why did the thought of her being passionately in love with another man stir up a nasty sensation in his gut that he couldn't identify? Was it jealousy? No. That was absurd. He had never felt jealous in his life.

'I saw her out with that man,' he told Jendi. 'At a very exclusive London club. I think we were even introduced. Was he a *prince*?'

Lady Geraldine made a dismissive sound. 'That's what he called himself. He was a long way down the tree of some obscure European royal family. He was certainly a very charming young man. And very sure of himself.'

'So what happened?'

'Charlotte will never talk about it. I didn't see her

for a few weeks. She said she had flu and didn't want to pass it on. And then she always had an excuse of being too busy at work to come to see me and when she finally did I was…shocked.'

'Why?' Nico leaned forward, unconsciously holding his breath.

'She looked…ill. So thin. And…' Lady Geraldine shook her head very slowly and when she raised her gaze to Nico's he could see tears in her eyes. 'You hit the nail right on the head, my dear. Her sparkle had gone. It was like it had been when she first arrived in my care as an orphaned child. When she was so lost and unhappy that she wouldn't even speak. For *months*.'

'She wouldn't speak to you?'

'Oh, no. She wasn't a tiny child any more. She would talk but only if we didn't talk about *him*. Siegfried. All she would say was that the relationship was over and it wasn't important. The only thing that mattered was her work.'

Lady Geraldine looked away. 'I thought if I gave her enough space that she would eventually talk to me about it, but it's been nearly six years and after the first attempt or two I had to give up. It's the one thing that's never discussed but is always there. The elephant in the room, you know?'

'The elephant?' How many odd English phrases were going to test him today?

'The huge thing. You can't ignore it because you always have to walk around it to get anywhere. But you're not allowed to mention it because, if you do, the door gets slammed shut and you can't get anywhere at all.'

'Hmm…' Nico was digesting the information. He was silent for a long time and when he spoke, his voice

was uncharacteristically grim. 'He hurt her,' he said softly. 'He hurt Charlotte badly, this *Siegfried*.'

'Yes.' Lady Geraldine dabbed at the corner of her eyes with her napkin.

'Physically?'

The gasp was shocked. 'Oh, *no*... If he'd done that, she would have gone to the police, surely?'

'But you said she looked unwell.'

'She'd had flu. There was a very bad flu going around that year. One of those bird varieties, I think.'

Nico wasn't listening. How could anyone have wanted to hurt Charlotte? She had been so beautiful. A girl testing the wings of womanhood. In love and totally trusting. What kind of bastard had he been and what had he *done* to her? Nico didn't believe the 'flu' excuse for a moment. And something was telling him that the pain of the broken relationship had not been simply emotional.

'I need to talk to Charlotte,' he said, his chair scraping on the stone-flagged floor as he pushed it back.

Lady Geraldine caught his arm as he turned to leave. Her age and state of health disappeared from Nico's awareness as he read her expression. It was the look of a mother as well as a grandmother. Ageless. She needed to protect her child and she wasn't sure if she should have spoken about her concerns. There was a plea in her eyes that Nico could read only too well.

'I'm not going to hurt her.' The words came out like a vow and Nico meant every one of them. 'I never would. That I can promise you.'

Charlotte was freezing.

An evening dress was entirely inadequate for a win-

ter's night in Venice but she couldn't go back inside. She could see that the evening was winding up now and people were leaving.

Good. If she waited a little longer, there would be no audience for when she had to go back in and face her grandmother after Nico had explained why he couldn't accompany them on the Orient Express.

She could see them through the tall, arched window. Their body language was intense as they leaned towards each other, oblivious to anyone else in the room. The fairy lights made the room seem like another world and Charlotte could see the Christmas images still scrolling against the far wall. Snowmen and sleighs. Christmas trees and prettily wrapped parcels. Happy people. Families. Parents with excited children.

Parents who had once been lovers. Engaged couples.

Charlotte was twisting the ring on her finger without realising it. She gave it a tug. Good grief…it was a tight fit. She was going to need soap to get it off. Maybe she should go into the bathroom and find some.

But then she saw Nico get to his feet abruptly and she saw the way her grandmother caught his arm. For a moment that seemed suspended in time she saw the way they looked at each other and the light was enough for her to see the expression on Nico's face. Such a *kind* expression. Loving. Intense. The kind of look someone might have if they were making a promise they intended to keep.

Or maybe he'd been apologising. Was he coming out to tell her it was safe to go back in now?

Charlotte's heart picked up as Nico came out onto the balcony. He moved with such grace, this man. A calm assurance that he could command his environ-

ment and protect anyone within it. Powerful but not intimidating because there was a softness about him. That slow, easy smile. The glint in those dark eyes that advertised the ability to find joy in life. To play.

That's what they'd been doing tonight and Charlotte couldn't deny that, for a while, it had been...fun. No. Fun wasn't the word. What had drawn her in had been the illusion. The need to taste something that was so seductive it was irresistible. The illusion of being in love. With Nico.

She had to turn her head and stop staring at him as if the charade was still continuing.

'Did you talk to Gran?'

'I did.' Nico was close to her now.

'Did you tell her the truth? Does she understand why you can't come on the train with us?' Charlotte couldn't repress a shiver. Was it the cold or the disappointment of failure?

'Not exactly.' Nico was shrugging off his jacket. He stepped closer and draped it over Charlotte's shoulders.

Her first instinct was to shrug the garment off with a dismissive shake. She wasn't a child who needed someone to take care of her. She could look after herself, thanks very much.

But the gesture had been unexpectedly thoughtful. *Caring.*

And the warmth was astonishingly comforting. Charlotte could feel her fingers creeping to the edges of the jacket to pull it closer around her. The warmth was the warmth of Nico's body. The slide of the silk lining against the bare skin of her arms and shoulders made it feel as though *he* was touching her.

It was disturbingly intimate now. Charlotte could

even catch a whiff of a scent that was pure male. Pure Nico? She had to close her eyes for a heartbeat as she tried to stop herself inhaling deeply.

'Your grandmother loves you very much,' Nico said quietly. 'She does not want you to be hurt…again.'

Again? Her eyes snapped open. Oh, my God…what had they been talking about in there? But Gran didn't know the truth so she couldn't have told Nico. She was safe.

So why didn't she *feel* safe?

'W-what did *you* say?'

Nico looked more serious than she'd seen him look all day. Even when he'd been arriving at a potentially fatal incident. The subdued look didn't sit well on a face that was made for laughter. Her heart skipped another beat.

'I told her that I would never hurt you.'

'So she still thinks that we're…we're *engaged*?'

Nico's mouth twitched. 'I'm afraid so. I couldn't bring myself to cause her pain.'

It shouldn't be such a relief. Not when Charlotte couldn't see any way out of this.

'And the train?'

Nico shrugged. 'I have a free day. I have to get back to London. Why not?'

'Because…it's impossible. How could we keep this up for thirty hours?' Charlotte had another try at tugging the ring off her finger, looking away from him as she did so.

She could see past Nico to where the final guests for the evening were leaving. Only her grandmother remained and the maître d' was looking concerned, helping the elderly woman to her feet. Lady Geraldine

was pointing towards the balcony. And now she was walking towards the door.

'Nothing is impossible,' Nico was saying.

'She's coming. She'll guess. She's not stupid.'

'She won't guess if you stop trying to remove that ring.' Nico caught her hands. 'If we…'

His hands moved, pulling hers up to his neck before he let them go. His hands kept moving, though, burying themselves in her hair. Cupping the back of her head and tilting it as he leaned in to cover her mouth with his own.

He was *kissing* her.

Just for show. To cover an awkward moment when Gran might have picked up on the tension between them.

Except…it didn't feel like a pretend kiss.

Or maybe it did, for that first, startled moment as their lips made contact, but then Nico's lips moved with a kind of question that Charlotte couldn't help responding to on some deep, instinctive level that totally overruled any conscious thought. Her lips parted beneath his and when she felt the touch of his tongue against hers all ability to control her thoughts vanished.

A fleeting hope that her grandmother would see them and stay well away to give them a private moment evaporated, along with any awareness of what was around them. Charlotte was completely lost in this kiss. Transported to a place she'd never been. A place where passion and tenderness combined to create an all-consuming fuel that could burn away anything and everything and leave only peace and fulfilment in its wake.

A kiss that promised everything. So much more than this touch of lips and tongues.

More…

And that was when Charlotte stopped being lost. She couldn't do more. If she tried, Nico would find out and he would know what was so wrong with her.

That she could go so far and no further. Because she was not a real woman. Real women liked going further. They weren't…*frigid.*

That did it. Just the tiniest echo of that hateful word was enough. Charlotte wrenched herself back from Nico's touch. His jacket slid from her shoulders and puddled on the stone terrace. She could turn to see what had happened, scoop up the jacket and try to collect herself before acknowledging her grandmother standing in the restaurant doorway.

'Oh…Gran… I'm so sorry. I…lost track of time.'

'So I see.' Lady Geraldine's smile warmed the winter's night.

Nico was rubbing his lips slowly with his forefinger, staring at Charlotte, but now he also turned towards the door.

'You must be tired, Jendi. Let me see you both back to your hotel.'

'That would be lovely, Nico. Thank you. We have an early start tomorrow. I think we have to be at the Santa Lucia station by nine a.m. to catch the train.'

It was Charlotte's turn to stare at Nico but he didn't meet her gaze. Instead, he put an arm around her waist as they began moving.

'No problem,' he told her grandmother. 'I'm an early riser.'

CHAPTER SIX

'WHERE IS HE?'

'I don't know, Gran.' Charlotte allowed a small seed of hope to blossom that Nico might fail to show up in time. Or maybe that odd squeeze in her chest was disappointment?

Yep. There was definitely an internal struggle going on here. The safest thing was to never see Nico Moretti again and that's what she should want. And, yes, she could try and convince herself that she only wanted him around, continuing this pretence of a relationship, because it was such a joy to see her grandmother so happy, but there was no way of hiding the real truth. Part of her—a big, rebellious part of her—simply wanted to be close to him again.

'Maybe something came up.' Like a bout of common sense? 'He doesn't have our phone numbers so he might not have been able to let us know.'

The train was already here at the station, the sleek, dark blue carriages with the gold trim, the coat of arms featuring two rampant lions and the lettering announcing that this was, indeed, the Venice Simplon Orient Express. As if anyone could mistake it! Among the ordinary modern European trains in the station, this

one stood out like a beacon. So did the attendants. The gold-trimmed blue uniforms looked positively military and the pillbox hats the stewards were wearing made them look ready for a fancy-dress party.

The check-in desk stood out on the grey concrete of the platform in equally startling contrast. A red carpet, of all things, with brass posts holding tasselled ropes to create an oasis of luxury amidst the mundane. Even the people milling around looked different. Like that young woman in a long coat that belonged to another era, its fur collar turned up around her neck. The people were generally better dressed, certainly, but that wasn't the only difference. There was an air of excitement that encased this part of the station and separated it from the rest. From the real world.

'I knew we should have offered to let him share our water taxi.'

'It would have been a bit of a squeeze with all your luggage, Gran.'

It had, in fact, taken an impressive tip to get the water taxi driver to leave his boat tied up and carry Gran's bags up the daunting flight of stairs leading into the train station from the road beside the canal. 'You did know you're only supposed to have one cabin bag and one piece of luggage to be checked in, didn't you?'

Her grandmother sniffed. 'If you're going to do the Orient Express, it must be done in style. Everybody knows that. Goodness knows how you get away with nothing more than an oversized handbag.'

Cabin luggage hadn't been all Charlotte had been carrying on her way to Venice, of course. She'd had her laptop bag to contend with as well. An accessory that was now lying on the bottom of a Venetian canal.

She could remember the expression on Nico's face as he'd realised what had happened. So apologetic, even though it hadn't exactly been his fault. The willingness to do whatever he could to put things right.

He was a kind man. And a generous one. The tailored suit jacket Charlotte was wearing again today suddenly felt tight. Scratchy, almost, as her senses replayed the sensation of the silk lining of Nico's jacket against her bare skin. A sensation that morphed almost seamlessly into remembering that kiss.

How kind was he? Kind enough not to reveal astonishment...*disgust*...when he found out what Charlotte was lacking?

And then there was that very tiny seed of what was definitely hope because that kiss had made her feel things that no other kiss ever had—even Siegfried's. And if just a kiss felt that different, maybe other things would feel different too and maybe...just *maybe*...she'd be able to—

Oh, *help*... Wasn't it enough that her memory of that little scene had kept her awake virtually all night? She couldn't allow it to keep distracting her like this. Charlotte balanced her cabin bag on top of Gran's biggest suitcase and grabbed the handle of the other with her free hand. With a determined shove she began moving the luggage towards a check-in desk that looked suspiciously like an antique mahogany piece. Lady Geraldine pulled the handle of her smaller bag as she followed.

'You're going to have to wear the same dress for dinner tonight that you had on last night, aren't you?'

'What was wrong with my dress?' It had been the first time Charlotte had worn the slinky, silver num-

ber but she'd been delighted with how it had looked when she'd put it on. How good it had made her feel.

'It's a lovely dress, dear. You just need more than one of them.'

It was a lovely dress. And if Charlotte was honest, she'd felt way more than simply 'good' in it. The way Nico had run his eyes over it more than once, as though the experience was a pleasure all in itself. Yes...that dress had made her feel *beautiful*. An odd experience for a woman who did virtually nothing to enhance her appearance in order to attract the attention of the opposite sex.

'Nobody's going to know I'm wearing it two nights in a row.' Charlotte smiled at the woman behind the desk and handed over the tickets.

'Apart from your fiancé.'

The woman behind the desk was smiling. 'You must be Lady Geraldine. We got your message. We're delighted to be able to welcome Dr Moretti on board to accompany you and your granddaughter.'

'Um...there could be a small problem...' Charlotte began. But the woman wasn't listening. She wasn't even looking at her and the expression on her face suggested that she was looking at something far more interesting.

A tall and extremely attractive man, perhaps?

'Cara...' The endearment was a caress. 'I'm so sorry I'm late.' Nico pulled Charlotte into his arms and then bent to brush her lips in a perfectly acceptable kiss for a public place. Except it lingered for just a heartbeat too long. And his eyes lingered on hers even longer. Charlotte dragged in a breath. The part of her that wanted to be close to Nico was winning. Doing a happy dance

inside her chest that made her heart thump and send extra blood up to warm her cheeks. The wash of relief was unmistakeable and hot on its heels was something she hadn't felt in years.

Excitement. The kind a small child would have creeping downstairs too early on Christmas morning and seeing the magic of the gifts under the tree. Gifts for *her*.

Did she dare to pick one up and rattle it? Tear off a tiny piece of wrapping paper to see if she could guess what was inside?

But what if it wasn't what she wanted? Maybe the anticipation was better than reality.

'I went to the hospital,' Nico explained. 'I knew you'd want to know how our man from yesterday was getting on.'

To her shame, no doubt due to the emotional roller-coaster the day had presented, Charlotte had barely given the man another thought. So much for her heart-felt presentation yesterday about the medicine they practised being about the people. But Nico was right. She could feel her face light up in her eagerness to know the outcome. This was the kind of excitement she was used to. *This* was what she needed to focus on.

'He's doing well.' Nico's smile was one of pure de-light. 'He had an angioplasty and half a dozen stents put in. His broken leg's been sorted and he's sitting up in the coronary care unit and you'd never know he'd been dead for a while. No evidence of any brain damage even.'

'Really? That's…astonishing. Our CPR must have been up to standard, then.'

'A little more than that, I think.' Nico put his arm

around Charlotte's shoulders as he turned towards Lady Geraldine. 'We are an amazing team. And here we are, about to have an adventure. I am the happiest man on earth.'

Lady Geraldine was beaming at them. The check-in clerk was smiling mistily but then she collected herself. 'Here are your boarding passes. We'll take care of the suitcases and you can take your cabin baggage with you. I wish you the happiest of journeys.'

Lady Geraldine merely nodded. 'It will be,' she said softly. She winked at Charlotte. 'All that remains to be seen is which of us is the happiest *woman* on earth today.'

Lady Geraldine needed some assistance to climb up the steps and negotiate the narrow corridor of the train carriage. The first impression was the glow of polished wood and brass. And lights. Lamps casting a soft glow. Fairy lights in honour of the season, looped at ceiling height on the internal wall and twinkling merrily. The doors had small wreaths festooned with artificial cherries and tiny golden bells.

Even more overwhelming than the warm glow of the wood and lights was a sense of confinement. The cabins were tiny with no more than a richly uphol-stered double seat and a tiny table beneath the window. A washstand was cleverly incorporated into a corner.

For most passengers this would have been their total space but with a suite, a door beside the washstand cab-inet was open, leading to the adjoining cabin where the seats had already been turned into comfortable-look-ing bunk beds with crisp white linen and soft-looking towels folded on the ends.

For one person, it would have been the ultimate

in spaciousness aboard the train. For a couple, it still would have been more than enough. To share this amount of space with Nico Moretti was something entirely different. There didn't seem to be enough oxygen in the small spaces.

Their personal steward served champagne as the train pulled out of Santa Lucia station while Charlotte was checking that Lady Geraldine was settling comfortably into her suite. Nico joined them as the steward pointed out features of the cabins, including the bell that would summon him for assistance at any time of the day or night.

'The maître d' will visit your cabin soon to take your lunch and dinner reservations. Our restaurant cars have tables for two or four people.'

'We are a party of three,' Charlotte informed him. And how lucky was that? No chance of an intimate table for two with soft lighting and too much champagne. If she could put up good enough barriers around that part of her that was so drawn to this man she would be safe from making a complete fool of herself.

Was that a significant look that her grandmother was sharing with Nico?

'This is your gift,' Charlotte added, for good measure. 'And we intend to share every possible moment of it with you. Don't we, Nico?'

Nico seemed to be relishing the champagne and he merely lifted his glass in a toast of agreement.

There wasn't room for three people to sit in one cabin. Charlotte sat beside her grandmother as they opened and perused the map of the journey. Nico stood near the door, apparently enjoying the scenery through

the corridor windows and chatting to other passengers as they went past.

They chose the first sitting for lunch and it was Nico who insisted on helping Lady Geraldine negotiate the route and cope with the sometimes jerky motion of the train. It took a long time to get through several carriages and through the bar car before they got to one of the restaurant cars, especially when everything had to be explored and admired.

'The bathroom is amazing,' Lady Geraldine declared after their first stop to wait for her, which was right beside her suite at the end of their carriage. 'The toilet seat is made of mahogany and everything else is brass. Even the cover for the paper. And it's all so clean and shiny.'

The resident pianist was not yet playing the baby grand piano in the bar but they had to stop there as well.

'Play something, Charlotte,' Lady Geraldine commanded.

'I can't do that.' Charlotte was horrified. 'I haven't played a piano for years and I'm quite sure it's not allowed, anyway.'

But the handsome young man polishing glasses behind the wooden bar grinned. 'Go ahead,' he invited. 'It's too early to bother anyone.'

'Please, Charlotte.' Lady Geraldine was heading for a nearby seat. 'For me? It's so long since I heard you play.'

And she might never hear her again?

'Yes… Please, Charlotte.' Nico's smile was mischievous. 'I'm curious about your splinter skills.'

Oh, for heaven's sake. Charlotte realised she wasn't

going to win and the best way of avoiding stress in getting through this voyage was clearly going to be taking the path of least resistance. She slid herself onto the piano stool and raised the lid on the gleaming keys. She had taken lessons for years as a child and playing for pleasure had been a feature of every visit to her grandmother's house. Until...until her life had changed overnight.

Her hands shook for a moment as she held them over the keys. Maybe the least stressful response would have been to refuse to do this but now it was too late and if she didn't, she might be expected to provide an explanation.

Flicking a glance upwards Charlotte knew that Nico had seen the tell-tale tremor of her hands. She willed them to be still. Willed herself to continue, much as she'd forced herself to start that presentation in Nico's presence yesterday. The only piece she could think of to play by heart was Beethoven's 'Moonlight Sonata'.

The first notes were tentative but the piano was beautiful and within a few bars Charlotte was drawn in to the haunting sound of the music. Her stiff fingers relaxed as she remembered the release that this had once brought her. The pleasure of doing something for herself that had nothing to do with work. Mindless and satisfying and restorative. Just...pleasure...

'Bravo...' Nico's eyes were full of admiration as the last notes died away.

'I knew those piano lessons were worth every penny.' Lady Geraldine held her hand out for Nico to help her to her feet. 'Now, let's go and have some lunch.'

The lunch was three courses of beautifully prepared

and presented food but Lady Geraldine only picked at hers and didn't touch the tarte tatin served for dessert.

'I'm a little tired,' she confessed. 'I think I'll go back to my cabin and rest for a while.'

'I'll come and keep you company,' Charlotte offered immediately.

'No. I might need some help to get back without being knocked off my feet but I need some quiet time. I might have a nap.'

Charlotte felt her level of concern ramp up. Gran hadn't eaten much and now she looked pale. Was she in pain?

It was Nico's arm that Lady Geraldine chose to lean on to keep her balance and they had to stop at frequent intervals to allow other people to pass on their way to the restaurants.

One of those people was another elderly woman whose head turned in surprise as she took another look.

'Lady Geraldine? Jendi?'

'Oh, my goodness. Winsome Black. What on earth are you doing here?'

'I could ask you the same thing. What an astonishing coincidence.'

Lady Geraldine's head shake was incredulous. 'It's a small world, isn't it?' She turned to Charlotte. 'Winsome's an old friend that I haven't seen for years. We worked together once on a huge fundraiser for that children's charity.'

'One Last Wish.' Winsome nodded at Charlotte. 'Such a worthy cause. They made wishes come true for terminally ill children.'

'This is my granddaughter, Charlotte,' Lady Geraldine said.

'And this is my grandson, Connor.' The good-looking young man, who was clearly aware of how much space they were all taking up in the narrow corridor, smiled at Charlotte and offered her his hand.

She shook it with an equally conspiratorial smile. They had something in common, didn't they? Here they both were in the company of grandmothers with... personality.

'Charlotte and her fiancé are keeping me company,' Lady Geraldine was confiding in Winsome. Her smile was poignant. 'This trip is my last wish...'

'Oh, surely not.' Winsome smiled. 'I seem to remember you telling me that age is only an attitude.'

Lady Geraldine opened her mouth but then noticed the human traffic jam they were creating in the corridor. 'We'd better get a move on,' she said. 'But we must get together, Winsome, and have a proper chat.'

'That would be lovely.'

'How about afternoon tea? We could meet in the bar at, say, four o'clock?'

'See you then.' With a smile, Winsome continued on her way.

Charlotte wondered if the arrangement might be too much given that her grandmother had already said she needed a rest, but the sparkle in the elderly woman's eyes chased away the worry that her condition was deteriorating and that this trip would prove too much for her.

'Oh, look...the queue at the gift shop has gone. Let's see what they have.'

Charlotte was quite happy to linger and look at the souvenirs available. The more time they spent doing

things like this, the less time she would have to spend with Nico, alone in their cabin while Gran had a rest.

You could buy hand-blown crystal glasses and crockery with the Orient Express insignia. There were salt and pepper shakers, travel accessories in blue velvet, photo frames and even jewellery.

Lady Geraldine chose a specially bound copy of Agatha Christie's *Murder on the Orient Express*. And then she ordered Charlotte and Nico to choose a gift for themselves.

'A selection of wine glasses would be a lovely engagement present,' she suggested.

'You are celebrating an engagement?' The tall man with a heavy accent who ran the gift boutique sighed happily. 'I tell everybody that this is the train of love…'

'This trip is the gift, Gran. Remember? We don't need anything else.'

But the tall man was putting things on the counter in front of Nico. 'For your beautiful lady?' he murmured. 'A special memory, perhaps?'

Blue velvet cases were being opened to display pearl necklaces on silver chains that had clasps engraved with the train's insignia. Silver and gold bangles were similarly engraved. A chain bracelet had tiny silver charms like a train carriage, a conductor's whistle and a pillbox hat but Nico was picking up another bracelet. He held it up to show Charlotte.

'Do you like this, *cara*?'

Tiny silver hearts linked together. A delicate piece of jewellery.

Romantic.

Charlotte opened her mouth to tell him that she didn't wear jewellery but out of the corner of her eye

she saw the way her grandmother was pressing a hand
to her throat. Holding her breath as she witnessed evi-
dence of the love her granddaughter had finally found?

'It's…lovely.' Let him buy it, she told herself. She
could reimburse him later.

Nico not only purchased the bracelet, he insisted on
putting it on Charlotte's wrist. His fingers brushed her
skin as he fed the rod of the clasp through the silver
circle engraved with the name of the train.

He smiled at her then. Just the way he had when he'd
sat at their table last night. As though she was the only
woman in the world for him. As if he was so deeply in
love that nothing else mattered.

She knew he was going to kiss her. The tall man
wanted it to happen. Her grandmother wanted it to
happen.

And, God help her, *she* wanted it to happen.

It was just a kiss and her lips were ready for it this
time, already soft and slightly parted. If she sat down at
a piano any time soon again, she would probably find
that her fingers were instantly ready for the release of
music too. The pleasure to be found. The connections
between her fingers and her brain and her heart had
unexpectedly been woken up after a very long sleep.

Like her lips had been?

Not that it was a passionate kiss, of course. Just a
gentle pressure. But the promise was there. And no
matter how fiercely Charlotte told herself that she
didn't want this and couldn't go there, her body was
defying her. The shaft of desire was so much more in-
tense after last night. How on earth was she going to
cope with the rest of this journey? Where were some
new barriers when she needed them?

At least Nico left her alone to do some more exploring after Lady Geraldine was settled back into her cabin behind a closed door. It gave Charlotte time to try and rebuild her defences. To plan how she could get through the next hours. Maybe one of them could sleep in here, on the seat? At the very least she could choose the top bunk so that she wouldn't have Nico climbing past inches away from her face. What did he wear in bed? Oh, God…imagine him climbing up wearing nothing but a pair of silk boxers or skin-hugging cotton knit underwear. And even with the highly unlikely possibility that he had a pair of flannelette pyjamas in his bag, she'd still be aware of him sleeping beneath her, wouldn't she? She would hear his breathing. Feel the warmth of his presence. *All* night.

Heavens, it was warm in here. Charlotte adjusted the central heating radiator beneath the window and even opened the top window a little for some fresh air. She was just beginning to feel calmer when Nico returned to the cabin.

He was carrying a bottle of champagne in a silver ice bucket. Two crystal glasses dangled from his other hand. He leaned against the door with a smile of invitation curling the corners of his mouth.

What woman would be able to resist?

Charlotte, that's who, with her grandmother safely shut away and all the good work of calming herself down undone in an instant.

It wasn't hard to glare at Nico as though he was committing an unpardonable sin. 'What on earth are you thinking?' she snapped. 'I hope you're not planning to get me drunk so you can take advantage of me again.'

* * *

Again?

Nico shoved the cabin door shut with his foot. The champagne had seemed like a good idea. They were supposed to be celebrating their engagement, weren't they? They didn't have to drink the damned stuff. And what was wrong with trying to make this journey as pleasant as possible, anyway?

What *was* Charlotte's problem?

'Take *advantage* of you?' He kept his voice quiet but allowed it to cool noticeably. 'Is that how you see this?'

Her voice was small. 'No.'

At least she had the grace to look embarrassed but it wasn't good enough.

'On balance, I suspect most people would consider you to be taking advantage of *me* right about now.'

'You agreed.' Charlotte had two bright spots of colour on her cheeks and her tone was accusing. 'This was all *your* idea—'

'I have gone out of my way to help you,' Nico interrupted, dumping the ice bucket and glasses on the table by the window, oblivious to the glorious scenery of the Italian Dolomites rushing past in the distance. 'And it is *not* because I have any intention of "taking advantage" of you. You are the complete opposite of the type of woman I find attractive.'

A curious expression changed Charlotte's features. She looked...hurt? Disappointed? Surely not. The expression was gone as quickly as it had appeared but it took the wind out of Nico's sails. His anger evaporating, he sank down onto the seat beside her. 'Do you want to know the real reason?' he asked.

'Mmm?' The sound was somewhat strangled but

Charlotte was looking at her hands, which were clasped tightly together in her lap.

'You fascinate me,' Nico said simply. An honest statement, dragged from a deep place, possibly against his better judgement.

There was a long moment of silence but Nico let it ride as he tried to shut down the implications. Why did this interest feel so very different from the attraction a woman usually had for him? Was it a threat?

Very slowly, Charlotte finally raised her head. Her eyes were a dark, stormy grey and they were wide and puzzled. Fearful, almost.

'Why?' The word was a whisper.

Why indeed?

'You're a beautiful woman, Carlotta.' The Italian version of her name came to his lips unbidden. 'You are also very intelligent and successful. I have a great admiration for your professional abilities.' He could feel a corner of his mouth quirk. 'You are also surprisingly talented at playing the piano.'

A snort of mirth escaped Charlotte as she shook her head, encouraging a lock of hair to escape the tight ponytail she was wearing today.

Nico couldn't resist catching that lock and smoothing it back behind her ear. 'I believe that people come into your life for a reason,' he added quietly. 'I find myself in an extraordinary place, if only for a limited time, and I have to wonder if fate has brought us together because we have something we can learn from each other.'

She was looking at him now as if he'd grown two heads. 'Like what?'

'I don't know.' Nico shrugged. 'Maybe it's your as-

tonishing grandmother I was destined to meet. To learn how one can make the most of life until the very end. Or how to face the prospect of that end with such dignity and courage.'

'Oh…' Charlotte caught her top lip between her teeth but it wasn't enough to stop tears rushing to her eyes.

Dio…he hadn't intended to make her cry. Nico extracted one of her still-clasped hands and held it between his own.

'Or maybe I need to learn about family,' he said. 'The love you have for your *nonna* touches me very much. Right here.' He brought her hand up to press it against his heart. 'I don't have a bond like that. Perhaps I pushed my mother away because of the childhood sadness of losing my father. Maybe that's why I never want to marry or have a family of my own because I can't imagine inflicting that kind of pain on children.

'But half of me is Italian and it doesn't feel right. I've ignored that sense for many years but seeing you with your *nonna* opened my eyes.' His smile was wry. 'I don't know if it will change how I live my life but it feels right to be helping you.'

'But you wouldn't inflict that pain on your own children.' He could feel the pressure as Charlotte started holding *his* hand instead of just letting hers be held. 'Because you'd know what it was like. And even if the marriage didn't work, you'd still keep your bond with your children. You'd fight for it. And win.'

She believed that. She believed in *him*. It gave Nico an odd frisson of…what, pride? Invincibility? Oh, yes…he could conquer the world if a woman like Charlotte truly believed in him. Except…

'It's not going to happen…' The admission was being torn from somewhere that had been so well locked away maybe he hadn't even been aware of it himself. 'The kind of love that leads to marriage… and children…can only happen if you can fall in love. I think…I think that I'm not capable of doing that.'

There it was. His deepest, darkest secret. Something that he'd never said to anyone. From the shocked expression on Charlotte's face she must realise the significance of his confession. But she didn't believe it.

'Why not?'

Nico had to swallow hard. Why was he putting himself through this? Because it seemed like a pathway to get Charlotte to open up about herself? If he stopped now, he'd never reach his goal.

'I love my mother,' he said quietly. 'I can't blame her for wanting to find happiness in her life and the men she falls in love with don't seem to be able to provide that for very long. But I loved my father too and, even as a child, I could see that he was destroyed by losing the woman he loved so much. Falling in love can create so much pain. You either end up being destroyed yourself, like my father, or destroying others, like my mother has—more than once.'

'That doesn't have to happen. Not if you choose the right person who can give you what you need.'

'What if you don't know what it is that you need? How can you possibly make the right choice of a person to be with for the rest of your life?' Nico shook his head. 'No. It's safer to never fall in love. Perhaps I'm lucky that I have that inability.'

Charlotte was still staring at him, a crease of concern between her brows.

'But you don't want to end up like Gran,' she said, with a wobble in her voice. 'Old and sick but with nobody to care about you. No child. No grandchild.' Her voice trailed away as if Nico wasn't supposed to hear her next words. 'That's what terrifies *me*…'

'So why are you alone?' Nico turned so that he could look directly at Charlotte. 'A beautiful, talented woman who should be thinking of having children of her own so that she can have grandchildren one day.'

There was no response other than a withdrawal Nico could both see and feel. As if the white witch from Narnia had waved her wand and turned his companion to stone.

Nico had bared a part of his soul here. A part that had never been shared before and never would be again. Charlotte wasn't going to be allowed not to take her turn.

'Tell me about Siegfried,' he said.

'No.' The refusal was absolute. Charlotte pulled her hand away and turned to stare out of the window.

Nico leaned back against the seat, letting his head rest on the lace-covered cushion. 'I'm a patient man,' he said lightly. 'We have the rest of today. And *all* night.'

He couldn't miss the way Charlotte's chest heaved as she gasped silently. Struggling for control? Interesting. He was getting somewhere, at least.

Nico watched her profile closely. 'We are in this extraordinary place and time and we never have to see each other again after tomorrow. I believe I have something to learn from you, Carlotta. And I think that maybe you have something to learn from me.'

He touched her arm and she flinched. Nico sighed. He should give up. Accept that Charlotte wasn't pre-

pared or ready to learn anything. Except he didn't believe that. She just had to unbutton herself a little more. And if she did that, maybe he would get the answers to the mystery of why she'd changed so much. And then his fascination with her would fade and his life could get back to normal.

'In order to learn something,' he offered carefully, 'maybe you have to be prepared to admit that there's something you don't know. To be open. And honest. Being honest makes you vulnerable, I know that. But I've been honest with you.'

Charlotte nodded. 'You have.'

'More than honest. I've told you something that I've never told anyone else. That I never *will* tell anyone else. Something that I see as...shameful. What kind of man am I if I cannot fall in love or be the kind of husband and father a woman would want?'

She was still struggling. Did she even realise that she was shaking her head very slowly? That her hands were gripping each other tightly enough to have cut off any useful supply of blood?

'You have the power to hurt me, Charlotte, if you chose to share that information with anyone. I'm trusting you not to do that.'

The slow headshake turned into an equally measured nod. A promise.

Nico lowered his voice to something just above a whisper as he touched her again. And this time she didn't flinch. 'You can trust me.' He cleared his throat and spoke more strongly. 'So...will you do me the honour of being honest with me?'

Dio, that had disturbing echoes of some kind of marriage proposal. Except it wasn't, of course, so he

didn't need to feel as if he was getting completely out of his depth.

Even when Charlotte raised her eyes to his and he could see that she wanted to tell him.

Wanted to trust him.

She was just having to gather so much courage that it broke his heart to watch.

'I loved him.' She finally choked the words out. 'I thought he loved me. But he wanted… I couldn't…' There was agony coating the words now. 'We weren't… *compatible.*'

There was another message in her eyes now. One that said Charlotte was unbearably alone in the world but that there was nothing she could do about it.

Nico sighed again, more heavily this time, as though utterly defeated. He held out his arms and gathered Charlotte to his chest.

And held her while she cried.

CHAPTER SEVEN

'THERE'S NOTHING LIKE a *proper* afternoon tea, is there?'
Lady Geraldine sighed happily as she stirred sugar
into her second cup and listened appreciatively to the
sound of silverware tapping against real bone china.
'Did you know you can buy these lovely cups and sau-
cers from the gift shop?'

'I'll have to have a look. I'm planning to go there
after this.'

Lady Geraldine couldn't help noticing the glow of
Winsome's smile. Her old friend certainly looked very
happy these days. She could return the smile easily.
She had a lot to be happy about herself at the moment.

Like meeting an old friend unexpectedly. Being on
her once-in-a-lifetime dream journey. Actually sitting
in this famous bar carriage with the pianist now in res-
idence playing some soft, classical music interspersed
with Christmas carols. Remembering Charlotte playing
on the beautiful instrument earlier when it had been
the first time she'd heard her in so many years. Could
it be that it was Nico who was bringing back the part
of her granddaughter she'd been missing for so long?

She picked up the elegant white cup with the blue
ribbon pattern around its rim and the VSOE logo under

a small crown. 'Maybe a set of these would make a lovely engagement gift for my Charlotte and her Nico.'

'You said they'd only met yesterday? In Venice? When they both saved that man's life?'

'Yes…' Lady Geraldine pushed aside that tiny niggle of doubt. 'But they'd met before. Years ago, at Charlotte's hospital. Fate has just thrown them back together and…' She sighed again. 'It's obviously meant to be. Like your Connor and…what was her name again?'

The conversation paused for a moment as the steward removed the plates that had contained tiny sandwiches and replaced it with a platter of warm scones, adding small silver pots of jam and clotted cream.

'Mmm…' Lady Geraldine eyed the cream. 'Proper Cornish clotted cream, by the look of that.'

'Kelsie,' Winsome said as she followed her friend's example and picked up one of the scones. 'Kelsie Summers. But I don't think she and Connor are about to fall into each other's arms like your Charlotte and Nico. She jilted him, in fact, fifteen years ago and I have the feeling he hasn't forgiven her.'

'Really?' Lady Geraldine had spread the jam and clotted cream onto her scone and was just about to take her first bite but the conversation had just become more enticing than the calorie-laden treat. 'They must have been very young. Oh, *do* tell…'

They both dropped their voices to a more discreet level and Lady Geraldine listened to the story with avid interest. Young love could be such a fragile thing, couldn't it? She had to hope that there wouldn't be any unforeseen twists in the road ahead for Charlotte and Nico.

She finally turned her attention back to her scone but her expression was thoughtful.

'We might be able to help things along,' she suggested.

'What do you mean?'

'The dinner seating is very strict, I hear.'

'It certainly is. I've tried to change tables at the last minute on some of my previous journeys and it almost never happens.'

'It's not the last minute yet,' Lady Geraldine said firmly. 'And if we both had a little chat to the maître d', I'm sure we could persuade him to juggle things a little.'

'In what way?'

'By making an extra table available. We've still got a lot of catching up to do, haven't we? We haven't even started talking about that terrible business with Deirdre Wilkins defrauding the charity so that she could run off to the Maldives with that "personal" trainer of hers.'

Lady Geraldine knew her smile would reveal how much she enjoyed an occasional bit of juicy gossip. 'If we asked to be seated together, that would mean leaving both your Connor and this Kelsie and my Charlotte and the lovely Nico alone at their tables.'

'Yes... If we could make sure they gave them a table for two or didn't put another couple to join them at one of the bigger tables.'

'It would be so romantic, wouldn't it? Everybody dressed up and the lighting all soft and lots of delicious champagne to add to the atmosphere?'

Winsome was smiling. 'Why don't we ask our nice steward to go and see if the maître d' might be able to spare us a minute or two?'

* * *

Charlotte drifted towards consciousness with reluctance.

She had never felt so comfortable. So relaxed. So *safe*. She was floating, supported by a strength she knew she could trust. Cradled against it and it was warm and…moving?

Yes. A steady, gentle movement like breathing. And there was an equally steady but gentle thumping against her ear.

A sound she normally only heard through a stethoscope.

Awareness of where she was kicked in. Or should that be who she was with?

Asleep on, in fact?

'Ohhh…' Charlotte pushed herself upright with a groan. 'I fell *asleep*?'

'You did.' There was amusement in Nico's tone. And a tenderness that touched something that felt raw inside Charlotte.

The last thing she remembered was bursting into tears and Nico holding her. She'd expected him to want more information about what had gone so wrong with her relationship with Siegfried. For her to define what she'd meant by being incompatible. But he hadn't asked anything. He'd offered her comfort instead, as though he understood. As though everything could somehow be put right.

And it had been too much for Charlotte. Her defences had collapsed completely and she'd sobbed out the tears that had been bottled up for years and years. And then she must have been overcome by sheer exhaustion and fallen asleep.

And he'd just continued to hold her?

'How long?' Charlotte put a hand to her hair, which felt like a rat's nest. She closed her eyes in disbelief and found that her eyelashes felt all clumpy when she blinked. She probably had mascara all over her face. She opened them again. The short winter's day was ending already and it was dark outside but their cabin was glowing in the soft light from a lamp on the table. 'How long have I been asleep?'

Nico was tilting his head to one side and then the other, stretching his neck. 'I wasn't watching the clock.' He smiled. 'I may have dozed off myself, in fact.'

Charlotte could feel a smile stirring. A joke about them sleeping together forming.

'Only until the steward woke me to tell me about Jendi.'

The smile and joke evaporated. 'What? Oh, my God…and you didn't wake me? What was wrong? Why—?'

Nico put a finger against her lips and the gentle pressure stopped her anxious flow of words.

'He merely came to ask if I could accompany her to the bar for the afternoon tea she had arranged to have with Mrs Black. As soon as he saw that I was… ah…otherwise occupied, he said it was no problem, he would accompany her himself and ensure that she didn't lose her balance.'

Charlotte couldn't believe she could have slept through the whole exchange. 'I'm sorry,' she muttered. 'I must have been more tired than I realised. I…um… didn't sleep much last night.'

'Of course not. You're worried about your *nonna*.'

'Mmm. That, too…'

She saw the flash of understanding in his eyes as he considered what else might have been keeping her awake. Like that kiss...

Distraction was needed. Charlotte looked around. The bottle of champagne was still sitting in the bucket. There were a few small cubes of ice floating on the water inside. Nico must have followed her glance.

'It may still be cold enough,' he said. 'Shall we have a toast?'

'To what?'

'To making this evening as enjoyable as possible? For everyone involved. It will be time to get ready for dinner before long, I expect.' Nico was dealing with the foil on the champagne bottle. 'We need to prepare ourselves to put on a good show.' The cork came out with a satisfying 'pop'. He smiled that slow, easy, irresistible grin as he filled the glasses and held one out to Charlotte. 'Dutch courage?'

'Will I need it?' And then Charlotte remembered what her hair and face must look like and she smiled ruefully. 'Don't answer that. I know I look a complete mess.' She took a sip of her drink. 'It's just as well I won't see you again after tomorrow. I would be mortified. I can't think of anyone who's ever seen me look this terrible.'

Apart from Siegfried, of course. Charlotte took a longer sip of the wine.

Nico touched his glass to hers. 'You are beautiful, Carlotta.'

He looked as though he believed the words. He was giving her *that* look again. Like the one he'd given her last night. And again, in the gift shop. But why?

There was no one around to see. He didn't have to pretend here.

And hadn't he told her that she was safe because she was so completely not *his* type?

She wanted to be his type. Heaven help her but she wanted Nico to kiss her again.

Dammit. Where were her safety barriers when she needed them? At the very least she needed to break their eye contact but it seemed impossible.

Charlotte searched for a barrier she could put up to protect herself but couldn't find a trace of one. All she could find was a memory of how it had felt to know that Nico had shared his shameful secret with her and how cathartic it had been to finally share her own with another living person. How it had felt to wake up in Nico's arms.

How was it possible to feel so vulnerable and yet so safe at exactly the same time?

She still couldn't break the eye contact either. And Nico wasn't looking away. Charlotte could feel the distance between them closing. The kiss that she wanted so badly was only a heartbeat away.

Until a knock sounded on the cabin door.

'Dr Moretti? Dr Highton?' The steward sounded as if the matter was urgent. 'I'm sorry to disturb you, but you are both needed.'

It was just as well the moment had been broken by the interruption.

Perhaps it had been a mistake to let Charlotte sleep in his arms for so long but what else could he have done?

The depth of pain he'd heard in those words '*not*

compatible'. They couldn't have had anything other than a sexual reference and for it to be so hard for Charlotte to have uttered them meant they were the key to the puzzle of what had changed her so much.

A horrible suspicion had formed in Nico's mind. Something unthinkable. So dark it couldn't be given a name. So horrific all he'd been able to do was hold onto this damaged woman as he'd tried to fit in the other pieces of the puzzle and control the rush of pure fury on her behalf.

He had to control it. Nico hadn't known if his assumption was correct. Maybe Charlotte would never tell him and even if she did, what on earth could *he* do about it?

Nothing, that's what. It was none of his business. Not his problem. But it would provide an explanation to the mystery and that was what he'd wanted, wasn't it?

So Nico had done nothing. Said nothing. As the minutes had ticked by he'd continued to do nothing and that was when he'd felt Charlotte's heartbroken sobbing subside. When the exhaustion in her body had taken over. When she'd slipped into a peaceful, bone-deep slumber.

He could have eased himself away at that point, found a pillow and blanket to make her comfortable on the seat. Or carried her to a bunk, maybe, and left her to sleep for an hour or two. What was it about this bizarre situation he'd been caught up in since early yesterday morning that made it impossible to walk away?

He could have ignored Charlotte when he'd first seen her crying on the terrace below his window. He certainly hadn't needed to come up with the dangerous notion of posing as her lover, let alone shoving a ring

on her finger. And he could have found an excuse not to accompany the women on this train journey.

But he hadn't. Every step of the way he had hesitated and then been drawn in deeper by something he couldn't explain. And if the steward hadn't rapped on the door at that particular moment, he would have kissed Charlotte again.

More than kissed her, actually. He could have asked gentle questions with his mouth and his hands that would have confirmed what he suspected was the answer to the puzzle that had intrigued him ever since he'd recognised Charlotte on that cobbled Venetian street.

He would have got answers to those questions, he was sure of that. Just as sure as he was of the fact that Charlotte had *wanted* him to kiss her. He had seen that desire darken her eyes and soften her lips and he'd felt that knowledge kindle his own flame because it was part of what intrigued him so much. The contradictions. The ice queen on the surface and the woman capable of such deep emotion within. Was the single, ultimately professional doctor desperately in need of physical release, possibly without being consciously aware of it?

Whatever. The desire had been wiped from her eyes the moment that sharp rap had sounded on the door and the tone of the steward's voice had told them that they were not only needed but needed urgently.

Charlotte's assumption was, of course, that Jendi had become ill. She moved swiftly to wrench open the cabin door.

'It's my grandmother, isn't it? She needs us?'

The steward nodded. 'Only you, Dr Highton. She's asking for assistance to get dressed for dinner.'

'But you said you needed both of us.'

'Yes. I'm hoping that Dr Moretti could come with me to see another passenger in the carriage who requires a doctor. He thinks he might be having a heart attack.'

Nico could actually feel his professional persona taking over. Smothering anything personal, like his desire to kiss Charlotte. There was still a flicker of something personal there, though. He stepped closer, needing to touch her, and put his hand on her shoulder.

'You go and help your *nonna*,' he told her. 'I'll deal with this.'

'But…' Was it his imagination or did Charlotte lean into his hand a little, as if she was trying to return the touch? Her gaze caught his and he could read the message so easily. She was reminding him of what he'd told her grandmother only hours ago. That, together, they made an amazing team.

'I'll send for you,' Nico said softly. 'If I need you.' He stepped past Charlotte into the corridor, where the steward was waiting anxiously for Nico to follow him. The last personal thoughts evaporated. 'What equipment do you have on board?' he queried. 'Oxygen? A defibrillator?'

'Yes. We have oxygen. And an AED.'

'Good.' Nico picked up his pace as they made their way to the cabin at the far end of the carriage. 'Show me which cabin and then fetch them for me, please.'

The man in the end cabin was in his sixties. His colour wasn't good and he was clutching a small red and white canister of glyceryl trinitrate spray in his hands.

His wife was beside him, looking even paler than her husband and virtually wringing her hands.

'How long is it since the pain came on?' Nico asked.

The anxious woman checked her watch. 'Nearly fifteen minutes.'

'And how many doses of the spray have been taken?'

'Two? Maybe three… I've lost count.' The woman was struggling to hold back tears. 'It's not working and…and they said that if it didn't work it could be a heart attack and we'd have to get Douglas to the hospital as quickly as possible.'

Nico had his fingers on the older man's wrist. His pulse was a bit rapid but quite strong and regular.

'Tell me about the pain.'

'It's like a bus parked on my chest. Right here…' Douglas pressed a fist to his sternum. 'It's hard to breathe.'

'Just in your chest?'

'Yes.'

'Have you ever had a heart attack?'

'Yes. Ten years ago. That's when this whole business started. But it's been stable. Always comes on the same way…and if I sit down and use the spray it… does the trick.'

He was starting to sound breathless. Thankfully the steward had returned now. He was carrying an oxygen cylinder in one hand and the small red case of an AED in the other. Hopefully the automatic defibrillator wouldn't be needed but it was great to know that such a lifesaver was available if it came to that. Even with the best team in the world performing CPR, it could only buy time. The only way to restart a heart was through defibrillation.

The best team in the world. Unbidden, a memory of Charlotte working with him on the man at the building site flashed into the back of Nico's mind. He shook it off as he uncoiled tubing and fitted nasal prongs to give Douglas some oxygen.

'This may help the pain,' he said. 'Are you on any medications?'

'Yes. Too many.'

'Can you tell me what they are?'

Douglas shook his head, closing his eyes and screwing up his face as though the pain was becoming unbearable. A sheen of perspiration was beginning to show on his bald head. Nico's heart sank.

'I've got them.' The anxious older woman was rummaging in a small suitcase. She pulled out a plastic bag containing numerous packages of medication. They were all things that a cardiac patient could be expected to be on.

'Have you had your aspirin today?'

'Yes.' It was his wife who answered. 'He's taken everything.'

'Let's try another dose of the GTN.' Nico took the canister from the man's hands. It was a bad sign if the spray that normally worked on his angina was failing to be effective but was it possible that it hadn't been used correctly? Nico rolled the canister in his hands, making sure the contents were mixed and then sprayed a dose into the air to check that the metered dose mechanism was working. The spray came out but, oddly, Nico couldn't smell anything.

He held the canister up and peered at the base. 'This spray expired two years ago,' he exclaimed.

'Oh, my goodness!' Douglas's wife clapped a hand to her mouth. 'Really?'

'Really.' Nico reached for the portable pharmacy in the plastic bag. Yes. There was a small box in there that contained a replacement canister. And the expiry date was a year away. He ripped open the box, took the lid off the canister and squeezed off a test shot. 'Open your mouth,' he directed Douglas, 'and lift your tongue.'

He gave Douglas two sprays under his tongue and then kept his fingers on his patient's pulse and watched his breathing while they waited. Within a matter of minutes Douglas started breathing more easily and deeply. The lines on his face relaxed and when he opened his eyes he actually smiled.

'It's almost gone,' he said.

'Oh…thank God…' His wife was crying. 'I'm so sorry, Doug. This is my fault. I should have thrown that old spray away as soon as we had the new one.'

'Waste not, want not.' Douglas patted his wife's hand. 'If you weren't so good at being thrifty we'd never have been able to afford this trip, would we?' He turned to Nico. 'Thank you, Doctor. I'm not having a heart attack after all, am I?'

'It certainly looks like nothing more than an episode of angina. Let's keep the oxygen going for a little while and see how you go. Someone can always come and find me later, too, if you're worried.'

The only person looking worried now was Douglas's wife. 'I'm so sorry to have disturbed your trip,' she told Nico.

'It's not a problem.'

'Is it your first time on the Orient Express?'

'It is.'

'Isn't it wonderful? Are you enjoying it?'

'Of course.' But Nico had to consciously smile instead of allowing a puzzled frown to crease his forehead. Enjoyment wasn't a word that he would have chosen to describe his state of mind so far. He'd started out being intrigued and then he'd been impressed by Charlotte's piano playing. He'd had a spell of being angry when he'd been accused of planning to take advantage of her and then he'd had that cold chill of horror when he thought he'd guessed her secret.

But the overwhelming emotion that he would remember from this trip was going to be the way he'd felt sitting in that cabin and holding Charlotte while she slept. The feeling of protecting her. Of knowing that she trusted him enough to fall asleep in his arms like that. That he could trust *her* enough not to ever share the personal information he had given her.

A good feeling.

An incredibly powerful feeling.

Even more powerful than the desire that had kicked in when he'd realised that Charlotte had wanted him to kiss her as much as *he'd* wanted to kiss her?

Yes. Strangely, it was. He was used to desire and he knew there were countless women in the world who could make him feel like that.

But that other feeling was completely unfamiliar. And deeply disturbing. Powerful enough to feel like it had a life of its own and could take control. Was this what falling in love was all about?

Nico couldn't answer that because he'd never been in this space before. He wasn't capable of falling in love. He knew that. But maybe he was getting a glimpse of what it might be about.

And it was disturbing enough that he never wanted to experience it again so maybe it was time to take charge and make sure he wasn't ambushed by any other strange emotions. The distraction of being a doctor for a little while was definitely helping. The fact that the train seemed to be coming to a halt was less helpful.

Had something happened? Maybe there was engine trouble or something on the tracks and he'd end up being on this train for a lot longer than expected. Just how long could he keep up the level of control he might need when he was sharing a compartment with Charlotte?

The steward, who'd been hovering outside the cabin while Nico treated Douglas, stooped to peer through the window. 'We're coming into Innsbruck,' he announced. 'I need to attend to other duties.'

Nico nodded. 'Thanks very much for your help.'

'I can put the AED away now?'

'Yes. Thankfully, I don't think we need it.' Nico raised his eyebrows as the train jerked and came to a complete halt. 'Why are we stopping?'

'We have to change engines whenever we come to an international border. This is a thirty-minute stop and most people like to get off the train and stretch their legs a bit.' The steward hurried off, probably to open doors and then to stand, looking very smart in his blue uniform, to give people another photo opportunity.

Douglas certainly wasn't going to be jumping off the train to stretch his legs right now. Nico adjusted the setting on the oxygen cylinder and settled in to watch the progress of his new patient.

The contents of Lady Geraldine's larger suitcase were spread out over the seat and hanging from the edges of the bunks as she chose her outfit for dinner.

'The long black taffeta skirt,' she decided. 'With the black, silk camisole and the velvet bolero jacket.'

'Very Gothic,' Charlotte smiled. 'Shall I do your hair so that you've got a bit of fringe covering one eye?'

'Don't be naughty, Charlotte Jane. The black is merely a canvas to show off my diamond jewellery. I'm going to need my necklace and the brooch that goes on the jacket. And I've got my bracelet and best rings in my jewellery case. Oh…we mustn't forget that darling little tiara either. The one I wore last night, remember?'

'How could I forget?'

Lady Geraldine eyed her granddaughter suspiciously. 'I don't think you're taking this seriously, Charlotte. This is the dinner of my lifetime and I intend to look the part.'

'Sorry, Gran.' Charlotte kissed her fondly. 'I want you to enjoy tonight as much as possible. Are you sure you're feeling all right? Did you have a good rest?'

'I had a lovely rest. And then I had an even better time having afternoon tea with my old friend, Winsome. We still have lots to talk about.'

'Maybe you'll see her again after dinner.'

Oddly, Lady Geraldine looked evasive now. 'Help me into my skirt, child. And then you'd better start doing something to get ready yourself. Fancy suggesting I wear my hair over my eye. Have you looked in a mirror recently? What have you and Nico been up to in your cabin?'

'Gran…' But Charlotte couldn't help thinking about the look in Nico's eyes just before the steward had interrupted them. About how much she had wanted that kiss to happen. Even now, the curl of desire the memory could evoke was enough to make her close her

eyes for a heartbeat. To make her lips curl in pleasure at the memory.

If that kiss had happened, would it have stopped there? Would she have wanted it to? The bite of fear that kicked in was enough to make her shake her head as if she could banish the hateful sensation.

She needed to try and locate at least a shimmer of her old armour. To pretend to be in control. Normal. Maybe it would help to make a joke of it. 'Have you *seen* the size of those bunks?'

'You're young,' Lady Geraldine said with a smile. 'I'm sure you'll cope.' She reached out and stroked Charlotte's cheek. 'Oh, darling. You're so in love with him, aren't you?'

Charlotte had to turn away. To find something solid to focus on as she felt the ground shifting beneath her feet with a curious spinning sensation. She lifted the hanger holding her grandmother's astonishing skirt with the ruffled hem down from the top bunk and pretended to notice some lint that needed brushing away.

In love?

Ridiculous. Nobody fell in love that quickly. She felt safe with Nico, that was all. He knew more about her than anyone. More than her grandmother, in fact, in a rather significant area.

She liked him. A lot. Who wouldn't? He was clever and kind. So kind that he'd sat, getting cramp, for hours, holding a woman in his arms because he hadn't wanted to wake her?

She trusted him, too. Who couldn't trust someone who put the kind of trust in you that led to sharing the kind of secret she could so well understand him wanting to keep to himself? Not that it was true, of course.

Nico was more than capable of falling in love if he'd only let himself.

And that feeling when she'd woken up in those arms. As if she had been floating in the most blissful place on earth. She'd never felt so safe.

So *protected*.

Superimposed on that memory came that look of desire in Nico's eyes when their lips had been drifting closer together in the moments before that rap on the door.

That mix of safety and desire was a chemical combination that could only mean one thing.

That...yes. She *was* in love with Nico Moretti.

No. Maybe it meant two things.

She was not only in love. She was in trouble.

CHAPTER EIGHT

MAYBE IT WAS her new awareness of how she felt about Nico. Or perhaps it was the incongruity of him appearing in these surroundings looking impossibly gorgeous in his dinner suit. Whatever it was, it completely stole Charlotte's breath away when she opened the door of her grandmother's compartment to his polite knock.

Did her grandmother actually bat her eyelashes?

'It's been a long time since I was escorted to dinner by such a handsome young man,' she said with delight. 'Charlotte Jane? You can have him later but I really do need Nico's arm while we're walking. This train is remarkably jerky at times.'

'No worries, Gran.' Charlotte smiled. 'He's all yours.'

But then her gaze caught Nico's and the smile got stolen away like her breath had been. Oh…Lord…that look in his eyes.

'I love that dress,' was all he said. 'I'm so glad you've worn it again, *cara*.'

Lady Geraldine made a tutting sound. 'I'm trying to train Charlotte to expand her wardrobe, Nico. It won't help if you tell her you're happy she's worn the same thing two nights running.'

'But it's true, Jendi.' Nico's smile for her grand-

mother was so warm and genuine that Charlotte's heart squeezed painfully. How could she not love a man who was clearly already so fond of her beloved gran? 'And I am an honest man.'

The comment did something strange inside Charlotte. Echoes of his voice telling her that he'd been honest with her and asking her to give him the honour of being the same with him. It was a bond she knew she could never have with another person. Did he feel the same? No. How could he when she hadn't shared the most shameful part of her secret? When she'd been less than completely honest?

But his gaze flicked past Charlotte's again. 'Most of the time,' he added.

All the time, Charlotte suspected. This pretence they were engaged in was an aberration. Sure, Nico had approached it as an amusing diversion but any control had been lost very quickly, hadn't it? At about the time he'd pushed that ring onto her finger, probably.

No wonder he was feeling uncomfortable but Lady Geraldine didn't seem to pick up on the loaded comment. 'I'm ready to go,' she announced. 'I want as much time to enjoy seeing everybody else dressed up as I can before I start feeling too old and tired.'

Or before she felt too sick and sore? Charlotte followed Nico as he carefully escorted Lady Geraldine through the rocking carriages towards the dining cars. She needed a break, she said, when they reached the bar car. She wanted to sit for a few minutes and enjoy listening to the piano. And…how nice…her friend Winsome was sitting at one of the side-facing seats and seemed to be saving space for her. Perhaps Charlotte could order a nice cocktail for her?

Charlotte perused the cocktail menu while Nico made sure her grandmother was seated comfortably. Heavens, but there were a lot to choose from. She'd never even heard of a Moscow Mule or a Planters Punch. Both her grandmother's favourites were there, though, so all she really needed to choose between was a Singapore Sling or a Gin Fizz.

Nico came back to the bar as she ordered a Gin Fizz. When he was only a step or two away the train gave a sudden and rather dramatic lurch. A cry rippled through the carriage as people spilt their drinks but the pianist didn't miss a beat of the Viennese waltz he was playing. And Nico's arm was right there to steady Charlotte as she lost her balance.

It was the first time he'd touched her since that almost kiss when they'd been interrupted earlier and it seemed to ignite a peculiar magic. How else could Charlotte explain the fact that a steadying touch morphed into an embrace that moved in time to the music?

They were dancing?

Yes. On a minuscule patch of blue carpet, in the space between the bar and the piano, Nico was very competently leading her through a confined version of a Viennese waltz. Charlotte could have laughed out loud. Except that this was giving her the same kind of feeling that she'd had when she'd woken from that deep sleep in Nico's arms, and she wanted to recapture that bliss for just a few seconds.

So, instead of holding her head in the correct position for a waltz as she'd been trained to do in those lessons Gran had insisted on when she'd been a teenager, Charlotte let herself droop enough to put her head

on Nico's shoulder. And he tilted his head so that it rested against hers. It was no waltz now. Just a slow, close dance.

To anyone watching, and no doubt that included Lady Geraldine and her friend, they must look like a couple madly in love. Nobody, meaning Nico, needed to know that it was actually genuine on her part now.

And maybe that was a good thing. Maybe...just a very small maybe...this didn't have to end when they got off the train in London tomorrow.

No. That tiny, unbidden seed of hope died away as Charlotte remembered Nico saying he never wanted marriage or children. That she was safe because she was so completely not his type of woman.

Oh, well...at least if Gran lived long enough for her to have to confess that the relationship wasn't going to work long term, she wouldn't have to pretend to be heartbroken, would she?

Oh, God...she really was in trouble now.

Released from Nico's arms to a round of applause from the crowded carriage, Charlotte headed back to the bar. She was going to order one of those potent-sounding cocktails for herself because she needed something strong if she was going to cope with the rest of this journey. She needed some bottled courage. Or stamina.

Moving towards Lady Geraldine's seat to wait for the bartender to bring the drinks, Charlotte found that introductions were being made. Winsome's grandson Connor was with a young woman called Kelsie, who was now sitting beside Lady Geraldine. They were discussing seating arrangements.

'Winsome and I have arranged a table for ourselves,'

Lady Geraldine said. 'We don't want to bore you young things with our gossip.'

The implications were immediately obvious. Nico and Connor exchanged a glance as if they were measuring each other up and considering the prospect of a foursome for dinner. Kelsie was watching the older women as if she knew there was more coming. And there was.

'So, instead, we have three tables,' Lady Geraldine smiled. 'One for each couple.'

Charlotte almost groaned aloud. 'I don't think you're allowed to change arrangements like that, are you, Gran?'

Lady Geraldine merely tapped the side of her nose. 'Wait and see where the maître d' puts us all,' she murmured. And then she winked at Winsome. 'Being old doesn't entirely deprive us of our ability to charm men into doing what we want, does it, Winnie?'

'Not at all, dear. As you say, age is only an attitude.'

Charlotte caught Connor's gaze and his expression said it all. This was a done deal and there was absolutely no point trying to make changes now. She was now faced with the prospect of being alone with Nico for a dinner that might go on for hours. An intimate, romantic kind of dinner. Her heart sank. One strong cocktail was not going to be enough.

Nico had to admire the persuasive powers of older women. Tables had to be at a premium on the train, even if there was more than one sitting for dinner, but here they were at a table that could seat four people and it was only set for two.

It was beautifully set with crisp, white linen, spar-

kling silverware and immaculate crystal that caught the soft light of the Tiffany lamp on the window side of the table. The carriage might be crowded with other diners but it felt like he and Charlotte were enclosed in a bubble of their own. He was glad that she hadn't had a different dress to wear because this silver sheath was gorgeous and so very appropriate for the season. It made her eyes look like a dark shade of silver instead of grey. Or was that because they were catching such a warm glow from the light?

Or perhaps it was the champagne he had ordered. She certainly seemed to be enjoying the Moët, even if she wasn't clearing her plate with each delicious course that arrived. He had polished off the entrée and then demolished the main course of traditional roast turkey with chestnut stuffing.

Conversation had proved easier than he'd expected, having been deprived of Jendi's company. They'd started out with the practical matter of sleeping arrangements for the night.

'I'll stay in the bar for a while,' Nico had told Charlotte. 'And then I'll come back to the cabin and sleep on the seat. You can close the connecting door when you go to bed.'

He'd asked if she knew what would happen tomorrow.

'We get to Paris around dawn,' she'd told him. 'When we get to the end of the French line for the Orient Express, we have to get off and there are special buses that we stay on for the channel crossing. The English branch of the train takes us into Victoria Station. I think we get in at about five p.m.'

As the plates for the main course were taken away,

Charlotte allowed her champagne glass to be refilled. Did her smile look a little forced as she held it up to Nico in a toast?

'What will you do?' she asked brightly. 'When we've arrived back in London? For Christmas Eve, I mean.'

Nico shrugged. 'I expect I'll go to work and catch up on any inpatients. I'm covering a big area for the next few days. I like to give my colleagues as much time as possible to be with their families over Christmas. And you? What will you be doing?'

Charlotte turned her head to look out the window, although there was nothing to see in the darkness.

'I'll go out to Gran's. Her estate is a good hour out of London. I'll stay with her for Christmas Day, of course, and then it'll be time to face up to what needs facing up to.'

Jendi's cancer. Dio…but it was going to be a difficult time ahead for Charlotte. Nico wanted to reach across the table and catch her hands. To offer to be there for her as a friend in the weeks or months ahead.

But this faux relationship wasn't supposed to continue, was it? Charlotte wouldn't want it to. Having her in a committed relationship with a potential family in the future might be at the top of her grandmother's bucket list but Nico could still hear the vehemence in Charlotte's voice when she'd declared that it was never going to happen.

So he said nothing. Instead, he followed Charlotte's example and stared out of the window. There were sparkles of light swirling outside in a mesmerising kaleidoscope.

'Look at that,' he exclaimed. 'It's snowing. It'll be a white Christmas for some people.'

'I love a white Christmas,' Charlotte said softly. 'It makes you feel like you're living inside a Christmas card. I think the best Christmas I ever had was one where Gran and I got completely snowed in and the electricity went off. We ended up cooking the chipolatas that were supposed to go in with the turkey on sticks on the open fire. I was only about nine but I was so impressed that Gran knew how to do stuff like get the fire going and cook sausages.'

'Sounds special.'

'What's the best Christmas you remember, Nico? Was it white?'

'No. It never snowed in our part of Italy.' Funny that to remember his best Christmas he automatically wiped out any year after he'd been whisked off to Ireland. 'It would get cold, though. I think the best Christmas I can remember was outside. We had a terrace with a long wooden table that was under grapevines. In the summer it was leafy and cool and in the winter there was an open fireplace big enough to roast an ox. For some reason we had Christmas dinner outside that year. Possibly because so many family members had gathered. There were aunts and uncles and cousins I never knew I had.'

'How old were you?'

'About six.'

'Did you have turkey?'

Nico shook his head. 'That wasn't traditional. We have the feast of the seven fishes on Christmas Eve and then on Christmas Day we have lots of pasta and then roast meat like chicken or beef. And potatoes.' He frowned. The food hadn't been what had made that Christmas memorable.

'There was music,' he continued softly. 'My father was at the head of the table and he was *so* happy. Between courses he would drag my mother away from the kitchen and dance with her in front of the fire. There were so many people. So much laughter. So much love...'

'Family.' The word was a whisper and Charlotte's eyes were as bright as he'd ever seen them when Nico turned from the view of the snow. 'It's what Christmas is all about, isn't it?'

'It was once...' Nico had to clear his throat. The memory of that particular Christmas was disturbing because it evoked a yearning he'd thought he'd put behind him many, many years ago. Part of the heartbreak he would never want to inflict on a child. Or a woman. Or have inflicted on himself ever again.

Dessert of a classic plum duff with crème anglaise and brandy butter came and went with a noticeably more sombre mood at their table. It was a relief when a steward came to tell him that Lady Geraldine was ready to be escorted back to her cabin whenever it was convenient for him.

'Or I can arrange another escort?' The steward tilted his head to include Charlotte. 'If you and your fiancé wish to stay longer?'

'No.' It was Charlotte who spoke up quickly. 'We can finish now.' She didn't meet Nico's eyes. 'If that's all right with you, Nico?'

'*Sì*. Of course it is.

The last thing Charlotte expected when she returned to her suite after helping her grandmother get undressed

and settled into her bunk for the night was to find Nico still there.

She had thought he would be long gone. Having a nightcap in the bar and ready to wait until he thought she was safely asleep before coming back to get what rest he could on the seat in this compartment. Not that she expected to get much sleep herself but it would have been a relief to shut the connecting door and have a space entirely to herself for a good few hours. No chance of losing control and making a fool of herself that way.

Now she was distinctly unsettled. Not only was Nico here but he'd taken off his dinner jacket and rolled up the sleeves of his dress shirt. His bow-tie was undone as well, hanging down beside the undone top buttons of his shirt. His hair was rumpled, as if he'd thrust his fingers through it more than once, and it was long enough since he'd shaved to give his jaw a dark shadow. He looked ever so slightly disreputable lounging on the padded upholstery of the seat.

And ultimately desirable.

Maybe that was why Charlotte's words came out more sharply than she'd intended. 'I thought you were going to the bar.'

Nico raised an eyebrow. 'It occurred to me it might be a good idea to wait until Jendi was asleep. What if she wanted to go to the bathroom and saw me abandoning my beautiful fiancée?'

Oh, God…this was getting way beyond a joke. Charlotte had had enough.

'It's not funny, Nico.'

'No…it's not.' Nico got to his feet. 'Shall I tell you the real reason I haven't gone to the bar?'

He took a step closer and Charlotte was pinned by the heat in his gaze. She still had a hand on the door to help her keep her balance as the train rocked, and Nico was swaying on his feet but his gaze didn't waver in the slightest.

She couldn't respond to the question but it didn't seem to matter. Nico was going to tell her anyway.

'I didn't want to,' he growled.

Charlotte didn't have to ask why not. She could see the see the answer in his face. Could feel the flicker of heat spiral deep in her belly. The words forced themselves out anyway, though, as she tried to buy enough time to process what was happening. 'W-why not?'

'Because I wanted this instead.' Nico closed the gap between them. He steadied himself with one hand over Charlotte's against the door but he slid the fingers of his other hand behind her neck and then up into her hair as he cradled her head and dipped his own so that their lips could touch.

His mouth felt familiar now. Safe. Charlotte knew that the touch of his tongue against hers would provide a pleasure so intense it was almost pain but her lips parted eagerly and her tongue met his halfway to begin the dance. And this time the give and take of the kiss changed into more than an exploration and taste of pleasure. This time it had an urgency that demanded more.

And that was enough to make Charlotte pull away. To snatch a gasp of breath and then shake her head.

'I…I don't understand…'

'Yes, you do, *cara*,' Nico said very softly. 'I want you.'

She shook her head again, more insistently. 'But…*why*?'

Nico leaned against the door. He still had a hand cradling her head and she felt his fingers move in a caress. 'Why wouldn't I?'

'Because I'm...not your type. You said so.'

Nico smiled *that* smile. The slow, lazy one. Except that this time it seemed to be gentle. Reassuring? 'I say stupid things sometimes.'

Charlotte had to drop her gaze. Dammit. The train seemed to have picked up speed and the way it was rocking made her more acutely aware of the proximity of Nico's body. Of how it would take nothing for her to fall just a little closer and mould her own body against his.

'This can't go any further,' she said.

'Why not?' The words were a whisper. A question, not an accusation. If she said the word Nico would stop but he genuinely didn't understand, and why would he? He must have seen her own desire for him. He had to be well used to reading those kinds of signals from women.

'Because...' Charlotte couldn't look up. She couldn't stop herself continuing either. Good grief...far from giving her the stamina to maintain control in a difficult situation, the amount of champagne she'd knocked back this evening was having the opposite effect. Her control had slipped so far she'd lost the handle for the door behind which she kept her secret so well shut away. She hadn't been completely honest with Nico earlier, had she? *He* had been with *her*. Guilt bubbled up inside her and something snapped.

'I can't do it,' she whispered. 'I...can't have sex. I'm...' No. There was no way she could utter that horrible word. A shudder went right through her entire body.

Nico's hand slipped out from her hair and he let go of the door. This was it. He was going to excuse himself and go to the bar for a stiff drink, and who could blame him?

But, instead, he gathered Charlotte into his arms and held her close to him. His mouth was close to her ear and he spoke softly.

'You've been hurt, *cara*,' he said. 'I know that. You've been raped, haven't you?'

Charlotte's gasp was shocked. 'No...it...wasn't rape. How could it have been? He was my...my boyfriend. I had chosen to be with him. I'd chosen to go to his apartment. It might have been my first time but I knew what was going to happen.'

For a long moment Nico simply held her in silence. Then he spoke gently. 'But it didn't happen the way you wanted it to, did it?'

'N-no.' Unbelievably, the tears were gathering again. After not having cried for so many years, she was certainly making up for it now.

'And when you wanted him to stop, he wouldn't, would he?'

'H-he said it wasn't his fault if I was frigid. He wasn't going to have his evening ruined by a—a tease.' There. The word had come out all by itself. 'And—and he was right. I hated it and...and when I tried again, more than a year later, with someone else...I couldn't do it...so he—'

'Was a stupid, arrogant bastard,' Nico whispered vehemently. 'Who had no idea what he was talking about and didn't deserve to be in the company of any woman, let alone someone like you.'

Charlotte felt his lips press against the top of her head. And then she felt Nico's hand under her chin and a pressure that made her raise her face to meet his gaze.

'It's not true,' he told her. 'You are a beautiful, *passionate* woman and all you need to do is believe that.'

Maybe there'd always been a glimmer of hope deep inside that that was true. Maybe when she'd tried again, it had been too soon. Or with the wrong person. Charlotte had always thought that she might have conquered her demons if she could have talked to someone professional about it but the shame of anyone knowing had always stopped her.

And now Nico knew. And he was still here.

And he was gorgeous and kind and he'd said that he wanted her.

They wouldn't be seeing each other again after tomorrow so would it really matter if it didn't work. She might never have an opportunity like this again. To find out…

Charlotte licked suddenly dry lips. 'Did you really mean it?' The words were incredibly hard to utter.

'That I want you?' Nico's eyes were so dark they looked black. His hands on her back slid lower until they cupped her bottom. He pulled her even closer so that she had no need of any verbal confirmation of his state of arousal.

'Oh…' Charlotte couldn't look away from his eyes.

'Do you trust me, *cara*?'

She didn't have enough breath to say anything. Instead, Charlotte stretched on tiptoe so that she could reach Nico's lips with her own. She slid her arms

around his neck at the same time as she felt herself being lifted off her feet and carried into the adjoining cabin and a bunk that would simply have to be big enough.

Well...

He'd been right, hadn't he?

Not just about the reason why Charlotte Highton's personality had changed so much.

He'd been right about the fact that she was a beautiful and passionate woman.

It was well after midnight when Nico eased himself out of the bed that was far too small for two people to sleep together comfortably. He got dressed again and let himself quietly out of the cabin with the intention of going to the bar for that long-postponed nightcap.

Charlotte was deeply asleep again, which wasn't surprising. She'd been on an emotional roller-coaster for the last two days and she'd had rather a lot of champagne tonight.

Had he taken advantage of her lack of inhibitions?

Or would she thank him for proving what she should have been able to believe in all along? That there was nothing wrong with her. Nothing she needed to be afraid of or hide from.

That was a minefield in itself. Charlotte was a passionate woman. The way she'd responded to him had been a joy. No...it had been by far the most tender lovemaking he'd ever experienced. So overwhelming that he could only hope Charlotte hadn't noticed she hadn't been the only one with tears wetting her cheeks in the aftermath. The way he'd felt when she'd started to touch him back... To offer herself so completely...

Even now Nico had no idea what to do with the sensations that made it hard to breathe. It had made him feel like he was the most special person on earth. As though she was the only woman in the world he ever wanted to be with again because he would never experience anything like this with anyone else.

He knew how ridiculous that was. The world was full of beautiful women who were eager to share his bed. But Charlotte was naïve in such matters. She might believe he was the only man who could make her feel like that. She might mistakenly believe she had fallen in love with him when she was now capable of having a fulfilling relationship with any man she chose.

It didn't have to be him.

He didn't want it to be him.

So why was he feeling so…uneasy? So in need of a stiff drink?

Because there was a voice in his head that was trying to insist that being with Charlotte for just a little longer wouldn't hurt? That he could, at least, have one more night like last night? Just to check whether it had actually been so extraordinary?

He knew perfectly well how wrong that would be. *That* would, without any doubt, be taking advantage of Charlotte, and Nico had far too much respect for her to even consider it.

The strange sound Nico heard as he made his way through the seemingly deserted carriages in the early hours of the morning only added to his disturbance.

He'd heard that sound before. The cry of a baby who'd only just entered the world.

A newborn on the Orient Express? Impossible.

The echo of that cry of new life stayed with him, though, imagined or not. And Nico didn't like it.

He didn't want a new life.

He wanted his old one back.

CHAPTER NINE

CHARLOTTE KNEW SHE was alone even before she'd surfaced from sleep enough to open her eyes.

Had it been a dream?

Her memories certainly had a dreamlike fuzziness to them. Sensations rather than clear thoughts, and the gentle rocking of the train beneath her seemed to encourage her to close her eyes and explore them. She could feel each one as clearly as if it was happening all over again.

The surprise of finding Nico in the cabin when she'd finally got Gran settled, so closely followed by a breath-robbing fascination generated by seeing him with his shirt buttons undone and his tie hanging loose. As if she'd interrupted him in the process of getting completely undressed…

The explosion of that sensation that had sent shafts of desire into every cell of her body when she'd seen the reflection of her own desire in Nico's eyes. When she'd felt his fingers steadying her head for the kiss that had sent her straight over the edge.

Into that abyss of fear and self-loathing. The feeling of falling without a parachute, knowing that death was

inevitable, as she'd uttered the words that had been her confession of her inadequacies as a woman.

The soft cloud that had gathered and cushioned that fall…first with Nico's words of reassurance and then the physical invitation to see how right they'd been.

And…oh…Charlotte had never known it could be like that. Maybe she'd had fragments of glimpsing it from haunting, erotic dreams but this had been reality.

Or had it?

Shifting a little in her bunk, Charlotte could feel the sweet, inner tenderness that could only be the result of having been passionately loved. With a small sound that was almost a groan, she let herself sink into the last sensation she remembered. Of falling asleep in Nico's arms again but this time feeling as though it was the only place in the world she could ever want to be. Falling asleep with the utter bliss of knowing those arms would still be around her when she woke.

Except they weren't.

How had Nico managed to extricate himself from this tiny space without waking her? He must have been very determined not to, which meant that he'd wanted to be alone.

Why? Did he regret what had happened between them?

Well…why wouldn't he? For heaven's sake, he'd been sucked into her private life because of her meltdowns in front of him. She'd cried all over him. Twice! He'd seen her with her panda eyes and he'd heard all the sordid details of her mortifying past. He must think she was needy and pathetic virtually all the time.

Did he think that she might remain clingy? That she

would try and keep him in her life longer than the period they'd agreed on? Ask him for more than he was prepared to give?

It was odd but the notion of being seen as pathetic and clingy was worse than revealing herself as physically frigid. Nico had shown her that what she'd believed about herself had been so not true.

What she needed to do was show him that any fears about how else she might behave were also untrue. She was in love with him, certainly, but that was *her* problem. It didn't need to be Nico's and he didn't deserve it to be. Not after giving her a gift so far beyond price by restoring her self-esteem.

Creating the magic that had been her night on the Orient Express.

She would have to thank him, of course, but she had to do it in a way that let him know he was not under any further obligation to her. And she needed to make him believe it. To present herself in a way that showed confidence and independence. The way she presented herself at a conference might be a good start.

With a determined shove Charlotte got rid of the bed covers and climbed out of the bunk. Finding herself naked was a reality check that made her blush. She'd never slept naked in her life and the comfort zone of well-fitting clothes had to be her first priority. Washing her face in the tiny corner basin a short time later, she eyed herself in the mirror. The smudged make-up and rat's-nest hair that advertised a night of totally wanton behaviour were the next things she had to take control of. Only then would she be able to face her day.

And Nico.

* * *

He was going to have to face Charlotte at some point. Having caught a few hours' sleep on the seat in the daytime area of the suite and making sure he was not there when Charlotte woke up, Nico had successfully whiled away a good portion of the morning with coffee and newspapers in the bar car.

Brunch was being served already in the dining cars and there was still no sign of Charlotte or Lady Geraldine. It wouldn't be that long before they reached Calais and would have to board the buses for travel to England via the channel tunnel. There would be no private cabins on the train leg to London, during which they would apparently be served afternoon tea, and they would be going in different directions as soon they reached Victoria.

Nico could well imagine how chaotic it was going to be in that huge station on Christmas Eve. It probably wasn't going to be much less private from the time they had to share a bus with dozens of other people. If he wanted a conversation alone with Charlotte, he would have to do something about it now. Clearly, she wasn't planning to come and find *him* this morning.

Their suite was empty and Lady Geraldine's door was closed but Nico tapped on it anyway. It was after ten a.m. Surely Jendi would be up and about by now?

Charlotte opened the door. For a long moment they simply stared at each other. Nico had to process the startling change from when he'd last seen Charlotte, asleep with her glorious hair spread across the crisp, white pillowcase, her lips devoid of any artificial colouring and swollen from so many kisses.

He was facing Dr Highton right now. Dressed in that

power suit he'd first seen her in when she'd been on her way to the symposium. She had her hair scraped back into that complicated knot arrangement that gave her the look of an air hostess and her make-up was perfect. No smudged mascara from tears being shed and her perfect lipstick made it look as though her lips had never been licked, let alone kissed.

And, apart from a flash of something that was gone too quickly to analyse, even her gaze looked professional. Impersonal enough to make Nico take a mental step backwards, at any rate.

'Is everything all right? It's…getting quite late.'

Charlotte wasn't meeting his gaze now. 'I can't believe I slept so late,' she said, loudly enough for her grandmother to overhear. 'No wonder you went off to find some breakfast. There's something about the motion of a train, isn't there? It makes you sleep so well.'

Nico raised an eyebrow. Surely Charlotte would realise that *he'd* had virtually no sleep.

'Is that Nico?' Lady Geraldine called. 'Bring him in, Charlotte Jane, for goodness' sake.'

There wasn't room for three people to sit. Charlotte remained standing as well.

'How are you this morning, Jendi?' Nico enquired politely. 'Did you sleep well, too?'

'Not bad.'

Nico could feel the tension emanating from Charlotte. She didn't believe that and she could be right. Lady Geraldine did look rather pale and she was gripping the windowsill with one hand, as though the movement of the train was making her uncomfortable.

'Apparently there was a baby boy born on the train last night, have you heard?'

'No...*really*?' Lady Geraldine turned and was unable to disguise her wince of pain. She ignored it, however, and her expression suggested that everybody else had better follow her example. 'How do you know?'

'The steward in the bar told me when he gave me the newspapers. He said that we'd be reading about the unexpected event on the Orient Express very soon. I actually heard it crying late in the night when I was walking through the carriage. Apparently the young girl had disguised her condition very well, by wearing a large, old-fashioned coat.'

'Oh...I think I saw that girl at the station in Venice,' Charlotte said.

'What on earth were you doing, walking around the train in the middle of the night?' Lady Geraldine asked.

'I needed to stretch my legs,' Nico said, after a moment's awkward silence. 'The bunks are...rather small, aren't they?'

'Depends on what you're doing.' Lady Geraldine managed a smile. 'I'm delighted that Charlotte felt the need to sleep in, I must say. It's probably been years since she hasn't been up at the crack of dawn.'

There was a very noticeable flush of colour on Charlotte's cheeks now and when she flicked a glance towards Nico the shutters were down. She was most definitely thinking about what had kept her awake last night. The relief at seeing what he now knew to be the real Charlotte peeping out was enough to make him try and hold that gaze. And convey the message in his smile that he agreed it was well worth remembering. Unforgettable might be closer to the mark.

'Oh, for heaven's sake...' Lady Geraldine flapped a hand at them. 'Go and make sheep's eyes at each other

in your own cabin and leave an old lady in peace.' The tone was authoritative but she was still smiling as she delivered the order.

Charlotte looked as though she was about to refuse but then shook her head and signalled Nico to go ahead of her. He stepped into their suite and she barrelled in straight after him, closing the door behind her.

'I don't want to leave her too long,' she said. 'I'm pretty sure she's not feeling nearly as well as she's trying to make out.' Biting her lip, Charlotte stared down at her hands. 'I *think* she wants me out of the way so she can take another dose of her painkillers.'

'Is there anything I can do to help?'

'I don't think so.' Charlotte shook her head. 'But... thank you...'

Nico had the distinct impression that the hesitation meant that Charlotte had something else she wanted to say. So he waited. Sure enough, her chin rose as she took a very deep breath.

'I don't mean just for offering to help with Gran...' The movement of Charlotte's facial muscles suggested acute embarrassment. 'Thank you for...you know...'

Nico raised an eyebrow. Was this it? So much for fearing that Charlotte might think she'd fallen in love with him! Was last night going to be a polite 'Thank you' and 'You're most welcome' kind of exchange?

He felt distinctly piqued even though he knew he should be relieved. But it deserved something more than that, surely?

He stepped closer. Close enough for them to be breathing the same air. He bent his head as if he was about to kiss her but stopped halfway there.

'I can assure you it was very much my pleasure.'

Her eyes widened and he heard her catch her breath but then she stepped back. Only a tiny step, admittedly, but it was enough to send a very clear message. Charlotte didn't want to be kissed again this morning. And there was enough tension in the air to make Nico wonder if she was trying to get back into her old comfort zone. That might explain the way she was dressed and the hairstyle that defied anyone to try and run their fingers through those long tresses.

'Don't....' The word escaped from him as a whisper. A soft groan almost.

'D-don't what?' she stuttered.

Nico had to close his eyes for a heartbeat. He hadn't intended saying this but maybe it needed to be said. 'Don't dismiss last night as a one-off.'

Oh... *Dio*...would she think he was asking to see her again?

Maybe he was...

With a mental shake Nico forced a smile to his lips. 'Don't ever stop believing that you're special. That what you have to offer would be more than enough for any man you chose to be with.' He straightened his spine and tried to keep his smile from faltering. 'There's a whole world of men out there, Charlotte. You'll find someone one day and you'll know he's the person you want to share your life with. Don't let your past hold you back.'

She was nodding. Blinking hard as though determined not to cry. And when she spoke, her voice was remarkably strong.

'Back at you, Nico Moretti.' Okay, her smile was a bit wobbly. 'Don't be afraid to fall in love in someone or let your past hold *you* back. You need to trust your-

self and find someone who can appreciate all you have to offer because…it's a lot.'

Find someone?

Someone else, she meant.

It was Nico's turn to nod. To smile. This extraordinary connection they had was because they'd shared things they'd never shared with others. It was a new experience—much as this train journey was new. Totally unrelated to normal life and it couldn't be expected to continue. They both knew that. At least, this way, they could part with special memories of their brief time together.

Charlotte was twisting the ring on her finger. 'I should give this back,' she said.

'There's no rush.' Nico shrugged. 'Despite your wise words, I'm not about to go hunting for a wife. And even if I found someone, I don't really think she'd want to wear such an old-fashioned ring.'

'It's a beautiful ring,' Charlotte said immediately. 'A family heirloom. A symbol of what's held you back even. *I'd* wear it.'

'You *are* wearing it.' He had to smile. 'Not that I gave you much choice about that.'

Charlotte's breath came out in a huff. 'I mean, you'd have to make sure that whoever you really give it to understands its significance. The promise. You'd have to tell her everything you told me.'

As if he was ever going to find someone to share soul-deep secrets with again. Once was enough. Like this train journey.

They were both staring at the ring.

'I'll have to take it off as soon as I get back to work,'

Charlotte said. 'I wouldn't be able to wear a ring like this even if I *was* engaged.'

'There's no rush,' Nico said again. 'Just see how things go with your *nonna*. You know where I work.'

Charlotte nodded again. 'At the Hammersmith, yes?'

'Yes. And it doesn't matter if I'm not there for some reason. You could just leave it with my secretary.'

'But…' There was a lot not being said here. About how long she might want to keep up the pretence. How long it would take for her grandmother to die. Her lips trembled. 'But it's precious…'

'I trust you.'

It wasn't hard to sound sincere. He'd trusted Charlotte with far more than a family heirloom, hadn't he?

The only sound for a long moment was the clack of the train wheels. Rhythmic and steady. Like a heartbeat. And then Charlotte raised her eyes.

'I trust you, too,' she whispered.

That was a lot bigger than the trust he'd placed in her, even by confessing what he knew could be seen as an inadequacy. Being a commitment-phobic male was far more socially acceptable than the stigma of having been labelled a frigid woman. Or having been raped. He was holding a secret that could potentially wreck her carefully ordered world. It was huge.

A gift that no one else could have given him.

Like the one he'd given her by showing her that it wasn't true? Being the man who'd had the privilege of holding her as she'd come apart in someone's arms for the first time?

They were even. Equals.

And, as long as he didn't do something stupid and make a fool of himself, they could keep this respect

for each other. Part as friends. They would get back to reality and their own lives soon enough.

It was time to lighten the atmosphere.

'I'm hungry,' Nico announced. 'Would you care for breakfast in the dining car?'

'Gran's ordered cabin service. I need to stay with her and see if she actually eats anything. You go.'

So the separation was to begin already. The count-down was on.

Fine. Nico knew that was sensible. What they both wanted. There would be plenty to distract them for the rest of the day because it was unlikely that they would be alone again together. They would probably never be alone together again. This was it. The last intimate moment he would have with Charlotte Highton.

He had to kiss her. Just a soft farewell.

'I won't forget.' It was a promise. A deliberately am-biguous one. Charlotte could assume he was talking about her wise words regarding his future. She didn't have to know that he meant *her.*

Her quiet words followed him like an echo that seemed to be picked up by the train wheels as he made his way to the dining car.

'I won't either.'

The rest of the journey seemed interminable.

Lady Geraldine was keeping up a brave face but she ate virtually nothing of her brunch and didn't touch the champagne or afternoon tea on the English leg of the trip. The weather was cold enough to make her look pinched and it was clearly a struggle to join the ex-cited conversations around them that were predicting

a genuine white Christmas as fat snowflakes began to fall more and more heavily.

'I'm just tired, love,' she told Charlotte. 'But I wouldn't have changed anything about the last couple of days. Not a thing.'

And Charlotte had been able to smile back and tell her grandmother that she felt exactly the same.

Victoria was heaving with people desperate to get to where they wanted to be for Christmas Day. It was Nico who helped collect their luggage and carve a pathway through the crowd to where Lady Geraldine's chauffeur had arranged to meet them.

They offered Nico a lift but he declined with palpable regret.

'I've made an appointment with a colleague at the Hammersmith,' he told them. 'You need to go in the opposite direction and it'll be bad enough already. I hope you don't get caught in a traffic jam or the snow. If I can't find a cab, I'll take the tube.'

He took Charlotte in his arms to say goodbye. For her grandmother's sake? Was that why he said that he was going to miss her and that seeing her again couldn't be too soon for him?

It wasn't why Charlotte returned his kiss and agreed that it couldn't be too soon for her either.

She meant every word.

The bleak feeling of watching the crowd swallow Nico only got stronger as they inched their way out of London.

Lady Geraldine took her hand and gave it a squeeze.

'I know it's hard, darling. It's such a shame that Nico's going to be so busy for a while.'

'Mmm…'

'You're lucky, though.'

'Oh?' Thank goodness her grandmother couldn't possibly have any idea of just *how* lucky her granddaughter had been.

'Yes. Much luckier than back in my day. You've got your mobile phones and…and Scope.'

Charlotte smiled despite herself as she sighed. 'Skype, Gran.'

'Whatever.' Her hand got another squeeze. 'It's not quite the same as the real thing, though, is it?'

'No. It's not.' There was an odd pain in Charlotte's chest as she tried to draw in a new breath.

Her heart starting to break perhaps?

CHAPTER TEN

CHARLOTTE'S FAVOURITE CHRISTMAS ever had been the one she'd told Nico about when they'd been snowed in and Gran had cooked sausages on sticks over the open fire in the drawing room.

Maybe, some time in the future, somebody would ask her about her *least* favourite Christmas and she knew that, coincidentally, it would also be one of the rare, truly white ones.

This one.

She stared out of the V-shaped gap in the snow piled on the sill of her latticed window and there was the eerie, early morning light that only a thick blanket of snow could create. There was nothing to disturb the perfection of the Christmas-card scene in the gardens of Highton Hall. The footprints on the lawn below had probably been made by a fox but if her grandmother had seen them in years gone by, she would have told a small Charlotte that they were the tracks left by Santa's reindeer.

The thought should have brought a poignant smile to her face but instead Charlotte felt the lump in her throat get bigger.

She had never felt this...bleak.

This lonely.

This...*empty*.

As if she'd lost something huge that she would never have back again. Like her heart? Or maybe it was part of her soul. The part that she'd shared with Nico. Yes. That's what it felt like. He had brought light into the darkest part of her being and, by touching it, it had somehow become his, even if he didn't want it.

Was that what love was? Giving away the most important part of yourself?

No... Charlotte found her picture-perfect view becoming blurry. It was finding someone who recognised that part. Accepted it. Made it better than it had been before simply by being there.

And it wasn't one-sided, that had been the clincher. Nico had shared that part of himself with her. The lonely little boy who was still there deep inside. The one who'd been hurt and had seen people he loved get hurt, and was determined to never be the cause of such hurt himself.

Nico thought he didn't know what he needed. That he couldn't possibly make the right choice of a person to be with for the rest of his life. He thought he was incapable of falling in love.

And maybe he had the kind of strength to hold himself back from that kind of surrender but it was blindingly obvious what he needed.

A tiny robin, its bright red breast a decoration in itself, fluttered into view and landed on the windowsill, tilting its head and to give Charlotte a cheeky glance.

'He just needs what we all need,' she informed the robin. 'To be loved.'

The robin fluttered off like an echo of laughter.

As if it was that simple...

It was. Charlotte had found that person, hadn't she? She had given him that part of herself she could never give to anyone else.

But it was that impossibly difficult at the same time.

Because finding someone that you connected with at a soul-deep level wasn't enough. They had to feel the same way or it could never begin to work.

And Nico didn't feel the same way. How could he when they'd only known each other for a couple of days?

But he didn't even want to *see* her again. Good grief, he'd told her that she could leave the ring with his secretary, if he wasn't around.

It had meant nothing. A bit of harmless pretence to make an old lady happy before she died. Repayment for the imagined debt of losing her laptop. A bonus of a one-night stand as well?

Charlotte forced herself to move. She couldn't stand here dwelling on how miserable she felt. It was Christmas Day after all. And her toes were freezing. Dressing quickly, she chose clothes for warmth, donning black woollen leggings and an oversized crimson pullover on top of a black bodysuit. No doubt her grandmother would expect her to change for dinner but that was a few hours away yet and it would be warmer downstairs when the open fires were stoked up.

Maybe Christmas dinner wasn't so far away after all. The rich aroma of roasting meat caught Charlotte's nostrils as she went downstairs. Betty, the cook, must be busy in the kitchen, probably under Gran's strict supervision. Charlotte would probably be given a laden

plate of bacon and eggs and an admonishment about the perils of laziness and sleeping in.

The Christmas tree in the huge foyer of this grand old house had coloured lights twinkling merrily and there were gifts beneath, enticingly wrapped in pretty paper and tied with bows of satin ribbon.

It looked like one of the festive pictures that had played against the wall of that Venetian restaurant... good grief, only three days ago? On the evening when she'd given in to the temptation of pretending that Nico was her lover. When she'd accidentally become 'engaged' to him.

The ring was still on her finger. Touching it, Charlotte found she could twist it more easily now. Because she was away from the efficient central heating of the Orient Express and in a huge, chilly ancestral home?

Or was it because she felt so cold inside? So bleak...

Whatever. She couldn't take it off yet, could she? Not on Christmas Day, when it would be the first thing Gran would notice. She would have to find a solution to this situation but not today.

And she couldn't let Gran see how miserable she was either. Pasting what she hoped was a bright smile on her face, Charlotte walked past the Christmas tree and went down the long hallway to the kitchen.

Betty was basting an enormous turkey. Her husband, John, was polishing silver serviette rings over newspaper spread on one end of the kitchen table. Her daughter was peeling Brussels sprouts and scoring an X into the stalks.

'I was just about to put some breakfast on trays and bring it up,' Betty said after Christmas greetings had been exchanged. 'I was getting worried.'

'Has Gran not been down yet?'

'Not a peep from her. And she's always the first up on Christmas Day.'

'I'll take her up a cup of tea,' Charlotte said. She was worried herself now. 'I expect she's just tired out after her big adventure.'

'You look a bit peaky yourself, pet.' Betty and her family had been a part of Highton Hall for as long as Charlotte could remember. They were more like relatives than staff. Family. Charlotte's smile was genuine this time.

'I'm fine, Betty. I just need a cup of tea, too.'

Betty had been patting her hand. Her jaw dropped.

'Oh…my…. Is that what I *think* it is?'

Charlotte held up her hand and the diamond flashed as it caught the light. Her heart sank. The game had to go on a little longer no matter how much worse it was going to make her feel.

'I guess I had a bit of an adventure myself, Betty. You'll hear all about it as soon as Gran's up, I'm sure.'

'I'd better.' Betty busied herself with a teapot and a china cup and saucer. She added a couple of tiny gingerbread stars to the saucer. 'Go on…tell Lady G that we're waiting to hear all about it.'

Her grandmother's bedroom was still dark.

'You awake, Gran? I've got a cup of tea for you.' Charlotte balanced the cup in one hand as she drew back the heavy drapes to let the bright, mid-morning light into the room.

And then she turned, and didn't notice how much tea she was spilling on the Persian carpet as she raced to her grandmother's bedside and dropped the cup and

saucer on the bedside table. Gingerbread stars floated in a saucer full of tea.

'Gran...'

Lady Geraldine was lying with her knees pulled up and the bedcover gripped between clenched fists. Her face was white with a sheen of perspiration on her forehead. Her pulse was racing. And weak. Her abdomen was swollen and hard to the touch. And it only took the lightest touch to make her cry out in agony.

'Oh...*God*...' Charlotte picked up the phone beside the half-empty cup of tea. She dialled only three numbers.

'I need an ambulance,' she said crisply as soon as her call was answered. 'It's urgent.'

Emergencies like heart attacks and strokes were no respecters of what day it happened to be.

Extreme weather was more of a problem on days when people simply had to be somewhere else for an important occasion and the number of accidents rose.

And there were plenty of people like him who had no family to be with and no desire to celebrate Christmas and carried on with stupid behaviour like getting into fights and getting beaten up or stabbed.

Worst of all, there were the people who found the season too much of a reminder of what they didn't have so the rate of attempted suicides always went up, too.

It was not a good day to be in charge of an emergency department but the staff always did their absolute best to make it as cheerful as possible, and Nico had always managed to join in and encourage them.

Why was it *so* hard this year?

Why did he feel so...bleak?

So...*empty*?

It was *ridicolo*. Ridiculous.

He had his life back the way he wanted it to be. *Needed* it to be.

So why did he feel so off-kilter? So *perduto*, almost?

And why was it always Italian words that came into his head when something stirred him deeply? The past was behind him and best forgotten. Even dredging up happy memories, such as the favourite Christmas he'd shared with Charlotte, was not a good thing to do. No wonder he couldn't settle into doing what he most loved to do and lose himself in the demands of his work.

He would go and do another thorough neurological check on the elderly gentleman in cubicle three who had fallen when he'd gone outside to sweep snow off the steps in preparation for his family arriving. He'd hit his head hard enough to need a period of observation before they could consider letting him go home to his Christmas dinner. Maybe it hadn't just been the slippery steps and the fall responsible for him losing consciousness either. Perhaps a more thorough cardiovascular work-up would be justified.

Imagine what would have happened in Venice if Charlotte hadn't been there to see beyond what others had seen?

'Incoming, Dr Moretti,' a nurse told him as she hurried past. 'Eighty-something-year-old female with an abdominal mass and acute bowel obstruction. She's tachycardic, short of breath and vomiting. GCS of thirteen.'

Dio... An elderly woman with a bowel obstruction that could potentially be due to a tumour? Was every-

thing today going to remind him of either Charlotte or her *nonna*? They were probably sitting in front of an open fire right now. Drinking mulled wine or eggnog, perhaps and listening to Christmas carols. Maybe there was a piano and Charlotte would be playing carols. Or maybe they were opening their gifts to each other.

Or…maybe something terrible had happened. Nico could see the ambulance team coming through the doors of his department now. He couldn't see much of the figure on the stretcher because she was bundled up in warm blankets and her face was covered by an oxygen mask. The person holding the bag of IV fluids aloft wasn't part of the paramedic crew, however.

It was Charlotte.

No. Could this be the beginning of the end for Jendi? Surely not today, of all days…

'Resus One,' Nico ordered, before the triage nurse had a chance to consider priority. 'And get a surgical consult down here stat.'

He ushered the entourage into the resus area reserved for major cases. There was no time for any more than brief eye contact with Charlotte as Nico listened to the handover from the paramedics and prepared to launch an investigative and stabilisation protocol that could deal with this emergency. There was no way he was going to let Lady Geraldine Highton die in his department on Christmas Day.

As awful as it was, this was just the kind of challenge he'd needed. That disturbing, *empty* feeling had completely vanished and Nico had never felt more in control. Or more determined to do his absolute best for his patient. And her family.

* * *

The waiting was the worst.

At least all the tension and drama and fear since the moment she'd found Gran in such a dreadful state had been balanced by the swiftness of action and the company of others. The paramedics had been brilliant, using a four-wheel-drive vehicle to get to the estate and then transferring Gran to a faster ambulance to get her into the city. The roads had been appalling with all the snow and traffic jams from a big accident on the M1. They'd had to stick to routes that had been cleared in the city and get to an emergency department that was not only open on Christmas Day but prepared to accept a major case.

It had taken too much time and all the while Lady Geraldine's condition had been deteriorating. It was becoming hard for her to breathe and her level of consciousness was slipping. By the time they'd arrived at the totally unexpected destination of the Hammersmith—*Nico's* hospital—she was unconscious and the situation was looking bad enough for Charlotte to be unaware of anything except the relief of getting to a place where they might be able to help her grandmother.

And then there'd been the drama of trying to get Gran stable enough for the surgeon to consider that operating might be an option on an eighty-two-year-old woman. There'd been fluid resuscitation and ventilation assistance, blood tests and scans and ECGs. People rushing in and out with the kind of controlled chaos Charlotte was all too familiar with, but this was her *gran* being treated and she'd never felt less like a doctor.

Waiting like this in an area set aside for the families of patients undergoing surgery was a new experience too. It was nerve-racking and felt interminable. There were only one or two theatres being used for absolute emergencies today and just a skeleton staff on duty so it felt like she was completely alone and she'd been here for what felt like hours. Surely the surgery was over by now? Why hadn't someone come to tell her what was going on?

Had they forgotten she was even here?

No... Charlotte could hear footsteps echoing in the wide, empty hallway outside. Coming closer. Someone was coming to see her and what they had to say could possibly be devastating news.

She couldn't move. Could only stand there, with her fingers pressed against her mouth to stifle a cry. Afraid to breathe. Unable to blink even.

And then a tall figure filled the doorway. A powerful presence entered the small space of the waiting room and...

And Charlotte wasn't alone any more.

'Carlotta...*cara*...' Nico gathered Charlotte into his arms and held her close. '*Grazie a Dio ho trovato voi.*'

He'd had to come even though he had no real news for her yet. Standing there, in the observation deck of the operating theatre, it had come back with a vengeance.

That empty feeling.

Had it really been the challenge of fighting for Jendi's life that had made it go away? The focus on medicine that was the most important thing in his life? Or

had it had been because Charlotte was so close to him again?

He had to find out. His shift in the emergency department was finished and there would be no professional distraction for him now. If he found Charlotte and that empty feeling disappeared then he would know the truth.

And it had. *Dio mio*, but it had evaporated like mist in hot Italian sunshine as soon as he'd gathered her in his arms and held her close to his heart.

The truth was irrefutable. It wasn't work he needed like the oxygen in the air he breathed. It was this woman. *Charlotte*. Without her, he would have that horrible, empty feeling for the rest of his life.

'Carlotta...' The word was a breath that got lost in her hair.

'I don't understand,' she said.

Neither did Nico. But it was wonderful. So joyous.

'I can't speak Italian, Nico...' She was wriggling in his arms, pulling back so she could see his face. 'What's happening?' Her breath was a fearful gulp. 'Where's Gran?'

How could he be so selfish? Nico stroked her hair and focused enough to change languages.

'There's a break in surgery. They're doing a biopsy of the tumour. It will be a bigger operation if they decide to try and remove it all and it would be too much of a risk if it's...'

She knew what he was saying. If the tumour was aggressively malignant, they would only attempt a palliative procedure to deal with the bowel obstruction.

But Charlotte's eyes had widened. 'The surgeon

thinks there's a chance it's not malignant? That it's…
benign?'

Was it cruel to give her hope or a gift that he could
share with her for at least a little while? The point was
moot because she knew the answer. They wouldn't be
interrupting surgery for the length of time it took to
use a technician on Christmas Day if it wasn't a good
possibility.

'Are you going back? Can you find out?'

Nico shook his head. 'They'll come and tell us. I
want to wait here with you. I…I *have* to.'

'You *have* to?' Charlotte's tone was as odd as his
had been. A note of wonder? *'Why?'*

'Because…' There was no point in being less than
honest with her. There never had been and never would
be. 'Because being with you…it makes the empty feel-
ing go away.'

'Oh…' Charlotte's gaze was holding his and he
could actually see it melting. Getting misty. 'It does…
It *so* does, doesn't it?'

'*You* feel it too?' A surge of emotion was threaten-
ing to explode inside Nico's chest. Gratitude? Relief?
Hope? No. It was bigger than any of those. 'I've never
felt like this,' he confessed. 'I don't know what this
is…but it's…it's…'

'I think it's love,' Charlotte whispered. 'I'm in love
with you and that's why I have the empty feeling when
you're not here.'

'I'm in love with you…' Nico tested the words out
loud. Strange and new but…yes…they felt right. He
tried them in Italian to make sure. *'Cara mia, innamo-
rata di te.'*

And that made them real but still unbelievable. 'How?' he whispered. 'How did this happen? So fast?'

'I don't know...' But Charlotte was smiling. Almost laughing, but there were tears in her eyes at the same time. 'But it's Christmas...and it's the most wonderful gift I could ever have been given. I love you so much, Nico. I've never felt like this before. It feels like everything that's ever happened to me, even all the bad things, were worth it because it led me here. To *you*.'

He had to kiss her then. Slowly. Tenderly. The bursting feeling inside him intensified and turned to molten joy. It was a long time before he could lift his head to look into Charlotte's eyes again.

'When I was in Venice,' Nico told her with a smile, 'a moment or two before I saw you at the accident scene I was having to push my way through the crowd and I heard this old woman and you know what she said?'

'No.' Charlotte was smiling up at him. A tear escaped and Nico let go of one of her hands so that he could brush it away for her. 'What did she say?'

'That it was almost Christmas. A good time for a miracle to happen. I think that's what this is, Carlotta. A miracle.'

Charlotte sniffed and the sound was so unromantic that Nico could feel himself fall even deeper in love with her. Had he really thought he was incapable of doing this? He was good at it. With a bit of practice he would be the best.

When Charlotte scrubbed at her nose, he caught her hand. The one with the ring on it. He seemed to remember it had been quite a struggle to get it onto her finger but it came off quite easily.

Charlotte went very, very still.

'You know what this is.' Nico had to clear the sudden gruffness of his voice away. 'Of all the people in the world, you are the only one who can know the symbolism of this ring. The…' His voice cracked again. 'The promise it carries.'

Her gaze clung to his. Her head dipped and rose again in a slow, solemn nod.

'I didn't give you a choice about wearing it before,' Nico continued. 'I'm giving you that choice now. Will you wear this ring, *inamorata*? Will you accept my promise?'

'Oh…*yes*, Nico.' Her hand was shaking as she held it out for him to slip the ring back on her finger. 'But…'

He stilled her words with a gentle finger on her lips. 'It's like your *nonna* said,' he murmured. 'It doesn't mean we have to get married next week. It's a promise of commitment. We can take all the time we need to make sure it's perfect.'

The sound of footsteps outside the waiting room sent a sudden chill down Nico's spine. Someone was coming to give them news.

What if it was bad news?

The only way this could be truly perfect would be to have Jendi at their wedding, wouldn't it? To see her, at some point in the future, cradle her first great-grandchild in her arms.

To know that the biggest thing on that bucket list of hers had been well and truly ticked off.

It was the surgeon, who'd come straight from Theatre to find them. He'd stripped off his gown and gloves but he was still in his scrubs and white gumboots. He still had a hat covering his head and neck.

But he was smiling. 'Your gran's a real trouper,' he

told Charlotte. 'Tough as old boots, in fact. She's come through this astonishingly well. You'll be able to go and see her in Recovery very soon.'

'Oh…thank God…' Charlotte was clinging to Nico's hand with a vice-like grip. 'And…and the tumour?'

'Benign. We got it all out. Can't see any reason why she won't keep ticking along for a good few years yet.' The surgeon's smile widened. 'Merry Christmas.'

Charlotte was sobbing in his arms now. Nico had tears on his own face.

Buon Natale, indeed.

The best ever, without a doubt.

EPILOGUE

CHRISTMAS WAS LONG GONE.

Lady Geraldine Highton didn't remember it at all. She remembered Venice, of course, and the magic of the Orient Express journey. How could she ever forget when it had made her most cherished dream come true? Her beloved Charlotte had found the love of her life.

And here they were, in the gardens of Highton Hall, in the springtime. Surrounded by daffodils and bluebells with the gentle perfume of apple blossom and tiny puffs of cloud in an otherwise blue sky making this day perfect.

Their wedding day.

They'd waited until she was fully recovered, bless them, and these last few months had been a gift in themselves. She hadn't been allowed to rely solely on the wonderful care Betty had co-ordinated. They'd both moved into Highton Hall themselves, despite the hassle of commuting to London for their busy working lives.

And somehow Nico had got out of all those overseas commitments that had threatened to keep him and Charlotte apart for the foreseeable future. They hadn't had to rely on that new-fangled Scope thing at all. It

had been, in fact, as if they couldn't bear to be apart from each other for a heartbeat longer than they had to.

And when they were together, they couldn't keep their hands off each other. Not that anyone minded today, of course. It was only expected that they would link hands when Charlotte had wound her way through the chairs set out in the bluebell woods under the ancient oak trees to join her husband-to-be in front of the celebrant. That Nico had immediately bent his head to place a lingering kiss on her lips might have been a tad premature but...he was Italian. What could one say?

And it wasn't as if Charlotte was wearing a veil to cover her face. She may have chosen a traditional, stunning white dress that made her look beautiful enough to bring a tear to anybody's eye, but she'd left her hair loose and flowing.

It had been a joke when Geraldine had offered her beloved tiara as the 'something borrowed' but there it was, sparkling in her blonde hair as a shaft of sunlight found a way through the unfurling leaves of the oak trees. A glint of silver on her wrist was the only other adornment Charlotte had chosen. That tiny ring of hearts that had the emblem of the Orient Express engraved on its catch.

Geraldine eyed the rings on her own fingers as she smoothed the skirt of her lovely new pink silk dress. Maybe she should tone down her own accessories? No. That would be tantamount to curbing all sorts of things. Acting her age even, and that would never do, would it?

She had to shift a little on her chair in the front seat as the proceedings started. There were still moments of discomfort as she recovered from the major abdom-

inal surgery that had removed that thankfully benign growth but she would never complain.

This was more than a bonus of time that she hadn't expected to have.

What had occurred during this last Christmas season had been the most amazing gift ever.

Although…

She'd interrupted something last night. A moment between Charlotte and Nico that had looked like more than an intimate goodnight on the eve of their wedding. Nico had had the palm of his hand on Charlotte's belly. She'd had her hand resting on top of his and the look they'd been giving each other was one of those that could speak volumes.

She hadn't let on that she'd seen them.

And she certainly wouldn't advertise the fact that her bucket list now had a new item on the top.

She was already the luckiest woman in the world, even though she knew her granddaughter would dispute that title. It would be her secret that she would be keeping her fingers crossed for another amazing gift next Christmas.

A gift they could all share.

A *baby*…

* * * * *

PERFECT RIVALS...

AMY RUTTAN

This book is dedicated to my agent, Scott, for telling me to take this chance and write this continuity story.

Thank you to Elisa, who patiently answered my questions while I was researching this book. Thank you so much for all your help!

And a huge thank you to the Medical team for assigning me Flo and Nate's story. They were an amazing hero and heroine and I loved every second in their world.

CHAPTER ONE

THIS TAKES ME BACK.

Dr. Flo Chiu remembered all the times she'd been raced to the hospital as a young girl. The familiar whir of a chopper coming in for a landing. Followed by the bump as the chopper landed, causing her to become nauseous. Even now, watching the helicopter, her stomach did a little flip. Everything reminded her of that moment. Something she hadn't thought about in a long time. The gray haze tinting the sky, as if it was promising rain, but this was Los Angeles. The haze was just smog. In Seattle, it would mean rain, and the day she'd flown in her own helicopter to a hospital helipad it had been raining. Hard.

And that was all she remembered of her emergent helicopter ride over Seattle. That, and her father screaming out orders in Mandarin to a helicopter pilot who only spoke English, but, then, when her dad was frightened he often put aside his second language of English for his native tongue. And when her dad was mad, the beautiful language she loved to listen to was quick and hard to follow. It had frightened her to hear him talk like that.

She took a deep breath and wrapped her arms around herself, trying to shake the thought away. Usually she wasn't this nervous about another surgeon coming in to

The Hollywood Hills Clinic, but this was not just any other surgeon. This surgeon was her competition. This surgeon had been brought in specially from New York at the request of her patient. And her patient happened to be the world-famous, award-winning actor Kyle Francis. An actor she'd always admired and had had a bit of a crush on when she'd been fourteen.

She'd watched a lot of movies when she'd been younger. Of course, there hadn't been much else to do when you were confined to a hospital bed. And Kyle Francis had been the perfect twenty-something rising star and heartthrob of her youth.

On the outside Kyle had aged well. His heart and lungs, on the other hand, hadn't. Which was why he was now a patient.

He'd collapsed at a press conference in Los Angeles and had been brought straight to The Hollywood Hills Clinic, where it had quickly been established that Kyle Francis was dying.

And that's where Flo had stepped in.

She was, after all, a world-renowned transplant surgeon, and that's just what Kyle Francis needed. Actually, what he specifically needed was a heart and lung transplant.

It was right up Flo's alley. She'd done many, and on worse cases than Kyle, but if they let it go much longer, Kyle would be a worst-case scenario and it would make the job harder.

She had been wheeling Kyle into the operating room to help stabilize him until she had been stopped.

That was when Freya had dropped the bombshell on her that another surgeon was coming.

"Another surgeon? Why was another surgeon called,

Freya? I'm a damn good surgeon. I can do this surgery on my own. You've seen me do one."

"I know, but this is out of my hands, Flo. Mr. Francis's management team has called in Dr. King from Manhattan. Dr. King's the one who has been treating his failing heart and lungs for some time. There's no negotiation. You'll have to work with Dr. King."

Flo couldn't really argue with that.

So that's why she was here, huddled in the elevator, waiting for the helicopter to land and deposit this Dr. King in her lap. He was probably some old-money type of surgeon, and she only hoped that he would be willing to work with her. Some of these big-city surgeons were a pain in the rump to deal with. They didn't think someone who was only thirty had the skill to be an excellent or extraordinary surgeon and a transplant specialist to boot.

The chopper landed and Flo ducked down, holding back the wisps of black hair that were escaping from her long braid as she headed out onto the helipad to greet this new doctor.

Please, don't be a jerk. Please, don't be a jerk.

She could deal with almost anyone but a jerk. Other surgeons tended to look down on her because of her size and her gender. That, and she looked a lot younger than her age. Even though she hoped this surgeon wasn't a jerk, she'd been warned about his arrogance so she braced herself for it.

The door of the chopper opened and her mouth almost dropped open in surprise. Dr. King was not at all what she had expected. He wasn't old at all. Probably in his mid-thirties. Tall, tanned and muscular. His blond hair was tousled and short. His face was chiseled, and the well-tailored gray suit molded his broad chest and thick muscular thighs almost perfectly. He was an all-

American high-school hottie. The kind of man who had probably got through med school on a football scholarship. The kind of man who would have ignored a perpetually sick, geeky wallflower like her at school dances. The kind of man she'd always secretly wished would look her way.

Johnny had been good looking, but not like this, and look how that had turned out. Flo shook her ex from her thoughts. He'd been gone for a long time and there was no place for him in her mind today.

Heat rushed to her cheeks when he turned to look at her. Light blue, almost ice-blue eyes fixed their hard gaze on her, as if assessing her and sizing her up in a matter of moments. It unnerved her, but also excited her. She almost wondered what it would be like steal a kiss from a man like this. And then she kicked herself mentally for thinking about the competition this way.

No matter how attractive she thought he was, he was still the competition.

All-American athletes like him were the kind of guy she'd always wanted to date. At least once in her life, because it wasn't the type of guy her father or mother would like if she brought him home. They hadn't been thrilled with Johnny either and he was a lawyer.

Focus. He's staring at you.

It was then she realized the chopper had already left the helipad and was headed away from the clinic toward LAX.

"Are you all right?" he asked.

"Fine. Dr. King, I'm—"

"I don't have time for pleasantries. You need to take me to my patient."

Great. He's a pompous jerk.

Well, an arrogant surgeon she could deal with. Her

father was an arrogant businessman in Beijing and Seattle. Flo's mother, who was American, was the only one who could get him to toe the line, and she'd taught Flo well. She'd taught her not to cower to arrogant men and to stand up for herself. Especially in light of the fact that Flo had been sick her whole life and people tried to walk all over her.

"As I was saying, I'm Dr. Chiu and I'm head of transplant surgery here at The Hollywood Hills Clinic. I've been treating Mr. Francis since his collapse last night."

Dr. King's eyes widened in shock. "Is that so?"

"Yes. Now, if you will follow me, Dr. King, I will take you to *our* patient." She got into the elevator and when he also entered, she pushed the button for the wing that housed Kyle Francis. It was the wing that had the most security to guarantee privacy for high-profile patients.

"Did you say 'our' patient, Dr. Chiu?"

"I did."

"I have to say I'm a bit confused. Kyle Francis has been my patient for a couple of years now. I'm the one who put him on the transplant list. He's my patient."

She grinned at him sardonically. "Oh, no. He's *our* patient. Mr. Francis's management team may have flown you in here, but the transplant wing is my wing. I'm granting you surgical privileges here, buster, and don't you forget it."

He grinned at her, amused, or at least she hoped so as those ice-blue eyes were twinkling. "Buster? I've never heard that one before."

Flo rolled her eyes, but smiled. "Sorry. Something I picked up from my mother."

The elevator doors opened up and Flo swiped her security card to open the doors to allow them entry to the

high-security wing. Kyle's large suite was at the end of the hall.

"So, when he arrived he was bradycardic. We got his breathing and rhythm stabilized, but it's apparent to me that his heart is failing and his time is running out. He needs to be put on a left ventricular assist device."

"An LVAD?" Dr. King nodded. "I can see why you would think that, but let's not jump to conclusions. We don't know what caused the collapse. He was stable when he left New York last week. And putting him on a left ventricular assist device complicates his transplant further."

"I am aware of that. I'm not jumping to conclusions. I've performed a heart and lung transplant before, Dr. King. I know what I'm doing. I know what I'm seeing."

"Then if you know what it is, why isn't he on a left ventricular assist device?"

Really?

"I was about to have him prepped for the OR when his management team put a stop to the procedure and insisted on flying you out here, Dr. King."

"Nate."

"Pardon?" Flo said as she picked up a tablet to bring up Kyle's chart.

"My name is Nathaniel, but you can call me Nate. And what can I call you, Dr. Chiu?"

"You can call me Dr. Chiu." She tried to step past him, but he blocked her path.

"If you knew my patient, you would know that he likes everything to be informal. It puts him at ease. So I think it's in the best interests of the patient that we address each other by our given names."

"My name is Florence, but everyone calls me Flo." She handed him the tablet with Kyle's chart.

He grinned. "Thank you, Flo. Let's see *our* patient, shall we?"

Flo gritted her teeth. This was going to be a trying ordeal and it had nothing to do with the complicated surgery that awaited Kyle Francis. Someone was going to die and it wouldn't be the patient if Dr. Nate King kept being a thorn in her side.

Nate didn't particularly want to be back in California, even though he'd grown up here and his parents now lived up in San Francisco. He hadn't been back to California since he'd started medical school, and that had been years ago.

He hadn't been in California since the accident. Since Serena had died when they'd been rock climbing on El Capitan in Yosemite National Park. He just couldn't be in the place where they'd fallen in love, the place where they'd lived for the rush, whether it had been surfing breakers in the Pacific Ocean, skiing at Mammoth Mountain or rock climbing.

Serena had been an adrenaline junkie, just like him.

And then, on a climb they'd done a hundred times before, a rope had given way and Serena had fallen.

His guilt still ate at him. He was so certain he'd checked all those clips, tightened the rope, but he couldn't recall actually doing it and her death weighed on him.

He'd realized then how recklessly he'd been living. So he'd taken the scholarship at Harvard and thrown himself into schooling. Nate had sworn over Serena's coffin that he would become the best damn transplant surgeon, focusing a lot of his research on regeneration and the means to sustain life longer when there were no viable donors.

People died every day while they waited on the transplant list.

Serena had died while she'd waited.

Don't think about her now.

Nate stared at the chart, at the scans they'd done on Kyle when he'd been admitted to The Hollywood Hills Clinic.

Dang. She was right.

Kyle needed a left ventricular assist device and he needed one right away. She was watching him as he scanned Kyle's chart. He snuck a glance, just a brief glance, at her and he tried not to smile. He didn't want to give her an inch.

She was feisty. There was a certain passion hidden deep in that petite frame. Her skin was almost flawless and her long black hair shone in the tight braid down her back, except for the few stray wisps that floated around her perfect oval face. Her eyes were dark brown, like chocolate, and they glinted as she watched him. Her full ruby lips were pressed together firmly, as if she was waiting for the moment to smirk at him when he announced that she'd been right.

Dr. Florence Chiu was intelligent, gorgeous and full of life. She didn't back down from him, even though he towered over her five-foot-five frame at six feet.

If he hadn't sworn off the idea of women in general, he would pursue a woman just like Dr. Chiu. He liked a bit of wildness as well as the fact she was a transplant surgeon. It was as if she was the perfect woman for him.

Don't think about her like that.

Just from a quick moment in Flo's presence he realized that she was a danger to his well-being. He was not looking for love.

He'd been hurt before. His heart had shattered when Serena had died, so Flo was off-limits. He was here to work. He was here for his patient and that's all that mat-

tered. Being the foremost transplant surgeon on the east coast afforded him the ability to further his research on finding other means of sustaining organs or life while patients waited for organs.

All that mattered to Nate was his career and he had to remember that. Love was not for him. He didn't deserve it.

He cleared his throat. "You're right, Dr. Chiu. He does need a left ventricular assist device. I assume, since you were prepping for surgery, that you have one ready to go?"

Flo nodded. "Yes. I can prep the OR in about an hour and we can get him in there and hooked up to the equipment. I'm sorry that your trip to California was a waste."

He cocked his head to one side and smiled at her. "Why is it a waste now?"

"Well, clearly I can handle this here. You came here and basically said I was right in the course of my treatment for Mr. Francis, so you can go back to New York."

Such tenacity.

"Oh, Dr. Chiu. I'm not heading anywhere. Mr. Francis is my top priority. There are other surgeons in New York who can run my service while I'm here. I'm staying and I plan to be in that OR with you and assist you in implanting the LVAD."

"You're kidding, right?"

"No. I never kid when it comes to my patients. I have been treating Mr. Francis for a couple of years. I'm the one who put him on the transplant list and I'll be the one performing his transplant, even if that means I'll be spending years in California. I'm not leaving his side."

Her mouth had opened to say something else when alarms went off and a code blue was called in Kyle's

suite. They ran into the suite and a nursing team was already working over him.

"He's crashing, Dr. Chiu!" Nurse Olivia Dempsey called out as she lowered the bed and the rest of the team rushed in with an AED and tray of instruments.

Flo jumped into action, rapidly firing off instructions as Kyle Francis flatlined. Nate wasn't leaving his patient.

He wasn't going anywhere. Even if it meant staying in California. Even if it meant being tempted constantly by Dr. Chiu. He was made of strong mettle. He could resist temptation.

Couldn't he?

CHAPTER TWO

DON'T DIE. DON'T DIE.

Flo glanced up at the monitors as she worked on Kyle Francis, and she tried not to think about the fact that Dr. Nate King was standing on the opposite side of the bed, working with her as they tried to stabilize him. If Kyle died, he'd judge her. He seemed like the arrogant type who would put the blame on her when really it was the management team that Kyle employed who would be at fault. They were the ones who'd put a stop to her helping him right away, insisting that Dr. King be flown in.

Making her and Kyle wait.

That wouldn't have happened if she'd been allowed to put in the left ventricular assist device when Kyle had first come in, and she was going to make sure that Freya and James Rothsberg both knew that. Especially if Kyle died.

Come on.

Right now she'd like to throttle that acting management team. Their delay might've cost Kyle his life.

"Come on," she whispered under her breath as she pictured all the thousand ways she'd torture Kyle's managers.

There was a bleep from the monitor as the sensor picked up a faint pulse. Flo gave an inward sigh of relief. Thoughts of murder and disemboweling some Hollywood yuppies dissipating for now.

"Good job, everyone!" She took off her latex gloves as the nursing team stepped in to make sure that Kyle didn't code again. "I need this man prepped and ready for surgery. I'm on my way to get an OR prepped. I want a repeat of his labs drawn."

"Yes, Dr. Chiu," said Olivia.

"Make sure that I'm informed of those labs as well, Nurse," Nate said, not even glancing in the direction of Flo's favorite transplant nurse.

Olivia looked at Flo for confirmation and she nodded.

Flo glanced at Nate, who was scowling as he monitored Kyle's vitals. She thought maybe she could sneak past him. She didn't want to deal with arrogance this minute. Moments like that just brought back the vivid memories of the time she'd collapsed during band practice. When her kidney had failed her at fourteen and she had been rushed to hospital.

They were jumbled memories, but her parents liked to tell that story about how she'd hovered near death. She'd needed a donor then and Kyle needed one now. But a heart and lung transplant match was tricky. The list was long and the United Network of Organ Sharing didn't care who Kyle was. Placement on the list was prioritized on who got on the list first.

There were other people waiting for a heart and lung transplant. Kyle was at the top of two lists, one for the heart and one for the lungs. He had to have both at the same time from the same donor.

At least the left ventricular assist device would stabilize Kyle while they waited. By the time her kidney had failed, dialysis had no longer worked for her. At least kidneys could be donated by a living donor.

You could live with one kidney.

Flo always had.

Her stomach twisted as she thought of that, because her time was so uncertain. She'd had this kidney for fifteen years now. How much longer until she was on her sickbed? On dialysis and waiting for another transplant?

Another precious gift so she could go on living?

Which was why she had to continue to live life to the fullest.

"Going somewhere, Dr. Chiu?"

Drat.

She turned around to see that Nate had followed her out of Kyle's suite. "I'm going to schedule our surgery."

"I'm so glad you said 'our' surgery."

Flo rolled her eyes and he fell into step beside her. "Really, I can handle this surgery on my own."

"I know you can, but what would be the fun in that?" Nate asked, his scowl changing into a teasing smile.

"Trust me. It's fun." She grinned back at him and he chuckled. He had a gorgeous smile, perfect white teeth against that tanned face. There was a faint scar that ran through his eyebrow and another on his chin.

Definitely a jock.

"So where can I get set up with a pager and scrubs? I wouldn't mind an office, either."

"You're not asking for much, are you?" Flo remarked.

"Well, if I'm going to be here a while I would like to continue my research."

"Research? What're you researching or is that a secret?"

"No. It's no secret. I've published several papers on regenerative tissues as well as robotic and mechanical devices to prolong organs and life while waiting for transplants."

Flo was impressed. She'd never read any of Nate's papers, but the premise was interesting.

"Well, if you're looking for a place to set up shop then you would have to talk to Freya Rothsberg, but she's gone home for the evening."

"Okay, I'll talk to her in the morning. I don't have to talk to her about getting a pair of scrubs, do I?"

Flo laughed. She couldn't help it. The jerk was charming. She pointed to the OR charge desk, where a nurse sat behind her desk and was electronically entering patients' details onto a vast surgical board. "No, just speak to that OR nurse and she'll point you in the right direction."

He smiled again, one that made her melt just slightly, before he headed off to get scrubs. She admired his well-defined backside as he strode away.

Don't think about him like that.

Flo had no time for romantic inclinations, because the one time she had and Johnny had found out that she had a chronic kidney disease because of her time in NICU, he'd run in the opposite direction, breaking her heart. He had crushed her completely. It was easier to guard her heart than have it mangled by someone you thought you loved and who loved you back. She'd bared her most intimate side to Johnny, but the moment he'd seen her scar, the game had changed. Attraction had been replaced by disgust and fear. Even pity.

So Flo had given up on the notion of love. Which was probably why she was still a virgin at thirty.

She didn't need it. Besides, if she involved someone else in her life they would tell her that her bucket list was crazy and no one was going to dictate to her how she going to live her life. She'd been given a gift when she'd been given that kidney and she wasn't going to spend the rest of her life like she'd spent her childhood, wrapped up in cotton wool by two well-meaning but overprotective parents.

No, she was going to live her life to the fullest, until her donor kidney failed and she'd go back on the list again. When she was waiting she'd have all these amazing memories to think about and not have any regrets if she died while on the list.

And no man was going to get in her way.

Not even the all-American hottie she had always pined for.

"Suction, please," Flo said.

"With pleasure." Nate suctioned around the area where Flo was working. Usually he was the one giving directions about suctioning or retracting, but instead he was the one on the other side of the table from the lead surgeon and it made him grind his teeth just a bit.

At least Flo had let him into her OR, because she was correct—she had every right to tell him to take off. She was the head of transplant surgery, he was just the patient's doctor from out east. Nate was very aware that he was in Dr. Flo Chiu's territory.

Scrub nurses and residents alike all respected and admired Dr. Chiu. Even though he should be bitter about the fact that she was working on his patient, he couldn't help but admire her surgical skill. Her tiny, delicate hands handled the heart with precision as she carefully sutured in the device. A device that would allow Kyle to live a bit longer.

"It's amazing how this can sustain his life," Nate remarked.

"Yes. It is. Medical research such as yours, Dr. King, is definitely valuable."

"You know, for a long time LVADs couldn't be used on children or women."

"I know, Dr. King."

"I know you do, Dr. Chiu, but maybe some of your residents in this room can tell me why LVADs couldn't be used on women and children in the past."

Flo shot him a look. "There are no residents here. The Hollywood Hills Clinic isn't a teaching hospital. All these surgeons are transplant fellows."

"Well, a fellow still has to learn under a seasoned surgeon." Nate glanced around the room. "Come on, someone has to know the answer."

"Would someone answer Dr. King, please? And maybe after this Dr. King would stop subjecting us to his pub quiz on cardiothoracic surgery."

There was laughter and Nate had to laugh to himself, as well.

Oh, she's feisty.

He liked that in a woman. Strong and not afraid to stand up for herself.

Flo wasn't afraid of much.

"The LVAD device was too large for the chests of women and children, that's why it couldn't be used on them in the past," a surgeon finally said.

"Right, thank you." Nate turned back to Flo. "See, this is why I'm doing my research and maybe this young doctor here would like to assist me while I continue with my research here in Los Angeles."

"Thank you, Dr. King," the surgeon said, stunned.

Flo shot him another look that said, *Are you kidding me?*

"I never questioned why you were doing your research, Dr. King. I admire it, but since Mr. Francis here will be stabilized, albeit bound to this hospital with his LVAD, maybe you could return to New York. I'll let you know when UNOS has a heart and lung ready for Mr. Francis." Flo continued with her work.

"Ah, but that's the thing. They won't be calling you, Dr. Chiu. UNOS will call me. I'm the one who put Mr. Francis on the transplant list."

Her head snapped back up and she fixed him with a stern look over her surgical mask.

That got her attention.

"You are persistent in your need to stay here, aren't you?" she said, with a hint of admiration in her voice.

"When it comes to my patients I am very persistent."

She looked up at him briefly and he knew by the way her eyes crinkled in the corners that she was smiling behind that mask. "Me, too."

"Dr. Chiu, I don't see why we both can't work together on Mr. Francis's care. We don't both have to stay at this hospital twenty-four-seven, waiting for a heart and lungs. Surely you have a life outside this hospital?"

"What're you implying, Dr. King? Are you implying I don't have a life?"

"On the contrary, I'm sure you have a life. Someone special."

"What?" she asked, not looking at him.

"A boyfriend."

There were a few titters in the crowd and Flo quickly shot them all a dirty look, which silenced the laughter.

"Not that it's any of your business, Dr. King, but I don't have a boyfriend. My work is my life."

"Oh, that's a shame."

Flo groaned. "Don't tell me you're one of those kinds of men?"

"What kind of men?"

"Men who think that a woman is worthless if she doesn't have a boyfriend or a significant other."

"No, I'm not. It's just…" Then he trailed off as he thought about Serena. "Life's too short."

She looked up at him, her brown eyes warm and tender as if silently agreeing with him. As if she knew personally how fragile life was, and he couldn't help but wonder what had happened in her life. Had she lost someone she'd cared about?

Nate certainly hoped not. That was a pain he wouldn't wish on his worst enemy.

"You're right," she said. "Life is too short. At least with this operation he won't be one of the ten to fifteen percent who die while waiting. It will give him a chance to beat the odds."

Nate nodded, but didn't say anything further as they worked together to attach Kyle's left ventricular assist device. Kyle was lucky that they'd brought him to Dr. Chiu, in light of the fact that he himself was based in New York.

There was talent here.

There was skill.

Together they could save Kyle's life. There were always variables when it came to heart and lung transplants, but maybe together they could succeed.

No. You can't. Not together.

Flo was the type of woman his old self would have pursued in a heartbeat and that thought scared him. If he had to work closely with her, then he would be tempted.

How could he not be tempted by a woman like Flo?

He had to keep his distance from her. It would be hard, but he had to put a wall between the two of them. It had to be professional. It had to be businesslike. That was all there was to it. Nate couldn't risk his heart again.

Risk was a dangerous thing and he wasn't willing to play around with that.

Look where his life of risk had gotten him.

Don't think about Serena now. You don't deserve to mourn her.

After the surgery was successfully completed, Nate didn't say much. He just scrubbed out and then tried to find his way off the surgical floor. He needed air. It took him a few minutes, but he found his way back up to the roof, to the helipad. Maybe the height would get him out of the LA smog.

It was hot out, different from New York, where the bitter remnants of March still clung to the city. He'd forgotten how much he missed the heat of California. He took a deep breath and tried to calm his jangled nerves.

He couldn't remember the last time he'd felt like this.

Since Serena had died he'd been busy burying his feelings in his work. He didn't usually connect with anyone, but Flo had got under his skin.

Even in the brief time he'd known her.

She made him forget. She made him forget how he had a tight rein on his emotions. Absolute control at all times.

"There you are," Flo said behind him, making him jump slightly.

"Why did you follow me up here?" he snapped.

"Don't get so testy. I followed you because I wanted to give you this temporary pass." She held out the scan card in her delicate fingers. "If you don't have this you can't get access to Mr. Francis or basically get around the hospital."

Nate sighed inwardly and took the scan card from her. "Sorry. Thanks."

"I guess I could've kept it and you would've been trapped here." A smile played at the corners of her lips. "You would deserve it, too, asking all those personal

questions during surgery. My team doesn't need to know about my personal life."

"I was trying to lighten the mood in there."

Since when?

In New York City he was always serious. Residents and interns alike quaked in their boots around him. He wasn't known for lightening the mood, or even chatting in an operating room. He didn't know what had come over him.

She crossed her arms. "There was no need for mood lightening in there. Besides, from what I hear, you're not exactly jovial all the time."

"Who told you that?" he asked.

"Mr. Francis, when he first came in and was stabilized. When he found out his management team had called you he warned me about you. He said you were a bit of an arrogant brute."

"I doubt he said arrogant brute."

"You're right," she said, a twinkle in her eyes. "It was much more colorful."

Nate chuckled to himself. That sounded like something Kyle would do. And when he glanced at Flo he could see a soft side to her. She gave off the appearance of being a tough cookie in the operating room, but there was a softness about her. A warmth.

Something he'd been missing in his life for so long.

"Thanks for helping me in there. I'm so glad he's stabilized. Let's just hope we can keep him that way until UNOS calls *you*." She smiled at him. "I'll leave you to it. If you need anything, just have me paged. I'll be at the hospital for some time still."

She turned to leave, but Nate reached out and took her elbow to stop her. Flo turned, a questioning look on her face.

"Thank you for being here to help my patient," he said. "I'm glad a surgeon of your caliber was here to help him. And I'll get UNOS to add you to the call list."

Her brown eyes widened in surprise and then she smiled, a pink blush tinging her round cheeks as she tucked an errant wisp of hair behind her ear. "Thank you, and of course."

Nate knew that he should let her go, only he couldn't. He felt mesmerized by her and without thinking he pulled her tight against and kissed her.

For one moment, while he tasted her sweet lips, he felt her melt against him, which prompted him to wrap his arms around her, deepening the kiss. Her petite body was pressed against his, his hands in her hair as he bent over to kiss her.

Nate wanted to take this further. If they had been back at his place in New York, he'd be scooping her up in his arms and carrying her off to bed to make love to her, but he was standing with her on a helipad in Los Angeles.

He was tumbling down a dangerous path.

Then he remembered what he was doing.

That this was not keeping his distance from her at all. It was the exact opposite.

He broke off the kiss and took a step away from her, running his hand through his hair, trying to calm the erratic beat of his pulse and the longing in his blood.

Flo stood there, just as shocked as he was, her fingers pressing her lips, her eyes wide.

"I'm sorry. I don't know..." He trailed off. He knew what had come over him and he was angry at himself for letting lust take over his senses, even for just one moment.

"No, it's okay," she said quickly. "The rush of the moment. I get it. We won't talk about it again, Dr. King."

And then, before he had a chance to say anything else, she turned on her heel and jogged away, putting the distance between them that he should've done in the first place.

CHAPTER THREE

FLO WOKE WITH a start and forgot for a moment that she was in an on-call room. Her arm had pins and needles because when she'd crashed, she'd crashed with her arm hanging over the side of the bed, clutching her pager, which was currently vibrating in her hand.

She glanced at it and saw that Freya Rothsberg was looking for her.

Drat.

She hoped it didn't have anything to do with sharing her office with Nate. She wouldn't have really minded or put up a fight before, but after yesterday Flo knew that sharing an office was a *bad* idea.

She'd been so surprised when he'd pulled her into his strong arms and kissed her. A little voice inside her head had told her to push him away, but she'd been unable to because the kiss had been the hottest kiss she'd ever had.

Every other kiss in her life, before Nate's kiss, had been chaste in comparison. The moment his hand had cupped the back of her head, his fingers playing in the wisps of hair at the back of her neck, it had sent a jolt of pure longing and desire through her veins.

And she'd wanted him.

That side of her that lived for the moment had screamed at her to take him. Though the sensible side

of her had reminded her that the last time she'd become close to a man, when she'd almost taken the plunge and had had sex, a certain scar had scared Johnny. It spoke to the world that she was ill. That her life was uncertain, and no one wanted to be tied down to a risk. Johnny had made that much clear.

He'd been afraid to touch her again after he'd seen the scar, and she'd told him why she had it hoping that would calm the issue, but it hadn't. It had just made it worse. Besides, what did she really know about sex? She'd never had it before.

It was good that Nate had broken off that kiss, though it was going to be hard to work with him. Especially if Freya insisted that they share an office.

Flo got out of bed, tidied her hair and brushed her teeth in the on-call room, then made her way to her office. Thankfully, her administrative assistant wasn't in yet, because Sally would certainly pepper her with a ton of questions about Kyle Francis and Flo's bedraggled appearance.

You slept in the on-call room again, didn't you?

Flo locked the door to her office and went to the closet to pull out the set of business clothes that she always kept on hand, because this wasn't the first time she'd slept over at The Hollywood Hills Clinic and had needed to make an appearance in front of the bosses the next day.

She tossed her scrubs in the laundry basket and then pulled on a reliable white blouse and pinstripe black pencil skirt. She traded her comfortable running shoes for her black heels and hoped no one would see the dents in her ankles from the elastic in her socks after wearing them all night.

Flo fixed her hair, putting it up in a bun, and then slipped on her white lab coat, attaching her security cards

and identification. With one last look she reached down and grabbed a tablet so she could bring up Kyle Francis's file, because she was positive that Freya would want to talk about that.

Once she had everything she quickly made her way through the halls of The Hollywood Hills Clinic to the boardroom, where Freya had asked her to meet her, which also had Flo's nerves on edge. She knocked and then entered the boardroom and tried not to blush when she saw Nate sitting in a chair at the table.

He was chatting to Freya amicably, but the moment Flo walked in those piercing blue eyes trained on her, and it took all her willpower to stop her knees knocking together. She would not let Nate get to her.

They were colleagues. That's it.

Besides, even if something came of it, once he found out she was a transplant patient herself, he'd run, like all the others had. Her uncertain future like kryptonite to men. Which was why she kept it to herself, both in her personal and professional life.

"Sorry for running late, Freya."

"No, it's quite all right, Flo. Please have a seat." Freya motioned to the seat directly across from Nate, on her left side. Flo sat down and tried not to look in Nate's direction.

"I understand Mr. Francis has been stabilized?" Freya said, sitting down at the head of the table and brushing her long hair over her shoulder in that refined way she had.

"He has." Flo pulled up Kyle's file. "The surgical report is here if you need it."

Freya held up her hand. "No, I'm not here to talk about Mr. Francis's surgery. I'm glad to know that he's been stabilized."

"I thought you wanted to talk about Kyle Francis? The page said there was going to be discussion about him."

"Well, it's indirectly about Mr. Francis." Freya brought up an image on the screen behind her with a click of the remote.

Flo almost fell out of her chair when she saw the headline of a local paper and the photograph that was underneath it.

Superstar Kyle Francis's doctors locked in a kiss while actor hovers near death.

"And then there's this one." Freya clicked the remote again and a close-up photograph of Flo in Nate's arms, lips locked, was emblazoned across a more reputable local paper with the caption underneath, *Love match between heart surgeons.*

"We're not heart surgeons," Nate joked, trying to defuse the situation. "We have cardiothoracic training, but we only transplant hearts when it comes to cardio care."

Freya fixed her sternest gaze on him. "Yet the world knows Kyle Francis is waiting for a heart and lung transplant."

"How did they know that?"

Freya sighed, "A paramedic leaked it. Not someone from our clinic thankfully, but still security and privacy measures at our clinic are now being questioned. Especially in light of a paramedic leaking the information about Kyle Francis's surgery and then a paparazzo snapping a picture of two surgeons making out on the roof of our clinic. Our reputation is on the line."

Flo's stomach twisted in a knot and she felt like she was going to be sick.

How could she have been so foolish? She liked to

live for the moment and take risks, but not when it jeopardized her career or the reputation of The Hollywood Hills Clinic.

"Freya, I'm so sorry…"

"There's no need to apologize, Flo. There's still a chance to solve this problem." She smiled at them both. "Which is why I'm so glad both of you are dressed respectably. We're going to hold a press conference in a few moments."

"A press conference about what?" Nate asked.

"We're going to talk about Kyle's procedure. We have clearance from his management team. It will be good PR for him. We're also going to talk about a pro bono case that both of you will be working on. We'll be working in conjunction with the Bright Hope Clinic to help Eva Martinez. She's a child in need of a kidney transplant. Her mother, a single mom and waitress, is a perfect match and is donating a kidney to her daughter. It's caught the attention of the media."

Flo's heart skipped a beat as Freya brought up the dossier of Eva Martinez. Eva was twelve. Just a couple of years younger than she herself had been when she'd needed her kidney transplant. It struck a chord deep in her heart.

"Of course," Flo said, finally finding her voice. "Of course I'm willing to work on a pro bono case for a child. That's no problem."

"Is that all?" Nate asked.

"No," Freya said quietly, crossing her arms and leaning back in the chair. "We have to address the issue of two prominent transplant surgeons kissing on the roof of The Hollywood Hills Clinic and being caught doing it."

"There's nothing between us," Flo said quickly. "It won't happen again."

Nate was eyeing her speculatively, as if she'd slapped him or something. "Of course. It won't happen again. It was an impulse after a long surgery."

"I don't need to know why it happened. I don't care if our surgeons date, but I do care about the fact those two surgeons were caught kissing on the clinic roof when we advertise privacy and security to our VIPs. So, I want you two to pretend you're in a relationship."

Flo blinked, because she couldn't believe what Freya was saying. "Pardon?"

"The Hollywood Hills dream team is going to save the life of Eva Martinez *and* Kyle Francis. The positive PR this will bring to The Hills is too good an opportunity to pass up. We need to restore our reputation. Until that reputation is restored and our clients begin to trust us again, your wagons are officially hitched together."

Nate knew he should refuse, get up and walk away. After all, he wasn't a surgeon at the clinic. He was only here because of his patient and that's why he couldn't leave.

He also didn't want to hurt Flo.

She was a surgeon here at The Hollywood Hills Clinic. Her reputation would be tainted because of this. He really didn't have much of choice. He might not like it, but it was just a prettiness. It wasn't like they had to *do* anything, and he didn't have plans to surf the local single scene in California. It wasn't going to put a damper on his style.

"Okay," Nate said.

"Okay?" Flo asked, shocked, and she fixed him with an *are you crazy* look.

"I'm fine with the pretense and I'm more than happy to help that little girl. The fact that a match has already

been found makes it all the easier. I don't mind working on a pro bono case."

Freya smiled. "Good. What about you, Flo?"

Flo was sitting back in her chair, still in shock. "I guess that's okay. I'm fine with the pro bono case and… yeah, I'm fine with the other angle."

"Good," Freya said, and stood. "I'll let the press into the press room and we'll get this conference started in ten minutes."

Nate watched as Freya walked out of the boardroom, leaving Flo and him by themselves. They didn't say anything to each other. There was lots he wanted to say to Flo; he wanted to apologize to her, because it was his fault they were in this situation. He was the one who'd been unable to control his desire for her.

He'd acted impetuously. Something he hadn't done in a long time.

This is why I need to maintain control and keep my distance at all times.

If he didn't maintain that tight control on himself, he acted irrationally and people paid for his indiscretion. Which was why he always tried to remain in control. Control of his life was the most important thing.

"Well, perhaps we should get to the press room."

"What was that?" Flo asked, her arms crossed.

"What was what?" he asked.

"Why did you agree so easily? I thought you would've put up a fight. I mean, you don't work for the clinic. You could just leave, go back to New York."

Nate snorted. "You'd like that, wouldn't you?"

Flo rolled her eyes. "This doesn't have anything to do with Kyle's surgery."

"Doesn't it?" Nate stood and leaned over the board-room table. "You've been trying to get me to go back

home since I first arrived. You don't like another surgeon sniffing around your territory."

Flo grinned. "You're right. I don't, but I had resigned myself to the fact you were staying. Honestly, if it were my patient I would probably do the same thing. What I don't understand now is why you're being so accommodating."

"Look, it was my fault what happened up there. I shouldn't have done it. I was an idiot and not thinking clearly. If I could go back in time and change the fact that I kissed you I would. It was a huge mistake."

A faint trace of disappointment crossed her face. "Okay."

"Let's just put on our best professional facades out there and play nice. Besides, I look forward to working on a kidney transplant with you. It should be a simple surgery."

A strange look passed over her face again, one he couldn't recognize as other than pain, but it was just fleeting as she stood up and straightened her lab coat. "Right. A nice pro bono case. Good PR."

There was a hint of bitterness to her tone.

"Are you okay?" Nate asked.

"Now you care how I feel?" Flo asked.

"Well, I am supposed to be your boyfriend. I might as well get into the act."

Flo shook her head and sighed. "Come on, then, Mr. Dreamboat. Let's get this press conference over with."

"That's Dr. Dreamboat to you," Nate teased.

Flo stuck out her tongue and they walked out of the boardroom and headed toward the press conference, with a lot of gazes fixed on them. A few whispers. So word had got out already about the "dream team".

Nate took Flo's hand and she flinched, so he leaned over, the scent of her soap tickling his senses.

"Relax, we're supposed to hold hands. We're a couple."

Flo nodded and then held her head high as they walked hand in hand to the press conference. Though he shouldn't like it, he did. Her delicate hands, the ones that had so expertly stitched in that left ventricular assist device just yesterday, were strong and soft in his.

And it felt right.

Too right.

The moment they stepped into the press conference they were met by a ton of flashes and questions being fired at them. Flo looked a bit shell shocked. Perhaps she wasn't used to press conferences, but Nate was.

He often spoke to the board and at conferences about transplant surgery. This was an old hat for him. The only thing that was a bit new for him, and unwelcome at that, was pretending to be Flo's significant other.

Well, it wasn't totally unwelcome to pretend to be Flo's boyfriend. What bothered him was that he wanted to act on it. He wanted another kiss. All the previous night in his hotel he'd thought about her, to the point he'd been unable to sleep and had spent most of the night in the hotel's swimming pool, swimming laps to burn off energy.

Energy that he'd wanted to spend in a different way.

Don't think about it.

"It's okay," Nate whispered in her ear, reassuringly. "Just smile. This is for The Hollywood Hills Clinic, remember?"

"Right," Flo said through gritted teeth, and she nodded as they made their way to the podium, taking a seat on either side of Freya.

He could do this. Keep his cool.

He could go with this charade.

He was made of strong mettle.

This was just an act. Just a risky, foolish act. One he should be keeping far away from.

CHAPTER FOUR

FLO'S PULSE THUNDERED in her ears. She didn't like crowds too much. Crowds like this just reminded her of junior high school when she'd been a sickly girl sitting off on the sidelines but wanting to be part of the action. Her mom had taught her to be strong, but that was usually in a one-on-one situation. There were a lot of people in this room. People who weren't doctors.

Stand her in front of a bunch of other surgeons, doctors and nurses in a conference setting and she was fine. Press? That was new territory. Especially given the fact that she was on the arm of the hottest man in the room.

And usually good-looking men didn't get to her, either. James Rothsberg was in the room and Flo had always found him attractive, with his golden blond hair, deep blue eyes and athletic frame. So what was it about Dr. Nathaniel King that made her feel so nervous?

Probably because you've never kissed James Rothsberg and have no desire to do so.

Whereas Nate King. Oh, yeah, she'd been fighting that craving since he'd first got off the helicopter.

Get a grip on yourself.

Freya was talking, but Flo really couldn't focus on what she was saying. She was talking about The Hollywood Hills Clinic and initiatives with the Bright Hope

Clinic. Flo glanced over and could see a petite woman with mahogany hair and hazel eyes smiling and nodding at everything that Freya was saying, and Flo recognized her as Mila Brightman, who ran the Bright Hope Clinic, but it was the look that James was shooting at Mila that caught Flo's attention immediately. There was underlying tension there, something Flo recognized as akin to her own feelings regarding Nate and their shared passionate kiss.

Flo couldn't help but wonder if there was something going on between James and Mila. James was usually so reserved in press conferences, so detached and cool, but this was different. Something was bubbling just under the surface of James Rothsberg.

Just like something was threatening to bubble out from her.

You can do this. Just stay focused.

All she had to do was keep reminding herself that as soon as Nate found out about her health condition, about how she had almost died from chronic kidney failure as a child because of complications from her premature birth and spending a month in a NICU, he'd turn tail and run. Like all of them did.

"And as part of the Bright Hope Clinic's collaboration with The Hollywood Hills Clinic, we're pleased to announce that our dream team of Dr. Florence Chiu and Dr. Nathaniel King, two of the best transplant surgeons in the country, will be taking on Eva Martinez's case while they continue to provide care to Kyle Francis." Freya motioned for Flo to get up and approach the microphone.

You can do this.

There was a round of applause and as soon as she got to the microphone she was hammered by a loud din of

questions being asked rapid-fire. James stood up and bent over the microphone.

"Please, one question at a time. I'm sure Dr. Chiu would be more than happy to answer all your questions." His tone was such that his word wouldn't be challenged. The din quieted down and he stepped away, leaving Flo up there by herself.

"You, sir. What's your question?" Flo pointed to a balding, pudgy man in the front row.

"Photographs of you and Dr. King have arisen that gives rise to questions about the state of security at The Hollywood Hills Clinic. Patients are wondering if their privacy will be protected and whether their doctors' focus will be on them, or will it be solely on who to hop into bed with next?"

Flo could feel her cheeks burning with a flame of embarrassment. "I can assure you that *my* focus is solely on my patients' care."

Nate stood up. "Dr. Chiu and I are in a committed relationship. We went on the rooftop after a successful surgery involving Mr. Francis and got carried away. Are you telling me that you've never got carried away celebrating with your significant other before?"

Nate then flashed a dazzling smile to the audience, which had them all laughing.

Oh, he was good.

"That still doesn't address the privacy and security concerns," the balding reporter called.

"The picture was snapped by a paparazzo from an office window across from the clinic. We can't control what happens outside our perimeters, but he was not able to get any photographs inside our facility, neither was he able to take photographs of our patients," Freya said.

"What about the paramedic that leaked the information?" another reporter asked.

"My understanding is he's been reprimanded and he will not be allowed back on The Hollywood Hills Clinic property in a capacity where he'll have access to confidential health information," James said brusquely.

Once they were satisfied another reporter stepped forward. "How long have you and Dr. King been in a relationship?"

"For a couple of months. We met to discuss Mr. Francis's care while our patient was in California to shoot a movie."

Nate nodded and touched the small of her back. Just the simple touch made goose pimples break out on her skin. Good thing he couldn't feel them.

"Can you tell us a little bit about Mr. Francis's procedure?"

"Of course. Mr. Francis is in congestive heart failure, but because he's been in heart failure for some time, this has put a strain on his already weak lungs. Mr. Francis had a pre-existing struggle with asthma for many years. Because his lungs are so damaged by the extra strain his heart is causing, he will require a heart and lung transplant. We were hoping to perform a domino procedure, but now that Mr. Francis is on a left ventricular assist device, he is no longer a candidate. We will have to wait for a set of lungs and a heart that matches Mr. Francis's blood type, but the LVAD will prolong his life while he waits."

Nate gave her a thumbs-up and Flo gave an inward sigh of relief. She sat back down next to Nate and he took her hand and held it. It was reassuring and made her feel good, but then she remembered this was all an act.

He'd pretty much said that he wasn't interested in her and that their kiss had been a mistake.

That's what you wanted, wasn't it?

"Now, if there are no more questions we'll conclude this press conference," Freya said. "Please make sure you take the statement with you. If you have any other questions, please don't hesitate to contact me. Thank you all for coming."

Flo took another deep breath.

"See, that wasn't too bad," Nate said, but he didn't let go of her hand as the journalists filtered out of the room slowly.

"No. It wasn't." She let go of his hand and got up to leave, but Freya and James were talking to the side and motioned for her over.

Oh, no. Now what?

"Good job, Flo," Freya said.

James nodded. "Yes. You handled that well."

"Thank you."

"I think that will help salvage the reputation of The Hollywood Hills Clinic and help reinforce our joint effort with the Bright Hope Clinic."

"I think it will," Mila said, joining them and extending a hand to take Flo's. "Dr. Mila Brightman. A pleasure to meet you, Dr. Chiu. I'm so pleased that you and Dr. King will be working on Eva Martinez's case."

"It will be a pleasure to do so," Flo responded.

"All this good publicity for the clinic will put my mind at ease," said Freya.

"A good thing, given your condition—" James cut off abruptly at the sharp stare from his sister and the surprised looks from the rest of the group.

"Well, since *some* people clearly don't know how to keep a secret, I guess the cat's out of the bag—I'm pregnant!" Freya announced.

James smiled sheepishly. "I'm so happy for you, Freya."

Then he turned to Mila and Flo noticed something pass between them. It was as if he wanted to embrace Dr. Brightman but held himself back. She couldn't help but wonder what was going on there, but, then, she liked her privacy, as well. She felt a bit humiliated that that private mistake of a kiss between her and Nate had been caught on camera so it wasn't her place to pry.

"Well, I'll leave you all to it," Flo said. "I'm going to go check on my new patient. I assume that Eva Martinez has been admitted to the transplant floor?"

Freya nodded. "Yes, thank you, Flo."

Flo walked away briskly. She was done with awkward situations. It was bad enough she had to be pretend to be in a relationship with Nate. That was uncomfortable, especially with the way he affected her.

She needed to focus on her new patient.

Eva's case struck close to home for her. Only, for Flo, it hadn't been her mother who had donated a kidney to her. Flo's kidney donation had come from a deceased organ donor. Being of mixed heritage had caused a bit of a cross-match problem for Flo. It didn't happen often, but Flo's case had been a hard one from the moment she'd been born prematurely thirty years ago.

If it hadn't been for that anonymous donor, who, of course, had sadly lost their life, Flo would've lost hers. Of course her *năinai* had always said she'd been a tough cookie from the moment she'd been born. Flo had been fighting her whole life. It's why she fought so hard for others; it's why she wanted to live in the moment.

Even though pretending to be Nate's girlfriend made her feel uncomfortable, because it was a temptation that she was in danger of indulging in, she was going to do what had been asked of her. What could it hurt?

It could hurt your heart.

Flo shook that thought away. This wasn't a serious relationship. It would *never* be a serious relationship. She didn't have serious relationships because of her health issues and she'd made her peace with that a long time ago.

Have you?

She caught sight of Nate in the hallway, talking with a group of doctors and what looked like members of Kyle's management team. Just the sight of Nate standing there made her heart flutter with insatiable need. She turned on her heel and quickly headed in the opposite direction.

Focus, Flo. She had to forget the carnal urges that Nate stirred in her. She had to remind herself that this was all an act. This would be fun. She could do this. What did she have to lose?

Pretending to be his was going to be so difficult. So dangerous. Even if she was a tough cookie, like her *năinai* said.

Nate glanced over his shoulder to see Flo retreating in the other direction, which was unlike her. She had never seemed fazed or frightened by anything before. She hadn't backed down from him when they'd first met.

He admired that about her.

Don't think about her that way.

He tried to turn his attention back the conversation he'd been having, not that he could really remember what he'd been talking about. It hadn't really been that important because all of his focus had been on Flo, and it bothered him that he was so absorbed with her that he'd agreed to play along with The Hills' ridiculous request.

His hospital in New York would never have asked him to do such a thing, but then again the hospital in New York wasn't a private upscale clinic that prided itself on the security of its clients. Neither did he like the

fact that Freya had conspired with Kyle's management team about the idea.

Only problem was, he wasn't a good actor.

A few years ago and he might've gone along with it, but now he liked to maintain control in all aspects of his life. One little slip and that reckless man he'd once been started to creep toward the surface.

And he couldn't let that happen. Only when he was around Flo, she made him forget his control. He lost all reason. That's why he'd pulled her into that kiss on the roof and got them into trouble in the first place.

They were in this mess because of him.

"Dr. King?"

Nate turned and saw James Rothsberg standing behind him. Beside James was an attractive redhead.

"Are we interrupting?" James asked sardonically.

"No. Not at all."

James nodded. "This is Dr. Mila Brightman from the Bright Hope Clinic. She wanted to meet you."

Mila stuck out her hand. "It's a pleasure to meet you, Dr. King."

"The pleasure is all mine."

It was then that Nate caught a flash of something in James's eyes, something akin to jealousy or a silent warning maybe to keep his distance, and Nate couldn't help but wonder if there was or had been something between Mila Brightman and James Rothsberg.

Not that it was Nate's concern, but he couldn't miss that underlying tension between them, the same current that ran between him and Flo.

It's all in your head. You're paranoid.

"I want to thank you and Dr. Chiu for working on Eva. She's a special child," Mila said.

"It's no trouble. I'm here and glad to help. If you'll

excuse me, I'm going to check on my patient." Nate extracted himself from that situation. The tension was uncomfortable and when he glanced back briefly he could see the awkwardness between James and Mila. They barely said anything, barely looked at each other before wandering off on their own separate ways.

This was exactly the reason why he didn't want to get involved with anyone. Especially not at work. His focus was surgery.

He should just tell Freya that he wasn't going to play along with this PR stunt, but where would that leave Flo?

Who cares?

Only he did. Just a bit, because it was his fault, his weakness that had got them into this situation. If he had been stronger he wouldn't have been tempted by Flo. He could've kept his distance. He should've kept his distance. He could do this.

Who are you kidding?

He had to get out of the hospital, had to head to his hotel and swim. He had to relieve this tension that was building up inside him, because if he didn't he was liable to crack and do something he would enjoy thoroughly but also deeply regret.

CHAPTER FIVE

WHAT AM I DOING? What am I doing?

The scent of chlorine stung her nose. She'd never really liked the smell of chlorine, probably because it reminded her of the many hours she'd spent poolside, watching her brother and sister swim competitively, something she'd never been able to do because she'd been sick for so long.

Thinking about her siblings swimming made her think about how she'd always wanted to learn how to dive. It was on her bucket list, but she'd never found the time.

And standing poolside at Nate King's hotel, watching said hottie swim countless laps, was not the time to start. She was having a hard time not staring at him, the way he moved through the water.

She'd wanted to talk to him before he'd left the hospital. If they were going to participate in this facade then she was going to get her facts straight. She was nothing if not efficient.

That's why she kept lists. She was organized, and when she did something, she did it right. If she was going to be Dr. Nate King's pretend girlfriend, she was going to do it right.

Except cleaning. She was a bit scatterbrained when it came to cleaning her apartment.

At least her office and workspace were organized.

He finished swimming and pulled himself out of the water at the far end of the pool. Flo tried not to stare at his muscular thighs and tight butt only covered in wet spandex. When he'd wrapped a white cotton towel around his waist, partially obscuring his six pack, only then did she hold her head high and walk toward him.

"Nate," she said.

He spun around in surprise, raking a hand through his dripping-wet beach-blond locks.

"Dr. Chiu."

"It's Flo, remember. We are dating after all." She laughed nervously, but he didn't smile. "I was hoping to talk to you before you left the clinic tonight but I just missed you. So that's why I'm here."

"About what?" he asked, picking up a second towel and drying off his face.

"About our 'relationship'." She used air quotes to emphasize it.

He groaned. "Now?"

"Are you busy? Do you have a prior engagement?" she asked, crossing her arms.

Nate dropped the towel he was wiping his face with and smiled, but that smile wasn't the cheeky one he usually gave her. It was a bit predatory and made her nervous.

"Would you be jealous if I did?" He took a step closer. "If I did, what would you do?"

"No. I'm not jealous, but for the sake of the clinic and our patients it would be bad form to have plans."

He chuckled and then snorted sardonically. "Would it? Don't you think this whole charade is bad form?"

Yes. Only she didn't say that out loud because she didn't understand PR like Freya and Mila did. Both of them thought this charade would be a good idea.

"We're just smoothing over a tricky situation," Flo said.

He arched his eyebrows. "Is that a fact? And have you canceled all your private engagements? Dumped your boyfriends?"

She sighed impatiently. "What is your obsession with my boyfriends?"

"Well, I don't think it would be good form for our charade if you had a couple of boyfriends lingering about."

"As I told you before, I don't have a boyfriend. As for private engagements, surgery is my life."

He grunted again and pushed past her. "How did you know where to find me?"

"Freya told me." She followed him out of the pool toward a bank of elevators.

"Of course she did." He shook his head.

"Well, shouldn't I know where my 'boyfriend' lives? Especially since we've been together for some time?"

"Good point. I never really thought about that. Deception really isn't my forte." The elevator doors opened and he stepped in. "Aren't you coming up?"

"To your room?" She hoped her voice didn't squeak too much because the idea of going up to his room was not on her agenda tonight. She couldn't go up to his room.

That was not part of the plan.

He grinned at her. That predatory grin again. "Yes. Play along, right? Isn't that what you told me?"

"How about I wait for you down here? We can have a drink in the hotel lobby."

"Now, how would that look to the paparazzi milling about at the concierge's desk?"

Flo glance over her shoulder and saw the press.

Hell.

She jumped into the elevator, the door closing just as

a photographer caught sight of them. That would've been bad and their cover would've been blown.

Nate was laughing at her. "Smooth move, Dr. Chiu."

"When did you notice him?"

"A while ago."

"You could've warned me."

"I did. That's why you're in the elevator now instead of waiting for me in the hotel's bar."

"I'd prefer to wait in the lobby bar," she mumbled.

"Why?" he asked.

Because it's safer.

"I don't know you. I don't think it's appropriate to go up to your hotel room."

Nate laughed. The elevator dinged and they stepped off. She followed him down the hall to the end. He swiped the key card and opened the door. Flo followed him inside, just on the off chance the paparazzi followed them up here. She shut the door and was surprised by the large suite. It was like a small apartment. There was a bedroom that Nate had disappeared into, a living room and small kitchenette.

She set her purse down on the counter and wandered to the huge windows, where the Los Angeles skyline lit up the night. It was a gorgeous night. Clear, but it wasn't like you could see the sky, not with all the light pollution from LA. Nate's suite had a large balcony and a hot tub tucked away in the corner.

"There are drinks in the fridge. I'm going to have a quick shower," Nate said from around the door of his bedroom.

"Okay, thanks."

Nate nodded and shut the door to his bedroom. It wasn't too long before Flo heard the shower on through

the closed door and she tried not to think about the fact that Nate was naked and in it.

This was a bad idea.

She could've just waited until he came to work the next day and talked to him there, but no. She'd got it in her head that this would be a better idea and now she couldn't remember for the life of her why she'd thought that.

Probably because she hadn't expected to find him half-naked, swimming in a pool, and then be forced to come up to his opulent suite and wait while he showered in the next room. This was an experience that was *not* on her bucket list.

Flo took a seat on the edge of the couch and just waited. She tried to keep her mind occupied on something else. Anything to take her mind off what was going on in the next room and how he'd looked just wrapped in a towel, fresh from a swim. The only men she'd seen built like that were either in the movies or magazines. She'd never seen one up close and personal.

She'd worked on Hollywood's rich and famous at The Hollywood Hills Clinic, but what was on screen versus reality had opened to her eyes to the whole magical mystery of Hollywood's elite. Photo editing was a beautiful thing indeed.

She often wished she could edit herself in real life. Maybe then she could erase the large scar on her abdomen and that way no one would ever need to know that she'd had a kidney transplant. That she'd been sick.

If Johnny hadn't known, he wouldn't have treated her differently.

Maybe they'd still be together. Then she wouldn't have kissed Nate and be in this situation, faking a relationship and being in his hotel room with him naked in the shower. In the next room. Of course, that's not how it had

happened at all, because that's not how real life worked. There had been no photo-editing solution and her disease had frightened Johnny away.

He'd made it clear he didn't want to get involved with her, not when there was a possibility that at any time in the near future that donor organ could fail and she might die. No one wanted to get involved with a woman who didn't have the greatest odds of staying alive.

Kidney survival rates were good, but they weren't perfect.

Kidneys could fail.

Especially when you'd had a chronic kidney disease as a child and had suffered kidney failure at fourteen. Following dialysis for a year and a near-death experience, she'd received her new lease on life.

And since that time she'd tried to live her life to the fullest.

Getting married and having a family had always been on her bucket list, until she'd learned the true nature of most men. When Johnny had run scared and left her heartbroken, she'd scratched that secret hope off her list.

A husband, romance and love were not meant to be. She'd made her peace with that, but now, because of a foolish and irrational moment on top of The Hollywood Hills Clinic, she found herself thrust into a situation she'd long given up on.

It's fake, though. It's not real.

Still, the idea made her uncomfortable because she was going to have to be really careful to keep her feelings out of it. She could have fun, but she couldn't let Nate get too close, because once Kyle Francis was on the mend, Dr. Nathaniel King would be returning to New York and she would be alone again.

"Did you want something to drink?"

Flo startled to see a freshly showered and dressed Nate standing in the doorway. He was dressed very much the same as he'd been when she'd first laid eyes on him. When he'd come out of that helicopter looking sexy as hell.

Don't think about it.

"How about we go downstairs?" Flo asked, tearing her gaze away from Nate.

"Well, first I think we should go over some ground rules for this whole charade, and I don't think that those ground rules should be discussed downstairs with paparazzi milling about. They were told we've been going out for some time. You can't be all skittish and embarrassed around me."

"I'm not skittish or embarrassed. I'm professional."

Nate rolled his eyes and shook his head. "You can't be professional with your boyfriend."

"Boyfriend sounds like we're in junior high or something."

"Lover, then?"

Warmth flooded her cheeks and her whole body quivered with the quick burn of arousal as an image of Nate, naked and pressed against her, filled her mind.

Lover.

That was something she was not intimately familiar with, but she wished she was.

She cleared her throat. "Fine. I can be relaxed around you."

Nate grinned, leaning over the polished marble counter in his kitchenette. "Can you?"

"Of course I can."

"Prove it."

"How?" she asked.

"Kiss me again."

* * *

Nate had no idea what had come over him when he'd asked Flo to kiss him. It had just seemed the natural thing to do and he'd be an idiot if he said he didn't want to kiss her again. Who wouldn't want to kiss her again? And he knew by the flush creeping up her long slender neck to her cheeks that she was feeling it, too.

She wanted him, but was holding back.

Like you should be, too.

And that was when it struck him that he'd done something he really shouldn't have, and that no woman since Serena had affected him this way.

He'd been attracted to other women, but he'd always managed to keep them at a distance. Then he'd met Flo. He tried to tell himself over and over again that the kiss on the rooftop had only been his relief at having been able to stabilize Kyle. They'd been able to extend Kyle's life while he waited for his new heart and lungs. That relief had caused him to let his guard down, so what was this?

This wasn't relief.

Even though he really didn't want to play in this charade that Freya Rothsberg had cooked up, he really had no choice, that's why he threw up his walls again. He was determined that even though on the outside, for all intents and purposes, he was Flo's significant other, he wasn't going to let her in.

He wasn't going to let his guard down around her.

At least, that's what he was going to do in theory. Twenty minutes with her and she was in his hotel suite, sitting on his couch only five feet away from him, looking as sinfully sexy as ever. Her long black hair, which she usually wore up, was loose over her shoulders. There was a bit of make-up on her, not much, but the red lipstick

on her lips just accentuated the fullness of them. Add the blush to those high, round cheeks and he was a lost man.

He forgot that Flo was off-limits to him, just like every woman had been since Serena. Yet here he was, asking Flo to kiss him again. And he wanted to kiss her. So badly.

"Pardon?" she said, breaking the silence.

"I think you heard me."

"I don't think that's a wise idea, Nate. Do you?"

It's not.

"Why? You want to show the world that we're together. We have to be at ease with each other so we can be believable."

What are you doing?

"Believable, but also professional. So I don't think kissing you is the wisest idea." She tossed her hair over her shoulder. "You certainly like to goad me, don't you?"

Nate's eyes twinkled. "Perhaps, but it's so easy."

She glared at him and then smiled. "I'm highly competitive and I don't like to have my buttons pushed."

"I gathered that, or it wouldn't be so easy to push them."

Flo nodded. "Perhaps we can go downstairs and get that drink? Discuss Eva's case and our plan of attack?"

"Okay, but still I think you should kiss me."

She grinned in a willful way that spelled trouble for him. "I do like to hear you beg."

He rolled his eyes as she walked past him toward the door. On one hand he was extremely relieved that she hadn't kissed him, but he knew that if he kissed her again he would lose himself completely and carry her off to his bed, which wasn't far away.

And taking her to bed would be good, so deliciously good, but only for a short time. He didn't want to hurt her,

not when they had possibly months of working together while they waited for Kyle's heart and lung transplant.

That would be awkward and horrible for everyone.

It was better this way.

That's what he had to keep telling himself to get over the smidgen of disappointment he had that she hadn't taken him up on his offer and kissed him.

Instead, as they walked down the hall toward the elevator, he reached down and took her hand in his. That small delicate hand that he'd admired so much during Kyle's LVAD surgery.

"What're you doing?" she asked, surprised.

"The paparazzi could be still downstairs. This way, there won't be any questions."

"Oh...right. Good point."

Nate could tell that she was nervous, and he liked that he had that effect on her. Serena had been the same when they'd first dated, but not for long. Maybe one date, because one date was all it had taken and they'd been in bed together and then heading off on a crazy adventure.

Don't think about Serena.

If he thought about Serena he'd pull away from Flo again and then the press would pick up on the fact that this was all just a charade. He had to remember what it was like to just let things happen and not control every aspect of his life, which was a hard thing for him to do because control allowed him to focus on saving lives.

There was no room in his heart for love or romance. Not again.

"You okay?" Flo asked as they rode down to the lobby in the elevator.

"Yeah, why?"

"I don't know. You just tensed up."

"I'm fine." He tried to give her a reassuring smile.

"I'm really fine, it's just that I don't like this. I don't like deception."

"I know. Neither do I, but it's for the clinic."

"Right. The clinic." The doors dinged and opened and they stepped out into the lobby. He knew that press guy was lingering around somewhere. It felt like there were a million eyes on them as they walked hand in hand toward the hotel's bar. Even when they found a private booth far in the corner of the bar, he still felt like they were under a microscope, and it made him uneasy.

It was only after the waiter had brought them their drinks that Flo said, "I feel like we're being watched."

"We are." He took a sip of his coffee. "Is this your first time working on someone as famous as Kyle Francis?"

"No. I've worked on some others, it's just The Hollywood Hills Clinic's security has never been breached before."

"Sorry about that."

Flo shrugged and took a sip of her water. "It's unfortunate but there's nothing we can do."

Nate chuckled. "Look at us, we've come to a bar and we don't even order alcoholic drinks."

"I don't drink," Flo said, and then she blushed, clearing her throat. "I mean, I have to get up early tomorrow and I don't want to drink tonight."

"Rounds?"

She nodded. "I want to check on Kyle and Eva, our two VIP patients."

"I'm not on rounds. I have privileges, but no regular patients beyond Kyle and Eva."

"You could always round with me." She smiled at him. It was warm, inviting and friendly, and now he could clearly remember why he'd kissed her on the rooftop. He wanted a piece of that. He wanted to feel that warmth.

"Sure. Thanks."

"No problem." She set her water glass down and glanced at the watch on her arm. "Oh, my, is that the time? It's almost ten."

"Ten isn't late."

"It is when you're rounding at five in the morning." Flo sighed. "I have to go."

"I'll walk you out." Nate signed the bill to his suite, the whole couple of bucks for the coffee, and walked her out of the bar to the hotel entrance. "Did you drive yourself?"

"I don't drive. I live close to the clinic. I usually just ride my bike."

"You don't drive?"

"I never learned, but it's on my bucket list." Then she blushed again.

"Bucket list? Usually that's for people who don't have a lot of time left. Unless I'm mistaken, Dr. Chiu, you have many years left."

"Oh, yeah, of course. It's nothing really. Just stuff I want to do before I... Anyway, I'd better go. The door-man can flag down a taxi for me."

"Sure. I'll see you tomorrow." Nate walked her outside and they stood there while the doorman waved down a taxi. When the taxi pulled up Flo turned quickly and pressed a sweet, light kiss against his lips. It caught him off guard and his blood heated. He fought back the urge to take her in his arms and deepen the kiss, make it last.

Which was a dangerous thing indeed.

"See you tomorrow," she said, not looking at him as she climbed into the cab.

As the cab drove away he stood there, his blood burning through his veins at just the simple butterfly kiss that had been brushed against his lips. So innocent, so sweet. It left him wanting more.

So much more.

CHAPTER SIX

FLO DOWNED HER second cup of coffee, which had two shots of espresso in it. She didn't know what had made her reach out and kiss Nate, because she'd had no plans to do that. Especially not after he'd basically dared her to kiss him in his hotel suite.

When he'd asked her that, it had taken all her will-power not to leap into his arms and kiss him again. To experience that heat and heady sensation he'd stirred within her since he'd first kissed her on the rooftop. Nate was incredibly sexy and Flo had never been attracted to a man so strongly before. So much so that she almost forgot herself and the fact that she'd sworn off all romantic entanglements.

Besides, Nate would run as soon as he realized what was going on with her. She tried to tell herself that maybe he would understand as he was a transplant surgeon himself, but then maybe that would make him back off all the more, because he would understand better than anyone what her body had been through.

Still, she'd been a fool and kissed him while waiting for the taxi, even though it had been for the press. She was pretty sure there would be pictures of them kissing and that would make Freya happy.

There was a lot of press camped outside The Holly-

wood Hills Clinic. She could see them lurking in shadows, waiting for something, anything, to give them juicy details about Kyle Francis and his surgeons who were in love.

Flo snorted. *Love. Sure.*

She didn't believe in love. Well, not for her anyway. Once she'd believed in love, but then love had turned on her. There was love. She'd seen it in her parents. They'd overcome a lot of odds and barriers in their way to be together. They came from different worlds yet that hadn't mattered to them in the end.

For them it worked.

Love couldn't work for her. Not when she couldn't promise any length of time to anyone. It wasn't really fair to someone else.

Flo groaned and crushed the empty coffee cup, tossing it in the garbage. Last week none of this had been an issue. Last week she'd been free of Dr. Nathaniel King. Last week she'd just been a great surgeon, with a stupid bucket list and a job that hadn't let her think about her personal life.

Last week she'd been happy. Now she was miserable.

Are you so sure about that?

"Flo!"

Flo turned to see Freya walking toward her. "Freya, I'm surprised to see you here so early."

"I couldn't sleep and had morning sickness." Freya held out a paper. "I'm glad to see that you and Dr. King are keeping up appearances."

Flo glanced down at the tabloid paper and saw photos of her kiss with Nate. That quick, impulsive kiss that had burned its memory on her lips and taunted her all night, which was the reason why she'd downed two large black

coffees with espresso shots, because she hadn't been able to stop thinking about it all night.

And now seeing it plastered over the tabloids reminded her of how hot that moment had been, and how foolish. She was willing to climb a mountain or do some other high-adrenaline sport, but when it came to the possibility of romance, she wasn't willing to let her heart get involved.

It was too dangerous.

"Ah," Flo said nervously. "Yeah, well, I thought I would pay Dr. King a visit to talk about our arrangement."

"Well, keep up the good work. Tomorrow night there's a dinner with some possible investors and they want the dream team to attend. It's business casual and will be at Dan Tana's at eight-thirty."

"Dinner? I...I have a shift tomorrow. Rounds in the evening."

"I have another doctor covering for you, one of your fellows." Freya glanced over her shoulder and waved. "Dr. King, can you come here a moment, please?"

Flo froze and was very aware the moment that Nate walked up behind her. She could smell the clean spicy scent of his body wash. She'd been very aware of it when she'd impulsively kissed him.

"Good morning, ladies." He had already changed into scrubs and had a white lab coat with an identification card. The white of the lab coat accentuated his tan and the blueness of his eyes.

"I was just telling Flo how pleased I was to see you two cooperating." Freya handed Nate the tabloid. Flo watched his expression carefully, but if it affected him she had no clue. He just nodded, smiled charmingly and handed the paper back to Freya.

"Just doing our part," he said.

"I was just telling Flo that there's a dinner tomorrow night at Dan Tana's. Business casual as we'll be meeting with investors." Freya tucked the paper under her arm. "I have to run. I look forward to seeing you both tomorrow."

Flo didn't even have a chance to say no, she didn't want to have dinner with a bunch of investors and pretend to be Nate's girlfriend, but she really had no choice.

Her job was on the line.

If she didn't play her part then people would stop coming to The Hollywood Hills Clinic, investors would stop giving money and the clinic could shut down. Then she couldn't help Eva, and she was very on board with this partnership with the Bright Hope Clinic and providing pro bono surgery to kids like Eva.

To kids who reminded her of herself.

"Dan Tana's is a nice place," Nate remarked. "I used to go there a lot as a kid."

"I thought you were from New York?" Flo said.

"I work in New York, but I'm a native Californian."

Flo snorted. "That doesn't surprise me. You have the look of a beach boy."

Nate fell into step beside her. "Where are you from?"

"Seattle," Flo responded, offhand. "Though my father is from Beijing and my mother is from the Deep South. They felt Seattle was a nice halfway point to raise their family."

Flo smiled as she thought of her family. She hadn't talked to them in a while as she'd been so busy. Actually, she was surprised that her father wasn't calling her cell phone every two minutes to question what was going on and why she was kissing men on rooftops.

Her parents had always been a little overprotective, trying to keep her wrapped up in cotton wool, like she

was some kind of fragile piece of crystal that was about to shatter into a million pieces.

Which was why when she'd got her kidney she'd rebelled a bit. Pushed the boundaries and decided to study medicine at Johns Hopkins across the country, almost a world away from her parents. After spending most of her childhood basically in a bubble, her first taste of freedom had been an amazing rush.

It's why she had the bucket list.

So many things she wanted to do. So little time.

"So you mentioned learning to drive is on this bucket list," Nate said casually.

"It is. I just don't have time to take lessons. My work here takes a lot of my time."

"I can teach you."

Flo laughed. "Yeah, right."

"Who better to teach you? I've driven in two of the busiest cities in America—Los Angeles and New York City."

"You have a point, but when? I don't have time."

"How about tonight?"

Flo cocked an eyebrow. "Tonight? You're going to teach me to drive tonight?"

"Sure. I can't take you out on the streets, but I know a place out of the city where there's an abandoned parking lot and plenty of room for you to make mistakes."

"Okay. I get off at three."

"I know." Nate took a step back away from her. "I have to make a phone call to my office in New York. I'll meet you up at Eva's room in twenty."

"Sure, leave all the grunt work to me," she teased.

He just smiled at her and disappeared down a hall, leaving her standing there absolutely perplexed about what had just happened. She told herself she was going

to be stronger. When she had to make public appearances with him, she was going to play the part of the girlfriend, but this learning-to-drive date she'd just made with him, that was just them. That wasn't something public.

It was just going be the two of them.

And that thought made her nervous.

Don't think about it.

She put her hands under the sanitary gel dispenser. Right now she couldn't think about that. Right now she had to be a surgeon. She glanced through the window to see Eva, so sick and in bed with an IV and looking so lost. Her mother was next to her, holding her hand.

It tore at Flo's heart. She'd been there.

She'd felt that way and her parents had been there. Only her mother hadn't been the one to give her a kidney, so she couldn't even begin to fathom the kind of strain that Ms. Martinez was going through or the amount of time it would take for both of them to recover, both emotionally, physically and financially.

Right now, this was Flo's focus. This was her passion, saving lives, especially giving a chance to a little girl who reminded her so much of herself that it was almost haunting.

"Good morning, Ms. Martinez and Eva. I'm Dr. Flo Chiu and I'll be one of the surgeons on your case."

The phone call back to New York had taken longer than expected, but by the end of the call he had been assured that all his patients were being taken good care of and that his practice was in safe hands. For so long Kyle had been his main focus, he didn't really have a lot of other patients who needed him as much.

Kyle had been very specific that Nate's sole focus was to be on him, and he paid him well enough that he didn't

have to take on too many patients, which meant he wasn't really missed in New York.

Nate didn't have friends in New York City. Colleagues, yes, but not any people he would consider friends. Neither did he have any family in New York. His parents were here in California and he definitely didn't have a significant other.

No one missed him and he didn't mind much.

He might've been chomping at the bit to get back to his practice, but being around Flo and working with her was exciting. It was fun, and that kiss she'd given him had kept him up all night.

So to take his mind off it he'd spent the night going over Eva's case. It had been a year since he'd done a kidney transplant with a live donor. Kyle had been his focus and any other cases he took on were usually complicated. Nate hadn't realized that for a long time he'd been focusing solely on the heart and lung. He'd had to brush up on his reading about kidney transplants. What concerned him most was that Ms. Martinez was a single parent. The sole breadwinner. Donating a kidney would put her out of commission for a long time. Weeks, for sure. Even if they did the retrieval laparoscopically and reduced her recovery time, she'd still be off for a couple of weeks.

Ms. Martinez was a waitress. She would need a month to heal from a laparoscopic procedure. She wouldn't be able to lift heavy objects and would still tire easily.

Even then, Nate wasn't sure that Ms. Martinez was a candidate for a laparoscopic procedure. He would have to do some more tests to be sure. Get some better MRI images.

Ms. Martinez could become destitute while she recovered. Being a waitress was a minimum-wage job, one that probably didn't have medical leave coverage.

Eva was pretty stable, so maybe in the family's best interests they should wait for a deceased donor.

When he got to Eva's room he paused in the hallway. He saw Flo sitting on the end of Eva's bed and she was playing cards with her. Nate smiled. When he'd first met Flo he'd thought she would be a bit uptight, reserved, but seeing her with Eva and playing a game of cards, well, he couldn't help but smile.

She was so warm with Eva.

There were so many layers to Flo; she was so intriguing. At times she was so prudish and then the next moment she was giving him a kiss that made him want her more than anything. Other times she was standoffish, but then could give a good quip that got through his thick-walled exterior. Back in New York City he had a reputation of being hardheaded. Someone you didn't want to mess with.

The moment he'd tried that with her, Flo had been right in his face and giving back as good as he could give her, but there was something Flo was hiding. She'd mentioned a bucket list and had then brushed it off as something silly. Only Nate knew there was something more there, and he shouldn't care what it was because he didn't want to get too close to her. He couldn't get too close to her, but he did care.

He wanted to know all of her, even though nothing could come of it. This relationship wasn't a relationship. It was just a facade. And when Kyle was on the mend and this pro bono case was done, he would pack his bags and head back to New York and his life.

Just like she would go back to hers, because this wasn't real. It was all fake.

And that thought made him sad, because just for one

moment he was wishing it wasn't all fake, that Flo and him were really dating.

Don't think like that.

He shook that thought from his head, disgusted with himself for allowing himself to think like that again. For letting his mind head down that path again. He was here to do work; he was here to save two lives.

This whole situation was temporary. There wouldn't be any permanence. There couldn't be any permanence to it.

He knocked on the door and plastered his best smile on his face. One he knew well and had practiced. A shield to the armor he wore every day to keep people out. "Am I interrupting?"

"Yes," Flo said, smiling and winking at Eva, who giggled. "Eva, this is your other surgeon. This is Dr. Nathaniel King."

Nate stood beside Flo and Eva smiled up at Nate.

"It's nice to meet you, Eva," Nate said.

"Nice to meet you, too, Dr. King." For a twelve-year-old girl she had excellent manners.

"You can call me Nate. I've just come to check your vitals. Is that okay?"

Eva's brow furrowed and she looked at Flo with concern. "Will it hurt?"

"No, this is just a vital check. No needles." Flo set down her cards and got off the bed, moving the swinging table out of the way. "Nate is super nice."

"I promise you it won't hurt at all." Nate pulled out his stethoscope. "I just want to have a listen to your heart first. Is that okay?"

"Sure." Eva sat up the best she could and Nate listened to her chest.

"Deep breaths for me, Eva." He moved his stethoscope and listened. "One more for me."

"Is that it?" Eva asked.

"Just blood pressure now."

Eva winced. "I don't like the squeeze."

"It's just for a second. It's nothing. Trust me, I would know," Flo said reassuringly, squeezing Eva's foot under the blanket. "You need to relax. Nate will get a better reading if you relax."

Eva nodded and Nate put the cuff on her and took her blood pressure. It was as good as it could be for a young girl in renal failure.

"Thank you, Eva. Do you mind if I borrow Flo for a moment?"

"Sure." Eva leaned back and picked up her cards.

"No cheating!" Flo warned, giving her a wink that caused Eva to laugh.

They stepped out of the room and Nate shut the door. Flo frowned and crossed her arms. "Is there something wrong? I checked her when I first arrived and her vitals were fine."

"Her vitals are fine. I was just hoping that Ms. Martinez would be around so that I could talk to her about her side of the donation."

"Ms. Martinez had to make some arrangements. She's going to be out of commission for some time, as well."

"That's what I wanted to talk to her about. Eva is stable, so why don't we wait for a deceased donor?"

Flo's brow furrowed further. "Ms. Martinez is a match. Her cross-match is the best I've seen in a long time. Why would we wait? Waiting just puts Eva in danger."

"Ms. Martinez is a single mother. She could continue working while Eva recovered here."

Flo shook her head. "The cross-match is almost per-

fect. A cross-match from a deceased donor wouldn't be as good. Ms. Martinez won't wait while her child sits on a list, she's done that. It's in their file. That's why she went to the Bright Hope Clinic, because she is the perfect donor for Eva. Eva is less likely to reject her mother's kidney."

"Less likely, though, Dr. Chiu. There's still a chance. There's always a high chance of rejection."

Flo's spine stiffened, her face unreadable. It was as if he'd slapped her across the face. "I'm *very* well aware of that, Dr. King. You don't have to remind me of that. I'm still head surgeon on this case. Ms. Martinez knows the risks. She doesn't want to wait, she doesn't want her daughter to get worse. It's her gift to give Eva. We're not going to discuss this matter further or try to convince her of anything different."

"I would feel better if I talked to Ms. Martinez all the same."

Flo glared at him. "Fine, but let it be on your head. I doubt you'll convince her. She wants to save her child and what she's doing is an amazing thing."

She tried to turn and storm off, but he grabbed her by her elbow. "What has got into you?"

"Nothing, I'm just annoyed that you're trying to talk a woman, who knows all the facts because her daughter has been fighting renal failure her whole life, out of saving her daughter's life."

Nate sighed. "I'm not trying to talk her out of it. I just don't want to see her lose her job."

"She won't," Flo said, calming down. "Her work is being compliant. Mila Brightman talked to them about the situation."

Nate nodded. "Okay. That's great. I'm glad she knows everything. I wasn't trying to endanger the patient. Please

trust me, because if you don't trust me here, you won't trust me in the OR and I need you to trust me in the OR when we work on Eva and Kyle."

Mollified, Flo nodded. "I trust you, Nate. I trust you as a surgeon. It's just…this is a touchy subject for me."

Intrigued, Nate let go of his grip on her. "Why?"

"I knew someone who suffered a long time, waiting for a deceased donor who was a good cross-match. A young girl, like Eva, whose parents would've given their kidneys, but they weren't a match."

Nate nodded. "I understand."

"Do you?"

"Yes," Nate said wearily. "I lost someone I cared for. Someone who was waiting on organs."

Her expression softened. "Then why wait now? It's just putting Eva at risk."

"You're right. We don't want Eva to suffer like your other patient. Like my friend."

"Right, my other patient. Well, I'd better get back to my game of poker. Eva cheats." She paused in the doorway. "I am sorry about your friend."

"Thanks," he said. "Okay, so I'll see you after your shift? Where should I pick you up?"

"The front doors. Though I hope you have space for my bike." She nodded and walked back into Eva's room.

There was a sadness about her. She'd obviously been affected deeply by her other patient to fight so strongly for Eva, to be so personally connected. And he couldn't help but wonder if the patient was someone close to Flo.

It was a close call. Flo didn't mean to let her emotions take control of her when they were talking about Ms. Martinez donating a kidney to Eva. She should've let him talk to her, not thought twice about it. It was Nate's

prerogative as a surgeon to talk to his patients and make sure they were informed.

She shouldn't have let it affect her so much, but the problem was, it did. Eva reminded her so much of her own time in the hospital, and if her parents could've given her a kidney they would've. Only her parents, her brother and her sister hadn't been cross-matches. Her *năinai* had been, but she had been too elderly, so her kidney hadn't been viable for Flo.

So she'd sat on the list, waiting for some poor soul to die.

It was a great gift that anonymous person had given her, but it also weighed heavily on her. That's why she was trying to live life to the fullest. And Nate had lost a loved one who had been waiting on the list and she couldn't help but wonder who it had been.

It's none of your business.

It may not be, but it gave some connection to Nate that hadn't been there before. It helped her understand him more. He got it. Even just a little bit, he understood the emotions, fear and pain of this whole process. It just made him all the more attractive to her.

She shouldn't be going out with Nate tonight, but even though she was emotionally drained from their spat, she was intrigued.

He was taking her somewhere out of Los Angeles, somewhere she would have a lot of room to drive. She could tick it off her bucket list and, really, what did she have to lose? Seeing Eva chained to her hospital bed had brought back too many painful memories for her, and she'd lashed out, almost telling him that it was she who had been that girl, clinging to life while she'd waited on the transplant list.

And that wasn't anyone's business.

Thankfully, she had been able to convince Nate that it was a former patient of hers.

There was a roar of an engine and Flo glanced over to see a vintage Corvette screech around the corner and pull up in front of the building.

She smiled when she saw Nate get out of the driver's side of the car. "Well, what do you think?"

"Where in the world did you get this?"

"Believe it or not, it's mine. I keep it in storage here. For when I visit. Will it do?"

Flo laughed. "I think so. Will there be room for my bike?"

"Yep. We'll toss it in the trunk, it'll be fine."

Flo wheeled her bike over and Nate took it from her and secured it in the trunk. She noticed he wasn't dressed in his business casual clothes. Instead he was wearing denim jeans, biker boots and a tight, black V-neck shirt. His eyes were obscured by aviator sunglasses. He was a typical Californian bad boy. Or at least how Flo had always pictured them. She didn't have a lot of experience with the bad-boy type of man.

He was too damn sexy for her own good and she had to keep reminding herself that he was off-limits.

She climbed into the passenger side after Nate held open the door for her. Flo had never sat in a sports car before. That was something else she could check off her bucket list. Nate slid into the driver's side and turned the key, revving the engine.

"You ready?" he asked.

"I'm always ready," she said.

He grinned and then took off out of the clinic's loop driveway and out into the streets. Flo's hair, which had still been in a bun, blew out of it and whipped around

her face as Nate drove through the streets of Los Angeles like a maniac.

When they stopped at a light Flo put her hair back into a tight ponytail. "I guess this is why women with long hair wear hats in these cars."

Nate chuckled. "Or scarves."

"I'm not wearing a scarf. Try not to drive like a lunatic."

"And what would you know about driving?" He revved the engine as the light turned green and then took off again toward the highway that led east out of LA and toward Vegas.

"You're not taking me to Vegas, are you? That's, like, six hours away!"

"No, it's in Barstow."

"Barstow! That's two hours from here."

"It's only four-thirty p.m. Do you have plans? I know for a fact you don't have an early shift tomorrow. You have a pretty decent one followed by a really nice dinner out."

She glared at him, but honestly she was glad for the car ride. She'd never been to Barstow. Heck, she'd never really been on a road trip. She'd always wanted to drive across the country. That was on her bucket list, as well. She wanted to drive Route 66 and hit every kitschy place she could. She also wanted to drive across the badlands and through Montana, Wyoming and maybe even up into Canada to Alaska.

She also wanted to do the drive in an RV and her family was *not* an RV type of family. Vacations were spent on a tropical beach somewhere, a place where Flo could rest and recuperate. A place of peace and tranquility.

Flo had had enough of peace and tranquility. She wanted to do things, see places. She wanted a collec-

tion of goofy postcards from places like the home of the world's biggest ball of string and Mount Rushmore.

Nate turned on the radio and Flo relaxed into the drive. She didn't have to say anything to him, she could just enjoy the sights of driving into the desert, watching the city trickle away into wide open spaces with the wind in her face and the sun at her back.

She forgot everything that had happened today, she forgot about her bucket list and limited time and for the first time in a long time she just relaxed.

"Hey, sleepyhead. Wake up."

Flo woke with a start and realized that she'd drifted off. The car was parked at a deserted drag strip and it was dusk.

And when she glanced at the dashboard she could see it was seven in the evening.

"How long was I sleeping for?"

"A couple of hours. You looked so peaceful I didn't want to disturb you."

"I'm so sorry."

Nate shrugged. "It's okay, but I thought you might want to *try* and drive a bit tonight before we have to turn around and head back to Los Angeles."

"Sorry." Flo got out of the car and stretched. "Where are we?"

"A buddy of my father owns this old drag strip. He's planning on refurbishing it, but he said we could come out here and practice driving around the parking lot. I'm not sure if he actually wants us to drive on the strip, though, so if drag racing is on that bucket list of yours..."

"It's not, meaning I've never really considered it."

Nate climbed out of the driving seat. "You ready to try your hand at driving?"

"Oh, yeah," Flo said, probably a little too eagerly. She

climbed into the driver's seat and did up the seat belt. Nate took her vacated spot in the passenger side. "What do I do first?"

Nate chuckled. "Turn the key in the ignition. That would be a good start."

"Ha-ha. I meant after that." She turned the ignition key.

"Whoa, don't jump the gun. Driving is an art form."

Flo snorted. "I find that hard to believe when any old schmuck can do it."

Nate rolled his eyes then placed her hands on the wheel. "Put your hands at ten and two and be quiet for a moment."

Flo stuck out her tongue. "What next?"

"Have you never been in the front seat of a car? Even fifteen-year-olds know this."

She grabbed the stick and put the car out of park into drive. It rolled forward a bit. "Which one's the gas and which is the brake?"

"Press it and you'll find out. Just gently."

"So no slamming?"

Nate arched an eyebrow. "Only on the brake, if needed."

"Okay." Flo pressed her foot down and the car lurched forward. She immediately jammed her foot down on the other pedal. "Whoa."

"There you go. Try again."

"Okay." Flo stepped down on the gas less and the car moved forward slowly. She smiled as Nate instructed her and she drove around the parking lot. Sometimes slow and sometimes fast, which caused Nate to shout out. But it was exhilarating.

She'd always wanted to drive, but her parents had refused to let her learn, even though by the time she was sixteen she had been two years post-op from her kidney

transplant and doing well. She'd begged and pleaded, but her father had not relented.

"Why do you need to drive? We have a driver who will take you wherever you want to go."

Her parents had been so stubborn and then when she'd gone off to college and medical school, she'd never really thought about driving and had just been happy to take public transportation and not have a driver take her around.

Learning to drive was way down the bucket list, though it was something she had to do before she drove across the country. It was nice that Nate had faith in her and was letting her try and drive. No one else had ever suggested that to her.

Not even Johnny.

Don't think about him. This moment was just about friends doing something fun.

It was laid back and easy.

It was fun.

And it was only temporary.

Nate allowed her to drive around until dusk turned to darkness and a smattering of stars spread out across the sky. They grabbed a quick drive-through dinner then parked back at the deserted drag strip, lying out on the hood of Nate's car. Flo couldn't remember the last time she'd seen so many stars.

She had been young and it may have been once or twice when they'd been driving somewhere late at night in the country. The details were foggy, but she remembered the night sky being flooded with brilliant light, and that's what she could see now.

It was beautiful.

She glanced over at Nate. His arm was behind his head and he was staring up at the night sky with the same kind

of wonder she was feeling. It made her heart skip a beat and she fought the urge to reach out and kiss him again.

It would be perfect if she did—kissing Nate under a star-filled sky—but she suppressed that urge and turned her gaze away. It was better that she didn't act on her impulse. There was no one else around. They didn't have to put on their act now. They were just friends.

And she wasn't even sure if they were friends, because she doubted she'd hear from him again once he returned to New York, and that realization made her feel sad.

"See, it was worth the drive, wasn't it?" he said, interrupting her thoughts.

"It was. You're right, this is great. I never see the sky like this in LA," she said with a sigh.

"It is. I used to come out this way with my dad. We'd find a campground out in the desert and watch meteor showers."

"Do your parents still live in Los Angeles?"

"No, they live in San Francisco. They love San Francisco and the lifestyle there. Why?"

"Just wondered. I mean, if they were here I'd ask why you're not staying with them."

"Would you stay with your parents if they were in town?"

"I wouldn't have a choice," Flo mumbled.

Nate chuckled. "Oh, really?"

"My dad grew up in Beijing and my mom in the deep south. They're quite overbearing and old-fashioned sometimes. They also drive me crazy."

"See, you wouldn't stay with them, either. Besides, maybe I have a bad relationship with my parents," he teased.

"Do you?"

"No," he said. "I care for them. I've just been so busy

in New York City. I never get to San Francisco. It's been a long time since I've been out this way. I forgot how much I love it out here. How I love the desert. I used to spend a lot of time out in the mountains when I was younger. I did a lot of rock climbing, too." Then his smile disappeared into a frown. "Well, that was a long time ago. I don't have time for that kind of stuff any more."

"I've always wanted to do rock climbing, or climb a mountain. Maybe Everest."

Nate shrugged. "It's hard work and dangerous."

"So?"

"It's on that crazy bucket list of yours, isn't it?"

"And if it is?" she asked.

Nate shook his head. "Why would you want to risk your life?"

"Life is meant to be lived."

"You can live your life without doing crazy things."

"What's the fun in that?" Flo teased.

"There's more to life than fun." There was a sadness to his voice.

"You okay?"

"Perfectly. Why wouldn't I be?"

"You sounded sad there."

"Not sad, just realistic. Well, we'd better get back to LA. Work tomorrow and dinner with potential investors." Nate slid off the hood and climbed back into the driver's seat. The moment was shattered and she blamed herself. Flo reluctantly got into the passenger seat. She didn't want to go back home to her lonely apartment. She wanted to keep driving. She wanted to spend the night on the hood of Nate's car, wrapped in his arms.

No. Not in his arms.

Nate was right. It was getting late and it was time to

head back to reality and LA. It was safer in LA, safer in her apartment far away from Nate.

"Thanks for tonight. It was fun," she said.

He smiled at her, but it wasn't the same easygoing, fun smile she was used to. It was subdued Nate again. "No problem. It was my pleasure."

Flo didn't say anything more to Nate as they headed west, back to the city, back to reality and back to the facade they were both very comfortable with.

CHAPTER SEVEN

"How much longer am I going to be holed up here, Doc? I'm supposed to start my stint on Broadway in five months. I have to prepare."

Nate glanced up from Kyle's chart. Kyle was sitting up in bed and doing better a couple days post-op from his LVAD surgery, but he still had a long way to go and even then he had an uncertain time ahead, hooked up to his machine as he waited for a new heart and lungs.

"I think it's in your best interests to cancel your stint on Broadway."

Kyle snorted and then winced in pain. "Are you crazy? This is a huge opportunity."

"One you'll have to pass up unfortunately." Nate crossed his arms. "You're hooked up to a machine. You can't leave the clinic. That machine is keeping you alive."

"The nurse said it was portable. She was having me walk around yesterday."

"Portable, but you still need to be monitored and you still need to be on oxygen a lot of the time. I don't see you tap dancing your way across a Broadway stage any time in the near future."

Kyle grinned. That famous smile that melted the hearts of many women, but which didn't work on Nate one bit.

He actually found it annoying more than anything else when Kyle tried to use that charm on him.

"There's no dancing. Besides, I could have a new heart and lungs tomorrow."

Nate pinched the bridge of his nose. "You could, but it still doesn't mean that you'll be up on your feet in a couple of weeks. You will be in the intensive care unit for a while, your body will have to heal from a long surgery, we'll have to monitor you for signs of rejection. It will be a long process of healing before you can return to the stage."

Kyle sighed and laid his head back. "I didn't ask for this."

"I know. I'm sorry."

"You paint a pretty bleak picture, Doc. At least that other doctor, at least she can give me some hope."

Nate frowned. "Was she the one who told you you'd be up on your feet in a short time?"

"No, she's just nice to look at." Kyle winked.

Nate laughed. "Thanks."

"Well, I don't have to tell you, right? I mean, I do keep up with gossip. You and her are a thing, right?"

Nate groaned inwardly. "Right."

"It's about time. You're always working; you never seem to have fun. I invite you to all my parties and you never come. Do you know how many beautiful women come to those parties?"

"I'm aware. Now, would you lie back and get some rest and either Dr. Chiu or myself will come in and look on you later."

Kyle grinned. "I hope it's Dr. Chiu. No offense, Dr. King, but I might just steal her out from under you."

"Sure you will. I'll see you later." Nate left Kyle's room and shook his head. Didn't people understand the

severity of transplant surgery? They thought that once they had a new organ things would go back to normal. That they'd be able to do all the same things they'd been able to do before, but it was a huge lifestyle change. The chance of rejection in Kyle's case was high. Granted, it was getting better all the time with medical advances, but surgery was still the *practice* of medicine, which meant things weren't perfect.

If only they were.

If only organs could be grown from patients' tissues and blood. If only there wasn't rejection. If only...

Nate scrubbed a hand over his face. He hadn't had a moment to turn to his research since coming to Los Angeles and he was annoyed. When he was in New York his research was his companion at night and that was all he needed.

Since he'd landed back in LA, he hadn't even glanced at it. His nights had been filled with Dr. Florence Chiu and his days had been filled with prepping Eva Martinez and her mother for their kidney transplant surgery, as well as monitoring Kyle Francis, who was his top priority.

The thing was, he didn't really miss his research. He'd enjoyed the last couple of nights with Flo. Maybe because it was just temporary, there was no permanence to it and it made him feel safe. Since there was no permanence there was less chance of heartache.

The only problem was, he wasn't sure if he wanted to go back to the way his life had been before. Empty.

You don't have a choice.

Nate groaned as he noticed the time. He had to grab his suit from the office he shared with Flo and try to make himself presentable for this dinner, which was the last thing he felt like doing today. Especially when this wasn't even his place of employment.

He was just a locum surgeon, just passing through.
It's your own fault. You had to kiss her.

And he'd wanted to kiss her when they'd been lying out under the stars. Actually, any time he was around her he wanted to kiss her. It was maddening. It was distracting and he wished he could act on it, but he couldn't.

Nate placed the tablet he'd been using back on the charging station and headed toward the office. He'd brought in his suit so that he could make a quick change here and drive Flo to the restaurant in West Hollywood.

He just wanted to get this dinner and schmoozing over with as fast as he could. Then he could come back here and force himself to do some work on his research. His research was his life. There was no room for anything or anyone else.

When he got to the office Flo was already in there and already dressed in a suit, her long hair up and smooth, instead of the usual wisps that framed her face. His gaze was drawn to her long slender neck. She wore a red silk blouse and a tight black pencil skirt, with black heels, the kind that had a red sole.

She was absolutely stunning and he knew that this dinner was going to be a challenge.

Flo glanced up at him. "You're not dressed yet?"

"I was just coming to do that."

"Where were you?"

"Checking on Kyle." Nate peeled off his white lab coat and tossed it on Flo's couch. She frowned, moved past him and hung up his lab coat in the closet. He couldn't help but smile to himself. "You're such a neat freak."

"Actually, I'm not. Just in my office. I like my workplace organized, but at home my decorating style is *There appears to have been a struggle.*"

"Is that a style?" he asked.

"At my apartment it is. I don't have time to tidy it much. And I'm rarely there."

"I would've never pegged you for someone who would live in clutter."

"It's not a sty, it's just not as organized as it is here." Flo crossed her arms. "I can't believe you're not dressed."

"Chill, I brought my suit here. I'll just go into your bathroom and change." He opened the door and saw toothpaste smeared on the porcelain of the sink, scrubs wadded up on the floor and an abandoned hair straightener. There was also some lingerie on the floor. He chuckled and picked up the delicate lace with one hand. "It looks like your office bathroom has the same style as your apartment."

Her cheeks went beet red and she snatched the flimsy garment from him. "Would you get ready, for the love of all that's good and holy?"

Nate didn't argue any further. It wasn't worth it, because the gleam in her eyes brooked no argument. He quickly changed into his suit and cleaned himself up, mostly to get the smell of hospital off himself.

When he opened the door to the bathroom Flo was waiting for him. Her gaze raking him from head to toe and a finger thoughtfully tapped her chin.

"You clean up nice."

"Thank you, Dr. Chiu. You do, too."

She smiled. "Well, let's get this over and done with."

"I think we should swing by Kyle's room. Make him jealous."

Flo arched an eyebrow. "What're you talking about?"

"He's trying to move in on my territory." And then he realized what he'd said. He only hoped that Flo took it as a joke.

"Your territory?" she teased. "Since when have I been your territory?"

"Since the rooftop, or have you forgotten?"

She rolled her eyes and took his proffered arm. They walked out of her office together and he knew, as they walked through the halls of The Hollywood Hills Clinic, that everyone was watching them.

Usually that would make him feel a bit uncomfortable, because he didn't like to be associated with any woman. He didn't want rumors flying about him, but he didn't mind walking through the halls with Dr. Florence Chiu on his arm, and in those heels she was almost as tall as him. He could smell her hair. It was lavender.

There was a limo outside and Freya was standing outside. She waved when they walked over to her.

"I'm afraid I can't go with you tonight," Freya said.

Flo frowned. "Why not?"

"I'm needed somewhere else. I'm sure you and Dr. King can handle this dinner. Besides, it's you two the investors want to meet. They know me." Freya glanced at her cell phone. "I have to run, but the limo is yours and dinner is on the clinic. I've already talked to Dan Tana's. Everything is a go."

And before either of them could protest Freya was walking off in the other direction, texting someone.

"A limo. Wow." Flo walked over to it and the chauffeur opened the door for her. She slid in and as she did so Nate caught a glimpse of her thigh. It made his blood heat and he pulled at the suddenly tight collar of his dress shirt. All he could think about was being alone with her in a limo and how much room and privacy there was for the two of them. "Are you coming, Nate? It's great in here."

"Yeah." He took a calming breath and tried to chase those dirty, bad thoughts from his mind. The last thing he

needed was to have an erection during a boring meeting with investors. Also because there was no way he could act on it. He hadn't planned on doing laps tonight at the pool, but now he was.

He had to seriously get a grip, but the more he tried to tell himself that the more his grip lessened.

Flo had never been to Dan Tana's. Actually, even though she'd been living in LA for a couple years, she really hadn't gotten out much. She didn't go to fancy restaurants, hadn't since she was a child, and she certainly didn't like investor meetings.

"You okay?" Nate asked.

"Why wouldn't I be?"

"Well, a moment ago you were pretty excited about riding in a limo and now you're stiff, on edge, like a rod is holding you upright."

Flo rolled her eyes and sighed, her shoulders dropping. "Fine. I don't like talking in front of crowds."

"Who said there will be a crowd?"

"Well, fine, a group of strangers. It makes me uncomfortable."

"You handled that press conference well," Nate said.

"No, I didn't. You did, though. I can speak to a crowd of doctors or nurses, anyone from the medical profession, but throw in people who aren't part of the medical profession and I just want to crumple up in a ball and cry."

Nate frowned. "That doesn't seem like you."

"How would you know?" She regretted the words. "I'm sorry."

He shook his head. "Fair enough. We haven't known each other long, but really it doesn't seem like you to be nervous like this."

"It is. Trust me." Flo began to tap her leg in agitation. "I have no idea what to say beyond 'Give us your money.'"

He reached out and put his hand on her knee to calm the tapping of her leg. It caused a zing of pleasure to race through her, his strong hand on her knee firing her senses. He moved his hand away. Her leg tapping had stopped and she was at ease.

Flo cleared her throat. "So what should I do? Do you have any suggestions?"

"Picture them naked."

Flo gasped and saw that devious twinkle in his eyes. He was joking with her. "You're crazy."

He shrugged. "There's nothing fundamentally different about talking to a press conference or investors. You're strong. You stood up to me the first day we met. Not many people have had the guts to do that."

"Why? You're not scary."

His brow furrowed. "Thanks for that."

"Why are you bothered by that?"

"You weren't scared when you met me?"

"No. Why would I be?"

"You just admitted large crowds make you nervous, but when you met me you weren't nervous?"

Flo felt her heart rate pick up speed. Of course she'd been nervous when she'd met him. He was gorgeous. He was the kind of guy who would never give a girl like her a second glance, so she'd been nervous when he'd stepped off that helicopter, looking so sexy. She just wouldn't admit it.

And she wouldn't admit that he made her nervous now, but in a much different way.

"No, I wasn't nervous. You're a surgeon, though, and only one man."

He frowned. "Most residents and interns are nervous

when they first meet me. They say I'm a bit of a monster. Cold. Detached."

"First, I find that hard to believe, and second, I'm not a resident. I'm a surgeon. I can deal with cold and detached. My father was a businessman, a CEO, and a lot of people feared him. My mom taught me to stand up for myself."

He grinned. "Then it should be easy to deal with a couple of investors. Just channel your inner dad and deal with them."

"You mean curse at them in Mandarin until they do what I want?" Then she laughed as she thought of her father. He'd tried for so long to get her to speak Mandarin, but she'd had no interest in learning it, except for the swear words.

He'd be horrified to know that's what she'd picked up in her endless classes in Mandarin. Of course, now she wished she had a second language under her belt and maybe that was something she could add to her bucket list.

"I think cursing at them will defeat the purpose." They shared a smile and the limo slowed down and stopped in front of the restaurant.

Flo took a deep breath and stared at the front of the restaurant.

You can do this.

"You can do this," Nate said, as if reading her thoughts.

"Maybe it shouldn't be me. Maybe it should be you."

He shook his head. "No, you're The Hollywood Hills Clinic's chief of transplant surgery. This is all you."

"Okay."

He nodded and opened the door, stepping out. Then he offered his hand and helped her out of the limo. As he held her hand he gave it a reassuring squeeze. It was

exactly what she needed at that moment. A vote of confidence from someone she admired.

Yeah, she could do this. She had to do this.

They were whisked inside the restaurant, which was decorated in deep, rich colors, and the concierge led them to a large patent-leather booth in the far corner where the investors were waiting. As she walked through the restaurant she felt a hand in the small of her back as Nate gently guided her. It made shivers of anticipation run down her spine. To make matters worse, he looked so darned good in a well-tailored suit.

It was maddening.

"Ah, Dr. King and Dr. Chiu, I am so glad you could join us. I'm Cecil McKenzie."

"A pleasure to meet you, Mr. McKenzie." Flo shook his hand and Nate followed suit.

"This is Ian Brownstone and Travis Fleming," Cecil said, introducing the other two men at the table.

Flo shook their hands and then sat down, Nate and the rest of the men at the table sitting down only after she had.

"I have to say we were quite worried when your story leaked in the press," Ian said. "The Hollywood Hills Clinic prides itself on privacy and protection of their clientele."

"It was an unfortunate incident," Nate said. "Thankfully one that was unfounded as Dr. Chiu and I were in a relationship."

Nate was so smooth with the investors. He was obviously used to this. Flo was, somewhat, but only from watching her father schmooze clients in his business. Schmoozing was not her thing.

"Dr. King wasn't fully aware of the clinic's strict guidelines on privacy," Flo said. "He is from New York."

That got a bit of laughter from the men at the table.

"Well, we're glad to see that it's all been smoothed over and, honestly, it's been spun in such a good way. We're also extremely impressed with the pro bono case you've both taken on with Eva Martinez. Can you tell us a little bit about that?"

"Of course, The Hollywood Hills Clinic is working with the Bright Hope Clinic and Eva is one of hopefully many more children who will benefit from this initiative. You know, of course, that cases like this will bring in more positive press for paying clientele," Nate said.

And he continued to talk to the investors, winning them over.

Flo was trying to pay attention, but again this wasn't her forte and, frankly, bored the socks off her. She was pretty sure that these men didn't want to hear about the science behind the surgery and that's what interested her most.

Also the journey, because she'd lived it.

Only it was better they didn't want to know about the emotions. The struggles one faced when undergoing an organ transplant, because then she would have to tell Nate about hers and that was something she would never do.

That was her scar to bear alone.

As the salads were being taken away her cell phone began to buzz and it was long distance.

"Excuse me, gentlemen. No need to get up." Flo pulled out her phone and slid out of the booth, walking to a secluded, quiet spot by the bathrooms before she answered the call. "Dr. Chiu speaking."

"Dr. Chiu, I'm calling from UNOS regarding your patient Kyle Xavier Francis."

"Please go on."

"We have organs for him. We need you to come to San Francisco and retrieve them."

Flo's pulse thundered through her ears as the words sank in. This was the moment. The magic moment where someone was given a second chance, but also a moment of reverence because it meant the end of a life.

A brave soul who was giving the ultimate gift.

"I'll be there within the hour."

CHAPTER EIGHT

FLO FINISHED HER conversation with UNOS and then promptly called The Hollywood Hills Clinic to ready a chopper to take them to the airport and to have a chartered jet be readied to fly to San Francisco. She also ordered her team and the nurses to stop feeding Kyle and prep him for surgery. It was amazing luck to find a viable heart and lungs so soon. It was a relief. Then she cursed herself for being somewhat optimistic. She didn't know if the organs were viable. Not until she examined them herself.

Focus. Don't rush.

They had a little bit of breathing time as the surgery wasn't scheduled to start for another hour and the heart and lungs would be the last to be taken out, and she was going to be the one to do it. She was very particular about that.

She headed back to the table. Everyone stood up again.

"I'm very sorry to have to do this, gentlemen, but there is a medical emergency and Dr. King and I need to leave right away. I do apologize."

Nate glanced at his phone and she could see the text message there confirming the news she had just received. "Gentlemen, I'm sorry we have to cut this evening short."

"Of course," Mr. McKenzie said. "Don't worry about

us, and you can tell Ms. Rothsberg that we're impressed and indeed interested in furthering our commitment to The Hollywood Hills Clinic."

"Thank you." Flo shook their hands briefly and then turned and walked away as fast as her heels would carry her. The limo was called and it only took five minutes for the car to pull up in front of the restaurant.

Nate told the driver to take them back to The Hollywood Hills Clinic.

"The chopper is waiting for us," Flo said, shaking her leg in impatience. "Mr. Francis is fortunate."

Nate nodded. "He is. I'm glad you had your phone on. I'm annoyed with myself that I put mine on silent."

"I never keep my phone on silent or I'd miss the calls completely. I never know when it's vibrating."

They didn't say much else to each other. There was nothing to say, because as soon as the organs were transplanted and Kyle was stabilized it would be the end of their charade. Which was a shame, because Flo did enjoy being around Nate. She liked working with him, too, but they both knew there was a time limit on this act.

It was good that it would be over and done with. Then she could get back to her normal existence. She could throw herself back into her work and not think about Nate so much, because she did. He also made her realize her loneliness.

And even though she hated to admit it, she was going to miss him.

The limo had barely parked and Flo was out, kicking off her heels so that she could run through the halls toward her office to throw on her scrubs and grab the heart and lung machine that would keep the donor organs alive and cool as they traveled back to Los Angeles. She began to undress, with the door to her office barely shut.

"Whoa," Nate said.

She spun around, just in her red lace thong and bra with her shirt covering her torso. Then she realized what she was doing and covered her scar the best she could with her blouse. What had she been thinking? How could she have been so lax about it? She'd never changed in front of people. Not even when she'd been a surgical resident. She always found an excuse to slip away into a stall and change. She didn't want anyone to see her scar and think that she was weak when she wasn't.

Nate was looking the other way, but he was clearly uncomfortable. And she quickly turned around so her back was to him and slipped on her scrub top, dropping the blouse that had hidden her scar. She prayed he hadn't seen it. She didn't want to get into a discussion about her scar. There was no time for that and she didn't want him to know.

"What?" she asked.

"I wasn't expecting you to strip down."

Flo rolled her eyes. "Don't be immature. We don't have time."

She breathed a sigh of relief that he hadn't noticed her scar, but then she'd had her back to him as fast as she could when he'd walked into the room, plus she'd covered it with her blouse.

Why, though?

She was being chicken. Nate wasn't Johnny and he could handle seeing her scar. Why was she so scared about telling him? He'd said she was strong, and for a moment she'd believed him, but right now she didn't feel so strong. Not when she'd been so afraid of him seeing her so vulnerable.

Part of having her bucket list was being bold and brave. How could she be either if she hid the truth from

the one person who might understand? Who wouldn't pity her?

Are you sure about that?

That doubt weasel in her head was stronger than she'd thought. It reminded her why it was better to be alone. To guard her heart like she'd been doing for so long. She couldn't go back to being hurt like that.

Still, she wished she could overcome her fear of people finding out about her illness. Maybe if she shared her experience then people would understand her deep connection and passion to saving those on the waiting list.

Maybe it would make her a better surgeon.

Maybe they would all pity you and question your abilities. Maybe they would think you were too emotionally attached to make a rational decision.

She shook those thoughts out of her head. "Are you going to get changed or what?"

"Fine." Nate shut the door and began to take off his clothes. First the suit jacket, which he tossed on the couch again, then the tie and the button-down blue shirt that brought out the color of his eyes.

Look away.

Only she was having a hard time trying not to look at him as she pulled on her scrubs. She'd seen him half-naked before, in tight swimming trunks, no less, with water running down his hard, tanned body.

Get a grip.

She pulled her hair up into a ponytail and grabbed her ID and jacket with "The Hollywood Hills Clinic" embroidered into it.

"I'm going to get the heart and lung machine. Shall I meet you on the helipad?" Flo asked, not looking at him as he kicked off his shoes and began to unbuckle the tight, tailored pants.

"Yep."

Thank goodness.

She snuck a quick glance at his tight backside and then shut the door, heading back up to her floor. When she got up onto the transplant floor, it was like a madhouse as people were scrambling and getting ready for the big show.

Flo stopped at Kyle's room. There were nurses hovering around him, more than usual. He saw her in the doorway and smiled.

"Do I understand there are organs for me?"

Flo nodded and walked toward him. "Yes, but remember, if they're not viable…" She couldn't even finish that sentence. She'd been over this with Kyle before.

He nodded. "I know. This could be one of those false starts you were talking about."

Flo squeezed his foot under the blanket. "I'm going to retrieve them with Dr. King. As soon as we land at LAX they'll wheel you into surgery. Dr. King will work on you, removing the LVAD, and put you on bypass."

Kyle held up his hand. "I understand. I'm more than ready, Dr. Chiu."

She smiled. "I'll see you in a bit."

A nurse handed Flo Kyle's chart on a tablet that was charged, and the means to transport the organs back. Flo took a deep breath and headed up to the rooftop. Nate was pacing and the helicopter was waiting.

It reminded her of the first moment she'd seen Nate, only this time they were riding off together and together they would save this man's life.

"You ready?" Nate shouted over the roar of the helicopter's blades.

"Ready."

He helped her load the equipment onto the chopper

before they got in. As soon as they were belted in the helicopter rose from the helipad and headed out over Los Angeles towards LAX, where the private jet was on the runway, waiting for them.

They didn't say a word to each other, not that they could've heard much over the noise of the blades. And when they were seated in the plane, they didn't say much either that didn't involve Kyle's surgery and the organ retrieval surgery. Flo would be the lead retrieval surgeon on the heart and lungs. She would hand the organs over to Nate, who would make sure they stayed stable and viable on their trip back.

Flo didn't mind. She didn't feel like talking.

She needed to keep focused on the task at hand and sent up a silent prayer for the lives that were being saved by this one person. It's what she always did even though she wasn't particularly religious, but still something she did.

When the plane landed there was an ambulance ready and waiting to whisk them off to the hospital, where the organ retrieval had started only ten minutes previously. Right now they were doing the laparotomy to make sure the organs were viable. If any organ wasn't viable then they could inform the surgeon who was retrieving the organ and the recipient could go back on the waiting list.

She fidgeted nervously as the ambulance raced through the San Francisco streets. She glanced over at Nate, who was absolutely comfortable. Or at least he appeared that way.

"You're not nervous?" she asked.

"Why would I be nervous? I've done this many times."

"What if the organs aren't viable?"

Nate sighed. "It would be too bad, but nothing I can stop. There's no use worrying about it. Why are you worried?"

"Because he's a big client. I wanted to do the lapa-

rotomy myself. I'm a bit controlling that way." That was part of the reason. She couldn't form the words and tell him that every time she went through the process she thought of the one time she'd gotten her hopes up and the organ hadn't been viable. The other kidney, which had gone to another recipient, had been fine, but the one destined for her hadn't.

And she almost hadn't survived her time on the waiting list again.

So she knew first hand what it would be like if she had to go back and tell Kyle that they couldn't retrieve his heart and lungs successfully.

When the doors to the ambulance opened, Flo jumped out and was ushered into the hospital by a resident, who took them straight through the hospital and to the ER. As she walked through the hospital she caught sight of a family.

A family in the waiting room.

A family that was grieving. They were holding each other up, mourning their loved one.

Her heart skipped a beat and for a moment she wasn't even there, because in her mind she was transported back to her own hospital bed, with hazy, tangled memories of her parents weeping and holding each other while she'd clung to life. The walk through the waiting room went in slow motion for Flo, her thoughts immediately going to her own donor.

She would never know who that person was, but if she did know she'd visit wherever they had been laid to rest and thank them.

Thank them for her second chance at life.

"Dr. Chiu?"

Flo shook her head and saw Nate was staring at her

with a concerned look and the resident was holding open the door to the OR floor.

"Sorry." She didn't glance back at the family. She couldn't.

She peeled off her jacket and hung it on a hook and then geared up, putting on a paper scrub cap and then scrubbing her hands. She glanced through the windows into the OR and saw the line of people waiting for organs.

"This will be fine," Nate said, scrubbing beside her.

"I know. It's just I don't like this part too much. I'm a surgeon and…" She couldn't even finish that sentence, because this was a life that wasn't being saved.

It was ending.

She preferred live donors. Like kidney, liver and sometimes lungs, when someone donated one lung to a loved one. There were rarely deaths in those retrievals. Those retrievals were done in love. There was a certain beauty to it.

There was a certain beauty to this moment as well, it was just that it had ended tragically for the donor.

She put on her mask and then headed into the OR, with Nate behind her holding one of the basins to collect the organs. She was gowned and gloved.

All she could do was wait. And she watched as organs were removed and people stepped forward to take them. They would be going off to different parts of the country. Saving countless lives.

"Dr. Chiu, we're ready for you now." The other surgeon moved to the opposite side of the table to assist. Flo stepped up. She closed her eyes and then went to work, but it didn't take her long. The bronchoscopy was done before the retrieval surgery to make sure that there were no signs of infection and the Gram stain came back clear.

It was now time to make sure that externally the lungs

were viable as the bronchoscopy only could see the lungs internally.

And as she carefully clamped and made ready to dissect she saw a dark spot. Her heart dropped to the soles of her shoes and she cursed under her breath as she felt the mass that grew into the pulmonary artery. She checked the heart and could see a minute dark spot beginning to grow.

Cancer.

Her stomach twisted in a knot and she tried not to be sick.

"I need to take a biopsy and I need it stat." If it wasn't cancer, maybe it was something benign and it would still be viable. She handed the specimens to the resident, who ran out of the OR to the lab.

Flo raised her hands, keeping them clean and rested while waiting, and tried not to curse. It couldn't be cancer. It just couldn't.

Nate came up behind her. "Dr. Chiu, what's wrong?"

"Look." She showed him the mass, the dark spots and where it spread.

Nate cursed, too. "Dammit."

Tears stung her eyes. If it had just been the lungs that were damaged, the heart could've gone to someone else. In Flo's case she couldn't take one and not the other, because it had to be one operation. Kyle's cardiopulmonary system couldn't stand the shock of two different surgeries. In his case it wasn't one or the other.

It needed to be both. The surgery had to happen at the same time.

Flo watched the clock, waiting for her answer. The donor couldn't be on bypass much longer. Even if the mass was benign, the organs would be useless if they

were kept much longer where they were because the donor was missing other vital organs.

It was a race.

The resident returned. "I'm sorry, Dr. Chiu. It's stage-four lung cancer and the tumor originated from the heart. There's no record of any of it in the patient's file so it's highly likely the donor was unaware he had cancer."

Flo closed her eyes and cursed. "Thank you, Doctor. Would you please take the patient off bypass."

Dammit.

She tried not to cry.

The resident nodded and Flo began to close up the donor.

"I can do that," the resident said.

"No. I want to do it," she said, hoping her voice didn't crack with the emotion threatening to overtake her. She didn't want to explain to the resident why she felt the need to see this through. It was her way of thanking the donor for the ultimate gift.

A way to process the loss.

A way to thank her own donor for her life.

In fact, everything she did to advance transplant surgery was a thank-you, but, then, one could never thank someone enough for the ultimate gift. Except to live life to the fullest. The heart and lungs were not viable. She had been afraid of this, because it had seemed too good to be true. They hadn't seen it on the laparotomy because it had been on the other side and hidden. The mass hadn't infiltrated the lungs yet.

Nate had left the OR. She didn't even know he'd left, but he came back in now. "I called the clinic and told them to cancel Kyle's surgery."

Flo nodded and continued to work. When the monitors flatlined, she sighed.

I'm so sorry.

The apology was for this donor and for Kyle.

"Time of death twenty-two thirty-five." She pulled off her mask, not able to control the tears threatening to escape. "Doctor, can you finish closing for me? I have to get back to Los Angeles and my patient."

"No problem, Dr. Chiu." The resident took over and Flo dragged herself out of the OR, ripping off the paper mask and jamming it in the garbage can. Then she tossed off her gown and scrub cap, angrily throwing them into the receptacle before kicking it.

Dammit. It was so unfair.

"Whoa, what's gotten into you?" Nate asked.

"The organs weren't viable. What do you think has gotten into me?" Flo snapped.

"It happens, Flo. Why are you taking this so personally?"

Flo just rolled her eyes and began to scrub vigorously. "I'm not taking this personally. It's just frustrating."

Liar.

Of course she was taking this personally, because it had happened to her. And when it had happened to her she'd resigned herself at that moment to the thought that she was going to die. She'd been tired of fighting. No fourteen-year-old, no child, should resign themselves to dying.

She only hoped Kyle didn't.

She wanted to give him hope. It was just that right now she didn't know how.

At least the donor had saved countless other lives, just not her patient's. She finished scrubbing and they walked silently back out to the ambulance, the machine empty.

She was not looking forward to disappointing Kyle.

"I'll tell Kyle," Nate whispered, as if reading her mind.

"Thanks." Flo climbed into the ambulance, exhausted and defeated.

"I'm sorry you're taking this so hard," Nate said.

"Thanks."

"Think about all the lives that donor did save, though." She smiled. "I know. I just feel bad for Kyle."

"He'll love it that you feel bad for him. He told me the other day that he's going to make a move on you."

Flo chuckled. "What?"

"That's what he told me. He really likes it when you come to check on him rather than me. He told me he was going to steal you away from me. Not that there would be any stealing on his part."

It was a sting, but it was the truth.

Nate wasn't hers and she wasn't Nate's. Still, it hurt all the same and she didn't know why she let it hurt. Nate couldn't be hers.

It was temporary.

She couldn't let Nate in. She couldn't risk her heart again.

"I'm afraid I'll still be disappointing him when I turn him down," Flo said.

Nate cocked an eyebrow. "Oh, really?"

"I don't date guys who have a broken heart." It had been meant as a joke, but Nate's smile disappeared like she'd hurt him.

"Right," was all he said, and didn't say any more.

An uneasy tension settled between them and Flo just let it be. She wasn't in the mood to discuss things further.

It was better this way.

It was better not to get involved and not to dig any deeper.

CHAPTER NINE

NATE KEPT HIS distance from Flo for a week. Even though he shouldn't have been bothered by her *I don't date men who have a broken heart* comment, it had stung. It had been meant in jest and if it had been anyone else he might've got a chuckle out of it, but Flo had been the one to say it.

It shouldn't bother him, because it's not like he was going to do anything about Flo, but it did, because he was slowly realizing he cared about her and that was scary.

How was she getting past his walls? He didn't know, but he decided after the failed transplant retrieval for Kyle Francis that it was best he stay away from her. So after disappointing Kyle and having a long talk with him, Nate threw himself back into his work at night. During the day he avoided being in the office. He found little corners to work in and the clinic had a nice research library tucked away on another floor.

At night, he worked on his papers and spent a lot of time swimming, but even then Flo's presence was there, and every time he got out of the pool he expected to see her waiting for him.

He had to get a grip and remind himself that there was nothing between him and Flo, but he did miss her companionship. He missed their friendship. And that's

why he was now standing outside her office, hesitating about whether to go in. Only he had to go in. There had been some whispers about whether or not their relationship had ended or perhaps was on the verge of ending, because it seemed the dream team was drifting apart.

Freya had noticed and Nate had just come out of a meeting with her, having assured her that the distance was nothing. He'd just been working and things between Flo and him were fine.

As fine as they could be for a fake relationship.

"The door is unlocked."

Nate turned to see Flo standing behind him, grinning at him, a sparkle in her eyes.

"You have a way of sneaking up on people, don't you?"

"I do." Flo moved past him and opened the door to her office. "You know this is your office, too, so you're allowed to come and go when you want."

"I know. I was thinking and you interrupted my train of thought." He walked into the office and Flo followed, shutting the door behind her. She took a seat behind her desk and put up her feet on it.

"Well, I'm sorry about interrupting your train of thought. You've been busy. I haven't seen you around much."

"I've been working on my research.

"What is your research about again?"

"Mostly working on ways of regenerating organs and also the possibility of robotic replacements."

She arched her eyebrows. "I'm impressed, Dr. King. I've thought along similar lines, too."

"I figured as much. You're just as passionate about transplant surgery as I am." He cleared his throat. "I just got out of a meeting with Freya and I think we need to talk."

Her smile faded. "I think I know. I had that talk with her, too."

Nate nodded. "Something happened after Kyle's failed retrieval."

"Yeah, I took it too hard. I'm sorry for acting that way." Only she didn't look him in the eye when she said that and he couldn't help but wonder if there was something else going on there. Something she wasn't telling him.

It's not your concern.

"Okay, and I do understand. It was hard on me, too. Hard to break the news to him," he said. "Freya wants us to make some public appearances together before the big gala fundraiser tomorrow night."

Flo sighed. "Oh. I forgot about that gala. I hate getting dressed up for those things."

"The investors we had that brief dinner with wanted to throw a gala to raise money for the Bright Hope Clinic and raise awareness for donating organs. We kind of have to be there."

Flo wrinkled her nose. "I know."

"So, before that gala, I think we should go out tonight. Make a few public appearances so the press will stop printing stuff about us drifting apart."

"Drifting?" A blush crept up Flo's cheeks. "Tonight. Sure. What did you have in mind?"

"Surfing."

Her eyes widened. "Are you serious?"

"Is that on your bucket list?"

"No, actually, but it could be. It sounds like fun."

"I took a look at our schedules. We're both off at three and I think we should take a drive out to Venice Beach, because it's nearby and I can show you a few things."

"You know how to surf?"

"I told you I'm a native Californian. Of course I know how to surf. I spent many summers on Venice Beach. Plus it's a pretty safe activity compared to tackling Everest or letting you drive again."

Flo chuckled. "I don't have a bathing suit here with me."

He frowned. "Well, I'm sure you can pick up something along Venice Beach. I don't have one with me, either."

She rolled her eyes but smiled. "Okay. It sounds good. I guess I can't really say no to that, but I didn't really have you pegged for the surfing type."

"Why?"

"You don't seem to take a lot of risks. Don't take it the wrong way, but when I talked about mountain climbing, you seemed pretty against any kind of risk-taking."

"I had a friend, she took a lot of risks. Maybe some risks she shouldn't have."

Flo tipped her head to one side. "What kind of risks?"

"Riding a motorcycle without a helmet, for one thing."

"I wouldn't do that one. I'm not that much of a risk-taker."

Nate grinned. "You want to climb Everest."

"Have you?"

"No." Only he didn't tell her that it had been on his list once. Back when he'd done foolish things, taken chances and lived life to the extreme. Of course that had been a long time ago. Now he was a surgeon and understood the kind of trauma that could be done to a body doing those things.

He shook those thoughts out of his head and decided to change the subject.

"Surfing isn't too bad, as long as you don't do too much of it at dusk when the sharks feed."

She sat up straighter, her eyes wide. "Sharks?"

"You'll be fine. I have to do a round because I promised James I would, but I'll see you at the front in an hour."

He chuckled to himself as he left her office and then stopped, because again she'd gotten through his walls. She made him forget that he didn't do things like surfing or rock climbing or even traveling hours out of town to drive around a drag strip.

That was the old him. Someone he'd buried years ago. Why couldn't he have suggested dinner or a movie?

That's not you, that's why.

But it was. It had been for a while now. Or at least he liked to think it was him.

Nate scrubbed a hand over his face, angry at himself for being so weak when it came to Flo. He was angry at himself for allowing the man he'd once been to come back, because that's not who he was now.

That man was long gone.

Flo walked through one of the shops at Venice Beach that sold bathing suits. Or rather pieces of thread that seemed to be woven together loosely. At least for women. It was bad enough that she'd forgotten herself for a moment and stripped down in front of him once. Something she never did, because she didn't want anyone to see her scar. If they saw the scar, they either knew what it was because they were a surgeon or they asked questions that she was not prepared to answer.

Which was why when the sales assistant kept bringing her bikinis, which were ridiculously skimpy, she turned them down.

"I want board shorts and a top that will cover my abdomen. I'm going surfing," Flo said.

The shop assistant frowned. "But this would look cute on you."

"Maybe, but, please, I just want board shorts and a top. It's only April. It's cold still."

The shop assistant sighed and went off to dig some out. Nate had disappeared next door into the store that catered to men and where he could rent a couple of surfboards for them. Hopefully he wasn't waiting for her.

"Oh, make sure it's not yellow. I heard that color attracts sharks."

"Oh, yeah," the shop assistant said, coming back with what looked like a one-piece wet suit. "Yum-yum yellow they call it on the Gold Coast in Australia. I learned that when I was studying over there."

Flo nodded. "Yeah, I definitely don't want to attract a shark."

"Well, this is a one-piece that is really popular with people who are looking for something more modest."

"I'll take it." Flo paid for it. "Can I wear it out?"

"Sure. The change rooms are in the back." The shop assistant handed her the bill. "Have fun."

"Thanks." Flo headed to the back of the store and quickly changed into the wetsuit. It was comfortable and most importantly it covered her scar. She packed her clothes in her bag and hurried outside to find Nate.

He was waiting beside his car, with two boards beside him and in a wetsuit, like her. Even though the wetsuit covered his gorgeous, muscular chest, it was tight in all the right places. He certainly filled it out well. Her cheeks heated and she tried not to think about the way he looked.

At least the scrubs at the hospital were loose on him. Shapeless.

Who was she kidding? He looked good in everything. It was almost criminal.

He smiled when she walked over to him. "Good choice, it's a bit chilly. It's only April after all."

"That's exactly why I picked it."

Liar.

She never really did think about the water being cold. Los Angeles was always warm and sometimes darned hot, but she didn't think about the water too much.

"You ready to go?" he asked.

"Just have to toss this in your trunk."

Nate opened the trunk and locked their stuff away, but pulled out a couple of towels.

"What're you going to do with your car keys?"

"My car is a classic. It was before computerized fobs." He pinned it to his wetsuit. "See no problem. Which board do you want?"

"As long as it's not yellow, I don't care."

Nate looked at her like she'd lost her mind. "You have an aversion to yellow?"

"Sharks like yellow."

"Who told you that?"

"I read something about it once. The shop assistant knew it, too."

Nate snorted and handed her a board that thankfully had no yellow on it. "Let's go then, you nut."

Flo stuck out her tongue and then jogged past him, the hot sand squishing through her toes as they headed toward the water. Thankfully there weren't many people out and about, so she wouldn't feel like such an idiot when she did a face plant or something.

She stood at the edge. The water was cold and lapped at her toes like it was taunting her. Nate set down his board and then knelt in front of her, his hands going around one of her ankles briefly.

"What're you doing?" she asked, startled.

"Proposing."

"What?"

"I'm adjusting your leash. The leg rope will keep your surfboard from being swept away if you fall, and you will fall."

"Thanks for the encouragement." She picked up her board.

"Have you ever surfed?" Nate asked as he wrapped the leash around his own ankle.

"No."

"Then you're going to fall. I haven't surfed in ages so I'll probably fall, too."

"I hope you do." And to prove her point she kicked some water at him.

"Hey!" He splashed her back, soaking her.

When she wiped the water from her eyes, he was already wading out into the water toward the swells.

What am I doing? What am I doing?

Yeah, she'd made a bucket list, but she hadn't done much about the bucket list. Though she had always had the intention of doing some of the stuff on it, her schooling and then her job had gotten in the way.

Maybe fear. Maybe Mom and Dad had been right. Maybe I shouldn't do this.

No. She wasn't going to chicken out. She'd spent her whole life being so protected and sheltered that she'd felt like she hadn't even really had a childhood. That's why she'd made the bucket list. She didn't know when her transplanted kidney might give up, but she had to *live*.

With determination she picked up her board and waded into the cold water after Nate, until she was beside him in waist-deep water.

"Glad you could join me." He smiled, that warm, charming smile that melted her heart.

"Let's do this. Show me how."

He nodded. "Okay, climb on your board. We're going to paddle out and then you're going to have to lift yourself up as fast as you can to ride the swell. Do you think you can do that?"

"I'll certainly give it a try." Flo took a deep breath and climbed on her surfboard, lying flat just like Nate.

She followed his lead, paddling out towards the swells. Thankfully they were small. She watched as Nate headed toward a larger one and, paddling faster, he leapt up with seeming ease and balanced as he rode the wave past her and toward the shore, before losing his balance and falling into the water.

Flo took a deep breath and aimed her sights on the next one. She did exactly what Nate had, paddling faster, and then tried to stand, only she couldn't. It felt like a ton of bricks was on her, and she got halfway up before the wave knocked her off her board into the water.

She surfaced, spitting water out of her mouth and rubbing it out of her eyes as she clung to her surfboard, which was now upside down.

Nate paddled toward her. "Good try. You almost got vertical there."

Flo groaned. "That was harder than I thought."

"I told you it's difficult. Do you want to stop?"

She grinned. "Not a chance."

They continued surfing until the sun began to set and she was absolutely exhausted, but that last time she stood on the board, albeit shakily, and rode the wave almost to shore, falling off in waist-deep water where Nate was waiting for her.

They picked up their boards and slowly carried them up the beach to where they'd left their towels. Flo sank down into the sand, using the towel to wipe the water

from her face. Nate knelt down beside her, his blond hair plastered to his face, but it quickly began to curl in the warm breeze. He undid the leash on her leg.

"Thanks. My legs feel like Jell-O," Flo said. All she wanted to do was sink into the warm sand and sleep.

"You were awesome." He smiled up at her, making her heart skip a beat. "Better than Serena the first time I showed her."

Then his expression changed to something unreadable.

"Thanks." She could feel the blush creep up her neck. "Who was Serena?"

"A friend. She passed away."

"Was this the friend who was waiting for the organs?"

He nodded curtly. "Yeah, she's the one who lived dangerously, until she couldn't."

"Sounds like she lived life to the fullest."

"Yeah," he snorted. Something had changed. A moment ago he'd been relaxed and having fun with Flo, teaching her how to surf, and then something had changed when he'd started talking about Serena and her death. She couldn't help but wonder if Serena had been more than a friend, and that thought made her feel a bit jealous, when she really had no right to be jealous about who he had been with in the past.

If he'd even been with her.

Nate's past paramours, living or dead, weren't any of her business, as long as it didn't interfere with the facade that they were dating and had been dating for some time. That was the extent of her relationship with Nate, beyond a professional one, and she had to keep reminding herself of the fact. Though it was hard to when she found herself enjoying her time spent with him. She wanted to get to know him more.

"Well, thank you for taking me out there and teaching

me how to surf. Albeit badly. I really had fun," she said, trying to defuse the tension that had fallen between them.

"I'll take these back to the rental place and I'll be right back. Just wait here." He picked up his towel and dried off his face and hair, before picking up both boards with ease and walking back to the shop.

Flo let out a sigh of contentment and watched the sun set below the line of the ocean. The sky was full of brilliant oranges and reds. It was so nice out here and for one moment she forgot everything. She closed her eyes and listened to the waves lapping against the shore. It was calming. It made her think back to that one summer her family had spent on Whidbey Island and a particularly sunny day in the Pacific northwest. It had been one of the happiest moments of her life.

One stolen moment from her childhood that her family had had. They'd had fun and had forgotten that she'd been so sick. It was like they had just been a regular family. Not a family constantly going from the hospital to work, to home. She opened her eyes to see the sun had set completely. She hadn't realized how long they'd been surfing and her stomach growled in hunger.

"Bring your towel, Flo, and we'll rinse the salt water off."

Flo turned around and saw Nate. Her breath caught in her throat at the sight of him. He'd unzipped his wetsuit and bared his muscular chest, his wetsuit hanging around his slender waist. The afterglow of the sunset made his tanned skin glow like he was a bronzed god.

Think about something else. Quick.

Only she couldn't.

"Okay," she said, hoping there wasn't a tremble in her voice. She grabbed her towel and followed him to the showers against the surf shop where he'd rented the

boards from. He pulled the cord and fresh water started raining down; she just watched him, mesmerized.

She shook off all the naughty thoughts that were going through her head and pulled the cord on the shower next to him, but nothing happened.

"It's not working?" he asked.

"Apparently not," she said, trying not to look at him. "I'll just wait until you're done."

"Don't be silly." And before she could say no he was pulling her under the water with him, their bodies close together. He ran his large strong hands over her, rinsing the sticky salt water from her body. Then he undid her ponytail, running his fingers through her hair, and she was frozen.

Her pulse roared through her body as he touched her.

No one had ever touched her like that.

No one else had run their fingers through her hair.

Then his hands came around and cupped her face, forcing her to look up at him. She realized how much he towered over her. His expression was unreadable but intense. It felt like time was standing still as she gazed up into his deep blue eyes. The water had shut off and the encroaching darkness caused the droplets of water in his hair to sparkle.

Kiss me.

Only she couldn't let him do that. It wouldn't be right, no matter how much she wanted another kiss, because she knew that kiss would lead to something more.

And she wanted that something more.

She wanted that night of passion.

Desperately. But it wouldn't be a smart move.

She broke the connection and stepped out of the shower, wringing her hair out. "That was great."

Nate cleared his throat. "Yeah, that was fun. I should take you home."

"That would be good." She picked up her towel and slipped on her flip-flops.

Nate did the same, wrapping the towel around his neck, but as they walked back to his car he took her hand. It sent a shiver of delight through her.

"What're you doing?" she asked.

"There's paparazzi here," he said in an undertone. "It's why I brought you into the shower with me."

And then she saw them out of the corner of her eye.

The shower had all been an act. The connection she'd thought they had hadn't existed. And even though it was for the best, it hurt all the same.

CHAPTER TEN

"NOW, THERE'S THE hot doctor the whole entertainment world is talking about this morning!"

Nate shook his head as he walked into Kyle's room at The Hollywood Hills Clinic. Kyle was looking worse and the left ventricular assist device was starting to take its toll on him faster than Nate liked. Now Kyle sported a nose cannula and was on extra oxygen support twenty-four hours a day.

"I can't say that I'm flattered that you're calling me a hot doctor, Kyle."

Kyle snorted. "Please. As if. It's in the papers."

"What?"

Kyle tossed a trashy magazine at him and Nate picked it up to see pictures of him and Flo surfing. The caption said: *Kyle Francis's Doctors Get Hot and Heavy.*

And the caption wasn't wrong. He tried to tell himself that he'd pulled Flo under the same shower as him because he had seen paparazzi taking pictures of them. He'd done it as a stunt, but then, when she'd been so close to him, she'd aroused him.

She'd burned his very soul.

Before he'd known what he was doing, he'd been undoing her ponytail and running his fingers through her hair. He'd wanted to kiss her. Badly. But that would have

been very bad, because if he'd acted on his impulse he wouldn't have been able to stop himself from making love to her right then and there.

He didn't like this loss of control. If he lost control, well, he didn't want to think about it. That carefree risk-taker he'd once been was long gone.

"She's really sexy," Kyle said, interrupting his thoughts. "You're a lucky guy. She's smart, too."

"Thanks," Nate muttered, suddenly feeling very jealous that a man like Kyle was calling Flo sexy.

So? She's not yours.

He shook those possessive thoughts away. "I came to check on how you're doing."

"How I'm doing?" Kyle asked. "Seriously?"

"Kyle, you've got to hang on. I know it's tiring…"

Kyle sighed loudly. "You know it's tiring? Do you? Have you ever waited for an organ?"

"Technically, yes. I've been waiting for yours for some time."

Kyle rolled his eyes and chuckled. "I guess you have. I'm trying my best, Doc. I'm trying."

Nate squeezed his shoulder. "I know you are."

"So what're you up to tonight?"

"Are you asking me on a date, Mr. Francis?" Nate teased.

"As if. Well, I guess sort of. You going to visit me tonight and keep me company?"

"I can't," Nate said. "Dr. Chiu and I are heading out to a gala tonight. I have to go rent a tux."

"Rent?" Kyle asked, horrified.

"Yes. I don't have my tuxedo with me. I wasn't prepared to attend any big parties out here."

"Pass me my cell, Doc."

Nate picked up the phone and handed it to Kyle. Kyle punched in a number.

"Hey, Martin. It's Kyle. Yeah, I'm good, man. Look, I need a favor. My doctor needs a tuxedo for tonight. He's about my size. I know I have something in my wardrobe. Can you bring a few of my choice ones from the last couple of award shows and we'll get him fitted. Great. Thanks, man." Kyle ended the call. "All taken care of, Doc."

"Who was that?"

"My personal assistant, Martin. Look, I never wear the same tuxedo to an award show or movie premiere twice. Usually at the end of the year I just donate them or give them to charitable auctions. They just sit there. I want you to have one."

"Thanks, Kyle. I really appreciate that."

"No problem. I'll have a nurse page you when Martin gets here and you can do a dying man one wish and show me which one you pick. Also, I would really like to see a picture of Dr. Chiu all dressed up."

"Yeah, that's never going happen, dude."

Nate turned to see Flo walk into the suite. She was smiling warmly at Kyle. "How are you today?"

"Dying apparently," Nate said.

Flo crossed her arms. "Kyle, we'll find you organs."

"I know, but can't I just milk that a little bit?" Then he flashed her that smile that melted the hearts of women everywhere. "Don't you have pity for me, Dr. Chiu? Just a bit?"

She rolled her eyes. "No one gets to milk anything around here. Haven't you heard the nurses refer to me as the difficult surgeon? I'm hard as nails."

"Somehow I don't believe that," Kyle said, grinning at the both of them.

Flo checked his vitals. "Well, Dr. King will see you

later and maybe if you're good I'll swing by in my dress. I'm getting ready here because the clinic is providing limos for everyone. So I'll take advantage of the free ride."

"Smart move." Kyle lay back down, looking exhausted.

"Get some sleep," Nate said. "I'll see you later."

He and Flo walked out of Kyle's suite and Nate shut the door.

"What do you think, Dr. King?"

"I think he needs organs sooner rather than later. He's not doing as well on the left ventricular assist device as I would've hoped."

She jammed her hands in the pocket of her lab coat. "I know. The LVAD gave his heart more time, but it's putting pressure on his lungs. They're deteriorating fast. I don't want to intubate him, his other organs wouldn't handle it for long. His chance for compartment syndrome and multi-system organ failure is high. Higher than I'd like."

Nate sighed.

Dammit.

Kyle was a nice guy. He may have been a world-famous superstar actor, but he was also a decent human being. He was in his mid-forties. That was too young to die all because he was on a waiting list.

Waiting.

Yet that's what had happened to Serena. Her injuries had been so extensive the only thing that might've saved her had been a new heart, but one hadn't become available, because she'd been so injured that the chances of her surviving a heart transplant had been low.

Then she'd gone into multi-system organ failure and she had gone before he'd even had time to process it all.

"You're thinking of your friend?" Flo asked gently.

"Why would you assume that?"

"Your expression. I may not have picked up my dad's flair for talking to a bunch of businesspeople, but I did pick up his knack for reading others."

Nate sighed. "You're right. I was thinking about her. Kyle's situation reminds me a bit of hers. I hate seeing Kyle suffer. I hate seeing him wait and slowly die when I know what the solution is. I could save him, but I'm missing two key ingredients."

"I know. Me, too. It's difficult waiting and feeling so helpless."

"Yes, helpless. I don't like that feeling very much."

"At least we can save one life tomorrow evening," Flo said.

"Eva?"

Flo nodded. "Everything is green lighted. It's time, and Ms. Martinez is ready and everything has been cross-checked. We're going to do the operation tomorrow night, because of Ms. Martinez's insurance."

"Okay. How is Eva doing?" he asked.

"She's good. She's scared and rightfully so, but I'm confident about this surgery. I did another MRI on Ms. Martinez, just to be on the safe side, and her kidneys are fine. I suggest you take the left kidney over the right."

"Sounds good."

Flo glanced at her watch. "I'd better run. Have some more rounding to do before the gala tonight. Shall we meet back up at Kyle's suite before we head down to the limo?"

"I thought you said to him, 'That's never going to happen, dude.' Changing your mind and wanting to impress the Hollywood actor?"

She laughed. "No, just letting him milk his situation a bit more."

Nate chuckled. "Okay. I'll see you here at four. That gives Kyle time to give us his best pointers for the gala."

She nodded as she walked backwards down the hall. "Right."

Nate ran his hand through his hair and headed back to the research library. He needed some time by himself, to collect himself before this gala. He was going to need all his wits about him to survive this and he certainly wasn't looking forward to wearing Kyle's tuxedo or trying on a bunch of tuxedos in front of him.

That wasn't his thing, but it was better than a rental.

At least now he didn't have to leave the hospital.

"I think that's the one, Martin. What do you think?"

Nate adjusted the cuff links and straightened the sleeve of the designer tuxedo Kyle had given him.

"I think so," Martin said. "It's the best fit. That's the one you wore last year."

Nate cocked an eyebrow. "Did you win an award in this one?"

"I did." Kyle chuckled and then waggled his eyebrows suggestively. "So it's a lucky tuxedo, too, if you catch my drift."

"I've been treating you for three years, Kyle. I *always* catch your drift." He glanced in the mirror in Kyle's luxurious private bathroom and straightened his bow tie.

Yeah, he could do this. He was uncomfortable, but it was just one night. He'd seen Flo dressed up before and this would be no different.

"Your date is here," Kyle called out.

Nate stepped out of the bathroom and then stopped in his tracks. He was not prepared for the visual assault to the senses that was waiting for him. He'd prepared him-

self to see Flo in a dress, but he hadn't quite prepared himself for this.

To have his breath completely and utterly taken away by her.

She looked a bit uncomfortable, standing in Kyle's suite. Her black hair swept up and off to the side, but it was the dress that caught his attention as his gaze hungrily devoured every inch of her.

Her dress was gray and flowing, with burn-out lace over top of it. The bodice was sheer with the lace strategically placed over her firm breasts. She spun around and her back was bare.

"What do you think, Doc?" Kyle asked.

Nate only briefly glanced at Kyle, who was grinning from ear to ear like a Cheshire cat. Normally Kyle's smugness about Flo would've bothered him, but he didn't care about Kyle or Martin or anyone else in the room.

He only had eyes for Flo.

And he knew at that moment he was a lost man.

Flo was shaking like a leaf; she only hoped that Nate didn't notice how nervous she was. She wasn't sure about the dress, but Freya had been the one to help her pick it out. She'd never worn anything so revealing before in her life.

She'd never gone to prom, so she'd never really dressed up.

Not that her parents would've approved if she had been asked by someone to go to prom. So this was her first real time getting dressed up to the nines.

Nate also made her nervous, because when he'd stepped out of that bathroom she hadn't been quite expecting a tuxedo or how *good* he looked. She'd seen him in a suit

before, but there was just something about a designer tuxedo that made her heart beat a little bit faster.

"Well, what do you think?" she asked. "Is it too much for the event?"

"No. Not too much," Nate said. He walked over to her and took her hand in his, causing a shiver of anticipation to race through her. "It's perfect. You look…stunning." He brought her hand up to his lips, placing a kiss against her knuckles, which made her blood ignite in flames. She knew from that moment she was doomed.

"Thank you," she whispered, finally finding her voice.

Nate took her arm. "Shall we?"

"Okay," she answered, feeling like everything she was saying sounded dumb.

"Have fun, you two!" Kyle called after them. "If I wasn't laid up in this bed, Doc, you know I'd be stealing Dr. Chiu from you, so you'd better—"

Flo didn't know what Kyle was going to say as the door shut behind them. Nate was grinning and she couldn't help but laugh.

As they headed to the front, where a fleet of limos was waiting for those who were going to the gala, Flo caught sight of Freya, James and Mila standing there, waiting for Flo and Nate to arrive.

Freya covered her smile with her hand, her eyes gleaming with pride. She moved her hand and mouthed, "You look beautiful," to Flo. Even James was looking at her appreciatively.

Nate led Flo outside. They had their own private limo—the surgical dream team heading to the big gala that would raise money for the Bright Hope Clinic and many more transplant surgeries.

So it was only fitting that Flo and Nate arrived separately from the other people from The Hollywood Hills

and Bright Hope clinics, and that made Flo feel like a bit like a Hollywood starlet.

The chauffeur opened the door and Nate helped Flo climb into the back. She adjusted her skirt and Nate climbed in beside her. The door shut and they were alone, except for the chauffeur behind the privacy screen.

Nate reached down and picked up her hand, holding it, his thumb circling the pulse point on her wrist, making her catch her breath just a bit.

"Kyle has good taste in tuxedos," she managed to say finally.

Nate glanced down and ran his free hand over his lapels. "Yeah, well, this is designer and apparently this is the tuxedo he won an award in last year."

Flo gasped. "You mean for *It's an Honest Truth*?"

"I guess so. I haven't seen that movie. Have you?"

"I have. It's a beautiful movie about the underground railroad. It made me bawl like a baby."

"I'll have to watch that," Nate said.

"Maybe we can watch it together later."

He grinned. "Maybe another day. Tonight I don't plan to watch much television. We do need to get a good night's rest for Eva's surgery tomorrow."

Flo nodded. "You're right."

For one moment she thought he was suggesting something else and she held her breath, but then again why would he? This was all an act. He'd made that clear the other night at the beach. But if he wanted to make love to her, she wouldn't stop him.

Act or not, for once she wanted to taste that forbidden passion. She wanted to know what it was like to take a man in her arms and feel that moment of connection. She wanted to experience what it was like to make love to a man. And she hoped they'd still be able to have that after

she told him and everyone else how important transplant surgery was to her.

Nate had lost a loved one. He'd understand.

Flo couldn't hold it in any more. If she was going to give herself to Nate there would be no way to hide her scar. She had to be brave. She had to tell him that she was the recipient of a donor kidney. She'd almost died waiting and that was why she wanted to live life to the fullest.

It was time to be brave.

Nate was not Johnny.

She could do this. The bucket list was nothing if she continued to hide and not act boldly. Taking risks and doing some crazy things were one thing, but how could she be true to herself if she was terrified to keep hidden a part of her that she was proud of?

That was no way to live any more.

And Flo wanted to live. She wanted to feel.

And have a man make love to her. She couldn't think of a better person than Nate. She trusted him, she'd grown to like him, and even though nothing would ever come of their one night together, she could have that stolen time.

They didn't say much else to each other. The drive to the iconic Beverly Hills Hotel was brief. Soon the chauffeur was opening the door to a red carpet. There were flashes from cameras as Nate helped Flo out.

The investors and The Hollywood Hills Clinic had gone all out, making it a red-carpet event. The whole hotel had been rented for the night. Freya had told her that everyone would have a room, so no one would have to drink and drive.

Of course, that wouldn't be an issue for Flo. She didn't drink. She couldn't because of her transplant. Alcohol would be destructive for her kidneys and that was one

thing she didn't mind missing. She had no desire to experience it.

Still, she might stay at the hotel, because when else would she be able to experience the opulence of old Hollywood by staying at a Los Angeles icon?

Nate placed his hand on the small of her back. This time, though, her back was bare and the brush of his hand on her skin made her gasp slightly. It burned even though it was hot out, but it burned in a different way. A way that made her body flush and tremble. He ushered her past the throng of press to the staging area, where couples were able to pose for their picture to be taken in front of a wall of sponsors' names.

Flo smiled as Nate put his arm around her and they posed for the camera. The surgical dream team. A force to be reckoned with.

Once their photo had been taken they were ushered into the hotel and led to the ballroom. When they entered it took Flo's breath away. On the ceiling there was a chandelier made of thousands of white flowers and twinkling lights.

There were flowers everywhere. White and sparkle lights filled up the ballroom. It was the most elegant thing she'd ever seen. They were shown to their table and took a seat with their investors.

The dinner was sumptuous, but all she could focus on was being in this amazing place with Nate by her side. He often took her hand. Champagne was poured, but she kept to water, even though there were a few curious glances. But she didn't care, because in a few moments she was going to get up there and ask a ballroom full of the rich and famous to give money to their charity and implore people to donate their organs, and she was going to tell them all why.

She was tired of hiding her kidney transplant. She never had before a man she'd loved had run from her because of it.

So Nate would soon know and she was okay with that. He was leaving anyway, but she couldn't hide it any more. He needed to know.

She wanted him to know, because maybe if then they connected in some way deeper than that moment she gave herself to him, it would mean so much more.

"Thank you all for coming here tonight," Freya said, getting the attention of everyone. "The Hollywood Hills Clinic is pleased to team up with the Bright Hope Clinic. It is our hope to continue to help this fantastic organization bring health care to those less fortunate."

There was a round of applause.

"Our first transplant operation with the Bright Hope Clinic is to help an underprivileged girl receive a new kidney, and to talk more about organ donation I am very pleased to introduce The Hollywood Hills' chief transplant surgeon, Dr. Florence Chiu."

Flo took a deep breath and stood up, making her way through the tables toward the stage. Freya stepped down and Flo was alone up there. The lights blinded her from those in the audience, but in the crowd she only saw one face. She focused on one person.

Nate.

"Hello, I'm Dr. Florence Chiu and I run the transplant surgery team at The Hollywood Hills Clinic. I'm also an organ recipient." Her breath was shaking and tears were threatening to spill down her cheeks, because it had been so long since she'd uttered those words without fear of retribution or even her own fear of admitting that her time was limited.

"I was born prematurely, and because of that I always

had health struggles. But when I was ten I collapsed and the doctors discovered my one functioning kidney was failing. I underwent years of dialysis as I sat on a waiting list. I had a couple of my own close calls, thinking that I was about to get a viable organ, only to find out that either the cross-match was negative or the organ wasn't viable.

"When I was fourteen, while I was lying in a hospital bed in Seattle, my time was almost up when my surgeon got a call from UNOS. A young man had died during a car accident, but he was an organ donor and his cross-match was almost perfect with me.

"Because of that young man filling out his donor card I'm here today, imploring you all to do the same. Because of him, I'm alive. I've been given a second chance and I chose to become a surgeon and help others like me. Like Eva. Medical professionals work hard to save lives, but you can save countless lives by donating your organs after your death. Also please think about donating financially to the Bright Hope Clinic and the amazing research that's being done in the name of transplant surgery. Hopefully one day donors won't be needed and lives can be spared while on the waiting list. Thank you for your time and enjoy your evening."

It was silent for only a moment, but then there was thunderous applause and a standing ovation, which made her cry, just for a moment.

She glanced over at Nate and he was standing, a smile on his face as he applauded her. There wasn't a sign of him feeling uncomfortable, or of him leaving because her future was so uncertain. He was still there and nodding his head in agreement.

He wasn't leaving and, best of all, he didn't look at her with pity.

There was no pity there.

She walked off the stage and shook hands with Freya, Mila and James, and then stood in front of Nate. He took her hand and kissed it again. Music started, because the dinner was over, and people began to drift out onto the dance floor.

Nate didn't say anything to her as he led her out to join them. People clapped as he spun her round and then pulled her close against him, his hand on her back.

Her knees were knocking together as she danced with him. So close to him. Her pulse raced and their gazes locked. The rest of the room was a blur to her, her only focus Nate.

All she saw was him. And she prayed her admission didn't drive him away.

"So that's why you don't drink."

She nodded. "That's why."

"Why didn't you say anything before?"

"Because I didn't want your pity."

"I don't pity you. There's only admiration here. I admire you," he whispered against her neck, making her body quiver with desire and relief. He was the first man who hadn't pitied her. Everyone pitied her.

Flo tried to swallow the lump in her throat, tears welling in her eyes. She didn't want to cry. Not now.

"Thank you," she said, finding her voice again.

"You make sense to me now," Nate said. "Before, you were so hard to figure out, but now... I get why you were so frustrated when Kyle's organs weren't viable. You've been there."

"I have."

He nodded. "You share my pain. Though it was a loved one I lost. I didn't almost lose my life."

"You still lost."

"I don't feel like I've lost at this moment," he whispered. "Being here with you, I feel...I feel like my old self again."

Her heart raced, adrenaline and desire coursing through her. If she didn't do this now, she might never do it. "I don't want to talk about that right now." And before he could say anything else she kissed him, but this was more than the featherlight butterfly kiss that she'd stolen from him when they'd been outside his hotel.

This was more.

This kiss was an invitation for him to take her, because what she wanted more than anything was to be with him. She wanted him to make her forget about her transplant, make her forget that she'd spent so many years sick and sitting on the sidelines.

Right now, she wanted to live.

He resisted at first, but only for a second, then his mouth opened against hers. His arms went around her, lifting her up on tiptoe as he deepened the kiss. His hands were hot on her bare back, holding her tight against him.

She'd never wanted someone as badly as she did Nate.

The kiss ended and she could barely catch her breath, her body quivering with desire. He rested his forehead against hers.

"Flo," he whispered.

"No, don't say anything." She took his hand and led him off the dance floor. No one was paying attention to them any more as people mingled, drank, danced and bid on the silent auction items. It was a perfect moment to lead him out of the ballroom to the elevators. She pulled the card she'd been given out of her wristlet and swiped it to summon the elevator.

Nate took her in his arms again and kissed her, pressing her against the wall next to the bank of elevators,

grinding his hips against her, letting her know exactly just how much he wanted her. And the fact that he wanted her that much made her feel faint.

He wanted her, just as much as she wanted him. If they weren't wearing so many clothes, if they weren't in a public place, she would have had him right here and now, but she wanted this to be slow. She wanted to savor this time, because this wasn't permanent.

It couldn't be permanent because of her medical issue.

So she was going to enjoy this moment. They got on the elevator and her pulse was racing as they rode up to where her room was.

This was really going to happen.

The elevator dinged and she pulled him out into the hallway. She was nervous as she led the way to her room. She opened the door and flicked on the light, just one. The door shut behind them and she was suddenly very aware of him so close to her.

A tingle of anticipation ran through her.

"Florence," he whispered, using her full name.

"Nathaniel." And that was all she had to say and she was in his arms again. Kissing him. No words were needed, because she knew they both wanted the same thing. She stood in front of the bed and he was behind her, undoing the clasp on the back of her gown, the small piece of sheer fabric that held her dress up at her neck and the hook at her waist.

Once the dress was undone, he ran his hands slowly over her shoulders, pushing the dress down and off.

"So beautiful," he murmured, pressing a kiss on her shoulder. His hands skimmed over her again, and he drew the dress down over her hips so that she was standing in a pool of fabric, wearing only her slip and heels. She hadn't worn a bra because her dress had been sheer.

She was vulnerable to him and that would've scared her before, but suddenly it wasn't scary for her. It was all too real.

And she wanted it. She pulled off her slip.

He gently turned her around and her hands instinctively went to the scar on her lower abdomen, but he grabbed her wrists and held them, stopping her from covering up the scar, like she'd done before. Like she'd been used to doing. She'd thought it was so hideous, a blatant reminder to the world of her weakness. That she'd been sick, that she wasn't perfect. Then again, who was perfect?

"You don't need to hide it from me." He dropped to his knees and placed a kiss against the scar, catching her off guard. "This is part of you. This is what makes you strong."

And when he said those words a tear did escape her eye and roll down her face. No man had ever made her feel so beautiful, so wanted as Nate did right now. He stood back up and held her close in his arms. He brushed the tear from her face with his thumb.

"Don't cry."

"I usually don't, but I can't help myself around you."

"You're strong. Stronger than I thought."

He kissed her again. It was urgent against her lips as he drew her body tight against his. She began to undress him, because there was no turning back for her. First she peeled off his tuxedo jacket, then worked on the bow tie so she could get to his shirt buttons. She wanted them open so she could feel his skin and run her hands over his chest.

He took her hands and held them in his own and then kissed her again. A kiss that seared her down to her very soul. Their bodies pressed together and warmth spread

through her veins, then his lips moved from her mouth down her body to her breasts.

She gasped in surprise at the sensation of his tongue on her nipple. Her body arched against his mouth and the pleasure it brought her. She'd never experienced anything like this before. Even though she was a virgin, she'd made out with a man before and it had never fired her senses so.

"I want you, so much," she said, and she was surprised that she'd said the words out loud, but it was the truth. She started to pull him toward the bed.

"Whoa, wait. I don't have protection," he whispered against her neck. "I didn't even think about it with you kissing me like that. I want you, Flo. I just never expected this."

Flo glanced at the jacket she had tossed away, cursing herself for not being prepared either, and then she saw foil from a strip of condoms sticking out from the breast pocket.

"What about those?"

Nate glanced over his shoulder and then shook his head. "Kyle. This is his tuxedo."

"I don't think he'll mind." Flo grinned.

"I don't care if he does. I wasn't going to ever ask him. I'm just going to take what I want." He scooped her up in his arms and carried her to the bed, laying her down and moving over her. She ran her hands over his partly exposed chest.

He sat up and whipped off his shirt. All that was between them now was his trousers and her underwear. Just scraps of fabric.

"There's something else I need to tell you," Flo whispered as he nibbled on her neck. "I'm a virgin."

He froze and she was worried that her virginity would be the deal-breaker. It wouldn't be the iffy future because

of the donated kidney, it would be because he didn't want to deflower a thirty-something virgin.

"How can that be?" he asked in disbelief.

She blushed, embarrassed to tell him this, but she hadn't wanted to spring it on him. He'd have found out soon enough. "Do you want to leave?"

"No, I just don't understand how someone as beautiful and sexy as you still is a virgin."

"It takes a lot for me to trust anyone with my past. I'm glad I shared it with you and that I waited."

He kissed her and she was lost, melting into him. "I'll be gentle."

Flo sighed and he moved off the bed. She watched him undress, her pulse racing as she drank in the sight of him naked. This was finally going to happen and she was more than ready.

Nate came back to her and slipped off her underwear before holding her tight against him. She trembled and he kissed her.

"Don't be nervous."

"I'm not."

He stroked her cheek and kissed her again, his hand trailing down over her abdomen and then lower. Touching her intimately. Her body thrummed with desire. She arched her body against his fingers, craving more. Wanting him. Nate moved his hand, pinning her to the bed as he shifted his weight.

"Do you want me, Flo?" he asked some time later, his voice hoarse.

"I do."

Their gazes locked as he entered her. She winced, but the pain was brief compared to all the procedures she'd gone through in her life.

"I'm sorry," he whispered.

"I'm not." She kissed him and he began to move gently. Slowly. He was taking his time. She wrapped her arms around him to hold him close as he made love to her. He kissed her again and then trailed his kisses down her neck to her collar bone. It made her body arch and she wanted more of him. She wanted him deeper and she wrapped her legs around his waist, begging him to stay close.

Her body felt alive. She had never thought a feeling like this would be possible. She had never thought that she would ever get to experience it. She'd hoped one day to, but the one man she had truly cared about had run from her when he'd found out about her past, and she wasn't the type of girl to hand over her first time to a random stranger.

Even though her relationship with Nate was not real and he'd leave once Kyle was gone, she was glad to have her first time with him. She trusted him.

Maybe love?

She shook that thought away. There was no room in her life for love.

There was just this moment.

She wanted to savor it. He quickened his pace and she came, crying out as the heady pleasure flooded through her veins. Nate soon followed and then rolled away, pulling her with him.

Flo rested her head against his chest, listening to his heart race.

Savoring her stolen moments.

CHAPTER ELEVEN

NATE FELL ASLEEP next to Flo. He hadn't intended to spend the night. He hadn't spent the night with anyone since Serena, and for one moment he had forgotten how *good* it felt to be with someone again. To spend the night next to someone, listening to them breathe.

Knowing that they were alive and not a ghost, haunting him.

He propped himself on one elbow to watch her sleep. A little crack of sunlight peeked through the drapes and a light warm breeze was blowing in through the sliding glass doors, but she was oblivious to all of it.

She was so beautiful with her ebony hair fanned out on the pillow, her plump lips pressed together in a pout and her delicate hands folded together on top of her chest. A strand of her silky hair curled around a pink nipple and he had to tear his gaze away from her, because he wanted her again.

It took all of his willpower not to wake her up and take her in his arms again, but he couldn't do that. He'd had a moment of weakness and that was all. There couldn't be any more. No matter how much he wanted it. Memories of being buried in her, wrapped in her arms, were still fresh in his mind. The feel of her tender, soft lips against

his, her nails down his back and her legs around his waist as he'd thrust into her fired his blood more.

Flo stirred and then opened her eyes to look at him, a blush creeping into her cheeks. "Good morning."

"Good morning," he replied. "I hope I didn't wake you."

"No. You didn't. I forgot you were there for a while. I didn't know where I was at first."

He chuckled. "You've already put me from your mind, then?"

"No, I just haven't slept that well in a long time." She stretched and rolled over on her side, tucking her arms under her head. "What time is it?"

Nate glanced over at the alarm clock behind him. "Six a.m. Early."

"Well, we did skip out on the gala early." Flo laughed softly. "Yes. I'm sure we'll get an earful when we get back to the clinic."

"Right. We'll have to head there soon. Today is the big day. Eva's transplant surgery."

Flo nodded. "It is."

"How are you feeling about it?" Nate asked.

"I'm feeling good."

He nodded. Everything about Flo impressed him, but it had all made perfect sense to him when she'd told the audience why they should become organ donors, why she didn't drink and why she understood her patients so well.

And why she felt every loss, why she connected with her patients so deeply. Then it occurred to him that she had a bucket list and had made several references to fleeting time.

"This bucket list of yours," he said.

"What about this bucket list of mine?" she asked.

"Why do you have it? Is it just for fun or something serious?"

"It's serious. I spent all my childhood on the sidelines due to overprotective parents who thought I might shatter at any moment. So I started compiling a list of all the things I wanted to do when I became an adult. I haven't done much because of schooling and work, but life is short. Failure rates are high. Who knows how much longer I have left?" Flo rolled over and began to pull on her clothes.

Who knows how much longer I have left?

"Flo, you realize that as you had your transplant at fourteen, you know you're doing quite well. You've come so far."

"I know," she said offhandedly as she put her long hair back in a ponytail. "Still, I do want to *live* while I have the chance."

"What else is on this bucket list? I know driving was on there."

She glanced over her shoulder at him. "You seriously want to know?"

"Sure."

"Well, you know about the mountain climbing, like Everest or walking the Annapurna trail. I would like to ride a motorcycle through Africa. Or swim with sharks."

"Hold up, you were terrified of sharks when we were surfing."

She chuckled. "I know, but this would be in a cage."

Nate sat there listening to her talk about all these dangerous things she wanted to do. Things that he'd done himself, so he knew for a fact how risky they were, and he couldn't figure out why she wanted to do these things. She'd been given a second chance, why would she risk throwing it all away by doing something dangerous?

"I also want to do some rock climbing and tackle El Capitan in Yosemite."

That caught his attention and caused his stomach to clench as the memory of Serena slipping out of his grasp as she'd fallen from the halfway point of El Capitan all those years ago. It made him sweat, made him sick to his stomach to think about Flo up there.

She could fall. She could die. Just like Serena had. And then what would he do? And the fact she evoked this feeling in him, these emotions scared him. Made him retreat further behind the careful walls he'd built for himself.

Walls that were there so he wouldn't get hurt again, because he never wanted to feel that kind of pain again.

El Capitan was too dangerous. Risking her life for all these foolish bucket-list ideas was too dangerous. Why did she have to do these things?

It's not your concern.

She was throwing it all away, but he couldn't tell her that because it wasn't his business. They weren't anything to each other. This whole relationship had just been an act to protect The Hollywood Hills Clinic.

Once everything was done with Kyle and Eva he'd go back to New York. That's where he belonged.

Besides, a fling with a colleague was probably on Flo's bucket list, he just didn't want to know that. It was better it was left this way.

Is it? She did give her virginity to you.

She had to get rid of it some time. He was just the one she'd chosen. He should've refused. He shouldn't have let her kiss him. He should've been stronger.

"Sounds like your bucket list is pretty sorted." He rolled out of bed and started to get dressed; he could feel Flo's gaze boring into him.

"Are you okay?" she asked.

"I'm fine. I just want to have a shower and go over some stuff before tonight." He zipped up his pants. "Maybe catch a nap. I didn't sleep much last night."

She laughed and then pulled on her dress from the night before. She had a change of clothes but she wanted to feel the fabric on her skin and to relive the memory of everything that had happened for just a little longer. "Can you help me with the back?"

"Sure." He took a deep breath, trying not to forget that she was off-limits to him. So he quickly did up the clasps that he had been more than happy to undo the night before. Once they were done up he took a step back, because he knew that if he didn't put distance between the two of them he was liable to fall back into that sweet trap again.

She turned around and touched his face. "Thank you again for last night. I'm glad it was you."

"I'm glad, too."

Are you?

"I hope you know that I don't expect anything. I don't—"

"I know," he said, cutting her off. "I appreciate it."

She didn't look convinced, but he didn't want to spend the day talking about this with her. He didn't have time for that.

What's done was done and he could move on.

Can you?

Flo walked back into the hospital. She'd gone home from the hotel, had taken a shower, a power nap and drunk a whole lot of coffee to get her up to fighting standard for Eva's big surgery this evening.

She wasn't going to let Eva down.

Flo was going to do everything in her power to make sure that this kidney stuck. That it wasn't rejected. Not that she had any power over that. Rejection happened,

but she was going to do her best to get Eva to fighting standard, as well.

As she walked to her office she caught sight of Nate, standing at a nursing station. He was typing something into one of the tablets and she could see a couple of the nurses eyeing him with admiration.

She couldn't blame them.

Just looking at him made her weak in the knees. Even more so now that she knew what was under those scrubs. She knew what he felt like and the memory of his lips on her skin, his body beneath her thighs, his hands in her hair made her blood heat and made her recall the pleasure he had made her feel.

Pleasure that she'd never thought was possible.

Her body responded to just the mere thought of him.

It scared her.

She was glad that Nate had been her first time. It's what she'd wanted and she kept telling herself that it was just a fling, nothing more. Yet the more she said it, the more ridiculous it sounded to her; the more she realized that being with him had probably been a huge mistake for her heart.

It was more than just a fling to her and that was terrifying.

Flo shook the little kernel of thought that there could be something more out of her head. They were just friends. Work colleagues. Both of them had always made that clear. There could never be any more.

If she tried to make it more than it was she'd get hurt. Hadn't she learned already that there was no room in her life for romance or any kind of emotional attachment beyond her immediate family?

Nate was all fine and dandy now with her kidney transplant, but he knew the facts. He knew that her time

was precarious. Eventually he'd leave for someone more stable.

So, no, there couldn't ever be any more between them.

Even if she secretly wished there could be.

She tore her gaze away from him and tried to make it to her office without being seen by anyone. She needed a few moments alone to regroup and prepare for Eva's surgery. There was a lot riding on it.

This was the first transplant surgery arranged between The Hollywood Hills Clinic and the Bright Hope Clinic. She knew there was some stuff from the past between the Rothsbergs and Mila Brightman, something about a wedding—Flo really didn't know. All she knew was she had to be on her top game.

This surgery meant a lot and the world would be watching.

She was well aware that the news of this surgery had reached far beyond Los Angeles, because the email from her father that morning and the countless text messages from her mother had let her know exactly how far the news had spread.

They weren't concerned about the surgery and whether or not she could pull it off. They wanted to know who Nate was and why she hadn't told them about her relationship with him. How could she lie to her parents? She'd never lied to them before. There was nothing to say about the relationship between her and Nate because there was nothing there.

Really?

There was something there, at least on her end, but she refused to admit it. She refused to give in to her emotions, because there was no place for them.

There was no place for love.

And putting a name to the emotions was out of the question.

She got to her office and sat down. The light on her phone was flashing and she had no doubt some of those messages had to be from her parents. The rest would be from various newspapers and magazines, wanting updates on Kyle's condition and her relationship with Nate. Flo had no time to deal with any of that.

She didn't want to deal with that.

Not today.

"I was wondering what time you were going to come in," Nate said as he barged into the office.

"I had a nap. You said I should nap."

"So I did." He set down the tablet he'd been carrying and sat down on the couch. "Are you ready for tonight?"

She nodded. "I think so. You?"

"I am. I did a few laps in the pool this morning after I got back to my place. I needed to take the edge off. I've done kidney surgeries countless times, but today… I don't know what it is but I feel a bit on edge about it. Like I'm under pressure."

"Yeah, I understand. I'm feeling the same way." Flo leaned back in her chair. "There's a lot riding on this."

Nate nodded. "Look, about last night…"

She shook her head. "I don't want to talk about last night. Not right now. I just want to keep my focus on Eva."

"Fair enough. Nothing from UNOS?"

"You mean about Kyle? No, nothing." Flo scrubbed her hand over her face. "Have you been to see him?"

"I have his recent labs here." Nate handed her the tablet. "It's not good."

Flo glanced at the vitals and the labs from first thing this morning to only an hour ago. Kyle's condition was deteriorating rapidly.

Blast.

"He needs organs."

Nate nodded. "He needed them yesterday. If it continues to climb this way he's going to go into multi-system organ failure and then there's nothing we can do. He'll die."

"Yeah, and the world will say we're responsible." Flo groaned. "What're we going to do?"

"There's nothing we can do. We just have to wait. It's the hardest part. We'll continue to draw blood, monitor his situation and just hope for the best."

"Have faith?" she asked.

"Yeah, that, too." He smiled at her. It was a kind and tender smile. It made her swoon. There were so many things she adored about him.

Stop thinking like that. Get a grip on yourself.

"It's hard to have faith. It's hard to sit here and wait for someone else to die so that our patient can go on living." It was the one thing she hated about the job.

"I know." There was a change in Nate's demeanor, as if he'd pulled away. He could barely look her in the eye. She didn't like that.

At least he's not pitying you, like everyone else.

"How are we going to attack this surgery? We've talked about our plan before, but never really firmed up details."

Nate nodded. "I think that I should retrieve it and you should reattach it."

"Have them in the same OR?" Flo asked. "We have an OR that is large enough and has been put on hold for me indefinitely."

"I think that's wise. Less travel time for the kidney. Less chance of contamination, and it minimizes the cold ischemic time or for something else to happen. This kidney is Eva's best shot."

Flo smiled. "Is it? And you're the one who wanted to wait for a deceased donor kidney."

"I know. You were right."

She grinned and leaned back. "Say it again."

Nate laughed and rolled his eyes. "You. Were. Right."

"I know."

"So does that plan work for you?" Nate asked.

"Yes. I'll let the surgical team know." Flo stood up. "For what it's worth, I'm glad you're going to be with me tonight. It's going to make the surgery so much easier having such a skilled transplant surgeon working with me."

"My pleasure," Nate said quietly.

She nodded and left her office quickly. If she stayed she might say a few other things that she wanted to say. Things that she wasn't sure she wanted to even admit to herself.

Like the fact that she was very close to falling in love with Nate.

Something she'd promised herself she wouldn't do when she'd slept with him, but that was easier said than done.

CHAPTER TWELVE

FLO STOOD AT the door to Eva's suite. The nurses were milling about, taking care of last-minute preparations on Eva. Eva looked absolutely terrified. Flo knew exactly how she was feeling and seeing the terror on Eva's face brought it all back afresh to her. At The Hollywood Hills Clinic she did a lot of transplant surgery and consultation on transplants. She'd even done a lot of kidney transplants with both deceased donors and living donors. But they had all been adults.

She hadn't worked on a child since her days as a resident and even then she hadn't done a kidney transplant on a child ever as a lead surgeon and not an assist. There were a few technical differences. Eva was twelve so it would be similar to doing the procedure on an adult, but, like Flo, Eva had been a preemie. Her vessels could be smaller, which meant Flo would have to try a different approach. She wouldn't know until she got in there and that was the maddening thing about surgery and the practice of medicine.

At least it was maddening for her.

Skill-wise, the surgery was the same. Ms. Martinez's kidney would be of adult size and the donor kidney would be placed in the same location as Flo's had been, the cradle of the pelvis. Technically, everything would go eas-

ily. Of that Flo had no doubt, but emotionally this was harder than she had ever imagined.

You need to talk to her.

Flo took a deep breath and headed toward Eva. The nurses finished up and left the room, and Flo took a seat on the edge of the child's bed.

"It's okay to be scared," she said.

Eva looked at her. "It is?"

"Of course, but I will tell you it will be okay. You'll feel better."

Eva shrugged. "How do you know it will be okay?"

Flo lifted up her scrub shirt. "See this scar?"

"Yeah."

"When I was fourteen I was the one in a hospital bed, waiting for a kidney."

Eva's eyes widened. "You?"

Flo nodded. "Me. Only my mom and dad weren't a match. I had to wait a long time. I almost didn't make it while I waited for someone special to give me a second chance. You're very lucky. Your mom was a match."

"I don't want my mom to get hurt."

Flo squeezed her hand. "She'll hurt for a while. You will, too, but it would hurt your mom far worse if she didn't do this and something happened to you."

Tears rolled down Eva's face and Flo hugged her. "It will be okay. You'll both heal and this will be behind you. Then I want you to do something for me."

"What?" Eva asked, wiping her eyes.

"I want you to live. Make a difference."

She smiled. "How?"

Flo shrugged. "That's up to you. I became a surgeon who helps people like us. Your future is up to you now, because you *have* a future, thanks to your mom."

"Dr. Chiu, we're ready to take Eva down now," a porter said from the door.

Flo nodded and then stood. "I'll see you in a bit and I'll see you on the other side. Just think, no more dialysis. You'll be able to play sports within reason, learn to drive. Go to dances."

Eva smiled. "That's a good thing."

Flo chuckled and walked out of the room and headed toward the OR floor. There were always risks associated with organ transplants. Always. The graft could fail, Eva's body could reject her mother's organ, but she had a good feeling about this surgery.

The allograft survival rate was high for those who got a living kidney compared to people like her who had received their kidney from a deceased patient. She also completely trusted Nate, who was doing the retrieval.

Before she had really got to know him, when he'd first arrived, she had looked him up. Read his research papers and discovered that he was one of the surgeons who could do a live donor kidney retrieval laparoscopically. Flo knew what a technical challenge it was to do a retrieval that way, but Ms. Martinez's recovery time would be exponentially cut in half.

She'd only be in the hospital two to four days compared to the six to eight weeks if it was done via laparotomy. They hadn't even been sure that they could do it laparoscopically on Ms. Martinez until after Nate examined her and found her health in good order. She was the perfect candidate.

The large OR was big enough to allow Flo to work on Eva and allow Nate and the laparoscopic equipment to be on the other side of the room.

She headed into the scrub room and ran into Nate, who was scrubbing up. He glanced at her. "How is Eva doing?"

"She's scared. Unsurprisingly." Flo stepped on the foot pedal to start the water. "I told her it would be okay."

"Normally I wouldn't tell a patient that, given all the variables, but I have a good feeling about this one." Nate smiled at her. "Ms. Martinez is very determined."

Flo nodded. "You can't get in the way of a mama bear protecting her cub."

"Is that what it is?"

"Sure, of course." Flo chuckled. "My mom was a force to be reckoned with in the children's hospital where I had my surgery done."

"I can see that. You're sometimes a force to be reckoned with." Nate shook water off his hands and grabbed a paper towel. "I think this will be okay. I'm very skilled."

"I know you are," she teased, causing him to laugh.

"I meant at laparoscopic surgery."

"I know." Flo glanced through the window into the OR. She could see Ms. Martinez on the surgical table, mouthing words with her eyes closed. It took Flo a fraction of a second to realize she was praying.

"I'll see you in there," Nate said, disappearing through the sliding door into the OR.

Flo finished her scrubbing and sent out her own silent prayer. She needed this to work. She'd promised Eva. As she finished scrubbing, Eva was wheeled in to where she got to reach out and hold her mother's hand, just briefly, before being taken to the opposite side of the OR.

She herself walked into the OR, where a nurse helped her into a gown and gloved her. Flo headed over to Ms. Martinez, who was crying.

"Ms. Martinez, it's Flo."

Ms. Martinez glanced up at her. "I'm sorry for crying."

"Don't be sorry. Everything will be okay. It will be

fine. I'll take good care of Eva and Nate will take good care of you. She'll come through like I did."

"You?"

Flo nodded. "Me, and I was only two years older than Eva at the time."

Ms. Martinez nodded and Flo walked toward Eva. The scrub team was going over the safety precautions and Ms. Martinez was put under general anesthetic. Flo glanced back once to watch Nate as he went into action.

That part was in his hands now. He'd retrieve the kidney and Flo had to prepare Eva so that when the kidney was brought across the room, she could start implanting it.

"Flo?" Eva said questioningly through the oxygen mask.

"I'm here, Eva. Can you count back for me? It's time to sleep."

Eva nodded and started to drift.

Flo turned to the nurse. "Insert a catheter and then a bag of methylene blue and Ancef. I want to make sure I can see her bladder and not hit the peritoneum or bowel."

"Yes, Dr. Chiu."

Flo took a deep breath and waited for the dye and the catheter. All she could think about was the time she had been on the table in Eva's place. Eva had a better shot than she herself ever had.

You're here, though. You beat the odds.

Once she had successful confirmation that everything was a go, she got ready to work. All that mattered was making sure that Eva had the best shot at success. When that press conference took place tomorrow afternoon, she wanted to walk in there and tell them that the first transplant surgery between The Hollywood Hills Clinic and the Bright Hope Clinic had been a complete success

and that mother and daughter would both make a complete recovery.

That was what Flo focused on as she worked and prepared the area.

As she readied the field where she would connect the kidney she heard, "Walking with the kidney."

She glanced up to see a surgical resident from the Bright Hope Clinic walking toward her with the kidney in a metal bowl full of ice. A perfect, healthy kidney, which had been taken from mother and was about to be implanted into the daughter.

Ms. Martinez had given Eva life. Twice.

It was a beautiful thing. It was a bit of joy.

The resident who was assisting her took the bowl from the other resident and prepped the kidney with solution, getting it ready for Flo to implant it in the intraperitoneum as Eva's external iliac vessels were too small. A slight change of plan, but one that Flo could easily handle.

"Walking with the kidney," her resident called as she carefully scooped up the kidney and handed it to Flo.

Flo cradled the kidney in her hand, marveling at it. Such an important organ. Just as important as any other organ and the most wonderful gift that she herself had been given. In time Eva would understand too what a gift she'd received.

A second chance at life.

Flo placed the kidney into the cavity and began the anastomosis. Eva's arteries and veins were delicate and her mother's donated kidney a little large, but she'd get it to work. Nate came over and stood on the other side.

"Can I assist you, Dr. Chiu?"

"Is Ms. Martinez okay?"

"She's on her way to Recovery. Everything is good and she came through beautifully."

Thank God.

"You can help," Flo said. "Her vessels are small and anatomizing to the aorta is a bit tricky. I was hoping she'd have larger vessels, being twelve, but her premature birth stunted some things."

Nate leaned over. "You're doing great and almost there." He continued to offer her words of encouragement as well as check on Eva's condition.

The blue dye allowed her to see the bladder when she attached the ureter.

And when she was done the kidney pinked up and a stream of urine shot out, letting her know that the kidney was functioning.

"Excellent job, Dr. Chiu!" Nate exclaimed as the surgical team applauded.

Tears stung Flo's eyes and she laughed when she saw that stream of urine. "Let's close her up."

Nate stepped in and they closed her up, making sure everything was where it was supposed to be. A pressure dressing was placed on the wound then Eva was rolled into the post-anesthesia recovery unit, where she would be extubated from her general anesthesia.

When that stream of urine had flowed, Flo had wanted to shout for joy, because the surgery had been a success so far, but there was still recovery and monitoring of Eva in the ICU to make sure that she didn't reject the organ or have stenosis or a clot. There were still so many risk factors for Eva, but so far she'd taken a step in the right direction.

There was still a long road to go, which was why Flo didn't want to give an update on Eva until tomorrow afternoon.

Right now she was exhausted.

She peeled off her surgical gown and mask, stuffing them into the appropriate receptacles, before scrubbing out.

Nate was beside her again.

"Good work, Dr. King," Flo said.

"Removing a donor kidney is easy—you had the hard job."

"Your job was just as technically challenging, Nate. Don't sell yourself short."

He smiled at her and toweled off. "How should we celebrate?"

"Celebrate?"

"We have to celebrate a bit."

"How about a pizza at my place? Usually I wouldn't have someone over to my place, but I'm wiped out and don't have the energy to bike home."

Nate laughed. "So that's why you're inviting me over. Sure. We can do that."

"Thank you." Flo dried her hands. "I'm going to check on them post-op and give my orders. Then pizza."

He nodded. "I'll meet you out front in an hour."

Nate watched Flo leave the scrub room.

What are you doing?

He really didn't know. After what had happened between the two of them last night and his absolute loss of control, he'd promised himself that would never happen again. For one moment, being with her now, he'd forgotten that he didn't do those kinds of things any more. They weren't a real couple.

He swore he wouldn't do things like surfing or racing or one-night stands again.

Nate strode toward the exit, mad at himself for letting

Flo in. It had been so easy for her to get past his defenses, under his armor. He couldn't let that happen tonight.

He'd celebrate with her because what they had just done together, saving Eva's life and completing a successful kidney transplant, was something worth celebrating. He could celebrate with Flo as her friend, because that's all it could be.

He had to remember to keep his distance after this.

He had to remind himself why he was here and that being in California was only temporary. His life was waiting for him in New York.

A lonely life.

A lonely life it may be, but it was what he deserved. He'd lived too recklessly as a young man and it had cost a life. Loneliness was the penance he gladly paid.

Or at least it had used to be.

CHAPTER THIRTEEN

"Did you check on Ms. Martinez?" Flo asked as she rummaged around in her fridge.

"I did," Nate said as he took a seat at her island. Flo's apartment was small and her tiny table was covered with an assortment of medical journals and papers. At least the piles were neat. She seemed to thrive on orderly chaos, if that was possible. So they were having their pizza celebration dinner at her kitchen counter. Which was fine.

If he didn't get too comfortable he wouldn't have the impetus to stay or linger.

"How was she?" Flo asked.

"Relieved." Nate smiled to himself as he recalled telling Ms. Martinez how well the surgery had gone. How her daughter was strong and stable in the pediatric ICU and being monitored, and that so far there wasn't any sign of rejection.

The joy on her face made his job worthwhile.

Though both he and Flo had their phones out in front of them. Ready to jump at a moment's notice if a call came from the hospital that something was up with Eva or Ms. Martinez. Or if there were organs for Kyle again, because Kyle was not doing well.

His time was running out and that weighed heavily on Nate.

He'd been Kyle's physician for a long time and watching Kyle slowly die was taking its toll on him. He wanted so much for organs to be found, but his hopes were waning fast. He was losing patience. He wanted organs for Kyle so Kyle wouldn't die and so he could go home to New York. There were too many ghosts in California for his liking.

Los Angeles brought up too many bad memories. He also had to get away from Flo. Distance would be the best for them.

"How about grape soda? It's not wine, but I can't have wine."

"Sure," Nate said. "You know that it's okay for you to have alcohol every once in a while."

Flo shrugged. "I know. Two units a day, but really I don't want to risk it. Alcohol raises your blood pressure and I want to keep my kidneys for a long time."

She set down a tumbler and poured some grape soda into it.

"I feel like I'm ten years old during summer vacation." He took a sip and winced. "Just as I remember."

"It's not that bad." Flo then pulled a piece of paper out of her pocket and set it down in front of Nate.

"What's this?"

"It's part of my bucket list. It's what I want to do to celebrate Eva's successful surgery. I told her that she needed to go on living when she recovered."

A sense of dread filled Nate as he unfolded the paper and found himself staring at a picture of El Capitan in Yosemite. The sheer rock wall brought back the moment, which had been over a decade ago, flooding back to him, like it was fresh and new all over again.

"Hold on, Serena. Please hold on."

"I can't. I can't."

Nate crumpled the picture in his fist, trying to drown out the screams in his head.

"What're you doing?" Flo asked shocked.

"This is a bad idea," Nate said.

"Why?"

"El Capitan is the tallest vertical face. It's three thousand feet high from base to summit. Do you know how dangerous it is to climb?"

"I'm aware of how tall it is, but a lot of people climb it."

"Skilled climbers, and even then they die!" he shouted at her. Didn't she get it? She'd been given a second chance at life, yet she kept wanting to do these risky and strange things. Why was she trying to end her life? She'd been given a second chance when Serena hadn't. Flo was reckless.

You were reckless once, too.

"What has gotten into you? Why are you so angry?"

"Why are you throwing away your life?"

She took a step back from him, confused. "Throwing my life away?"

"Yes. You've been given a second chance so why are you risking your life, doing these dangerous things? Why do you even need a bucket list?"

"I need a bucket list because I don't know how much time I have left," she snapped.

Now it was his turn to be confused. "You said that before. What're you talking about? You had a kidney donation. Is your kidney failing?"

"No, but you know the failure rates. How long can a deceased organ really last? It may not last a lifetime. I've already surpassed fifteen years. I don't have many left."

"Do you hear yourself? You've passed fifteen years and aren't in renal failure. Why are you risking your

health, wanting to do dangerous, stupid things? You avoid alcohol and I would say that's a lot safer than climbing El Capitan. You're throwing your life away."

It was like a slap to the face. She'd thought he would understand her passion to try new things. She'd told him how she'd spent her life on the sidelines, watching and never able to participate. Flo had thought he understood her.

She'd thought that he didn't pity her, but apparently she'd been wrong, because he was treating her like a fragile thing. Like she was about to shatter at any moment if she continued to try and live her life.

"I'm not throwing away my life. I'm living it until I can't any more."

"You still have years left, but if you continue down this trajectory, you won't. You'll get yourself killed and what kind of thanks would that be to your organ donor?"

He was stifling her. Just like her parents always tried to do. This was why love and romance wasn't for her. Fall in love and suddenly that other person tried to control your life. "How dare you? You don't know me."

"Don't I?" Nate rubbed his face.

"No. You don't. I'm making the most of my time. I'm not being ungrateful by putting my life at risk. I'm living my life to the fullest."

"No, you're not, because you don't understand the consequences."

"And you do?" Flo asked.

"I do." His expression changed from one of anger to one of sadness.

"I'm sorry you lost a friend while they waited on the list, but this isn't the same thing."

"Of course it is. They wouldn't have acted so recklessly."

"I'm not reckless. And what would you know about that? You're so rigid and guarded. You said you used to climb mountains, so why don't you any more? What happened?"

Nate sighed. "Before I entered medical school I lived like you. I took risks. In fact, the riskier the better as far as I was concerned, and my girlfriend Serena lived the same way. We were adrenaline junkies. We were also experienced rock climbers. We were always at the gym, practicing rappelling. We knew what we were doing until we didn't.

"Then, during a climb, halfway up El Capitan, Serena's rope slipped, the carabiner failed and she fell. She died in the hospital with multiple injuries, needing organs, but there were none to be had and she was far down the list because of her trauma. It was my fault she died. I don't remember if I checked everything as thoroughly as I should've. That's why doing these risky, foolish things is a waste, Flo. You're risking your life for a second of adrenaline. A minute of thrill. That's it. Life is not worth that."

Flo was saddened to hear his admission. He'd been carrying around guilt for so long that it had eaten away at him. She'd thought he was pitying her, trying to hold her back, like her parents did, because he didn't think she could physically do it, but it was something more.

He was afraid for her.

He was angry at her.

Nate claimed that she was wasting her life by doing such risky things, as if her time was up. And maybe he was right, but he was wasting his own life, letting the ghosts of the past hold him back. He was hiding behind walls of guilt and pain.

It was tragic Serena had died and that he blamed him-

self, but he was throwing away his own life by not living. Two people had died on that mountain, Serena and Nate.

"You have lots of time left, Flo. Don't risk that time by doing something stupid," Nate snapped.

"You're one to talk."

"What's that supposed to mean?"

"It means at least I'm out there, trying to live."

He snorted. "That's not living."

"And hiding behind guilt, letting guilt keep you back from ever having happiness again, is living? Maybe you're the one who needs to start living again. Maybe you need to take some risks."

Nate didn't say anything else to her. He just turned on his heel and left her apartment. The door slammed behind him.

Flo sighed. It had hurt, saying those things to him. She hadn't wanted to, but he'd said some hurtful things to her.

Only he's right.

She bent down and picked up the crumpled picture of El Capitan. Did she really want to do this?

No. Not really. She'd picked it because it had been the most advanced thing she could think of. Nate did have a point. Why was she so adamant on doing stuff she wasn't capable of doing? Maybe after some training she could tackle El Capitan.

Maybe Nate was right about it all.

Had she been so bent on proving to the world about what she could do, because for so long everyone she cared about had said she couldn't, that she was really risking this precious gift she'd been given? And in that pursuit she'd pushed away everyone, including the man she was in love with.

The realization hit her hard because even though she didn't want to fall in love with Nate, she was in love with

him. And she had been so scared about him pitying her or keeping her from doing what she wanted that she'd pushed him away.

The tears began to flow down her face and there was no stopping them.

All these years she'd thought she'd been living her life, but she really hadn't been.

Flo didn't sleep well that night so instead she headed back over to the hospital and spent the night in the ICU next to Eva, watching her urine output and monitoring her vitals. There was no sign of Nate and it was better that way.

After what had happened between the two of them, Flo doubted she'd ever see him again outside work and the facade they had to put on. Even then, they seemed to have convinced the press a while ago that they were indeed dating, because the furor had died down.

There was no story to tell.

No scandal.

Everyone was just waiting for organs for Kyle Francis.

All she had to do was get through the press conference about Eva and, thankfully, she could present good news. She just hoped that she could hold it all together in front of Nate. Her heart was racing as she entered the press room. Freya and Mila were waiting for her and a smattering of press was assembled.

Flo shook their hands and smiled, silently letting the two of them know that the surgery had been a success. That she was here to deliver good news rather than bad. She glanced around, but Nate was nowhere to be seen.

And she was a bit disappointed.

What did you expect?

Flo took the podium and the din of chatter died down. "Thank you all for coming here today. Last night at ap-

proximately nineteen hundred hours Eva Martinez and her mother were taken to the OR at The Hollywood Hills Clinic where a successful live donor transplant took place. Ms. Martinez went through a laparoscopic left kidney retrieval performed by Dr. King and came through her donation with flying colors. Her surgery was minimal compared to an open dissection method."

As she said his name the door opened and he slid in, standing at the back. His face was unreadable as he leaned against the wall with his arms crossed.

Ignore him.

"I performed the anastomosis of Eva Martinez's kidney with implantation onto the aorta and IVC, intraperitoneal."

"Can you explain why you chose that method over using the external iliac vessels?"

"I approached it this way because Eva's vessels were too small given her age," Flo said. "Pediatric external iliac vessels can be too small sometimes."

The reporter nodded and jotted down notes.

"Eva is doing well in the ICU and is expected to a make a full recovery."

There was applause and that's when Nate began to make his way to the front. Her heart sank. She prayed it wasn't Eva.

"I'm sorry for interrupting," Nate said. "Dr. Chiu, can I speak with you a moment?"

Flo stepped away from the microphone and Nate leaned over, whispering in her ear, "There are organs for Kyle across town."

Then, before she could say anything further, he moved away from her, like he couldn't stand to be near her, and left the press room. Everyone was watching her, the room silent.

"I'm afraid I have to leave. Thank you, everyone." Flo

quickly turned on her heel and ran out of the press room, ignoring the rapid-fire questions of people asking if this was about Kyle. She'd let Freya and Mila deal with that mess. They were better at it.

Right now she had an important job to do.

Kyle didn't have much time left. He needed those organs.

Please, God. Let them be viable this time.

And since it was across town she'd get there in time to perform the examination of those organs herself this time.

Nate was waiting outside the press room.

"I'll prep Kyle. You go and get the organs," he said quickly. Then he handed her her cell phone. "You forgot this in your office. You almost missed the UNOS call."

"Sorry. Okay, and thanks."

He nodded, but he wouldn't look at her. "Call me when you have the organs. There's an ambulance waiting for you."

Before she had a chance to say anything else he turned his back on her and walked away, off to prep Kyle. Flo headed to where the ambulance was waiting for her. They had the equipment she needed and once she was in the back of the ambulance the paramedic shut the door and the siren blared. They took off across Los Angeles.

Flo's heart hurt, but, really, what had she expected?

She'd ruined her chances with Nate. After Kyle's surgery, he'd return to New York and she very much doubted she'd see him again.

It nearly killed Nate to see Flo. He'd planned to keep his distance from her today, but then he'd got the message from UNOS and had had to face her.

At least he had the excitement of telling Kyle about the organs to distract him.

It killed him to watch Kyle suffer. But now he had a real chance.

Kyle was conscious, but barely, as Nate walked into his room.

"Hey, Doc," Kyle whispered.

"Good news. We've found organs again. Dr. Chiu is on her way to retrieve them. This time they're not so far. Only across town. We need to get you prepped and into the OR."

Kyle smiled weakly. "That's great, but forgive me for not holding my breath. Also because I can't really. Bad lungs."

Nate chuckled. "Yes. Please, don't."

"So, you never did tell me how the tuxedo worked out."

"Didn't I?" Nate said, trying to ignore Kyle's questions. He didn't want to talk about Flo here. It was too raw.

"No. You didn't. Come on, what happened?"

"We went to the gala and raised money."

Kyle rolled his eyes. "Come on. There's been sexual tension between you two from day one. You're telling me nothing happened?"

Nate shook his head. "Really not going to talk about this with you."

Kyle grinned. "I knew it. How was it?"

"We have to draw some more blood from you before you go into the OR. I have your blood type ready and standing by for surgery."

"Come on," Kyle said. "Why don't you want to talk about your relationship with Dr. Chiu?"

"Because there is no relationship. It was a ruse. I kissed her accidentally on the rooftop once and then had to pretend I was in a relationship with her, but really there's nothing there."

Kyle's eyes narrowed. "You're such a bad liar, Doc. You care for her."

He's right.

Actually, it was more than caring for her. Nate loved Flo. He loved how strong she was. Even though she was a bit pessimistic about her own donor kidney, she still was out there, trying to live, and what had he been doing with his time? Hiding away behind guilt.

"I don't."

"I don't know why you're not admitting it when it's…" Kyle trailed off, his eyes rolling into the back of his head as he collapsed.

"Kyle?" Nate tore off his white lab coat. "Kyle?"

The monitors went nuts and Kyle flatlined.

"No, Kyle! No." Nate lunged forward and hit the code button. He lowered Kyle's bed and began CPR compressions. He couldn't shock the LVAD with an AED. As he fired off instructions for medicines, he continued his compressions.

Oh, God. Oh, God.

Kyle wasn't going to survive his own transplant surgery. No, he couldn't let his friend, his patient die. He just couldn't.

Come on. Come on.

The monitor picked up a heart rate, but every time Nate stopped compressions, Kyle crashed again.

Dammit.

His phone began to ring and a nurse picked it up.

"Dr. King, it's Dr. Chiu. She's got Mr. Francis's organs and they're viable. She said to get him into the OR."

Nate cursed under his breath and jumped onto Kyle's bed, not stopping his compressions. "Get us to the OR, stat."

The team moved quickly and Nate continued his chest

compressions on Kyle as they rolled them out of his suite and to the OR.

Nate hoped that Flo would get to them on time.

CHAPTER FOURTEEN

FLO HAD HEARD on the way back to The Hollywood Hills Clinic that Kyle had crashed. She moved as quickly as she could, yelling at people to get out of her way as she raced to the OR. When she got to there she learned that they had Kyle stabilized and Nate was performing his cardiectomy.

She scrubbed and then entered the OR. One of her younger surgeons was taking the organs and readying them for transplantation. A nurse helped Flo into her gown and she was gloved. She approached the surgical table and could see that Nate was about to remove the LVAD.

"The organs look good?" Nate asked, not looking up.

"They did. They're viable."

He nodded. "I will have the heart removed and then we can place it and work on the lungs. It will be a long haul."

"I know," Flo whispered. "Look, about—"

"I don't want to talk about it. Let's focus on Kyle, shall we?"

"Of course." Flo took her place as assist to Nate and she watched him work with bittersweet sadness, knowing that soon he would be going back to New York and she wouldn't see him again.

Even though she had resisted the idea of them pretend-

ing to be a couple to protect The Hollywood Hills Clinic, these last weeks had been the best time of her life. She'd had that bucket list for so long, but she had never really done anything about it.

Until she'd met Nate.

Not that he'd done anything risky with her, but he didn't treat her like she couldn't do things. He encouraged her, he treated her like she wasn't going to shatter at any moment, like her parents had always done.

She'd never minded being by herself. It was easier than risking her heart, as she had learned earlier on, but now that she'd had a taste of being with someone she cared about, someone she loved, she was going to miss Nate.

She was going to be lonely for a long time.

Focus.

Flo returned to the task at hand. They removed the left ventricular assist device and then went about removing Kyle's damaged heart. He was put on bypass and then they removed the lungs. The donor organs, which were in the icebox on a heart-lung machine, were brought forward. Flo took on the lungs while Nate worked on the heart.

No words were needed as they worked seamlessly together. It was like they'd been doing this kind of surgery together for years. Kyle lost a lot of blood, but blood was ready on standby for transfusion.

It was a grueling eight hours, but Flo didn't feel it. Adrenaline fueled her and when breaks were needed she took a shot of espresso, which was kept just outside the OR. Two transplant surgeries in a row and she was feeling exhausted.

"Remove the clamps," Nate said. "Let's take him off bypass."

Clamps were removed and the bypass machine was

CHAPTER FOURTEEN

FLO HAD HEARD on the way back to The Hollywood Hills Clinic that Kyle had crashed. She moved as quickly as she could, yelling at people to get out of her way as she raced to the OR. When she got to there she learned that they had Kyle stabilized and Nate was performing his cardiectomy.

She scrubbed and then entered the OR. One of her younger surgeons was taking the organs and readying them for transplantation. A nurse helped Flo into her gown and she was gloved. She approached the surgical table and could see that Nate was about to remove the LVAD.

"The organs look good?" Nate asked, not looking up.

"They did. They're viable."

He nodded. "I will have the heart removed and then we can place it and work on the lungs. It will be a long haul."

"I know," Flo whispered. "Look, about—"

"I don't want to talk about it. Let's focus on Kyle, shall we?"

"Of course." Flo took her place as assist to Nate and she watched him work with bittersweet sadness, knowing that soon he would be going back to New York and she wouldn't see him again.

Even though she had resisted the idea of them pretend-

ing to be a couple to protect The Hollywood Hills Clinic, these last weeks had been the best time of her life. She'd had that bucket list for so long, but she had never really done anything about it.

Until she'd met Nate.

Not that he'd done anything risky with her, but he didn't treat her like she couldn't do things. He encouraged her, he treated her like she wasn't going to shatter at any moment, like her parents had always done.

She'd never minded being by herself. It was easier than risking her heart, as she had learned earlier on, but now that she'd had a taste of being with someone she cared about, someone she loved, she was going to miss Nate.

She was going to be lonely for a long time.

Focus.

Flo returned to the task at hand. They removed the left ventricular assist device and then went about removing Kyle's damaged heart. He was put on bypass and then they removed the lungs. The donor organs, which were in the icebox on a heart-lung machine, were brought forward. Flo took on the lungs while Nate worked on the heart.

No words were needed as they worked seamlessly together. It was like they'd been doing this kind of surgery together for years. Kyle lost a lot of blood, but blood was ready on standby for transfusion.

It was a grueling eight hours, but Flo didn't feel it. Adrenaline fueled her and when breaks were needed she took a shot of espresso, which was kept just outside the OR. Two transplant surgeries in a row and she was feeling exhausted.

"Remove the clamps," Nate said. "Let's take him off bypass."

Clamps were removed and the bypass machine was

shut down. Nate glanced at her and Flo nodded and sent up a silent prayer.

Come on.

As the machines started, Kyle's new donor heart pinked up and began to beat. His lungs moved as he took breaths. There was clapping and Flo laughed out loud.

Nate was grinning behind his surgical mask—she could tell by the way his eyes were crinkling. "Let's close him up, Dr. Chiu."

"Indeed, Dr. King."

They finished closing up Kyle, inserted drains and tubes and had him off to the post-anesthesia recovery unit. Later, if there were no problems, he would be moved up to the intensive care unit. Flo didn't plan on leaving the hospital at all. She was going to monitor Kyle all night. She peeled off her gown and disposed of it before scrubbing.

"I'll stay with Kyle tonight," Nate said. "He's my patient after all."

"Are you sure?" Flo asked. "I don't mind staying with him."

"He's not your patient. He's mine. I want to monitor him and when he's strong enough we'll take him back to New York. That's what he wants. He wants to go back to New York to recover. His parents are there."

Flo nodded and finished scrubbing. "We've managed to keep things quiet but we should speak to Freya and Kyle's people about giving a press conference about the surgery."

"You're not going to be there?"

"No."

Nate sighed. "For what it's worth, I'm glad you were in there with me."

Tears suddenly and unexpectedly stung Flo's eyes, but she wouldn't let them fall. "Me, too."

Nate left her alone and she leaned over the sink of the scrub room, letting the tears fall. Tears of regret, hurt and most of all relief.

She didn't want him to go, but she'd ruined that.

So it was best he went. Besides, how could she love a man who didn't want to be loved in return? A man who still clung to the past and punished himself for that?

The answer was that she couldn't.

Nate didn't bother changing or shaving. He just made sure his scrubs were clean. If the public wanted a press conference so badly after he had just finished an eight-hour surgery, then they could see him like this.

He walked into the press room, blinded a bit by the flashes, and took the spot at the podium.

"Thank you all for coming. As you are aware, a donor for Mr. Francis was found in a hospital about forty minutes away from The Hollywood Hills Clinic. Dr. Chiu retrieved the heart and lungs, which were found viable. After removing Mr. Francis's left ventricular assist device, Dr. Chiu and I successfully removed Mr. Francis's damaged heart and lungs and replaced them with the viable organs."

"How long did the surgery take?"

"Approximately eight hours. Mr. Francis will be in the intensive care unit for some time."

"How is his prognosis? Will he make his Broadway debut?"

"His prognosis at this moment is stable. The next forty-eight hours will give us a better picture," Nate said. "As for his Broadway debut, that will be on hold for some

time. Mr. Francis's recovery will be long and he will be on anti-rejection drugs for the rest of his life."

"Where is Dr. Chiu?" someone shouted, and as Nate glanced at the man he saw Flo, in her street clothes, sneak into the back of the room. No one noticed she was there.

Seeing her made his pulse race.

Why had he had to ruin it? Why did she have to live so dangerously? The loss of control he felt around her was too much for him to bear. He had to put distance between them, even though he loved her.

"Dr. Chiu is monitoring our patient in the ICU."

"Once Mr. Francis is stable and returns to New York, what will become of your relationship with Dr. Chiu? Is this the end of the dream team?" There were a few chuckles.

"We'll see how a long-distance relationship goes." He glanced to where she was standing, but all he saw was Flo's back as she left the press room.

It killed him to hurt her.

Why did he have to hurt her?

Because you can't lose her, too.

And that was it. She was so determined to *live* her life and he wasn't. He was too scared to move forward. Too scared to lose someone he loved again that he was willing to damage his own heart.

"Now, if there are no more questions about Mr. Francis's surgery, I would really like to get back up to the ICU floor and monitor my patient." Nate excused himself, even though there was still a barrage of questions coming at him. He ran out of the press room to try and catch Flo.

There was no sign of her.

He cursed under his breath and made his way up to the ICU. When he got there, he checked on Kyle. He was still

intubated, but his vitals were good. For someone who had just had a heart and lung transplant, he was doing well.

And Nate could recall the way his friend's heart had stopped under his hands. How he'd almost lost him.

"Serena, come back to me."

Only there had been no heartbeat under his hand when he'd held her. There had been nothing, just the sound of the doctor pronouncing her time of death.

When he held Flo in his arms, she was alive. She was here. Serena would want him to live on. She wouldn't have liked him living as he had been for the last decade.

Serena had been full of life.

She'd lived life to the fullest, just like Flo wanted to, and he'd never called Serena out on what she did. He'd never called her selfish for risking her life. Yet he did that with Flo.

Flo, who had fought so hard for her life.

She deserved to live it the way she wanted, and who was he to get in the way of that.

Because you don't want to lose Flo the way you lost Serena.

And that was the crux of it.

Only he didn't think he had much of a shot with Flo any more. Not after the way he'd been treating her, and he wasn't sure if he was brave enough to let Flo live the life she deserved to live. Maybe it was better for them both that he'd be leaving soon.

Flo hadn't seen Nate in three days. At first she'd thought he'd gone back to New York, but she learned from Freya that Nate was still in LA. He seemed to be working the opposite shift from her.

Which was probably for the best.

Maybe if she didn't see him again it would hurt less when he left for real.

Yet as she stood in her office, staring at the white lab coat neatly folded on the couch—his lab coat, with one of his scrub caps tucked inside—it hurt so much.

She'd thought she'd been in love before, but that wasn't true. The pain she'd felt after Johnny had left her had been nothing compared to this ache she was feeling.

I have to get out of this office.

She headed up to the ICU floor, where Kyle still was, although he would be moved back down to his suite soon if he kept doing as well as he was. Nate wasn't anywhere to be found, so Flo walked into Kyle's room.

Kyle opened his eyes and smiled, but winced just slightly. He was trying to show her that he wasn't in pain. She'd heard from one of the ICU nurses that he was trying to put on a brave face.

Flo couldn't help but chuckle. "How are you today, Mr. Francis?"

"I think I've told you to call me Kyle."

Flo nodded. "So you did. So how are you today, Kyle?"

"Sore," he whispered. "Tired. I don't think I've ever been this tired before in my life."

"Your body is healing and trying to get used to a new heart and lungs. That's a big deal."

"So I've heard." He rolled his head to one side. "How did it go, in your opinion?"

Flo sat down on the end of his bed. "It went as well as I expected. You're not showing any signs of rejection or any other post-op complications. I think that if you stay stable, tonight we can take you back to your private suite and in a month we'll have you back on that plane to New York."

"Oh," Kyle said, and he looked disappointed.

"I know you wanted to make your debut on Broadway but—"

"No, it's not that." Kyle swallowed hard. "I'm terrified, Dr. Chiu. I'm terrified at this gift I've been given."

A lump formed in Flo's throat. She understood what Kyle was feeling. There were so many times she felt that way, too. It was overwhelming.

"I understand. It's a gift that you can never send a thank-you note for. The greatest gift of all."

Kyle nodded. "That's it exactly. What if something happens...?"

"You can't live your life with the what-ifs. I lived like that for so many years." Flo sighed. "I had a kidney transplant at fourteen and I was grateful for my second chance and wanted to live, but I let my fear of life ending at any moment drive me. I felt that if I was going to die I was going to die on my own terms and not let an organ determine when that was going to happen."

"You've had a transplant?"

Flo nodded. "I know how you feel. The weight of having an organ from someone who died, it's a precious thing and I don't want you to squander it, Kyle. Live life, but live it to its proper fullest. Don't push away loved ones because of the off chance that your life might end. I mean, we never know how long our second chance at life will last, but living that second life alone...it's a life not worth living."

A tear ran down Kyle's cheek.

"That's it exactly. How long can this last?"

Flo shrugged. "I don't know. There are so many factors, but I think if you take care of yourself and the gift that you've been given, you can live a long while yet."

"Does this fear ever go away?" Kyle asked.

"No," Flo said. "It never goes away, but if you have

someone who loves you and you love them then it makes it all worthwhile."

"Thanks, Dr. Chiu."

"Flo, remember?"

Kyle smiled. "Flo. Although I prefer to call you Florence, if you don't mind. I fell in love with a girl from Florence. She was the love of my life."

"What happened to her?"

"I let her go. The worst mistake of my life, but maybe Broadway will have to wait a little while yet. I think when I get back on my feet I'll be heading back to Italy. I want to see if I can track her down in Florence."

"I wish you all the best, Kyle." Flo got up and left Kyle's suite before she started bawling. She wished she hadn't pushed Nate away.

She wished she could have a second chance and tell Nate how she felt, that she wanted him and that she wouldn't risk her life in such a way any more.

For so long she'd lived her life saying that she wouldn't let anyone control her, tell her what she could and couldn't do, but really that didn't matter in the long run. What mattered was love.

What mattered was not pushing away those who loved you.

Life was not worth living without love.

Nate stood in the shadows and watched Flo walk away. Her head hung low and her hands were jammed in her pockets as she walked toward her office. When he'd first met her she'd held her head high and run through these halls with purpose, with drive.

This Flo was just as heartbroken as he was.

He'd come up to check on Kyle before he'd planned on finding Flo. He'd wanted to say goodbye and thank

her again, but when he'd come to Kyle's room in the ICU he'd been shocked to hear her open up to Kyle.

To say the same things he felt about her.

He was scared. He'd been living a life of guilt and fear for so long, but that was no way to live. Flo lived a different fear, but she lived a fear nonetheless.

She just didn't let it stop her from living. Whereas he had.

He loved Flo and if she forgave him, he would spend the rest of his life making it up to her. So instead of making a stop to see Kyle he chased after Flo.

"Dr. Chiu," he called out.

She stopped and turned around, surprised to see him. "Dr. King? I thought you'd left for the evening."

"No, I was working in the research library. Can we talk?"

Flo nodded and he took her arm, leading her to her office. When they were both inside he shut the door.

"I'm sorry, Flo," he whispered.

"Sorry for what?" she asked.

"Sorry for trying to stop you from living your life."

"Nate," she sighed. "You didn't."

"I did. I just... When you said you wanted to climb El Capitan I became terrified. I couldn't lose you, Flo. Not after losing Serena. I couldn't bear it if I lost you."

She gasped. "What?"

"I love you, Florence Chiu. I think I loved you from the moment I first met you. I just wouldn't let myself."

"You could still lose me, though, Nate."

He shook his head. "I don't care. I know the risks, but I don't care what will happen. I doubt anything will happen to your donor kidney, but if something happens I will be right by your side. I'm not going anywhere. I'm

here for the long haul. You breathed life into me again. You saved me."

"I thought I pushed you away. I've pushed away everyone. I thought I had so much to prove with that dumb bucket list, but I have nothing to prove. I let my fear rule my heart."

Nate took her in his arms and held her close. "I love you, Flo. I'm not going anywhere."

"I love you, too."

He tipped her chin and kissed her, holding her tight in his arms. She was alive. She was here and she was his.

A relationship that had started out as a facade, all because the person he used to be, the man he'd thought he'd buried a long time ago, had snuck out and kissed her. When he'd been told that he would have to pretend to be in a relationship with Flo he'd felt nervous, because he'd known that if he spent time with her he'd fall for her.

In her he saw who he used to be.

And he missed who he used to be.

With her, he could be so much more and he planned to never let her go.

Flo laid her head against his chest and sighed. "So what happens now? A long-distance relationship?"

"No, I think I'll be moving to LA. James offered me a job."

"Oh, he did?"

Nate nodded. "Also, I could really use a vacation."

"Vacation? I don't know the meaning of that word."

"I think you should learn. I think we both need a two-week vacation once Kyle is stabilized. I think we should accompany him to New York City, get him settled and my stuff dealt with, and then drive back out here. What do you think?"

"Drive across country?"

He nodded. "It was on your bucket list."

Flo groaned. "Don't even talk to me about that bucket list. It's done. It was for someone who thought she was dying. I have time."

"How about an anti-bucket list."

"What's an anti-bucket list?"

"A list of things we do while we *live.*"

Flo chuckled. "I like that idea much better. That's better than my bucket list. You're better than my bucket list."

And then she kissed him again and this time he didn't let her go.

EPILOGUE

One year later

FLO TOOK A deep breath and stood at the edge of Whistlers Mountain in Jasper National Park, staring eastward out at Canada. It wasn't Everest, but it was the highest mountain she'd ever been up, and the fact she was standing at the top, the air so cold and clear, was amazing. She could see for miles and miles. The sun was above them, but it was still morning and it was chilly. Which didn't surprise her as there was snow up at the summit of Whistlers.

Nate came up beside her and sighed, slinging his arm around her shoulder as he stood beside her on the top of the mountain, looking out at the small town of Jasper spread below their feet.

"It really is in the shape of the letter J." Flo pointed. "I didn't believe the hotel clerk when she told us."

Nate chuckled. "So untrusting."

"I trust people." She took a step away from him. "Although you have been acting mighty suspicious lately."

"I have not. See, you're totally untrusting."

"Well, you have been surprising me a lot lately. It's so unlike you." Flo grinned. "All this risk-taking."

"It's not really risk-taking, and are you telling me you don't like this surprise?"

Flo laughed and wrapped her arms around Nate. "I liked the surprise trip to Canada and I liked the surprise of climbing a mountain, even if we didn't really climb very far and it wasn't really that difficult."

"I thought taking a tram would be a nice foray into mountain climbing."

She raised an eyebrow. "The private cabin with the spring-fed hot tub is really nice, too, but it seems a bit posh. Did Kyle give you the idea?"

"He did. He knows the owners and managed to finagle a deal for us." Nate kissed the top of her head. "He wanted to do something to thank us for saving his life. He's doing a play on Broadway, but passed on the singing and dancing for now."

"That's good. I love Kyle, but he's not a singing and dancing type of actor," Flo said. "Don't tell him I said that though."

"I won't, or he'll be heartbroken. He still threatens to steal you away from me."

Flo snorted. "I'd like to see him try."

That earned her another kiss. She sighed and saw more people were taking the hour-long hike up to the summit of Whistlers. They moved off the path and headed out toward the glacier, trying to keep off to the side to enjoy their stolen moment of privacy.

Since Nate had started work at The Hollywood Hills Clinic and since their successful surgery on Kyle and the little girl Eva Martinez, people had been flocking to Los Angeles, wanting the dream team of surgeons to work on them.

Flo couldn't remember when she'd been so popular. Nate had also managed to get some more grant money for his research and he was starting a huge clinical trial at The Hollywood Hills Clinic. They hadn't had a proper

vacation since they'd driven across the country together after saving Kyle's life.

They'd flown with Kyle to Manhattan and got him set up. They'd closed down Nate's practice in New York and moved him back out to Los Angeles. It had been a crazy road trip, and they'd stopped at a lot of touristy places on the two-week drive back to Los Angeles.

They had seen the Liberty Bell, had ridden on a river boat on the Mississippi. Had spent a night in the French Quarter in New Orleans, had seen Graceland and the Grand Canyon. They'd hit as many states as they could on their way back to Los Angeles. They'd even spent a night in Las Vegas before they'd meandered their way up to Seattle so that Nate could meet her parents and, of course, her *nainai*.

Surprisingly, her parents got along well with Nate. Usually both her mother and father disapproved of her dating anyone because of her health problems, but apparently that was all in the past because they wholeheartedly approved of Nate.

And Nate got along well with them.

After Seattle they'd taken a trip down to San Francisco, where Nate's parents now lived. Flo had been nervous, she'd never gone and met parents before, but they were delightful. When they'd returned to Los Angeles they'd found a bigger place near The Hollywood Hills Clinic so they could live together, and then they'd both thrown themselves into their work.

They hadn't killed each other yet.

It had been a great year.

Then last week Nate had surprised her by telling her he'd cleared her calendar. Their patients were all stable. No one was currently in dire need of organs and if they

were, Nate had brought in one of his colleagues from New York to cover for them.

He'd booked two weeks off for them. They'd flown into Calgary, Alberta and then driven up to Jasper National Park, where a very private cabin had been waiting for them. The only connection they had to the outside world was a television that was hooked up to an old DVD player. The cabin had a large selection of old movies for them to watch if they got bored.

So far, Flo was not bored.

They had been hiking, they'd been to the Miette Hot Springs. They'd been white-water rafting and out to dinner. In fact, Flo was feeling a bit tired.

She was used to mountains, having grown up in Seattle, but she'd never been to the top of one. So even though she was exhausted from the supposedly relaxing, romantic vacation, she was glad to be standing at the top of this mountain, drinking in the sights around her.

Mountain climbing had been one of the things at the top of her bucket list and she knew this moment was hard for Nate, given his past. So even though they technically hadn't climbed Whistlers, other than an easy walk to the summit, the gesture was appreciated all the same.

"Thanks again for bringing me..." She trailed off when she saw that Nate had dropped to his knees. Her heart thundered in her ears. Maybe she was hallucinating. Maybe this was altitude sickness and she should get down off the mountain. "What're you doing?"

"Proposing."

She sighed in relief. "Oh, right, just like when we were surfing. Are we going to walk out on the glacier and you have to attach some kind of strap to me?"

He looked at her strangely. "No, this isn't like when we were surfing."

"What?" She began to shake. "Are you…what?"

He pulled out a box. "Flo, I'm actually proposing."

"Marriage?"

"Yes. Flo, I asked your dad's permission before we left. He was okay with it. He gave us his blessing, as did your mom. The question is, will you marry me?"

She couldn't answer him as she stared at the silvery diamond ring. She hadn't been expecting it. It was something she'd never thought twice about, because it was something she'd thought she'd never get to have, and now she was staring at it and she couldn't even find her voice.

All she could do was nod. Nate grinned and slipped the ring on her finger and then kissed her hand, followed by her lips.

"I'll take that as a yes, since you didn't fight to take the ring off."

Flo laughed and wrapped her arms around his neck, pulling him down to her so she could kiss him again. "Yes. That was most definitely a yes."

"I love you, Flo Chiu. You brought me back to life. You reminded me that life was worth living. I wanted to bring you up to the top of a mountain, in a place that was new to both of us, a halfway point for both of us, a place that would just be ours, and ask you to be my wife."

Now the tears fell down her cheeks. She'd been so guarded all her life, never showing her fear or any of her emotions. She hadn't wanted her parents to worry and she hadn't wanted to be looked at like she was weak, so she'd guarded her heart until the day that helicopter had landed on the top of The Hollywood Hills Clinic and changed her life forever.

Since then, it was hard for her to lock those emotions away.

She didn't want to lock that piece of her away.

She looked down at her ring, sparkling in the bright morning sunlight at the top of the world, or at least the highest she'd ever been, and she couldn't believe what a year it had been. Full of changes, full of opportunity, and even though her future was still a bit uncertain, she knew that she had the strongest man at her side. Her rock.

"Well, at least my suspicions about you were well founded."

"How's that?" Nate asked.

"I knew you were up to something. I just never expected this."

"Well," he said, pulling her tight against him, "it was risky. I mean, your dad did lecture me for a long time about wanting to marry his little girl. I also had to put up with your sister and brother. Thankfully your mother and *nainai* were easy on me."

"Yet you still took a chance on me."

He nodded. "You're a risk I'm willing to take, because you're the surest thing in my life and no matter what the future holds for us, I want us to be together forever."

"I feel the same. Though you might change your mind in a few months' time."

He frowned. "What're you talking about?"

"Wedding preparations. My mom told me horror stories about trying to plan her wedding with Dad. Do you really want to even attempt that? I mean, my grandmother in Atlanta is just as stubborn as my *nainai* and when you put the two of them together..." Flo shuddered. "Your mom is so nice. I think she might get eaten alive."

Nate laughed out loud. "How about neither?"

Flo was intrigued. "What are you proposing now?"

"A trip to Vegas after Jasper and eloping."

Flo laughed out loud. "I love it and I'm totally in.

Though you've probably just ruined your relationship with my parents and grandmothers."

"It was your *nainai*'s suggestion, actually."

Flo chuckled. "When do we leave for Vegas?"

"Tomorrow. I have it all arranged."

"You were so certain that I was going to say yes, then?" she teased.

"Yes, it was a risk I was willing to take."

* * * * *

THE DOCTOR'S
DATING BARGAIN

TERESA SOUTHWICK

To Maureen Child, Kate Carlisle, Christine Rimmer
and Susan Mallery, the best plot group ever!
Thanks for the friendship. And the fun. (Wine, too.)

Chapter One

"I'm in so much trouble."

Ben McKnight sat in the twilight shadows on the rear second-story deck of Blackwater Lake Lodge. The angry blonde who'd just stomped up the wooden stairs from the lush grounds below obviously was too caught up in her snit to notice him. She continued to mumble to herself as she paced back and forth in front of the redwood railing.

"Is it me?" she grumbled. "Do I attract trouble like black pants pick up pet hair? Or lint? Or fuzzballs? What is my problem?"

Then she lashed out with her foot and connected with one of the sturdy, upright posts anchoring the railing. It was a solid kick and after a few seconds the message traveled to her brain. When it got there, she blurted out, "Damn it! Now my foot's broken."

Beautiful, angry women who talked to themselves were not in Ben's wheelhouse, but broken bones he knew some-

thing about. He stood and walked out of the shadows into the circle of light cast by the property's perimeter lights.

"Maybe I can help."

She turned and gasped. "Good Lord, you startled me. Where the heck did you come from? I didn't know anyone was here."

"I figured that. The talking to yourself sort of gave it away."

"That happens when you don't want to talk to anyone else." She limped closer. "Who are you?"

"Ben McKnight. *Doctor* McKnight. I'm an orthopedic specialist at Mercy Medical Clinic."

"Call me crazy, but I didn't think it was in a doctor's job description to scare a person to death."

"True. *Do no harm* is the cornerstone of the Hippocratic Oath."

She pressed a hand to her chest and took a deep breath. "Then your bedside manner could use a little work, Doctor."

"Sorry." He watched her put weight on the foot and wince. "For the record, I don't recommend kicking things as a communication technique. Especially when you're wearing four-inch heels. Next time I'd use my words if I were you."

"What am I? Five?" The tone was full of irritation that seemed completely self-directed. "Okay. That was childish."

"Would you like me to take a look at the foot?"

"No. I'm fine. Completely over it. I'm calm and tranquil."

"I could tell," he said dryly. "All the pacing, stomping and trash talk were a clear indication that you're totally in your Zen place."

"I didn't mean for anyone to see that. It's been a bad

day and when that happens, I come up here to decompress. Pretty much every night. My serenity spot isn't normally occupied."

"Since I'm trespassing, the least I can do is listen." It would give him a chance to look at her mouth.

"Thanks, but I really have nothing to say."

"All evidence to the contrary. Look, whether or not you feel like talking, you should probably sit for a few minutes and elevate the foot. There could be swelling."

"Did you learn that in medical school?" She limped toward the two chairs nestled in the shadow of the lodge.

Ben put his hand under her elbow, mostly to help take some of her weight, but partly to touch her. "Actually, that's basic first aid. Every coach of every team I've been on since I was five has preached ice and heat for an injury."

"How many teams have you been on?"

She lowered herself into the Adirondack chair and leaned back with a sigh. There was a matching natural-wood ottoman and he cupped her ankle in his hand, then lifted it, resting it on the flat surface before slipping off her high-heeled shoe.

"A lot." Ben sat on the ottoman beside hers.

"What sports did you play?"

"Soccer. Basketball. Football. My senior year I was on the Blackwater Lake High School team that won state about fifteen years ago."

"So you're a local boy?"

"Yes."

"How come I haven't seen you around?" she asked.

"I just got back."

"Do you have family in Blackwater Lake?"

"Father. Older brother, younger sister."

"That qualifies." She thought for a moment. "So, I can't help being curious. You have family close by, which makes

me wonder why you're sitting in the shadows on the deck all by yourself. Did you have a dinner date here at the lodge and she left in a huff? Are you a guest here at the hotel? Or just stalking someone who is a guest?"

He laughed. "I'm a guest. Staying here while I'm having a house built."

"Too old to live at home?"

"Something like that," he said.

The clouds drifted away from the moon and the deck was bathed in silver light, giving Ben a better view of the blonde. She was prettier than he'd thought, with a small face and deep dimples. Her eyes looked blue, although he couldn't tell the shade, and tilted up slightly at the corners. Her hair was straight, and cut in layers that framed her face and fell past her shoulders. Her arm through the light sweater she wore had felt delicate and small-boned. Although the heels gave the impression of height, she barely came up to his shoulder, which made her not so tall.

Suddenly he wondered who he was talking to. He didn't even know her name. On top of that, she was the one asking all the questions. "Are you sure you don't want to tell me why you're so ticked off?"

"There's nothing to say."

"For starters you could define the mess you're in."

"I was hoping you didn't hear that," she said.

"Nope. Sorry. Every word. And let me quote here, 'I'm in so much trouble.' Should I be afraid to get too close? Are you at the top of an assassination list? On the run from law enforcement? A CIA spy doing covert surveillance?"

"Right, because so much happens in Blackwater Lake that the government needs to surveil." There was a suggestion of sarcasm and the barest hint of mockery in her tone.

"You don't like it here?"

She met his gaze. "Let's just say it's not New York or L.A."

"So define trouble. You could be pregnant," he pointed out.

"You have quite the imagination." Her lips turned up at the corners in a brief show of amusement. She had an awfully spectacular mouth when it wasn't all pinched and tight. "And that would be a miracle since I haven't had sex in—"

"Yes?" He looked at her and waited.

"That's really none of your business."

"Maybe not, but now I'm awfully curious."

"Be that as it may," she said, "you're a stranger and I'm not in the habit of sharing personal information with someone I've barely met, Dr. McKnight."

"At least you know my name. That's more than I can say about you."

"Camille Halliday." She looked at him expectantly, as if waiting for recognition. Actually more like bracing for it, as if the information would be unpleasant.

The name did sound familiar, but he couldn't place it. "It's nice to meet you, Miss Halliday."

"Likewise, Dr. McKnight. Now, I really should be going." She slid the punting foot off the ottoman and gingerly tested it on the deck.

"How does it feel?"

"Several of my toes hurt," she admitted.

"Can you walk on it?"

"I have to. Work to do."

"At the hotel?"

"Yes."

"In what capacity?" he wanted to know.

"I run the place."

That's when her last name clicked. Her family had made

a fortune in the hotel and hospitality industry. "You're one of the Halliday hotel chain family."

"Among other things," she said a little mysteriously. After sliding her other leg off the ottoman, she moved forward in the chair and tested more weight on the foot. Drawing in a breath she said, "That smarts a little."

Ben realized he didn't want her to leave yet. "I'd be happy to look at it for you. Sometimes taping a couple toes together helps."

"Thanks for the tip. Taping a toe I can handle." Her words implied there was a whole lot more she couldn't handle.

"Okay. But if you don't want me to examine it, at least sit for a few more minutes and take the pressure off."

She sighed, then nodded. "I can sit, but that won't relieve any pressure."

"You're not talking about the foot now, are you?"

"No." She caught the corner of her bottom lip between her top teeth as she stared out over the back grass and the thick evergreen trees beyond.

"What's wrong? Might help to get it off your chest."

"It might, but I can't. One of the first things I learned getting a master's degree in hotel management was never unburden yourself to a guest."

"I'm not really a guest," he said. "It's more like a lease until my house is ready."

"Why didn't you do that?" she asked. "Rent a place, I mean?"

"Oh, so you get to ask questions but I don't? How about a quid pro quo?" He met her gaze. "You tell me about your trouble and I'll spill about my living arrangements. What can it hurt?"

She stared at him for several moments, then nodded. "It's pretty common knowledge that this property in the

hotel chain isn't doing well financially. My father gave me six months to stop Blackwater Lake Lodge from hemorrhaging money or he'll close it down."

"I see. So you have half a year."

"Not anymore." She blew out a breath. "I've been here two and a half months. The employees are intractable and do their own thing. Personnel turnover is too high and we bleed money in training until a new hire is competent enough to pull their own weight. I think someone is skimming money from the books, but I'm so busy putting out fires that I can't get to the bottom of it. And I'm running out of time."

"Do you have a personal attachment to this property?"

"I'd never seen it until January." She sighed. "But my father is testing me. If I can pull this off, I'll get a choice assignment somewhere that's not in the wilderness of Montana."

"Ah." Making the lodge successful was her ticket out of here.

Ben could understand. Once upon a time he couldn't wait to shake the dirt, mud and mountain air off, but he didn't feel that way now.

"So, why are you back here?" she asked.

"To build a house and put down roots. Blackwater Lake is a great place to live." When she stood, he did, too. "Can't see renting something, settling in, then moving again. I'm focused on expanding Mercy Medical Clinic and providing quality health care for the town and the tourists who come here to visit."

"It's a really noble goal." She touched his arm to steady herself while slipping her shoe back on, then limped toward the stairs. At the top she turned and said, "Good luck with that, Doctor. Now I really have to say good-night."

After she disappeared from sight, he heard her uneven step as she walked down the stairs.

Ben found her intriguing and was sorry she'd had to leave. Still, the quid pro quo had put everything in perspective. He was staying and her objective was to get out of town as fast as possible.

That was too bad.

Until last night Camille hadn't known Ben McKnight existed and now she wondered how he could have been staying in her hotel without her being aware. He was tall, funny and as good-looking as any man she'd met in L.A. or New York, and she'd met a lot of men, according to every rag sheet tabloid paper on the planet.

Now Dr. Ben McKnight was having dinner in the Blackwater Lake Lodge restaurant where she was filling in as hostess. The last one had quit and it was hard to run a five-star establishment without a greeter and seater. Hopefully the interviews she had tomorrow would be productive. Fortunately it was Sunday and not busy. At least it hadn't been until Doctor Do-Good had arrived and asked for a table by himself.

Since then at least four women, two from the lodge staff and two civilians, had come in, sat with him, written something down on a small piece of paper, then handed it to him. Since they were small scraps of paper, she was pretty sure the information wasn't their medical history.

At the moment he was sitting by himself and the place was practically empty except for a couple lingering over coffee and dessert at their table near the stone fireplace.

Cam just couldn't stop herself. She strolled over to where she'd seated him a little while ago and smiled. "Did you enjoy your dinner, Doctor?"

Ben nodded. "I did. The food here is excellent."

"Amanda will appreciate hearing that. She's the chef." And someone Cam had coaxed here from New York. The plan was to prove herself in six months and the two of them would get their pick of prime assignments in one of the Halliday Hospitality Corporation's other properties. "Can I get you something from the bar?"

"No, thanks. I'm on call for the clinic."

"Are you expecting broken bones tonight?"

"Mercy Medical Clinic docs rotate the responsibility of being available to triage emergency calls."

"Excuse me?"

"We take information and decide if the patient on the phone needs to see a doctor and which one could best take care of them. If it's an orthopedic problem, I'm their guy. Otherwise Adam Stone, the family practice specialist, is up."

Cam was "up" all day and night here at the lodge. It wasn't the same as life and death, but she had to be available to deal with any crisis situation. Her performance was being evaluated, and Dean Halliday, her father and president of Halliday Hospitality, didn't grade on a curve.

"Maybe dessert and coffee?" she suggested. "I happen to know the chef makes the best seven-layer chocolate cake in Montana."

"Is that a fact?" Dark brown eyes teased and taunted.

"Slight exaggeration. But if it's not the best you've tasted in Blackwater Lake, this meal is on the house."

"Can you afford to take the chance, what with losing money and all? Or," he added, "I could lie just to get the meal comped."

"You could."

It wouldn't be the first time a man had lied and taken advantage of her, but she'd been younger then. Naive. Vulnerable. All of that was a pretty way of saying she'd been

stupid and her judgment about men sucked. But she was going to prove herself here in this little backwater town or die trying.

She gave him her best smile, the one that showed off her dimples. "But if you don't tell the truth, we'll both know."

"You're on." He laughed and showed off his own considerable charms.

His teeth were very white and practically perfect. The pretty people she'd once counted as her closest friends all had cosmetic work to make their smiles perfect, but Ben's looked like nothing more than good genes. There were streaks in his brown hair that came from the sun and not a bottle at the salon and the bump in his nose kept him from being too pretty. He had a natural ruggedness about him that had nothing to do with acting technique and everything to do with being a manly man. Again with the good genes.

Cam had promised herself after a teenage run-in with police that she'd never again do anything she'd regret. Last night she broke that pledge. She regretted not letting Dr. Ben McKnight examine her foot. Not because she needed anything more medical than an aspirin and a bag of frozen peas for swelling, but simply to feel his big, competent hands on her leg.

Focus, she told herself. Glancing around, she saw Jenny, the lone waitress tonight, and signaled her over. The server shot her a dirty look, then moved to the table and smiled warmly at the doctor.

"What can I get you, Dr. McKnight?"

"Miss Halliday has talked me into a cup of coffee and a piece of Montana's best chocolate cake."

"Excellent choice," Jen said. "I'll bring it right out."

"I should walk back and get it myself," he said. "It's going to add an extra mile to my run in the morning."

"You look fine to me." Jenny smiled and there was definite flirtatious eyelash-batting going on.

Cam held in a sigh and made a mental note to add an item to the staff meeting agenda. Friendly, but not too friendly. It was a fine line.

She looked down at the customer and gave him her professional, but not too friendly smile. "You may have to run an extra mile, but I promise the cake will be worth it." Then she turned away.

"You're leaving?"

"I have work to do."

"Is the place that busy? Can you keep me company?"

"From what I saw you had plenty of company during dinner, Doctor."

He shrugged. "People in Blackwater Lake are friendly."

"Is it just me or merely a coincidence that all those friendly Blackwater Lake people were of the female persuasion?"

"Are you jealous, Miss Halliday?"

"What if I were, Dr. McKnight?"

"I'd be flattered," he said.

"And I'd have a target on my back. Enjoy your dessert," she said, turning away.

"Whoa, not so fast, Cam. Do you mind if I call you that?" Without waiting for an answer he pointed to the chair at a right angle to his. "It's just plain mean to make a cryptic remark like that, then walk away."

"I have no reason to stay."

"Aren't you supposed to be friendly to your guests?" he asked.

"The first rule of hospitality," she confirmed. "And I have been. But there's a line that shouldn't be crossed."

"Isn't the customer always right?"

"Yes, but—"

"So, sit. Take a load off that foot." He looked down at her legs in four-inch heels. "Nice shoes. How is the foot, by the way?"

"Fine." She didn't take him up on the offer to sit because that wasn't professional. But she didn't leave, either.

"Tell me about the target on your back."

"Obviously you were smart enough to pass medical school. Do you really not get it?" That was tough to believe. A man as good-looking as he had to have had opportunities. He'd probably left this small town for college a naive guy of eighteen, but surely he'd been around the block a time or two since then. "You're quite a catch."

"What am I? A fish?" The twinkle in his eyes said he knew where this was going and wasn't the least offended.

That was fortunate because in the hospitality game one always aimed to please. "You're a doctor and not hard on the eyes—"

"Did you just say I'm cute?"

"I said the women in this tiny little town might perceive you that way and you probably make a decent living as a doctor."

"Are you asking?" He rested his forearms on the white-cloth-covered table.

"I'm not interested. But clearly a number of women are. A single guy—" She stopped as a thought struck her. "You aren't married, are you?"

"Nope."

"Divorced?"

"One would have to have been married for that to be the case."

"So you've never been married."

Before Camille could continue the line of questioning, Jenny brought over his cake and the assistant waiter delivered a saucer and cup, then filled it with coffee.

"Anything else I can do for you?" Jenny asked.

"No. But thanks." Ben gave her a smile.

The waitress returned it and moved behind him where she leveled Cam with a look that if it could kill would render her a rust-colored stain on the floor.

Ben forked off a piece of cake then put it in his mouth, his eyes never leaving hers. After chewing and swallowing, the sound of pleasure he made was almost sexual. Since her January arrival in this state that was so close to Canada, she'd never once been too warm. Not until now. And she very much wanted to fan herself.

Steady, girl. What were they talking about? Oh, right. He'd never been married.

"What's wrong with you?" she asked.

"Excuse me? I believe I just proved your point about this being the best cake in Montana."

"I'm not talking cake." She folded her arms over her chest. "You're handsome, smart, a doctor who returned to his hometown to practice medicine. Approximately thirty-five—"

"Close," he confirmed. "Thirty-four."

"Apparently I'm out of practice. And don't interrupt me. I'm on a roll. You're thirty-four, not married and never been married. What's wrong with you?"

"Am I gay, you mean?"

"That's not what I asked, but—"

"No. I'm not."

"That's a relief." She realized that thought hadn't stayed in her head and added, "I mean, for the single women in Blackwater Lake who went to all the trouble of giving you their phone numbers."

"How do you know that?"

"I've been watching them hand you slips of paper too

small to be a résumé or autobiographical novel. And I did catch a glimpse of numbers."

"You're very observant."

"Attention to detail is the hallmark of the hospitality business," she said, irritated at how much she sounded like her father. "So, how does someone who looks so good on paper escape personal entanglements unscathed?"

The twinkle in his eyes vanished and the warm cocoa color turned almost black. "Who says I did?"

"So you have a story." It wasn't a question.

"Doesn't everyone? You go first."

"Nice try." She shook her head.

If he was curious he could just Google her. There was plenty documented on the internet that she'd never live down no matter how hard she tried. Or he could ask the hotel staff. They'd be happy to share.

And judge. The employees had made up their minds about her based on tabloid stories and entertainment gossip. They'd decided she was too shallow, too spoiled, too short and too blonde to be taken seriously.

Why should Ben McKnight be any different?

Chapter Two

"I don't think it's broken, but I'll know for sure after I look at the X-ray."

"The garage is really busy right now so I'm holding you to that not-broken thing."

Ben hadn't expected to start the week treating anyone in his family, but he had been wrong. Sydney McKnight sat on the paper-covered exam table cradling her right hand. His little sister was a pretty, brown-eyed brunette who loved fixing cars as much as he liked fixing people. As a little girl she'd followed their father around McKnight's Automotive and learned from the best mechanic in Montana.

"You know," he said, "if you wanted some big brother time, we could have done lunch. It would have been a lot less painful for you."

"Not if you made me buy." She winced as he probed the swelling. "In my opinion, what this clinic really needs is

a neurologist. You need to have your head examined, find out why it's so big."

"Seriously, Syd. This is nasty. What happened?"

"An accident at the garage." She shrugged. "There was a wrench involved. My hand slipped. Occupational hazard."

"And aren't you lucky big brother the doctor is back to take care of you?"

"We've done all right."

Without you, he thought. Ben knew she hadn't meant to make him feel guilty for leaving, but he did anyway. His father had encouraged him to do what was necessary for his future the same way he'd nurtured Sydney's love affair with cars. Eventually Ben had gone, but now he was back. Where he wanted to be.

The exam room door opened and nurse Ginny Irwin walked in. She was in her late fifties and had blue eyes that missed nothing. Her silver hair was cut in a short, no-fuss style. It suited her no-nonsense attitude.

"Hey, Syd," she said.

"Hi, Ginny." His sister started to lift her hand in greeting, then winced and lowered it.

"I've emailed the X-rays to the radiologist at the hospital and it will be a while before we get the report. But here are the films, Ben." Ginny had known him since he was a kid and didn't feel the need to address him as *Doctor*.

He liked that. Adding *Doctor* to his name didn't make him a better medical practitioner. No polite protocols or assembly-line medicine, just solid personal care to, sometimes literally, get people back on their feet.

"Let's take a look." He put the films on the lighted view box. He wasn't a radiologist, but in his expert opinion there was no break, although he took his time studying all the small bones, just to be sure.

"Don't keep me in suspense," Syd said.

"I have to look at the full range of densities. It can go from white to black and I need to evaluate the contrast ratio for a diagnosis."

"Please don't go all medical techno-speak on me," Sydney begged.

"It's not broken."

"Good." Ginny almost smiled, then looked sternly at the patient. "I don't want to see you back in here, Sydney Marie."

"Yes, ma'am. I'd salute, but this Pillsbury Doughboy hand would just punish me."

"In so many ways. Take care," Ginny said, just before slipping out the door.

"She scares me," his sister said. "So I'll ask you. Can I go back to work?"

"Really?" He folded his arms over his chest. "I'm the weak link? Do we need to get Ginny back in here to keep you in line, Sydney Marie?"

"I'm happy to stay in line if you'll just tell me what I have to do so I can get back to work."

"Take the rest of the day off. Use ice and over-the-counter pain meds. When the swelling goes down you can work."

"That's it? You're not going to do anything? No quick fix? What kind of doctor are you?"

"The kind who replaces hips and fixes broken bones, sometimes with surgery. I have a piece of paper that says it's okay for me to do that."

"Just asking. I guess you'll come in handy for water- and snow-skiing seasons." She settled her injured hand on her thigh. "Speaking of that…how do you like living at Blackwater Lake Lodge?"

The mention of his living arrangement turned his thoughts to the lady who was in charge of the place where

he lived. This wasn't the first time she'd crossed his mind and every time it happened, the thought was followed by a vague regret that she wouldn't be around very long.

"Did I say something wrong?" Syd's eyes narrowed.

"What? No. Why?"

"You look funny."

"Define funny," he said.

"I don't know. Sort of goofy. Sappy. Like you walked down the hall at Blackwater Lake High and saw the girl you had a crush on."

"Interesting diagnosis, Doctor."

"Am I right about a woman being involved?" she persisted.

"Yes."

"I'd clap my hands in excitement, but…" She looked ruefully at the puffy extremity. "Who is she? Anyone I know?"

"Do you know Camille Halliday?"

"Everyone knows her." Syd's expression said it wasn't in a good way. "She's the hotel heiress."

"I know. Met her Saturday." And he'd seen her again at dinner last night. He wondered if she was having another bad day.

"Are you aware that she has a certain reputation?"

"What kind of rep?"

"Partying. Hanging with a wild crowd. Name always in the paper and not for sending mosquito nets to Africa to wipe out malaria. She even went to jail. Although they let her out early."

"Good behavior?"

"Overcrowding," Syd answered. "You didn't know about this stuff?"

"No."

"Have you been living under a rock?"

Sort of. "Las Vegas is surrounded by rocky mountains and rocks are frequently used for landscaping, what with water being scarce in the desert. But none of that qualifies as living under one."

Unless you counted working too hard to think about anything else. Now he had time to wonder about Camille Halliday. What his sister just said didn't fit the ambitious, hardworking woman he'd met. "Was this jail thing recent?"

"No. She was in her teens."

Ah. "And where did you get all this unimpeachable information?"

"The tabloids." Syd grinned shamelessly. "I love to read them. A guilty pleasure."

"Then here's a headline for you. Don't believe everything you read." He slid his fingers into the pockets of his white lab coat. "I found Cam to be bright, funny, focused and a serious businesswoman. Sexy, too."

His sister's eyes narrowed. "Do you have the hots for her?"

No. Maybe. Irrelevant. "She's got her sights set on bigger and better things. Blackwater Lake Lodge is where she's proving herself. She can't wait to move up the career ladder, preferably to a city with a more impressive population."

Syd's dark eyes gleamed with plans he knew he wouldn't like. "That's a relief."

"Why?"

"Here's the thing. You're not getting any younger, Ben."

"Yeah. I think they taught us that in med school," he said dryly.

"No. Seriously. You should think about settling down."

"I'm building a house. Doesn't that count?"

"Good start." She shifted her tush on the table and the

disposable paper rustled. "You should think about a woman to go along with it. And I just happen to have some suggestions."

His sister and every other female in this town had ideas. There'd been matchmaking vibes since he'd touched down. Even Cam had noticed women giving him their phone numbers. "Why am I not surprised?"

Syd ignored his sarcasm. "Annie Higgins is pretty and fun."

"Isn't she divorced with three kids?"

"So?" His sister obviously saw the negative in his expression because she moved on. "Okay. Darlene Litsey has never been married. She has a great personality."

"Personality? Isn't that code for a deal-breaking flaw?"

"Maybe she's a little controlling," Syd admitted. "Okay. I've got the perfect woman for you."

A vision of Cam Halliday flashed into his mind. Specifically her expression when he'd eaten the sinfully good cake. He'd have sworn it was a look of pure lust, but that could just be wishful thinking.

"Are you paying attention?" Syd demanded.

"I'm all ears."

She eyed him critically. "They are a little big. I wasn't going to say anything…but you're a doctor. Surely there's something you can do to fix them."

"Very funny. Now that I think about it, what woman would want to go out with Dumbo?"

"Don't sell yourself short. You've got a lot to offer." She did that critical appraisal thing again. "Handsome, in spite of the ears. Funny, except to me. And you're a doctor."

Cam had said almost the same thing last night. "So?"

"A woman wants to be taken care of. Goes back to caveman days. Picking the biggest, strongest Neanderthal/

Cro-Magnon who can hunt, gather and beat the crap out of anyone who tries to take what's his."

"None of that pertains to me," he protested.

"Sure it does. Modern man just pays people to do all of the above and you can pay better than most. I happen to know you got a couple of bucks when you sold your practice in Las Vegas."

"You could say that."

When he finished medical training, Ben had researched areas of the country for a place to practice medicine. Las Vegas was booming and there was a scarcity of doctors in his field. He set up an office, built a solid reputation all over the valley, hired more doctors to make the business end of it more lucrative, then sold it to the partners. The deal made him a millionaire and wise investments had more than doubled his net worth. He never had to work again if he didn't want to.

Except he loved what he did. Long hours and hard work had earned him the freedom to use his knowledge to help people without having to practice cookie-cutter medicine. He could take his time and give patients the personal attention he wanted to.

"Ben, Emily Decatur is really nice."

"I remember her from high school. She works at the Lodge."

"Right. And you live there. It's a sign. It's convenient."

Cam Halliday worked where he lived, too, and somehow that seemed more convenient to him. "I'm sure Emily is great, but there's no spark."

"Three strikes and you're out. I just provided you with a list of perfectly lovely women and you found something wrong with every one." Syd's frustration was showing. "If you don't want a woman, why did you come home?"

"I'm not sure those two statements actually go together."

"They do in my mind. Las Vegas has a bigger dating pool than Blackwater Lake, so why are you here?"

"Believe it or not, dating isn't my reason for coming back."

"I get it." She was angry and frustrated in equal parts. "You're not looking at all. This is about Judy Coulter, isn't it?"

"My main squeeze in high school and college." After that not so much.

"Yeah. The same one who strung you along for years then married some ski bum she'd only known a month. And moved back East with."

All of that was true and it hurt at the time. But he'd gotten over her a long time ago. "She did me a favor, Syd."

"She broke your heart. How is that a good thing?"

"She didn't break my heart. When I started med school there were no distractions. I put all my energy into school and becoming the best doctor possible."

"You are pretty good," she grudgingly admitted.

"I thank Judy for that."

His sister frowned. "If you were really the best, you'd make my hand better right now."

"Only time can do that," he said gently.

"Speaking of time and healing, I just thought of someone else for the dating list—"

"Stop. I've barely unpacked."

"Oh, pooh," she scoffed. "It's been a couple weeks. You have a duty to date someone."

Now he was getting frustrated. "Right back at you, sis. Who are you going out with? Do I know the guy?"

"I'm taking a break from men."

"Why?"

"I don't want to talk about it."

There was a story. Ben saw it in her eyes, but wouldn't

push. If he set a good example, maybe she'd back off, too. "Okay. So you understand where I'm coming from."

"Not really. You've had a very long break," she started.

He barely held back a groan. She was like a bulldog with a favorite bone. How long would it take before she decided to let this go? He wasn't opposed to dating, just wanted to do it in his own time, his own way.

He would go out when he met someone who intrigued him as much as Camille Halliday.

With a four-inch heel in each hand, Cam walked out of the bedroom into her suite's sitting area. All the bigger, more expensive lodge rooms were on the top floor and she liked living here a lot. It was big, a convenient distance to work and the mattress was soft and comfy. Love seats covered in earth-tone stripes faced each other in front of the fireplace. There was a small kitchen and a cherrywood table in the dining area.

She stopped in front of the mirror over a small table in the entryway for a last check on her appearance before starting the day.

"Hair?" She nodded with satisfaction. "Check."

Something about the water here in Montana brought out the best in her shoulder-length layered style.

"Makeup? Check." It was flawless. She had the money to buy good skin care products and cosmetics and had paid big bucks for a professional makeup artist to teach her the techniques for perfect application.

"Clothes? Dressed for success." She loved this lavender suit with the pencil skirt and fitted matching jacket. The heels matched perfectly.

"It's Tuesday," she reminded herself. "Maybe today I'll get staff cooperation. And maybe I'll flap my arms and fly to the moon."

All those power of positive thinking seminars had been a waste of time for this exile in Blackwater Lake. So far the information and methods hadn't achieved any measurable real-life results.

She was about to slip her heels on when shouting in the hallway shattered the silence in her room. "It's too early for this," she groaned. "Rocky and Apollo Creed couldn't make it just one day without going a couple of rounds?"

Cam opened her door and hurried into the carpeted hall barefoot. Patty Evans and Crystal Ames, a housekeeping team on the staff, stood two inches apart, shouting into each other's faces. They were in their early thirties and about the same height, which made them quite a bit taller than Cam, but she couldn't spare the time for her shoes.

She tried to get between them, but they pretty much ignored her. "Ladies, this is unprofessional."

"Stop flirting with him." Patty's hair curved under in a brown bob. She wore the black pants and gray, fitted smock shirt that was the department uniform.

A honey blonde, Crystal had her hair held back with a big clip. "I wasn't flirting. Just being friendly. You're paranoid." She waved her index finger in the other woman's direction. "And you need your head examined."

"There's nothing wrong with my head," Patty retorted. "I know what I saw. You always want what's mine."

"You're imagining things." Crystal moved even closer.

Patty lifted her chin defensively. "Stay away from Scooter."

Someone named Scooter was worth coming to blows? Cam had to break this up. The most expensive lodge rooms were nearby. Unprofessional behavior like this was inappropriate anywhere, but especially here. Social media being what it was, negative information could go viral on the internet and she had enough problems without that.

"Ladies—" She put a hand on each of their shoulders and used gentle pressure to move them back an inch or two. "That will be enough."

Patty's blue eyes blazed. "It's not nearly enough. Not until she backs off my boyfriend."

"How many times do I have to say this? I'm not coming on to him." Crystal jammed her hands on her hips. "You've got quite an imagination. Get over it."

"Stop it." Cam raised her voice which she hated to do, but a sharp slap to snap them out of it wasn't an option. "This is unacceptable—"

A door opened behind them. "Hi."

Cam held in a groan. It was only one word, but she knew that deep voice. Before she could turn and respond, the two housekeepers relaxed their combative body language.

"Hey, Ben." Patty smiled. "I heard you were back in town and staying here."

"It's been a while." Ben was wearing surgical scrub pants with a long-sleeved white shirt beneath the matching shapeless blue top. "How are you, Patty? Crystal?"

The blonde flashed him a flirty smile. "Fine. How've you been?"

"Good. It's great to be back."

"We should get together for a drink and catch up."

He nodded. "After work some time."

"Sounds good." Patty looked at her partner. "Speaking of that, we've got to get busy."

"Right. Catch you later, Ben."

"Have a good one." He returned their wave before the two women moved down the hall to where the housekeeping cart was pushed against the wall.

"I'm sorry you had to see that," Cam said.

"I actually didn't see anything. Hearing is a different

story." He leaned a shoulder against the doorjamb that was right next to hers. "Are you still in trouble?"

"Tip of the iceberg. Those two are on a very long list of employees who do their own thing."

"So, that's a yes to trouble?" His dark eyes sparkled with humor, no doubt the memory of the other night on the deck.

"It is," she admitted.

"Are you going to kick something?" When he looked down at her bare feet, his gaze turned decidedly, intensely sexy and suggestive.

"No. It was a lesson. I'll use my words. Right after I get my shoes." Every time she saw him it felt like a power struggle and she didn't like feeling at a disadvantage. She also didn't like the little shimmy in her heart when his eyes went all hot and smoldery. That couldn't be good. "I have to get to work."

"Don't let me keep you."

She nodded, then looked up. "And Ben?"

"Hm?"

"I'd consider it a personal favor if you forgot about the little disagreement. I really am sorry you had to see that and I intend to talk to them." For the umpteenth time. If only she could promise him it wouldn't happen again.

Ben glanced down the empty hall where the two women had been. "I take it Patty and Crystal don't get along?"

There was no point in denying what he'd just witnessed for himself. "I referee practically on a daily basis." Then his words sank in. "You know their names."

"We went to high school together."

"I see." Small-town life, she reminded herself. "They're good at their jobs. When not arguing."

"Those two haven't gotten along since Crystal stole

Patty's boyfriend before prom and she missed the high-light of high school."

Cam wouldn't know. Her teen years had been erratic and traditional school wasn't in her frame of reference. "That's good information."

"I've noticed that housekeepers here at the lodge work in teams."

"It's efficient."

He nodded. "I know what you said about personnel turnover and the cost of training. Obviously you feel it's important to retain those two. So it might be a good idea to split them up."

"It crossed my mind, but I've been working in—what did you call it? Triage? Dealing with the most important things first. Operating in crisis mode."

The longer Cam stood looking up at him, the more she noticed how handsome he was. How easy he was to talk to. How good he smelled. How safe he made her feel.

That was something she hadn't felt since losing her big brother when he was only nineteen. Since then men had come on to her, using her to get their name in the paper. Famous by association. But there was something trust-worthy about Ben.

He folded his arms over his chest. "You should be used to crisis mode."

His voice was pleasant and teasing, but her stomach dropped at the words. It had been too much to hope for. "Why?"

"Your tabloid history is pretty colorful."

"So you know about that."

"I Googled you."

"That's a lot of information to wade through." Disap-pointment sat like a stone in her gut.

"Not so much after you went to jail."

It was hard, but she managed not to wince. She would never be able to erase her infamous past and the lies that were part of it. She knew the truth and could set the record straight, but she couldn't make him believe it.

"Being in a cell, even segregated from the general population, was more scary than I can tell you. I was grateful for early release and determined not to go back. Ever. I returned to college."

"Coincidentally, that was about the time all the stories dried up."

"Photographers still stalked me, waiting for a screwup to document and sell papers. But I was more determined to get an education and have a career. Accomplish something. Do more than be famous for being famous."

"Good for you."

Right. The words sounded supportive, but she knew better. Everyone wanted something.

"I really have to get to work," she said.

"Me, too." He straightened and looked down at her. "I'd like to see you later."

"That's not a good idea." The door to her suite was right next to his and she headed for it now. Over her shoulder she said, "Have a wonderful day."

In her room she leaned against the closed door and dragged in air. Since college the nice guys had shunned her. Classes, studying and getting exemplary grades were all she had. The loneliness and isolation hurt deeply, but she'd learned valuable lessons. She needed a solid, successful career because that would be all she had, all she could count on.

It was time to focus on that career. Making Blackwater Lake Lodge into a lucrative property in the family hotel chain was her ticket out of this town. It would get her

away from the handsome, sexy doctor who was nothing more than another nice guy who wouldn't want to bring her home to meet his family.

Chapter Three

Ben McKnight had never pictured himself as a Chamber of Commerce sort of guy, but here he was at the monthly Blackwater Lake meeting. He'd been interested in hearing Mayor Loretta Goodson's plans for growing the community, expanding Mercy Medical Clinic and eventually building a hospital here in town. Being in on that project from the beginning was one of the reasons he'd come back. Blending the best and newest medicine with a small-town, hands-on approach was exciting and rewarding.

Apparently he wasn't the only one interested in long-term planning. It was a standing-room-only crowd in the council chamber here at City Hall.

"I think we've thoroughly covered all the information about the architect hired to draw up the plans for the Mercy Medical Clinic expansion. The town council and I liked the work she showed us, but she also has the lowest fee. McKnight Construction will be doing the building. Is there

any further business or questions?" The mayor, an attractive woman who looked thirty but was probably ten years older, glanced around the room. Her shoulder-length, layered brown hair caught the overhead light as she turned her head. She smiled, but it didn't quite reach her gray eyes. "All right, seeing no raised hands, that concludes the meeting. There are refreshments in the back. Thank you for coming, everyone."

Almost instantly chair legs scraped and talking commenced as people stood and filed out of the room or to the table filled with coffee and dessert.

Ben had been at the clinic late setting a patient's broken arm and barely made it to the meeting. With no time to eat, he was starving. After grabbing a couple cookies and a brownie, he looked around. Against the wall he noticed Cabot Dixon, an old high school friend, talking to the pretty redhead who owned the marina store on the lake and was engaged to Adam Stone, the family-practice doctor at the clinic. He moved toward them and Cabot grinned.

"I heard you were back in town, Ben."

"Good to see you, Cab." He set his coffee on the seat of a chair and shook the other man's hand.

"Do you know Jill Beck?"

"I do. How's that little guy of yours?" Ben had met them at the clinic when they visited Adam at work.

"C.J. is great." Her blue eyes glowed with pride and pleasure. "Adam is keeping an eye on him tonight. Tyler's there, too."

"How old is that boy of yours, Cab?"

"Seven. Can't believe it. I remember when he was hardly bigger than my hand and I was trying to figure out which end to put the diaper on and which one to feed."

"You've done a great job," Jill said, "because he's healthy and happy."

"It was one day at a time, one crisis at a time." He shook his head at the memories. "Seems like yesterday he was a toddler."

"I look forward to seeing him. Preferably not at the clinic."

"From your mouth to God's ear," the man said fervently.

Ben knew Cabot had been married and his wife took off right after the baby's birth. Apparently, in addition to a husband and newborn son, small-town life wasn't her thing. And speaking of that... In his peripheral vision he noticed a flash of red. Camille Halliday was a few feet away from the refreshment table, by herself and holding a cup of coffee. She stood out like a fly in milk.

The people in this room were dressed in denim and flannel. Mayor Goodson had on a navy blue blazer with her jeans to negotiate the line between casual and professional. There was an occasional pair of khakis, and Ben was in scrubs, but that was as formal as anyone got.

Cam was wearing a stylishly short, snug skirt and fitted red jacket with a ruffle at the waist. Her four-inch red come-and-get-me heels made her legs look longer than he thought they were and shapely enough to make his fingers tingle to know for sure.

Jill must have noticed where he was looking. "Camille Halliday is prettier in person that she is in photographs."

"I'll have to take your word." Ben forced himself to look away. He took a chocolate chip cookie from his plate and bit into it. After chewing and swallowing he said, "I've never seen pictures of her."

"Really?" The redhead looked surprised. "She's been all over magazines and tabloid news."

"I've been busy." He shrugged. "Barely put it together when I met her at the lodge. I'm staying there until I build my house."

"I'd steer clear of her." Cabot's eyes were dark with suspicion.

"Have you met her?"

"No. And that's fine with me."

"I can't help wondering what she's doing in Blackwater Lake." Jill sipped her coffee. "It's painfully obvious that she doesn't fit in here."

Ben noticed that people were looking curiously at her, but no one ventured over. She looked a little lost and the stubborn lift of her chin said she was trying not to be.

"I'm going to talk to her," he said.

"Bad idea." Cabot shook his head in warning.

"Why?"

"She's way out of your league."

"That would be a problem if I were looking for something serious." He already knew that was a waste of time, because the lady had her sights set on bigger and more high-profile than here. "But there's no harm in being friendly."

"Yes, there is." His friend looked like he'd rather take a sharp stick in the eye.

"I'd go with you and introduce myself," Jill said, "but I have to get home. Although I'm sure Adam has everything under control."

"And I have to pick up Ty and get him home. It's a school night. And I'm your ride," Cabot reminded her.

"That, too."

"Okay, then. I'll see you guys later."

Cabot's expression was filled with fraternal sympathy. "You're a braver man than I am."

Ben laughed and said his goodbyes, then picked up his coffee and dropped his empty dessert plate in the trash before heading in Cam's direction.

There was relief in her eyes when he stopped in front of her. "Hi, Ben."

"Cam." He sipped cold coffee. "How are you?"

"Fine."

He hadn't seen her since yesterday morning when she'd broken up the housekeeping hostilities. "Is there a cease-fire at the lodge?"

"For Crystal and Patty there is." That implied not so much with the rest of the staff. "I paired them with other people. They weren't happy, but I pulled rank."

"I think it was General Colin Powell who said that to be an effective leader, sometimes you have to tick people off."

"I'd just settle for a little respect," she said ruefully.

Ben wondered at the twinge of protectiveness he felt. This big-city girl was more than capable of looking after herself. Rich, beautiful and experienced, according to the press. But there was a look in her eyes, an expression that said she was a little out of her depth.

"So, what are you doing here?" he asked.

"I already told you—making the lodge profitable."

"No, I meant why did you come to the Chamber of Commerce meeting?"

"Oh." She shrugged and what that small movement did to her breasts in that tight-fitting jacket should be illegal. "I thought it couldn't hurt to be here to see other business owners in action. Maybe it would spark marketing ideas in the mountain milieu. Promotion strategies for increasing spring and summer bookings. And get a jump on fall and holiday reservations."

"Throw everything at the wall and see what sticks," he agreed.

"Pretty much." She tossed her half-empty cup in the trash beside the table. "I like Mayor Goodson. She's smart

to open up some of the town's property for sale and development."

"Maybe. It's going to be a juggling act, though. Growing, but not so fast that we lose the qualities that make life here special."

"Bigger means more people can enjoy special."

"Not always," he disagreed.

"For the sake of argument… Didn't the mayor say that as far as health care escalation goes, right now a grant for the money to add on to Mercy Medical Clinic is the best she can do? An actual hospital needs enough of a population to support it. Bigger would be better for everyone."

"That's true. As much as I'd like to see it built, going too big too fast makes for a weak foundation that won't support the existing residents. Everything collapses."

She opened her mouth to say something, but before any words came out the lights went off and on. He looked around and noticed there were only a few people left in the room.

"I think they're throwing us out," he said.

"Looks that way." She took a cell phone from the small purse hanging by a handle from her wrist. "I need to call a cab."

"You don't have a car?"

"Not one with four working tires. I had a flat. The good news is I noticed before leaving the lodge parking lot."

That meant she took a cab here. "I'm surprised you went to the trouble of showing up."

"I didn't want to miss the meeting."

Anything and everything possible to get the job done and move on, he thought. He'd moved on, made his mark, and when he did it felt as if something was missing. They said you could find anything in Las Vegas, but that wasn't true for him. Contentment couldn't be bought at a high-

end store on the Strip. But clearly Cam had things to do, places to go. Except right now she didn't have the wheels to get there.

She started to press numbers on her phone. To call a cab.

"I'll drive you back to the lodge," he said.

"I can't ask you to do that."

"There was no asking involved. I offered. Seems silly to pay for a ride when we're both going to the same place."

She smiled for the first time and it was like sunshine. "I'd appreciate that very much. Thanks."

"Okay." He pointed to the rear exit. "I'm in the back lot."

They walked side by side through the room and outside. His Mercedes SUV was one of the last cars there. He pressed the button on his keys to unlock the doors and the lights flashed.

"Nice car," she said.

"Thanks. I like it." He opened the passenger door for her.

She hesitated, obviously wondering how to get in without flashing the goods. He was going to hell but couldn't stop the anticipation coiling inside while he waited for her to maneuver up and in with that short skirt.

"Thank goodness for running boards," she said.

Lifting one foot, she stepped on it and took the hand hold just inside, then settled her butt on the seat. She swung her legs in and reached for the seat belt.

Ben hadn't seen much more than everyone at the Chamber of Commerce meeting. Maybe a couple extra inches of bare thigh, but that was it. Disappointment snaked through him along with a growing desire to see what she looked like out of that chic suit clinging to every curve. That wasn't likely and it was the kind of regret a guy would carry for a long time.

"Nicely done, Miss Halliday."

"Thank you, Dr. McKnight."

He shut the door and walked around to the driver's side, then got in and started the car. A few minutes later he parked at the lodge and they walked into the lobby with its big stone fireplace, cushy leather couch and chairs and the reception desk off to one side. When he started for the elevator, he assumed she'd be coming, too. Their rooms were side by side.

"This is where I say good-night."

"You're not going up?" he asked.

"Later. Work to do."

When she shrugged, he felt a stab of desire shoot straight through him. "It's late."

"I know." She smiled and it was a little tattered around the edges. "But thanks to you, I'm back earlier than expected. I appreciate the lift. Good night, Ben."

"Sweet dreams." He watched the unconsciously sensuous sway of her hips and heard the click of her heels as she walked away and knew his dreams would be anything *but* sweet. Then he thought of something. "Cam?"

She turned. "Yes?"

"My father owns an automotive repair shop in town and my sister works there. I'll have her check out your tire."

"That would be great. My Mercedes is in the employee lot, and probably the only car there with a flat tire. Just have her let me know the cost."

"Will do. Don't work too late," he cautioned.

"Okay." She walked into her office behind the registration desk and shut the door.

The two of them couldn't be more different, but that didn't stop Ben from wanting her. It seemed to get more intense every time he saw her and she worked where he lived. She'd spend the night right next door. It was just a damn shame that she wouldn't be in his bed.

* * *

"Hello?"

Cam looked up from the spreadsheet on her computer monitor when the voice from the registration desk outside the office door drifted to her. In a perfect world there would be a front-desk clerk on duty, but her world wasn't perfect. She was getting used to that particular customer tone, a combination of surprise and annoyance that they'd been waiting longer than necessary for someone to check them into the hotel.

"Damn it, Mary Jane—" Cam had been through this too many times not to know the woman had abandoned her post yet again.

She hurried out and plastered a big friendly smile on her face. A man was standing there and did a slight double take.

"Hi, there," she said. "I hope you haven't been waiting too long."

"A few minutes." He was alone, in his early forties, balding and twenty pounds overweight. He didn't look irritated, which was a good thing.

Cam's motto was never give the customer a reason not to come back. "How can I help you?"

"I'd like to check in."

"Of course. What's the name?"

"Stan Overton."

She pulled up the reservations screen on the computer. "Here you are. Three nights?"

"That's right." He wasn't much taller than she. "Would there be a problem extending my stay?"

If only, she thought. "Not at all. We'd be happy to take care of that for you."

"Great." He glanced around the lobby. "I've never been

to Montana before and I might want to hang around longer."

"I'm sure you're going to love it here." She pressed some keys and pulled up his information. "What brings you to Blackwater Lake?"

"A combination of business and pleasure," he said vaguely.

"Did you want to use the same credit card?"

"Yes." He pulled out his wallet and handed it over. "Have you been in town long?"

It felt like forever. But she wondered why he would ask. Was "greenhorn" tattooed on her forehead? "Long enough to appreciate how special it is."

"What's your favorite restaurant?"

"I could be prejudiced, but the best place in town is the five-star restaurant right here at the lodge. The chef is from New York."

The man leaned an elbow on the high desk that separated them. "What do you like to do here? On your day off, I mean?"

"What's a day off?" She hoped he would take the remark in a teasing way, but it wasn't a joke.

"I know what you mean." He laughed. "But what I'm asking is if you only had a short amount of time here, what would you see?"

"The lake is beautiful. I'm told the fishing is good." She printed out a summary of the hotel's daily room rate and policies. "I'll need your signature and if you could initial the places I indicated…"

"Sure thing." He scrawled an indecipherable name. "I did some research on the Net and what I found said there are hiking trails and places to camp. Is there any place you would go? Somewhere not to be missed?"

Now she was starting to get irritated. Was he just

friendly or hitting on her? That was just… Ew. Or maybe he didn't get out much. The worst thing anyone in hospitality could do was to show impatience.

"To be honest, I can't recommend any outdoor activities from personal experience. But we have a variety of brochures and the concierge desk is right across the lobby. Dustin would be happy to help you. One key or two?"

"One."

She put it in a folder and handed over the packet and receipt. "Third floor. The elevators are right around the corner." Forcing a charm into her smile that she didn't feel, she said, "If there's anything the staff can do to make your stay more pleasant, don't hesitate to ask."

"Thanks. It's starting out great." He nodded and walked away.

Cam let out a breath and saw Mary Jane Baxter rush around the corner. She stopped short for a second, then just looked guilty.

"I just left for a minute, Miss Halliday. I didn't think I'd be missed."

"You never do."

"I'm sorry."

That statement should have been followed by something along the lines of it would never happen again. Cam was just about to the point of making sure it didn't. "Mr. Overton just checked in. Would you please finish up the paperwork?"

"Of course."

The woman handled people and paperwork flawlessly—when she was there. The disappearing without a word was a chronic problem and needed to be managed, but not when Cam was this angry.

"Are you going to be here for a while?"

"I—" She nodded.

"Good. I'm going to take a fifteen-minute break."

Cam turned on her heel and headed for the exit and the rear of the property. Breathing deeply of the clean, fresh air, she climbed the wooden stairs up to the second-floor deck. Her serenity spot. She looked down at the green grass and beautiful flowering plants in the fast-growing shadows. It was six o'clock and the sun had disappeared behind the mountains, taking the warmth with it, and that was just as well. She needed to cool off.

Just as the irritation started to dissolve, she heard the sound of footsteps, heavy ones. A man's walk. There was someone behind her.

"You look ready for a knock-down, drag-out with that railing, but I don't recommend it."

Ben. The corners of her mouth turned up, which was a minor miracle. She turned. "And yet again you're trespassing."

"I saw you at the registration desk, but you were gone before I could flag you down."

"So... Stalking?" She lifted one eyebrow.

"More of a house call. Someone to use your words with."

"McKnight in shining armor strikes again."

"You look like someone broke the heel off your favorite shoe. What's up?"

"Same old thing. Personnel insubordination." She leaned an elbow on the railing. "My clerk at the registration desk disappeared again."

"Again?"

"I know employees are entitled to breaks. That's not a problem; someone is assigned to cover the desk for a scheduled break. But with her it's chronic, unscheduled disappearances. Every two hours she's gone without a word. It's flaky and irresponsible. And I might have to let her go."

"That doesn't sound like Mary Jane Baxter."

"You know her?" She should stop being surprised by that.

"From high school. The blessing and curse of a small town." He shrugged. "She was student body president. Smart, efficient. Every two hours?"

"Like clockwork," she confirmed.

He looked thoughtful. "Now that you mention it, I recall that she's hypoglycemic."

"Can you dumb that down for those of us who didn't go to med school?"

"Her blood sugar dips and she needs to eat regularly."

"So it's a recognized medical condition?"

"Yeah."

"I'm not a monster who'd keep her chained to her post until she passes out. I can be fair, but only if I know what the problem is." Cam threw up her hands in exasperation. "Why didn't she say something?"

"Maybe it's famous heiress intimidation syndrome. All the symptoms are there."

"I'm a very nice person," she defended.

"Then try talking to her like one."

Cam thought about it and nodded. "Can't hurt. Thanks for the suggestion."

"You're welcome."

Now that she was calmer, she remembered that he'd planned to flag her down. "Was there something you wanted?"

"Yeah." For just an instant intensity darkened his eyes and then disappeared. "My sister checked out your tires."

"And?"

"They're practically new and she couldn't find any damage. No evidence of puncture, but the cap was missing.

Syd's guess is that someone deliberately let the air out."
He frowned. "Probably a prank."

"Is it still considered a prank when a disgruntled employee does it?" Her sigh had an awful lot of defeat in it.

Obviously Ben noticed because he slung an arm across her shoulders. "They'll come around. Give it time."

She leaned into him for a moment, soaking up the comfort he offered. Again he made her feel safe, made her miss her big brother. He'd taken care of her in a way her father never had and she missed him every single day. But Ben wasn't her brother and a hum of awareness vibrated through her that suddenly didn't feel safe at all.

She pulled away from him. "It's been almost three months and things here at the lodge are worse than ever. In my experience, people either don't like me or they pretend to be my friend in order to get something from me."

"Betrayal leaves a mark."

She wasn't going to confirm or deny. "What do I owe your sister?"

"Nothing. She took it to the shop and put air in the tire then brought it back."

"A house call?"

He shrugged. "Call it public relations. If anyone here at the lodge needs a good mechanic, put in a good word."

"Okay. Please give her my thanks and tell her that I appreciate what she did very much." She started toward the stairs. "My break is over."

She didn't want it to be over because being with Ben felt like a sanctuary.

"I'll see you around," he said.

Not really a good idea. He was right about betrayal. The mark it left on her was about not being able to trust anyone. Ever. That wasn't much of a problem here, since

everyone fell in the hating her camp. So that made her wonder why the hometown hero was the only one in town being nice to her.

Chapter Four

"I put a patient in exam room one. And I use the term *patient* loosely, if you know what I mean."

Ben looked at the disgusted expression on nurse Ginny's face and was afraid he did know what she meant. It was another single woman faking a sprained ankle or wrist or something else as an excuse to put the moves on him.

"Does she have a casserole?"

Ginny grinned, a sign she was enjoying this way too much. "Yes."

"Okay. Is there a chart?"

"Uh-huh." She handed it over. "The home phone number is highlighted and underlined and asterisked."

He looked at the paperwork inside the manila folder. Cherri Lyn Hoffman. Twenty-five. Worked in accounting at the Blackwater Lake power company. Single. Discomfort in right ankle. "Well, I guess we should see what's wrong with her."

"Or not." Ginny headed down the hall to the break room. "Aren't you coming with me?"

"You're a big boy. I think you can handle this." She kept walking, then turned into the last room and disappeared.

Ben sighed as he knocked once on the exam room door. "Miss Hoffman?"

"Come in."

He did. In this Victorian house donated to the town and turned into a clinic, the rooms were bigger. There was a sink in the corner and walls filled with charts and posters. One for nutrition, with portions of fruit and vegetables dominating. Another was a skeleton with bones labeled.

The patient was sitting on the paper-covered exam table with her legs dangling. Brown hair fell to her shoulders and teased the tight white T-shirt. Some shiny stuff sparkled on the front of it. A denim skirt the size of a postage stamp hit her just below the curve of her thigh and barely covered her…assets.

He left the door open, then went to the sink to wash his hands. "Hi, Miss Hoffman. I'm Dr. McKnight."

"Please, call me Cherri."

And you can call me Dr. McKnight, he thought, but couldn't say it. "What seems to be the problem?"

"I think I twisted my ankle."

"Let me take a look." He sat on the rolling stool and moved toward her, and the very high heels she was wearing. That was the first clue she was faking. He looked at both legs. "Which one hurts?"

"The left."

He looked in the chart where Ginny had noted that, per the patient, the injury was to the right ankle. "I don't see any swelling or trauma."

Cherri stuck her leg out. "Maybe you can feel something."

He could feel it was a sham without touching her or looking at an X-ray. "Why don't you walk across the room for me?"

"All right."

She slid to the step at the end of the table, then stepped to the floor with an exaggerated wince as her right leg took her weight. Turning toward the doorway, she limped on the right leg. After a pivot she came back and favored the opposite side before stopping at the exam table next to him.

She blinked her big blue eyes. "What do you think, Doctor?"

God, he hated this. Several times a week this happened. He wanted to tell her not to waste his time. This wasn't a game and he wouldn't order needless diagnostic tests or prescribe medication for a nonexistent condition. But he was a professional and couldn't say any of that.

"I don't think it's serious." He kept his tone neutral with an effort. "When it bothers you, take over-the-counter medication for pain. Elevate it and alternate cold and heat."

"Thank you. I'm so relieved it's nothing serious."

It *was* serious, but not in a way she would understand. He stood and headed for the door. "All right, then. Have a good day."

"Wait." She moved quickly to stop him. "Don't I need to see you again? Another appointment? Or something?"

"No. I'm sure you'll be fine."

She lifted a covered casserole dish from the chair next to the door beside her purse. "This is for you. I thought you being a bachelor and a busy doctor that you might like something home-cooked."

"Thank you." He took it but couldn't manage a smile. "Goodbye."

"Are you going to call me? To see how I'm doing?"

"I'm sure you're fine."

Before she could stop him again, he walked out, down the hall to the break room. Once safely inside, he shut the door. There was a refrigerator on the wall beside it and he opened the freezer, then shoved the food in with the five or six others there. The fridge was running out of room.

Ginny was sitting at the oak table having a cup of coffee. "We usually leave that door open."

"I know." If only it had a lock.

"Are you hiding?"

"Damn straight," he said.

"How'd it go with Cherri Lyn?"

"Same as always. Couldn't keep the limp consistent." He leaned back against the counter. "That's actually a good thing, because otherwise it would have been tempting to order unnecessary X-rays just to be sure."

Ginny's blue eyes sparked with mischief. "So, are you going to call her?"

"Of course not. What she did is inherently dishonest. You can never trust someone like that."

Talking about trust made him think of Cam, who clearly had issues with it. As far as he could tell her checkered past was isolated in her rebellious youth. Anyone should get a pass on that. Now she seemed straightforward and sincere. He couldn't picture her faking a medical problem. In fact, he'd seen her do a number on her foot and refuse to let him look it over. He wouldn't mind seeing her any time, for any reason. Or no reason.

He looked at Ginny. "I'm losing my patience."

"From where I'm sitting, patients of the female persuasion are on the rise here at Mercy Medical Clinic."

"You know what I mean." He snapped out the words, then drew in a deep cleansing breath. "Sorry. But I'm really frustrated with this situation. This is a medical facility,

not a speed-dating event. I have a professional reputation to maintain."

"You've got a reputation, and being a doctor is only part of it. The other part is bachelor."

"You're enjoying this, aren't you?"

"Yes." She grinned.

"Well, that makes one of us. The thing is, it could be dangerous. What if I blow someone off who really has a medical issue because of all the women who are faking it?"

"They shouldn't have to fake it if you're doing it right."

"Ginny—" he warned.

"All right." She held up her hands in surrender. "This is the thing. It's your own fault."

"Mine?" That hit a nerve. "What did I do?"

"How can I put this delicately?" She thought for several moments. "Tough love time. And I do love you. A doctor who isn't married and doesn't have a girlfriend is fair game for every marriage-minded woman or matchmaking mother within a five-hundred-mile radius of Blackwater Lake."

"God help me." He shook his head. "And there's no immunization?"

"Nope."

"So, you're saying I need a wife?"

"Or steady girlfriend."

"That's just wrong," he said.

"Are you gay?"

"No."

"Confirmed bachelor?" she persisted.

"Not exactly."

"Then, what exactly are you?"

"Just a guy who wants this to stop."

"Then you need to hook up with someone so the women will leave you alone."

"I haven't met anyone to go out with." No one except Cam Halliday and she'd only be around another few months. She was leaving town.

And just like that he realized she would be perfect. It wouldn't exactly be faking it, not if she knew exactly what was going on.

The best part was that no one would get hurt.

Try talking to her like a very nice person. Cam recalled Ben's advice as she waited for the employee in question. When she heard the knock on her office door, she swiveled her chair away from the computer and called out, "Come in."

She hoped Ben was right about this, because so far nothing had worked. Her role model had taught her the scare-the-crap-out-of-employees style of management. Her father had managed family the same way.

The door opened and Mary Jane Baxter took a hesitant step forward. She was a very attractive blonde in her early thirties, with blue eyes and square black glasses. "You wanted to see me, Ms. Halliday?"

"Yes. Thanks for coming, Mary Jane." She folded her hands on her desk. "There's something I'd like to talk to you about."

"All right."

"Please shut the door. And have a seat," she added.

The woman's expression said she was terrified, but she did as instructed and they faced each other across the desk. But Mary Jane's leg was moving nervously and she looked everywhere but at Cam.

What would Ben do to put her at ease? Probably ask a personal question.

"How long have you worked here at Blackwater Lake Lodge?"

"Almost eight months."

"Are you married?"

"Yes."

"Children?"

"Yes." Mary Jane almost smiled. "A girl and a boy."

"That's really nice. Are they in school?"

"When the youngest, my daughter, started first grade, I decided to go back to work."

The woman still looked tense enough to snap in two. What else could she try? Mary Jane was already scared, so maybe it would be effective to do the exact opposite of her father. Take down the barriers.

Cam stood, rounded the desk and sat in the other chair beside her employee. *And stop keeping her in suspense.* "I might as well come to the point. We need to talk about your unscheduled breaks from the registration desk. Because that's the first place our guests see, there really needs to be someone behind it at all times to greet and take care of the customer."

"I know." Mary Jane twisted her fingers together in her lap. "My husband was laid off recently. I really need this job."

"You're good at it. When you're there, your performance is exemplary. Efficient. Friendly. And you have a fantastic way of calming down the most irate customer. My issue is with you disappearing."

"It won't happen again. Really, Ms. Halliday—"

Cam held up a hand. "The thing is, I was talking to Ben McKnight and he mentioned that you need to eat every two hours for health reasons."

"I can't believe he remembers that." Her leg stopped moving. "It's true. I get lightheaded if I don't have something regularly."

"Is there a reason you don't keep snacks at the desk?"

For just a second there was a wry look in her blue eyes. "There's a company rule against it."

"A stupid rule. Fortunately I can do something about that." Cam tapped her lip thoughtfully. "Keep whatever you need in a drawer. Obviously if a customer is there, don't grab a handful of cheese puffs, but you already know that. In a discreet way, do what you need to do to take care of yourself. I can't afford to lose you."

"Really?"

"I wouldn't say it if I didn't mean it." Cam figured she had nothing to lose by putting it all out there. Again, the opposite of Dean Halliday Senior. "This hotel is in financial trouble."

"There were rumors," the other woman admitted.

"I'm here to turn things around. Part of that hinges on employee retention. Training is expensive and time-consuming. If I can't do what I'm supposed to, the property will be closed down or sold. A lot of jobs will be in jeopardy. Maybe I shouldn't say anything, but the situation is serious."

Mary Jane nodded. "Not knowing what's going on is the worst. Thanks for being honest. I appreciate it."

"So, we're okay and on the same page? Just to make it clear, if you need to leave the desk, for any reason, just let me or someone else know to cover you."

"Of course. Thanks, Ms. Halliday—"

"Please call me Cam."

"Okay. Cam. And I'm M.J." She smiled, a genuinely warm look.

It was the first friendly expression she'd seen in Blackwater Lake from anyone other than Ben. This talking like a nice person was working for her. And that made Cam wonder.

"Can I ask you, M.J., why you didn't just come and talk to me about this?"

"I was intimidated. You're the Halliday Hospitality heiress. Famous. And I'm just—me." She pushed her black glasses up more firmly on her nose. "I didn't want to ask for special treatment."

Cam smiled at the fact that Ben was right. "It's not special treatment from my point of view. Frankly, I'd rather have you on your feet than passed out behind the desk. Just be healthy. That's an order."

"Yes, ma'am." She saluted smartly.

Cam laughed. Since a fragile connection had been established, this might be her only chance to find out a little about her McKnight in shining armor. "Ben said he knew you in high school."

M.J. nodded. "And we went to college together. He could have gone out of state anywhere because his grades were scary good. But he didn't."

"Why?"

"Didn't want to leave his girlfriend. Judy Coulter." There was a sharp edge in her voice when she said the name. "For a smart guy, he was really stupid over her."

"Oh?"

"He'd been accepted to medical school in California and proposed to her so they could go together. She turned him down. Said she wasn't ready yet. Six months later she met a ski bum. Arrogant jerk talked about the Olympic team as if he'd made it. Said he was going to be a star and make a fortune in endorsements. She married *him.*"

"Ouch." Poor Ben. What kind of idiot would turn her back on a man like him? "Did he take it hard?"

"I heard he nearly flunked out of med school." She shrugged. "But he didn't. And he got the last laugh."

"How's that?"

"The bum didn't make the Olympic team and Ben made a bundle on his medical practice in Las Vegas. He sold it before moving back here." M.J. smiled. "He really dodged a bullet."

"Sounds like it."

Cam couldn't help wondering if he felt that way. There was something about that first love. Not in her case, because no one had ever loved her for herself. It was the Halliday name and wealth that were the draw.

But that was old news. The good thing was she was doing girl talk and employee bonding. It felt good, really good. And she had Ben to thank for it. And she would.

"She moved back to Blackwater Lake a few months ago," M.J. added.

"His old girlfriend is here in town, too?"

The other woman nodded. "I haven't heard that they've seen each other, but it makes you wonder."

Yes, it did. But Cam couldn't afford to get sidetracked by stuff like that.

"I'm really glad we cleared the air, M.J." She stood and started for the door.

"Me, too."

"There's something I think you should know."

"What is it?" Cam met her gaze.

"The guest that you checked in. Mr. Overton. He's been asking the staff a lot of questions."

"Has he been inappropriate with them?" That's the last thing she needed.

M.J. shook her head. "Mostly he's been curious about you and your family."

"Most people are," Cam said. "But we're just people who put their pants on one leg at a time. Like everyone else."

"I just thought you should know. I have to get back."

She smiled at her employee. "Keep up the good work."

"Thanks, Cam."

After dinner in her suite, Cam was too excited to stay put and decided to get some air. She grabbed a sweater and went out in the hall, her gaze drawn to Ben's door. It was tempting to knock, but he was a paying customer and disturbing a guest's privacy was something a Halliday would never do.

She left the lodge by a rear entrance and walked up the back steps to her serenity spot. It was the first time since coming to Blackwater Lake that she'd come here when she didn't need to find her serenity. She was in the best mood and realized it was about possibilities. There were still mountains to climb and hurdles to get over, but those were for another day. This was a time to savor even minuscule progress.

At the top of the stairs, she automatically looked around for Ben. The last two times she'd been up here it was to get her temper under control when she'd had a bad day and he'd helped her do that. Today was a good day and things continued to go her way when she saw him in the same place he'd been the night he startled her.

"Hi," she said.

"Hey." There was no automatic grin or welcoming smile.

"I was hoping I'd see you." She walked closer.

"Oh?"

"Yes." She sat in the Adirondack chair beside his. The spotlight illuminated his expression and it wasn't happy. He looked a little broody. "What's wrong?"

"I'm trespassing. This time I've got a reason. I'm borrowing your serenity. I hope you don't need it tonight."

"I don't, actually. Bad day?" she asked.

"You could say that."

"Want to talk about it?"

He shook his head. "Not when you look like that."

"Like what?"

"Like you're *not* dying to kick the snot out of something." He settled his linked hands over his flat abdomen. "I was hoping I'd see you, too. There's something I'd like to talk to you about."

"What?"

"You first. Tell me why you're smiling from ear to ear."

"I took your advice," she said.

"Good for you. I'm glad it worked out. What advice would that be?"

"I talked to Mary Jane—M.J."

"What happened?"

"You were right. She was disappearing to eat because she couldn't have food at her desk. There's a company rule against doing that, so I made a unilateral decision to change the rule. Now she's going to keep snacks with her. The conversation went really well. You were right about something else, too. She *was* intimidated by me, but I think she's reassured now."

"I'm glad." He didn't sound glad. He sounded crabby.

Maybe she could cheer him up. "It's all because of you that we're okay now. Thanks for the suggestion. I owe you one."

"Funny you should say that." He looked at her and there was a spark in his eyes. "I have a favor to ask you."

"I'm in a really good mood. Ask away."

"I'd like you to be my pretend girlfriend."

Chapter Five

Cam stared at him for several moments. Surely she must have heard wrong. "Did you just say you want me to be your *pretend* girlfriend?"

"Yes. What do you think?"

It was a good thing she was already sitting down. "I think I'll pretend you didn't just ask me that."

"Why?" He sat forward, all semblance of relaxation disappearing. Tension rolled off him in waves. "You said I was cute. And a good catch because I'm a doctor. Is there something wrong with me?"

"Not on the outside, but I'm thinking a psych evaluation might not be a bad idea."

"That's harsh. It's not like I asked you to run away and get married."

"For reasons I can't even begin to explain, that would be less shocking." She stared at him, waiting for the easy smile. Disturbing though it was, she would even prefer that

hot, smoldery look in his eyes that made her a little weak in the knees. She didn't see either, just the frown indicating something was bothering him. "Tell me what's going on. You don't look like yourself, Ben."

"If only that were true."

"Stop being cryptic and—dare I say it?—a little sulky, a tad pouty. Tell me what the problem is."

"Okay." He met her gaze. "Women won't leave me alone."

She waited for more explanation or a punch line indicating that he was joking. Neither happened and she couldn't help it. She started laughing. When his expression grew more intense she said, "You can't be serious."

"Why not?"

"Because most men would give anything to have a problem like that."

"I'm not most men." Now he looked downright glum.

"Sorry." She got a grip on her grin and did her best to be as solemn as he was. "I agree that you're not most men."

"Why do you think so?" He gave her a sideways glance, a flicker of interest breaking up the gloom.

"For one thing, you're the only man in town who's even friendly to me."

"What else?"

"Talking to you about my problems actually made me feel better. And you had helpful, commonsense advice that was useful."

"It's not that big a deal." He shrugged it off.

"It is to me. Nothing about my childhood, family or internship for my father was normal, so practical is a new experience."

Dean Halliday Senior didn't understand a pragmatic, down-to-earth style of management because he'd never

lived in that world. And neither had Cam until arriving in Blackwater Lake, Montana.

Ben rested his elbows on his knees. "Good to know."

"Okay. So. Now that I've boosted your ego to the breaking point, tell me what this is all about. Why is it a problem for you that women won't leave you alone?"

"If I was at The Watering Hole—"

"The what?"

"It's the local bar on Arrowhead Way and Buffalo Boulevard."

"Ah." She nodded. "I don't get out much, what with working all the time. You were saying?"

"If I was sitting at the bar and a woman started a conversation, I'd happily participate. It's public. It's expected. It's honest. It's a way to meet people."

The Fireside restaurant here at the lodge was public. Maybe it was just that all her life she'd endured photographers ambushing her wherever she went, whatever she was doing, because she'd been concerned that his privacy was violated when he'd been eating alone.

"So you didn't mind that strangers walked over while you were having dinner the other night and handed you their phone numbers?"

"No. I was fair game."

"So call one of them to be your pretend girlfriend. Or, and here's a novel suggestion, maybe a real girlfriend."

"Not a good idea."

"None of this is," she pointed out. "Seriously, Ben, this is like a wacky sitcom episode."

"I'm desperate." He looked it. "Women show up at the clinic with phony ankle injuries or holding their wrists. They're not particularly good at faking it and can't remember which limb is injured."

"Wow. What's the world coming to. No pride in lying anymore."

"Go ahead. Kick a guy when he's down." There was a flash of heat in his eyes but it wasn't lust. More like anger. He stood up. "I guess it was unrealistic to think you'd understand and take this seriously."

"Ben, think about it—"

"For what it's worth, walking in the other guy's shoes is good training when you're developing a management style."

When he started to walk away she surged to her feet and put a hand on his arm. "Don't go. Help me understand. Take me for a walk in your shoes. I'll be good." She held up her hand, palm out. "I swear."

He dragged his fingers through his hair. "Every woman in this town has a mother, grandmother, daughter, niece or friend of a friend and knows of someone I should meet."

"They're just looking out for you."

"More like marriage on their minds. It's like I have a duty to pick one. Even my sister is trying to fix me up."

"So let her." Cam wasn't a good candidate for this. She was damaged goods, so wrong for the hometown hero.

"Maybe I'm old-fashioned, but I want to be the one asking for a phone number when I'm ready."

To her it sounded more like he wanted to control the situation and that could have something to do with the high school sweetheart who threw him over for a ski bum. She could see where he'd be cautious, but that was a long time ago. He was too well-adjusted and normal now. Not to mention too smart and sophisticated not to have gotten over it. Maybe he was the stubborn kind who just didn't want to be told what to do, and wanted to make things happen in his own time, his own way.

"I get that. But—"

"Wait. There's more and it's what's really important." His mouth pulled tight. "When someone comes in to the clinic, I'm obligated to help. I've sworn an oath and this ongoing scenario could potentially affect my ability to do no harm."

"How?"

"These women are taking up appointment time, faking an orthopedic problem to get my attention. And they bring food."

"The way to a man's heart—" She saw the warning look and said, "Sorry. Go on."

"The situation is creating an atmosphere of doubt, for me and the staff. If there's any question in my mind, I'm bound by that oath to order diagnostic tests. X-rays. CAT scan. MRI—magnetic resonance imaging. They're expensive and possibly unnecessary. Exposing someone to needless radiation. Also, there's a very real possibility that under these conditions a real medical condition could be missed."

"Sort of like the boy who cried wolf so often, eventually no one listens."

"Exactly." He rested his hands on his hips. "On top of that, it's disrespectful to the clinic, to me and to patients who need my help."

"So say something to them."

He shook his head. "I will if necessary, but it's awkward. Especially if I'm wrong. I'm concerned about my career. You can't understand what it's like to be a doctor, but I know we share a common interest in doing the best job possible."

He had her there. She'd told him about her ambitions and what the stakes were for her. But that brought another question to mind. One she'd sort of asked already.

"Okay, I see your dilemma." She recognized skepticism

in his expression and added, "Really. But why not ask one of the women who gave you a phone number? Why me?"

"Because they all live here in town and you're leaving."

Any flattery she might have felt at being asked just evaporated. *Be still my heart,* she thought. "I'm not sure what difference that makes."

"This is a small town. You can't keep up a pretense for long. The truth would come out and spread like the flu on crack."

"Secrets do have a way of not staying secret. What makes you so sure that would be any different with me?"

"Like I said—you're leaving. We both know that so neither of us would have unrealistic expectations. All the cards on the table. No one gets hurt."

"Okay. All sensible reasons. But here's a thought. When I'm gone, what are you going to do? When the whole thing starts all over again?"

"Good question." He nodded thoughtfully, as if that hadn't crossed his mind. "I could claim you broke my heart. Spread the word that I need space and a very long time to get over you."

"That could just throw kerosene on the fire. Women are nurturing by nature and would be absolutely convinced that they're the one who could take away your pain and rabid to do just that." She met his gaze and shrugged. "Just saying."

"I'm the new guy in town. A novelty. If I'm off the market for a while, maybe this intense interest will die down. An affair would take me off the radar."

Her heartbeat stuttered. "Since when did it become an affair?"

"Bad choice of words. I meant girlfriend."

"Title only?"

"As God is my witness." He blew out a breath. "Basi-

cally it will buy me time. If I'm wrong and things get out of hand after you're gone, I'll come up with a plan B."

If she agreed to this screwy dating bargain, the deck was stacked in his favor. He would get everything and she got nothing. Unless they really did have an affair. At least then they would have sex. It had been an awfully long time since she'd had sex. She couldn't speak for him, but a man as handsome as Ben probably hadn't gone without.

"So far this is all about you," she said. They were standing close together and she looked up at him. Way up. "Not to be too selfish, but what's in it for me?"

"Unfettered access to practical solutions to your personnel problems."

"And this is valuable to me—why?"

"Because I know these people. I grew up here. I can help you build a bridge over troubled waters."

"You've already done that out of the goodness of your own heart."

"I could clam up next time you seek out my advice." He shrugged. "A man's gotta do what a man's gotta do."

So he wasn't a true friend. He wanted something from the Halliday Hospitality heiress after all. Just like everyone else. Granted, his motive was more noble than most, and she suspected deep down this was partly about the woman who'd tossed him aside for a jerk. But still he wanted something. Except she'd sort of grown accustomed to talking with him and didn't want to slam the door on that. Another three months without a friendly face was an incredibly lonely proposition.

"You know this is completely nuts."

He looked surprised. "Does that mean you'll do it?"

"It means I'll think about it."

"Thank you."

He pulled her close for what she'd thought would be a

thank-you hug, but it wasn't. He kissed her. His lips were soft, warm, appealing. The touch lasted a shade longer than simple gratitude warranted and then he pulled away just before she melted against him.

"Have dinner with me tomorrow night and give me your answer." His voice sounded a little raspy, a little husky. "What do you say?"

"Okay, I guess."

But she would be crazy to agree to this. Ditto on looking forward to it.

At promptly six-thirty the next night, Ben left his suite at the Blackwater Lake Lodge and walked next door. He knocked and Cam opened up almost immediately, as if she'd been waiting.

"Hi."

"Are you ready?" he asked.

"As I'll ever be." There was a distinct wariness in her voice. Cam looked at his jeans, white shirt and sport coat. "Where are you taking me?"

"Don't make it sound so ominous. There's a nice little place in town called the Grizzly Bear Diner."

"Sounds kind of ominous to me. Am I overdressed?"

"You look beautiful." And that was an understatement.

She took his breath away, which made no sense since she was wearing what she always did to work—a suit. The narrow skirt was lavender with a matching fitted jacket and she had on beige patent high heels. Her makeup was impeccable. There was nothing out of the ordinary in her appearance, so the shift in his awareness level must be coming from him. The more he'd thought about it in the last twenty-four hours, the more he really wanted her to say yes to his idea.

"Okay. Let's do this," he said.

She nodded, but he was pretty sure someone being led to the guillotine would look happier than she did.

They walked to his car in the parking garage and he handed her inside, then walked around to the driver's side and slid in behind the wheel. Ben backed the SUV out of the space and headed for the exit that would take them to downtown Blackwater Lake.

"Is there a reason we're not going to Fireside here at the lodge?" she asked.

He glanced over at her and smiled at her expression. "Yes."

When he didn't elaborate she said, "I'm guessing the food's not better. Best seven-layer chocolate cake in Montana. Just saying."

"It's not fine dining, if that's what you're asking. My criteria for tonight is a locals' favorite because it's always busy."

"I haven't agreed to this insane charade yet."

"I'm aware of that. But I think I can win you over."

"Pretty confident, aren't you?"

"Power of positive thinking." He grinned at her. "Plus, whatever your decision, being seen there together will keep everyone off balance, and that can't hurt."

"By 'everyone' you mean women."

"Men talk, too."

The signal light at the intersection of Main Street and Pine Way changed to green and Ben turned left into the parking lot. The diner was on the corner and the whole block was lined with businesses—Potter's Ice Cream Parlor, Tanya's Treasures, Al's Dry Cleaning. He parked and shut off the ignition, then got out and walked around to open the passenger door. Cam was just sliding out.

"You should know that I always open the door for a lady."

"Even a pretend girlfriend?"

"No exceptions." He thought for a moment and added, "Well, my sister."

"Because she works on cars?"

"No. She's my sister and that would just be weird."

Instead of the expected laugh, her forehead creased in a frown. "I wouldn't know."

"You don't have siblings?"

"Actually, I have a sister. My older brother died when he was nineteen."

"I'm sorry."

"Me, too."

He settled his palm at the small of her back and guided her to the front entrance of the Grizzly Bear Diner. It was Friday night and the place was packed.

They stopped at the podium displaying a sign that said "Please Wait to Be Seated." There was a young woman wearing a green collared shirt with a grizzly bear on the pocket. Her name tag said *Bev* and she was probably somewhere in her twenties. She looked Cam up and down but said nothing to her.

"Party of two?" she asked him.

"Yes."

Bev checked her clipboard. "It'll be about fifteen minutes."

"That's fine."

When he started to give his name Bev interrupted. "I know who you are, Dr. McKnight."

"Okay. This is Camille Halliday."

"I know who she is, too. But I didn't know you knew her. Go figure." But this time she nodded politely and said, "Nice to meet you, Miss Halliday."

"It's Cam." She slid him a glance and said, "Thanks. You, too."

People were waiting behind them, so they moved aside to clear the area. "So what do you think of the place?"

"The decoration clearly incorporates the diner's name and establishes a brand."

Ben glanced at the bear wallpaper, the laminated menus with grizzlies on the front and grizzlies tucked on the side of the greeter's podium. There was even a glass case with plastic bear toys and logo T-shirts and hats.

The bell over the door rang and a middle-aged man with a beer belly walked in. Cam smiled and nodded at him.

"Friend of yours?" he asked her.

"Stan Overton. He's a guest at the hotel. He's never been to Blackwater Lake before and was asking me about the sights."

"What did you tell him?"

"That I haven't been here long enough to see the sights," she said wryly.

"I'm guessing you didn't add that you don't intend to be here long enough."

She smiled up at him. "I kept that to myself."

The bell over the door rang again and Adam Stone walked in with a pretty redhead. He spotted his clinic coworker and smiled. "Hey, Ben." The family practice doctor did a double take when he noticed Ben was with Cam. Clearly he knew who she was. "You've met my fiancée, Jill."

"Nice to see you." Jill had grown up in Blackwater Lake but was younger and their paths hadn't crossed then.

"This is Camille Halliday."

"I didn't know you knew each other." Jill looked from Ben to her and smiled. "So, you're the competition."

Cam shook her hand. "Sorry?"

"I'm sort of in the hospitality business. I rent out the apartment above my house. Adam was my tenant when he

first came to town last year. It's how we met." She looked a little self-conscious in the presence of the Halliday Hospitality heiress. "Bad comparison. No way I'd put you out of business."

"I'm relieved to hear that."

Cam flashed a charming smile that would fool the general public but Ben knew better. Jill's rental apartment wasn't really competition, but Cam was concerned about the property's future in a less than robust economy.

"Do you two want to join us?" Adam asked.

Ben met Cam's gaze and shook his head. "Thanks, but we have some things to talk about."

"Another time," Jill said, holding her fiancé's hand. They wanted to be alone, too, but probably not for the same reason.

"Dr. McKnight?" Bev walked over to them with two menus in her hand. "If you'll follow me, I'll show you to your table."

"Thanks." Again he settled his hand on her back. Partly it was being a gentleman, but mostly he just wanted to touch her. He liked touching her and not just her back. A blast of pure yearning poured through him when he thought about touching her everywhere.

The path to their table took them past the counter with swivel stools, then all the way to the back of the diner. He felt Cam's body tighten with tension as people stopped talking to look first at her, then him.

He leaned down and whispered, "Everything will be fine. You gotta have faith in me."

"Words that strike fear in a woman's heart," she said under her breath.

So the lady had trust issues. He could win her over. His plan was foolproof.

She looked relieved when they were finally seated at

a table across from each other. After unrolling her paper napkin from around the silverware, she put it in her lap.

"Smells good in here," she admitted. "I'm hungry."

"Me, too." He looked at her lips, full, defined and incredibly kissable. The lust not only hadn't subsided, it compounded. "I think you'll like—"

"Ben?" A woman passed the table, then backed up a step. "Ben McKnight?"

He recognized the brunette. "Hey, Tanya. How are you?"

"Fine. I heard you were back in town." She looked at Cam, speculation in her green eyes.

"This is Camille Halliday. Tanya Smithson. We went to high school together," he explained.

"Nice to meet you." Cam's eyes were cool as she looked at the other woman.

"I didn't know you knew our Ben," Tanya said.

"We met at the lodge. How's your store doing?" he asked, wondering when he'd become "our Ben."

"Hanging in there. I own the gift store next door. Tanya's Treasures."

"Right," Cam said. "I saw you at the Chamber of Commerce meeting."

"That's why you look familiar." There was a hint of nerves and a suggestion of guilt in her voice. "I didn't know you and Ben were acquainted."

Cam slid him a flirtatious smile. "We've become good friends."

"Really?" She glanced at her watch. "Unfortunately I have to run. Just took a quick break for a bite to eat." She smiled at Cam. "I hope you'll drop by the gift shop and say hello."

"I'll do that." When the woman was out of earshot, Cam's eyes narrowed. "That was quite an about-face. She

went out of her way to ignore me at that Chamber of Commerce meeting. She had to walk around me to get to the refreshment table and didn't bother to introduce herself. Whatever happened to courtesy and old-fashioned friendliness?"

"Like I told you. There's the heiress intimidation factor." He grinned. "And you weren't with me."

"If I hadn't seen it with my own eyes, I'd never have believed it."

"What's that?" he asked.

"I've been here for weeks and no one smiled at me. But with you it's like something shifted in the universe. Attitudes altered. You're the cool guy. The hometown hero."

"Stick with me, kid. You'll see that we can really help each other out."

She nodded thoughtfully. "If you can work that kind of magic at the lodge... I mean, change attitudes and rally cooperation just by being my pretend boyfriend, I just might be able to pull off salvaging that property."

"Does that mean what I think it does?"

"Before I give you an answer, you need to know that this isn't a joke to me."

"I never—"

She held up her hand. "My brother was the Hallidays' young prince. He was being groomed from birth to take over running the corporation. When he died, the job fell in my lap and I didn't want it. After that I made choices and they weren't good ones. But now I'm all grown up and it's important to me to step up. For my family. For my brother."

"I understand. And I'm sure you'll do a terrific job."

"Maybe." She folded her hands and set them on the table's paper placemat. "I don't know how to do it right. Dean Junior would have aced being the boss. He'd have made our father proud if he'd lived. I can't do it as well as

my brother, but I'll do my best. And if that means winning hearts and minds in Blackwater Lake by pretending to be your girlfriend, then that's what I'll do."

"Let's shake on it." He held his hand out across the table.

She put her fingers into his palm and her eyes widened. Clearly she felt the sparks, too. She was more fascinating every time he talked to her and talking wasn't the only thing on his mind.

He was sick and tired of all the women throwing themselves at him, but this woman could come on to him any time she wanted. He would be very willing to oblige.

Chapter Six

At the Grizzly Bear Diner cash register, Cam stood beside Ben while he paid for dinner. Later she would settle with him for her half of the meal, which had been delicious, and worth being here for more than just the food. She couldn't swear to it, but her impression was that the friendliness quotient from people in the diner had gone up by a lot since she'd walked in beside the handsome doctor. With luck this—*liaison* was the best word she could come up with—would thaw out her stubborn, opinionated employees and convince them to help her save their jobs here in town and get her a better one somewhere else.

After signing the credit card receipt, he took her elbow and ushered her out the door. Spring was on the way, but the air was still cool and she shivered.

"Are you cold?"

"Just for a second." And thanks to him not as much as she'd been since coming here. "The fresh air feels good."

"Would you like to walk a little? I can give you a guided tour of downtown Blackwater Lake."

"I've seen it. But walking sounds good. I'm so full."

They strolled past Potter's Ice Cream Parlor and its brightly lit interior. There were little round tables with chair backs shaped like hearts. Colorful prints of sprinkles, cones and scoops were scattered on the walls. A glass case was filled with different flavors of ice cream.

"So I guess you don't want dessert," Ben said.

"Not even the best seven-layer chocolate cake in Montana." She groaned. "I can't believe I ate the whole Mama Bear burger."

"I can't believe you ordered it." He slid his fingers into the pockets of his jeans. "I have to admit I misjudged you."

"How so?"

"I figured you for a gourmet greens and goat cheese kind of girl. That hearty appetite of yours was a pleasant shocker."

"Why pleasant?"

"Because there will be more dinners and I'm not a fan of eating with someone who takes one bite and pushes the rest of the food around the plate."

Cam liked to eat. She liked good food. But she tried to make sensible choices, not deprive herself. She was glad he favored a normal, not stick-thin type. But what pulled her up short was the mention of more dinners.

As they walked she glanced up at him. "I don't understand. Why do we need to go out to dinner again? We've been spotted. As the cops on all those TV shows say, we've been made."

"And we'll need to build on that—otherwise the plan won't work. It's what a dating couple does."

Cam realized she hadn't thought this through. She'd been so caught up in the power of his aura and how just

walking in it gave her Blackwater Lake street cred. That's what had convinced her to agree to the bargain. So far it was working, but she hadn't considered what came after.

"Hm." She caught her heel in a sidewalk crack and stumbled a little. His steadying hand was warm, strong and masculine, and desire knotted in her belly. He was the kind of guy a woman could count on. Heck, the town counted on him. "Our Ben," they'd said. But she wasn't the kind of woman a hometown hero like him made promises to. "Maybe we should figure out exactly how this is going to work."

"We're dating," he said. "Don't tell me a girl like you has never dated before."

"Of course. But it was spontaneous. Not calculated."

She glanced into the big picture window of Tanya's Treasures. Ornate silver picture frames, collectible figurines, crocheted tablecloths and delicate crystal lamps decorated the window. It looked like a charming place. The owner was behind the register counting bills.

"What are we going to *do?*" she asked.

"This isn't rocket science. We'll just do the things a man and woman do when they date."

Her insides quivered at the thought of that. It was the whole sexy gray area of this bargain. Men and women did a lot of very physical things when they dated. But she wasn't going there. Keep this conversation generic.

"I know what people do in New York and Los Angeles. What is there to do here in Montana?"

"Same things. Dinner. Movies. Watching movies at each other's houses."

"We don't have houses," she reminded him.

"You have no imagination," he scoffed. "Your house is right next to mine. It's handy."

That fact was beginning to concern her the most. "But

sneaking back and forth between rooms won't get us seen by the gossip-loving people in town."

"That's true. But it would be fun."

"This is *pretend* dating," she pointed out. "We're not supposed to have fun."

"That's too bad." He grinned. "Because I'm having a great time."

So was Cam. That was the other problem. Too much fun in the past always bit her in the backside. "Let me re-phrase. The whole point of pretend dating is to be seen in public doing public things."

At the end of the block instead of crossing the street, by mutual unspoken agreement, they turned and started back toward the diner.

"I think we should hold hands," he said.

Really? Because shaking on their bargain and feeling the heat of his touch sizzle all the way to her toes wasn't enough fun for him?

"No one is watching us," she protested.

"You never know." His voice was solemn, but laced with teasing.

"There's no one around."

"But the night has a thousand eyes."

"That's just creepy. And Blackwater Lake may be many things, but *creepy* isn't an adjective I'd use to describe it."

He laughed and slipped her hand into his, linking their fingers. They were strolling past the gift shop again. "Think of this as good practice. A chance to get used to each other. Make it look more real—"

Cam was just beginning to relax with the touch when she felt him tense. "What's wrong?"

"I can't believe it." He was staring down the street at a woman waiting for the signal light at Main Street and Pine. "Of all people—"

"Who?"

Cam followed his gaze and saw the light turn green. The woman, tall and slender with dark hair, crossed the street. She passed the diner and glanced in the window as she walked.

Ben leaned down and whispered into her ear. "It's time to kick this bargain into high gear."

"What?"

He stopped dead in his tracks, right under a streetlight, and pulled Cam into his arms. "This is another public thing dating people do all the time."

In the next instant his lips were touching hers. Even if her mouth hadn't been otherwise occupied, she wasn't sure forming a protest was possible. His fingers tunneled into her hair as he cupped her face in his palm and brushed his thumb tenderly over her cheek.

His body felt solid and strong and wonderful pressed against hers. Her heart started a weird thumping as he nibbled quick little kisses over her mouth and jaw, inching toward her neck. His breath tickled her ear and raised tingles that raced over her shoulders and down her arms, settling in her belly. A moan built inside her, but the click of a woman's heels on the sidewalk beside them trapped the sound in her throat.

Ben lifted his head and stared at her as he drew in a breath. Deep down she felt a small flicker of satisfaction that she wasn't the only one feeling *something*. It was a really good kiss. Unfortunately it didn't last nearly long enough.

The footsteps stopped. "Ben? Is that you?"

He straightened and looked at the woman. "Judy Coulter?"

His ex-girlfriend. The one M.J. had told her about. Cam stared up at him as the realization hit her that he'd rec-

ognized this woman before the kiss and that's why he'd pulled her into his arms.

"Ben McKnight." She smiled up at him. Darn it, she had a beautiful smile. "It's been a long time."

"So you're back in Blackwater Lake?"

"Yeah. And so are you. How long has it been?"

"I'd have to do the math." He laughed.

"You were always good at it." She finally tore her gaze from his and gave Cam a look she was all too familiar with. It said you're the airheaded infamous heiress, the one whose only talent is turning outrageous antics into outrageous stories for the tabloids.

Ben looked between them and slid his arm around Cam's waist, intimately nestling her to his side. "Judy, this is Camille Halliday. She's working at the lodge."

"I know who she is." Unlike at the diner, this woman's attitude didn't warm up. That changed when she looked up at Ben. She was very warm to him. "Now that I see you, it seems like yesterday that we were prom king and queen."

"High school was a lot of years ago," he said.

"We used to date," Judy informed Cam.

And you're the moron who threw him over for a ski bum, Cam thought. It might be a long time ago for Ben, but it was new to her and she wanted to get even on his behalf. She wanted to tell the witch what she could do with this walk down memory lane. She wanted to protect him.

She snuggled against him and gazed adoringly into his eyes, seeing the amusement there. "Ben and I are dating now."

"Really?" Large, dark eyes glittered with dislike until she looked at Ben. "I didn't realize that spoiled heiresses were your type."

When he started to say something, Cam put her hand on his chest to stop him. "I've got this."

"Oh?" Judy gave her a dismissive stare.

"Yeah." Cam gave it back to her. "If you were his type, honey, you wouldn't be his *ex*."

"It's getting late, sweetie," Ben said to her. "We have work tomorrow. See you around, Judy."

They walked away and she knew the ex-girlfriend was watching because it was several moments before she heard the clicking sound of high heels on the sidewalk behind them. Cam was angry and upset, but mostly with herself. She wasn't sure where the inclination to protect him had come from. He was nothing if not a nice guy, and a woman like Judy was a cobra. Still, he was a big boy and didn't need Cam coming to his defense. He'd only kissed her to get his how-do-you-like-me-now? moment.

He'd used her. At least it was for revenge, a cause she could get behind, but being used was never fun. Especially for someone like her, who'd been manipulated and tossed aside too many times to count.

But not again. This time she was using him right back and would get something out of the bargain, too.

After clinic hours on Friday, Ben pulled his SUV into McKnight Automotive and stopped beneath the covered area connecting the office to the work bays with hydraulic lifts. That part of the business was shut down for the day with chains across the opening to keep cars out. It was ghostly quiet since all the employees had gone home. He planned to leave his car for servicing in the morning and get his sister to drop him off at the lodge on her way home.

He opened the heavy glass door and walked into the office. There was a high counter where several computer monitors sat. On the wall was a Peg-Board with hooks to hold customers' keys, numbered to link them with the correct vehicle. To the right there was a lounge with chairs

and a TV. A side counter held a coffeemaker and a refrigerator underneath it was stocked with water and soda. A vending machine had candy, chips and nuts. It was a comfortable place to wait while your car was being worked on.

"Hi, guys."

Tom McKnight looked up from his paperwork, and immediately grinned, obviously happy to see him. Syd's expression was guarded, which meant happy to see him, something on her mind.

"Hi, son." His dad turned off his computer and slid off the high stool in front of it. He held out his hand and after grabbing it, he pulled Ben into a quick hug. "Good to see you."

His father had just turned sixty, still a handsome man with brown hair that was liberally sprinkled with silver. There were crinkle lines at the corners of light blue eyes that would always show the shadow of sadness from losing his wife too soon. She'd died from complications of childbirth after Syd was born. As the face of McKnight Automotive, he dressed professionally in a long-sleeved yellow shirt, coordinating striped tie and sharply pressed khakis.

"What can I do for you?" he asked.

"The SUV needs an oil change and tire rotation. Can you do it first thing in the morning if I leave it overnight?"

"Sure. Can you spare it?"

"I'm not on call, so if Syd will give me a lift to the lodge..."

"I'm happy to." She looked up from the computer, clearly having listened to the conversation. "But why can't your main squeeze come and get you?"

Ben met his father's gaze and saw the question reflected there, too. Main squeeze? What was she talking... Oh. Right. Cam. So they'd heard about the diner. He'd forgotten how fast word spread in Blackwater Lake, even though

that's what he'd been counting on. Apparently the plan was working even better than he'd hoped.

"Cam has her hands full at work and I don't want to bother her." The first part was true or she wouldn't have agreed to the bargain. As far as bothering her? He hoped that kiss was bothering her as much as it was him. He looked at his sister. "Besides, you go right past the lodge on your way home."

That was also true.

"What makes you think I don't have plans? A date?"

"You told me you were taking a break," he reminded her. "Speaking of that, how's the hand?"

She flexed her fingers. "Good as new. You were right about giving it time."

"Glad to hear that."

"Bev Thompson from the diner was in today." His father gave him the what-the-hell-are-you-doing? look. "I didn't know you were going out with that hotel woman."

Hotel woman? That made Cam sound like a room-by-the-hour girl and Ben felt a quick spurt of anger. "When I lived in Las Vegas it wasn't my habit to run past you every woman I went out with."

"You're not in Vegas anymore." His father loosened his tie. "This is where you grew up."

Ben decided not to debate the point. "Cam is a dedicated businesswoman. Ambitious, conscientious and smart."

Syd's eyes widened a little at his sharp tone. "Looks like you hit a nerve, Dad."

"I didn't think taking her to dinner was breaking news or that you guys needed advance notice. It's my private life."

"In Blackwater Lake nothing stays private," his father said, stating the obvious.

Ben knew that but hadn't been prepared for the part of

the plan where his family would find out. As fast as word got out about them dating, it could get out about them being a phony couple. He had to play this just right. Best to stick with the truth wherever possible.

"Things with Cam and me happened pretty fast."

That was true. He hadn't planned to kiss her, but when Judy appeared out of nowhere it had seemed like an excellent idea. After the fact he wasn't so sure, because the taste of her had made him burn for more.

Tom McKnight looked at him long and hard, then nodded. "You're a grown man and I guess you know what you're doing. But I can't help worrying about you. It's what a father does."

"There's no need, Dad. But I appreciate it."

"Comes with the territory, son."

Ben looked at Syd. "About that ride home…"

"Let me change and I'll be right with you." She headed out of the office toward the employee area.

"Why is Syd taking a break from men?" he asked when his sister was out of earshot.

"Beats me." Tom shrugged. "You'd think in a place that can't keep a secret someone would know. If they do I haven't heard."

"I guess she'll talk when she's ready." Speaking of ready… Ben could barely recall the time before Syd was born when his mother had been with them. To his knowledge, his father had been alone ever since she died. "How are you, Dad? Anyone *you* want to tell me about? Are you seeing anyone?"

"I have friends and some of them are of the female persuasion. But your mother was the only one for me." He smiled, but it didn't fool either of them. Tom McKnight was the kind of man who loved fiercely and only once.

Ben wondered if that was a quality he'd inherited, but

seeing Judy again went a long way toward answering part of that question. He felt absolutely nothing for her and wondered now why it had hurt so much when he'd heard she married someone else.

"Your ride is here and it's leaving." Syd had changed out of her overalls into snug jeans, a camisole top and red blazer. She'd transformed from a scrappy little mechanic into a beautiful, sophisticated woman. They said clothes didn't make the man or woman and that was true as far as character, but the change in his sister was truly amazing.

He slid his arm across her shoulders and resisted the familiar urge to rub his knuckles across the top of her head. There would be hell to pay now if he messed up her hair. "You're a very stylish grease monkey."

"I'm sure there's a compliment in there somewhere, but I'll have to dig it out later." Her eyes twinkled when she looked up at him. "Are you ready to go?"

"Whenever you are. I'll see you tomorrow, Dad."

"Since I'm holding your car hostage, I'll look forward to it." He lifted a hand in a goodbye gesture.

Ben followed his sister to the parking lot and got in the passenger side of her sporty red compact. He moved the seat back for more leg room and noticed how close Syd was to the steering wheel. She was a small woman, like their mother.

She fastened her seat belt and turned on the ignition. Before they reached the exit, the doors automatically locked. "Now I've got you where I want you."

"Should I be afraid?"

"A smart man would be. I want to know what's really going on with you and that woman. Consider yourself lucky that I didn't push this in front of Dad."

"Her name is Camille and we're friends who enjoy each other's company."

"Trying to decide whether or not to take it to the next level?"

"Exactly," he agreed.

"Is she seeing anyone else?"

"No." He hadn't actually thought to ask her that question.

"Are you?"

"No." That he was sure about.

Syd shook her head and tightened her hands on the steering wheel. "I don't buy it. She's not your type."

That's what Judy had said. And how did they figure that? "What *is* my type?"

"Not a hotel heiress who went to the slammer, I can tell you that."

The slammer was a long time ago and everyone was entitled to a second chance. Cam had definitely made the most of hers. "Have you been talking to Judy Coulter?"

"I wouldn't waste my breath on that...witch." She glanced over at him. "Why?"

"Cam and I ran into her."

Syd glanced at him. "You're trying to change the subject, but it won't work."

"What exactly is the subject?"

"Your personal life. I have questions. Starting with: For a guy who's been avoiding a serious relationship for a very long time, you picked the wrong woman to break the dating fast."

"That's not a question, it's a statement," he pointed out.

"The question is implied," she shot back.

"How do you know I haven't dated?"

The question *was* a diversion to get her off the scent. When had his sister become so perceptive? Ben hadn't counted on that either.

"I listen. You should try it sometime." She flashed him

a grin. "The thing is, I tuck away information. And women just know this stuff. There hasn't been anyone serious for you, not since college. Now the first one you pick is the type to get her name in the papers for all the wrong reasons?"

"For the record, I don't have a type."

"And it has to be said, that's all the debate strategy you've got?"

"Yes." The less he said, the better. "No type."

"Baloney. You have one and Cam Halliday isn't it. There's something fishy going on here."

"To quote you, baloney. There's nothing fishy about an attraction to a beautiful, brainy woman with a terrific sense of humor," he defended. And a body that makes a man's palms sweat.

What else could he do? If this ruse was going to work, everyone had to believe they were a couple. When the message spread and sank in, women would back off and leave him alone. He'd get peace and quiet at work. Was that really too much to ask?

"She is pretty," Syd conceded. "And a great dresser. I'd give almost anything to have a shoe wardrobe like hers. But I'll have to reluctantly take your word for the rest."

The rest was a petite package who'd kissed him back. A kiss that packed a punch and he hoped she'd "hit" him with it again. The fact that she turned him on would make it really easy to play the part of her boyfriend.

"It sounds like you're smitten."

"I definitely am," he agreed.

"Then you should bring her to dinner Sunday night. It's family night. We'd all like to get to know her." She pulled the car into the Blackwater Lake Lodge and braked to a stop by the front door.

Ben released his seat belt and tried to think of a way out

of this one. It would be easy to play his part with people who didn't know him, but him and Cam spending time with his family was a recipe for disaster. If he put up a protest the way he wanted to right now, it would be like pouring kerosene on the flames of his sister's curiosity. She was already suspicious and would want to know why he was hiding Cam from them.

He hoped he didn't regret this. "That sounds great. What time and what can we bring?"

"Dad's barbecuing and we'll eat around six. Why don't you bring that seven-layer chocolate cake from the lodge restaurant that everyone in town is raving about?"

"I can tell you from personal experience that it's fantastic. We'll be there at five-thirty."

"Great." Syd smiled with a satisfaction that was unnerving. "We'll see you then. Can't wait."

"Me either. Thanks for the ride."

"Any time, big brother."

Any time little sister had an ulterior motive, was more like it, he thought, watching the taillights on her car move out of sight. He blew out a breath. It was put up or shut up time. He was going to take his fake relationship out for a spin with his father, older brother and baby sister—the three people on the planet who knew him best. If they weren't fooled it was game over.

Now all he had to do was talk Cam into it.

Chapter Seven

Late Sunday afternoon Cam was sitting in the passenger seat of Ben's car and not a particularly happy camper. Even though he'd said something about more dinners, she'd been hoping that no further action would be required from her for this bargain. Was it too much to ask that gossip from the diner sighting of them together would hold everyone for a while? At least long enough for her to get over that kiss?

"Tell me again why I have to meet your family and eat Sunday dinner at your dad's?"

Ben glanced over at her, then settled his gaze back on the road. His dad lived just outside of town, not too far from the lake, and the way was winding. "Red flags will be raised if anyone asks about us and my family hasn't met you. It's what a normal couple would do."

"Is it what you and Judy did?" There was just the tiniest bit of shrew in her tone and that wasn't a particularly good thing. Was it jealousy? Or annoyance that he'd only kissed her to make some kind of statement to his ex-girlfriend?

"Judy and I were just kids." Was it imagination or did his jaw just clench? Did he still have scars from what happened? "Now, a few pointers about the McKnights."

Ah. He didn't want to talk about the ex. Cam wasn't sure what that meant, but was happy to change the subject.

"Anything you can tell me will help," she said.

"Remember, this is just a low-key dinner. All very normal."

"I wouldn't know about normal. Nothing about my life ever was. Especially after my brother died."

He shook his head in sympathy. "As annoying as they can get at times, I can't imagine losing one of my siblings. That must have been hard."

"It was." Her heart caught as an image of Dean Junior's handsome, teasing face flashed into her mind. "But before I'd even dealt with the loss, the burden of responsibility that he was supposed to carry shifted to me. In the blink of an eye I was the oldest child of Dean Halliday. As such, I was expected to take over the reins of Halliday Hospitality Inc. someday." She gripped her hands in her lap. "I rebelled."

"All kids do."

"But I elevated it to an art form. Sneaking out of the house in the middle of the night to party with friends I knew my parents didn't like." She cringed, remembering the chances she'd taken. "That resulted in more than one ultimatum."

"They were worried about you."

"No. They worried that company stock prices would drop. I didn't care about anyone but myself then. All I could see was that the kids I thought were cool wanted to hang out with me."

"Every kid goes through that stage."

"I bet you didn't."

"Sure I did." He glanced over and met her gaze. "To me that all sounds pretty normal."

"Not when the police get involved. There were brushes with the law. Then I was in the wrong place, wrong time, at the wheel without a driver's license and someone in the car had drugs. The judge didn't believe I didn't know. And my last name is Halliday. He decided to make an example of me."

"That was a long time ago."

"Yeah." She looked out the window, at the scenery going by. The trees were green and serene and when he drove around the lake, the sight of sunlight turning the surface of the water to shimmering blue took her breath away. "I grew up and discovered I have a head for business."

She glanced over at him and lost her breath again for a different reason. Ben McKnight was an incredibly good-looking man. He would turn women's heads in Hollywood or New York, cities that had some of the most handsome, sophisticated men in the world. As far as her head was concerned, she was having trouble keeping it on business because of him.

"Cut yourself some slack," he suggested. "You turned your attention to school and proving yourself to the corporation. That means you're focused. And you're going to need to be for the McKnights."

"Now you're scaring me."

"My family has to believe we're a couple or no one else in town will buy the act." He glanced at her. "No pressure."

And if the act was outed, any strides she'd made with the employees at the lodge would disappear. Any career ambitions she'd had would go up in smoke because she would fail the test her father had given her.

She nodded emphatically. "Okay. We're a couple. Got it."

"You should also know that my sister is already suspicious."

"Great."

"We're almost there."

"And the hits just keep on coming," she mumbled.

He turned off the main road into a tract of homes. After following the road around a curve, he stopped the car at the curb of a small house with gray siding and white trim. The tops of the pine trees behind it were visible over the roof. In the front a large expanse of grass was green and manicured. There were three vehicles in the driveway— a small, sporty red compact, a big black truck and a silver Cadillac sedan.

Ben met her gaze. "Here we go."

"I can hardly wait," she muttered.

After exiting the car, he took the boxed seven-layer cake, then put his hand at her waist, guiding her up the drive to the covered porch. Cam could feel the heat of his fingers through her wool blazer and satin blouse. The touch skewered rational thought just when she needed it the most. He knocked on the door and it was opened almost immediately.

A beautiful, brown-eyed brunette stood there. "Hi. Glad you guys could make it."

"Me, too." Ben put his free arm around Cam's shoulders. "Syd, this Camille Halliday. Cam, my sister, Sydney."

"It's nice to meet you." This is the one who was suspicious. Cam smiled and held out her hand. "Thanks for fixing my flat."

"You're welcome." The other woman shook it as she looked over her outfit, including the black silk-blend slacks and Jimmy Choo heels. An expression somewhere between admiration and envy slid over her face. Sydney was wear-

ing jeans tucked into brown calf boots and a long-sleeved yellow T-shirt.

Two men came up behind her. One was a handsome, slightly older version of Ben and the other a good-looking guy who had a strong resemblance to his sons. Both wore jeans, boots and T-shirts. Ben wore essentially the same outfit, which should have been a clue that Cam was severely overdressed. Her heart sank because you didn't win hearts and minds by not fitting in.

She shook hands with both of them. "It's a pleasure."

"All mine," Alex said, smiling. He was a local building contractor. "I can't imagine what a woman like you is doing with my brother."

What gave her away? She hadn't really done anything yet and the jig was up. Then she realized the two men were grinning at each other so she deduced that his comment wasn't about their charade but simple good-natured sibling teasing.

Obviously feeling her tension, Ben tightened the arm he still had around her shoulders. "Don't mind Alex. He's okay when you get to know him."

"Don't keep her out here on the porch, Ben." His father smiled. "Come on in, you two."

"Thank you, Mr. McKnight."

"Call me Tom." He stepped aside as they walked in. "What would you like to drink? Beer? Wine? Soft drink? Iced tea?"

"I'd love a glass of white wine if you've got it."

"Chardonnay?" Sydney asked.

"Perfect."

As they followed the other three McKnights into the kitchen, Ben took her hand. It felt weird and wrong and fake and wonderful. She really liked the strength of his fin-

gers, the warmth and the tingles. The you-and-me-against-the-world touch took a little energy out of her nerves.

Alex pulled a bottle of wine out of the refrigerator and expertly used a foil cutter and corkscrew to open it. Like his brother, he was an extraordinarily good-looking man. Like most women would, Cam glanced at his left ring finger, which was bare. He was probably single and she made a mental note to find out from Ben if Alex was having the same problem with women throwing themselves at him.

"Here you go," Alex said, handing her a glass of wine.

"Thanks." Their fingers brushed and she felt no tingles or anything out of the ordinary. It was a totally different and distinct experience from when she touched Ben and that shouldn't be. The terms of their bargain didn't allow for heat and tingles when touching.

Finally everyone had a drink and Tom said, "Let's go outside."

"Sounds good, Dad." After setting the cake on the counter, Ben slung his arm across her shoulders again, as if they'd been going together for years instead of days.

He was surprisingly good at this pretending thing.

The rear yard was just as beautiful as the front. It felt like a park, with an expanse of grass surrounded by shrubs and flowers. The wooden fence held back a forest of pine trees.

On the covered back porch there were two wrought-iron love seats covered with pads and a couple of matching chairs. Cam and Ben sat side by side, thighs touching and sparks flying. The closeness caused a hitch in her breathing and she sipped her wine to cover it. Alex took one of the single chairs closest to her and Tom sat with his daughter across from them.

"So, Cam, how do you like Blackwater Lake?" Alex

took a drink from his longneck beer. The label read Moose Drool. Ew.

"It's a beautiful place." She glanced at Ben. The twinkle in his eyes told her he knew she was lying. That wasn't fair. The town *was* beautiful; it just wasn't New York or L.A. "We drove past the lake and with the sun shining, the surface looked like glittering diamonds."

Sydney's smile was supposed to look friendly and to her family it probably did. But a woman could see the cynicism around the edges. "Diamonds are a girl's best friend."

"I couldn't agree more." Cam met her gaze. "A girl who doesn't like jewelry is a quart low on estrogen. Call me shallow, but I can't be friends with someone like that."

"Well put," Sydney agreed, grudging respect in her eyes as a smile turned up the corners of her full lips.

"I know my sister is outnumbered by the boys and taking advantage of having another woman around," Alex said. "But please tell me we're not going to discuss the latest feminine hygiene product."

"I think he just challenged us," Cam said. "Sydney, do you want to start or should I get the ball rolling with what's new in shapewear these days?"

That got an actual laugh from the McKnights' lone female. "High five, Cam."

"Well, well…" Alex glanced between the two women. "That sounds a lot like a seal of approval from my little sister, and I agree. Camille, a lady as pretty as you should feel right at home in a place as beautiful as Blackwater Lake."

"Thank you." If he talked like that to all the girls, they'd be lining up to contract his house-building services and a whole lot of things that had nothing to do with construction.

"Hands off, bro. I saw her first." Ben threaded his fin-

gers through hers and settled their linked hands on his muscular thigh.

The resulting wave of heat almost kept her from noticing the slightest edge to his voice and the possessiveness of the gesture. Was this real jealousy, or was he pretending? It was the sort of thing an actual boyfriend might do and felt very real. So real she had to remind herself that this was just make-believe.

Sydney's gaze narrowed as she studied them. "Is anyone else starving? I think it's time to cook the steaks, Dad."

"Okay. I'll fire up the barbecue."

"I'll take care of everything inside." She stood. "Do you want to give me a hand, Cam?"

This was a test, Cam thought. "Of course."

"Me, too," Ben said.

The three of them went into the kitchen where Syd pulled an already-put-together salad from the refrigerator. "Why don't you two set the table?"

"Okay." Ben turned toward the cupboard nearest the natural pine table in the kitchen's eating nook. "I'll show you where everything is, sweetie."

"Thanks."

Was she supposed to add an endearing nickname, too? This phony-girlfriend thing was harder than she'd thought. Play-acting for his family was a lot of pressure, but if they passed this test, fooling the rest of Blackwater Lake should be easier. But the McKnights seemed like a wonderful family. There was a part of her that wished this wasn't an act and normal could be hers.

"So, Cam," Syd said, setting a bowl of potato salad on the table. "Do you like the outdoors?"

Was this a trick question? "I love the fresh air here in the mountains. But work keeps me pretty busy. I don't get out much."

"So you haven't been camping yet?"

"No." That was the truth. Not once ever in her life had she slept without four walls surrounding her that included a bathroom with running water and electricity. She looked at Ben for guidance, but he was just taking plates down from a shelf and the rattling kept him from hearing the question. "Like I said, there hasn't been much time off since I got here."

The look in her brown eyes said Syd was just getting started. "Ben loves backpacking, fishing and camping, don't you, big brother?"

He set the five plates on the table, which was big enough for six people, and put one in front of each chair. "Yeah. I've missed doing that."

"Isn't that one of the reasons you moved back here?" his sister persisted. "Camping, fishing, being outdoors?"

"It is," he agreed.

"Have you ever camped out, Cam?"

She looked at Ben again, unsure how far this pretense should go. It was all a big lie, but lacing everything with some truth would make the ruse easier to pull off. "Since my family owns a hotel chain, the only camping out we did had room service. But it's something I've always wanted to try."

A little truth followed closely by a whopper of a lie.

Ben moved close and settled his arm around her waist. Tension was evident in his body. "As a matter of fact, I'm taking Cam backpacking next weekend, right, sweetie?"

Cam's gaze snapped to his. This was not what she'd signed up for, and definitely not spelled out in their verbal agreement. It did, however, fall into the category of convincing his family. If they were convinced, people in town would be, too.

"Right," she said, shooting him a glare.

Syd pulled a platter of raw steaks from the refrigerator. "Ben, would you take this out to Dad?"

"Yeah." He took it and opened the door. "Be right back."

Then Cam was alone with the suspicious sister. Ben's dad had seemed happy that his son was happy. His brother appeared to approve of her. Sydney McKnight was the lone family holdout and kept staring as if she expected an alien to pop out of Cam's chest.

"There's something fishy going on," she said.

"I guess that happens when camping and fishing are involved." Cam winced at the stupid joke.

The serious expression on Syd's face didn't change. "Just so we're clear, if you break my brother's heart..."

"What if he breaks mine?" That was an automatic response, but for the first time Cam realized it was a possibility.

She liked Ben more every time they were together. That was potentially a problem, because the longer she had to keep up the pretense of being his girlfriend, the more she could see herself falling for him, for real. And now they'd been maneuvered into a weekend trip.

Maybe they could just pretend to go camping.

Cam was standing at the front desk with M.J. and Glen Larson, the general manager. He was tall, dark and nice-looking, in his early twenties and a recent college grad with a brand-spanking-new business degree. The three of them were looking over upcoming bookings. Summer was only a couple months away and she'd feel a lot better if reservations increased.

Shaking her head Cam said, "I have to figure out a way to pitch the positives of Blackwater Lake Lodge to travel professionals and online sites."

"I can help with that," Glen offered. "I've got some ex-

perience in web marketing. There's a way to make sure this town and the lodge come up first in the search engine when someone is looking for information on Montana."

"That would be great." She smiled at him, his earnestness and willingness to help. Cooperation was a nice change and there was little doubt that she had Ben McKnight to thank for it. "If you need extra time to work on it, let me know. I can handle some of your management responsibilities. And if necessary and you're okay with it, I can authorize limited overtime."

"Thanks, boss." His surprised tone said he hadn't fully expected teamwork or support from her.

"Okay, now for the employee appreciation dinner next week. We need—"

Her two employees smiled at someone behind her; she'd been concentrating so hard she hadn't heard anyone approach. Then strong hands on her shoulders gently turned her and she saw Ben standing there. Her heart did a little skip and shimmy when he smiled.

"Hey, beautiful." He was looking at her mouth.

"Hi." She blinked up at him, wondering if the glow growing inside her was visible to the naked eye. "It has to be said that there are rules against non-employees being behind this desk."

"Rules were meant to be broken." He took her hand and settled it in the bend of his elbow. "But I respect you and your work so I'll just have to lure you out into the neutral zone and away from all this."

"Good luck with that, Doc." Glen slid his hands into the pockets of his charcoal slacks. "M.J. and I have been trying to get her to go home for an hour."

"He's right. She works too hard. All work and no play..." M.J. lifted one eyebrow to make her point.

"I love what I do and it doesn't feel like work," Cam protested.

"Still—" Ben gently tugged her around the desk to the lobby side. "I've got you now, my pretty. And we have shopping to do."

"Shoes?" she asked hopefully.

"Yes." His eyes twinkled. "Hiking boots."

"What did I ever do to deserve this?"

"She's a wilderness virgin and needs stuff. I'm taking her camping," he explained.

Because his family, specifically his sister, was torturing her. "Lucky me."

"Sounds like fun." M.J. walked into the office behind the desk and returned with Cam's purse and handed it over. "Go. Work will still be here in the morning."

How many mornings after that would it be here if business didn't pick up?

"Okay." She started to turn away, then thought of something. "Wait. One more thing. What's happening with the employee dinner? I know the restaurant chef is handling all the food. Do we know—"

"Today is the deadline for RSVPs," M.J. said. "I'll get the head count to Amanda. I formed a volunteer committee to decorate the conference room. We'll keep it simple. It's being handled. Go. Fly. Be free."

"Thanks." She saluted. "See you guys in the morning."

Ben walked her out the front door to where he'd parked his car, then handed her inside. He went around to the driver's side and got in. "This will be fun. Trust me. Don't look like the Olympic rifle team is going to use your designer shoes for target practice."

"It feels that way."

"You're such a glass-half-empty person. Where's that stiff upper lip?"

"There's not enough Botox or filler on the planet for that when you're talking boondocks and backpacks."

He laughed, which meant one of them was having a good time. Actually, she was, too. Who'd have thought?

Ben drove into town and pulled into the parking lot behind the large sporting-goods store. After getting out of the car, they headed for the rear entrance, where he held the door for her to precede him inside. Straight ahead was a locked glass case displaying rifles, pistols and some lethal-looking hunting knives.

Cam stared at the weapons, then up at her pretend boyfriend. "About that whole execution thing? Are you sure camping isn't like that?"

"You'll be completely safe," he assured her.

She shook her head. "I think we need to renegotiate the terms of this bargain."

Ben glanced around to see if anyone had heard the incriminating statement, then took her elbow and led her to a secluded corner behind a rack of quilted down vests and cargo pants.

"The agreement is perfectly clear," he said calmly. "There's not really anything to define. We're making it up as we go along, but everyone needs to believe you're my girlfriend."

"And two nights of sleeping on the ground is going to convince them?"

"Yes."

"Can't we go to a hotel in a big city far from here and just tell everyone we backpacked into the mountains?"

"You mean lie?"

"We're already doing that," she pointed out. "After the first whopper it gets easier."

"My sister isn't completely buying us as a couple. She knows I like the outdoors and anyone I go out with would

have to be willing to try it. And the trying it part has to be convincing. A lie only works if you wrap it in enough of the truth."

"So, I need snake bites, scratches and dirt under my fingernails so she'll believe?"

"Yeah." He shrugged. "Either that or things go back to the way they were."

That meant a return to uncooperative lodge employees and the cold shoulder from the rest of the town. She shuddered. Things had been noticeably better since she'd "been with" Ben. There was an actual *volunteer* committee, for goodness' sake. She was beginning to have a glimmer of hope for upward mobility in her career.

And that was just her. If the deal fell apart, women would start throwing themselves at Ben again. Now there was a thought that she wasn't crazy about. Oddly enough, she liked it a lot less than being able to bring only what she could carry on her back for a whole weekend in the mountains. If she didn't know better, she'd call what she was feeling jealousy. But that wasn't part of the bargain.

"Wow, I think all the fresh air here in Blackwater Lake is beginning to affect my reasoning ability."

He looked amused. "Why?"

"Because I, Camille Halliday, am going to buy camping stuff. The world has gone mad."

He grinned. "Let's do this."

About an hour later, they had backpacks, sleeping bags, a lightweight tent and the sturdiest and chicest hiking boots money could buy. The wiry, gray-haired man at the cash register put the newsmagazine he was reading down on the counter. He must have been the owner, because he was practically quivering with excitement at all the stuff they piled up.

"This be all for you, Doc?" He looked at Ben, then her.

"I think so, Mr. Daly."

"Got your sunscreen and mosquito repellant?"

"Do you have anything that will discourage snakes?" Cam asked.

The owner laughed. "She's a pistol. Got a great sense of humor."

"Yes, she does." Ben put his arm around her shoulders and squeezed.

Cam was getting far too used to that. She liked feeling his strength and that big, warm body close to hers.

"So what's the damage, Mr. Daly?"

The man gave them a very impressive total and Cam started to pull a credit card out.

Ben stopped her and said, "I've got this."

"We'll settle up later." She had skin in this, too, and couldn't let him do that.

He shook his head. "It's settled now."

Unsettled was more like it, Cam thought when her heart started beating erratically. But it was stupid to do that. This was just him playing a part, showing people that he wasn't Mr. Camille Halliday, but a man with deep pockets of pride who paid his own way and hers. Wouldn't it be nice if it weren't an act at all? Talk about make-believe.

The man put the smaller items into bags and slid them across the counter. The newsmagazine caught underneath the plastic bag and fell on the floor at her feet.

"I'll get that." Cam picked up the paper, absently looking at the front as she handed it back. Her hand froze as something caught her attention. She read the headline and her stomach knotted until losing her lunch along with her sense of humor was a real possibility.

There was a picture of Ben kissing her outside the Grizzly Bear Diner and the headline screamed, "Halliday heiress hot for hug-a-licious hunk."

Chapter Eight

Ben wanted to put his fist through a wall when he saw the headline and Cam's stricken look, but she was upset enough for the both of them. He decided to try and keep it light. "Good alliteration."

"I'm so sorry." She glanced at him, then skimmed the article some more. "I was so sure that I was off the rag-sheet radar. This is awful. M.J. even warned me that the guy was asking questions."

"What guy?" Anger curled through him.

"Stan Overton, the sleazy guy we saw at the diner that night. Obviously he was following me and snapped this picture. I was so sure it was all behind me. If I'd thought for a second you'd be involved, I'd never have—"

Ben touched a finger to her lips. Partly because he hated to see her so upset about this trash, but also to keep her from revealing their secret. Mr. Daly was watching intently.

"Let's go put all this stuff in the car," Ben suggested.

She looked at him, then the man, and comprehension flared in her eyes. "Okay."

Together they carried all the bags to his SUV and stowed them in the back. Then he put her in the passenger seat and jogged around to get behind the wheel.

"I'm so sorry, Ben. I should have known better than to get you mixed up in this."

"It was my idea, remember?" He was angry, but not with Cam. It was with the bottom-feeders who victimized someone like her. She'd been through the devastating loss of her brother and hadn't been allowed to act out without every move ending up on the front page. If her family hadn't had money, no one would have cared. "You've got to shake this off. Don't let them get to you."

"I'm not worried about me. Although when my father sees this, and he will, my odds of getting a better assignment at a bigger property are about as good as managing a motel on the moon." She met his gaze. "You need to find someone else to run interference for you."

He didn't want someone else. "Don't be hasty."

"Seriously. Associating with me could jeopardize your credibility at the clinic. I couldn't stand being responsible for that."

"You underestimate the people of Blackwater Lake. They can separate personal from professional."

The outside parking lot lights illuminated the shadow of betrayal in her eyes and Ben badly wanted to make it go away. If they hadn't been sitting in the car, he would have taken her in his arms, so it was probably a good thing they were here.

She shook her head. "This is a lousy situation without recourse. The public believes that someone with monetary resources is fair game for their entertainment. In their minds the question becomes: Is the crown too tight? Are

the jewels too heavy?" She sighed. "So I just have to suck it up. If it ruins my life, there's not much I can do. But I won't let them take you down, too. You need to distance yourself from me—"

"No."

She blinked at him. "What?"

"You don't need to protect me. I can take care of myself."

Distance was the last thing he wanted. Taking care of her was the first order of business. This protective instinct was usually reserved for his patients. He channeled it into his profession. With Cam it was personal, more than he'd expected.

"I'm sure you can protect yourself, but dealing with negative tabloid publicity isn't something they taught you in medical school." She wadded up the newsmagazine. "They twist the truth or print outright lies. I'm a demanding diva who cracks the whip. I broke up a perfectly good housekeeping team because they talk too much."

"Yeah," he agreed. "They talk at the top of their lungs."

"That part was conveniently left out because it doesn't sell papers. I've dealt with it all my life. But they'll try to dig up dirt on you, too. It's best if we don't see each other and cancel the camping—"

"Let me stop you right there." He took her hand and the delicacy of her fingers and wrist twisted him up inside. "A backpacking trip is just what the doctor ordered. We'll get away. Let the dust settle. By the time we get back, the whole thing will have blown over."

"That would be running away, and Hallidays don't do that."

"Neither do McKnights."

She was quiet as she studied him, but didn't pull away

when he linked his fingers with hers. "Don't be a martyr, Ben."

"The thought never crossed my mind." He laughed, then turned serious. "Don't let them win, Cam. It's an opportunity. I can show you how beautiful Blackwater Lake is so you can pass it on to guests at the lodge. First-person experience."

"You're saying this is all about business?"

"Exactly." Sort of. Although it was feeling a little more personal than he'd expected.

"Okay, then. Let's go backpacking."

"I must have been high on clean air when I let you talk me into this." Cam walked the uneven trail beside Ben.

There was a slight grade and that took them steadily uphill. Fortunately gym workouts and stair-stepper sessions had kept her in good enough shape so as not to be embarrassed. But at the fitness center you didn't have to carry on your back all the stuff you needed for one night and two days in the mountains. Ben had shown her how to attach her sleeping bag to the lightweight frame.

"You're going to love this," he predicted.

"Wouldn't it be easier to be airlifted in by helicopter?"

"Of course. But there are several problems with that scenario. First and most important, the trees are too thick for a chopper to get through." He looked down at her. "Second, while hiking you get to appreciate the beauty and awesomeness of these spectacular mountains. And—"

"There's more?"

"No pain, no gain. You'll appreciate it a lot more where we're going if it's not easy to get there."

"So it's like banging your head against the wall? Feels good when you stop?"

"Something like that." His gaze was assessing as he

looked her over, checking for fatigue. "Are you sorry yet about insisting on bringing the wine?"

"Never." She shook her head emphatically. "Just because this is the wilderness doesn't mean we have to be uncivilized."

"Unlike the offensive bottom-feeders who write stories for the rag sheets."

"Yeah. Like them." She brushed the back of her hand across the perspiration on her forehead. Wearing a baseball cap, she'd pulled her hair through the opening at the back, getting it off her neck. "That still makes me mad enough to spit."

"Self-control," he warned. "You don't want to dehydrate."

"Gotta love the great outdoors. And, speaking of that, it seems pointless to put myself through this when there's a very good chance that tabloid story will put an end to my career before it even gets started."

Ben handed her one of the refillable water bottles that was strapped to his pack. The plan was to refill them at the stream where they'd set up camp. "I disagree about your downward career trajectory."

"This will not endear me to employees who already think I'm a privileged, ditzy diva. And you don't know my father."

"Then he doesn't know marketing strategy. You're famous. Any publicity will be good for the lodge and the town, too. Local businesses will be grateful for all the customers you bring in and you didn't have to pay for it."

"Not out of pocket, but there's still a price." Self-esteem. Reputation. Dignity. Respect.

"The people who know you won't believe that trash. And everyone else doesn't matter."

"It's easy for you to say that because your life has never

been turned upside down by someone who stalks you with a camera then writes lies about the pictures that are flashed all over the world."

"Speaking of that…" He pulled out his digital pocket camera. "Everyone in town is expecting pictures of us."

She snorted. "We could stage them. Photoshop everything. Paparazzi do it all the time."

"I'm not an underhanded reporter trying to make a buck by slandering a celebrity. And it's the most natural thing in the world for us to take photos on a camping trip. We're supposed to be a couple."

"About that…" She took a drink of water, then looked up, but couldn't see his eyes behind the aviator sunglasses. "I wouldn't blame you if you changed your mind about the bargain. It's not easy being my boyfriend."

"So far it's been pretty stress-free."

"Because we're pretending. What happens because of that picture of you kissing me will be very real. Now you're a target, too. If there's anything to find they'll drag your name through the mud." She handed back the water bottle. "I'd like to apologize in advance for that."

"You have nothing to be sorry for." He hooked the bottle on his backpack. "And don't worry about me. I'm a big boy. I know what I'm getting into."

"No offense, but you really don't. They'll say that you're only with me to kick-start your medical practice in backwoodsville. Or you came back to a small town because you weren't good enough to make it in the big city. Possibly that a love affair gone bad turned you into Grizzly Adams, a recluse who can't hack it anywhere else. They make stuff up. That's what they do and it's the reason I've been single so long."

"Because of unscrupulous reporters?"

"Yeah." She glanced up at him as her boots scraped

across the dirt trail. "They make up front-page lies and the truthful retraction is buried on the second-to-last page days later. But trash sells. Some guys wanted to be with me to get their name in the paper, to get noticed by producers, directors, people who could fast-track a career." She shrugged. "Other guys didn't want anything to do with me because the circus that is my life could spill over into theirs. I've found it's just easier to be on my own."

"Again, I need to remind you that this bargain was my idea."

"Only because you didn't fully understand what dating me would entail."

"There's some truth to that." He nodded. "But we've spelled out the rules and both of us know why we're doing this. I *am* using you for my career—to keep women from turning my medical practice into a farce."

"And I'm using you to rehabilitate my image with everyone in Blackwater Lake. As far as I can see that tabloid story makes us zero for two."

"I think you're wrong." He glanced down. "The goal was to spread the news that I'm not available. One picture is worth a thousand words."

"I hope you still see it that way after you fully experience the fallout from this. Believe me, you're going to be relieved that this relationship is fake."

Cam looked up when he didn't respond to that statement and realized that part of her wanted him to refute what she'd just said. Part of her wanted him to say that so far it had been fun playing out their secret arrangement. But she didn't get that vibe from what she could see of his face.

There was an intensity tightening his jaw and with the stubble darkening it, he looked decidedly uncivilized—in the sexiest possible way. Her heart stuttered and her stomach shimmied in a way that had become unfamiliar,

a way she'd put aside because that was easier than giving her heart to a man only to be disappointed yet again. She was attracted to Ben McKnight and it had nothing to do with the agreement they'd made.

Wanting him wasn't part of the bargain, but that didn't stop it from being true.

"Are you warm enough?" Squatting by the campfire, Ben put more kindling and wood on the glowing embers.

"Yes."

The fire was lovely, but Cam was plenty warm admiring how the glow of the sparks highlighted the lean, rugged angles of his face and broad, muscular shoulders. She was warm from the tips of her toes to the top of her head from watching the competent way he'd set up the tent and arranged the sleeping bags inside while she'd gathered rocks and arranged them in a circle for the fire. They'd refilled water bottles, then Ben had fished in the stream, eventually catching the trout that he'd cooked.

"That fish you made was as good as anything I've eaten at the lodge's five-star restaurant."

"Too bad we don't have Montana's best seven-layer chocolate cake for dessert."

He looked over his shoulder and grinned before standing, looking all masculine mountain man. In two steps he was beside her, then lowered all that lean strength to a sitting position next to her, so close that his shoulder brushed hers. Sparks from the friction felt as real as the ones she'd seen when he stirred up the campfire.

"At least there's wine." She sighed and it had nothing to do with the absence of cake and everything to do with the presence of this sexy, competent doctor.

He made her feel safe and she hadn't thought any man could make that happen. They were sitting on a blanket

with their backs braced against a fallen log, legs stretched out in front of them, holding plastic wine glasses.

"If I'd known fish was the main course, I'd have brought a nice white instead of Pinot Noir. But when you're roughing it in the godforsaken wilderness, beggars can't be choosers."

"Has anyone ever told you that you have a finely tuned flair for the dramatic?" He shook his head. "We're a couple hours' hike from town, not on an expedition to the wasteland of the North Pole."

"Still…" She finished the wine in her glass and refilled it from the bottle beside her. When she held it out to him, he shook his head.

"What do you think of camping so far?" he asked.

"It's not hideous."

He laughed. "Wow. I'm not sure the Blackwater Lake Chamber of Commerce and Visitor Guide is going to want that as a slogan for their advertising campaign. I can see it now—'Come to Montana. It's not hideous.'"

She laughed, too. "Let me frame that comment better so you'll understand where it came from."

"I can hardly wait to see how you can spin it to rehabilitate that remark."

"It's about me, and I don't mean that in a self-centered way." She took a sip of wine even as the relaxation from the first glass slid through her. "I wasn't sure how I'd hold up just getting here. Would I collapse in a heap on the trail? Break a leg? Snake bite?"

"I can't believe how optimistic you are."

"Seriously. I didn't know if I had the stamina and intestinal fortitude. Heck, I had no idea if I was in good enough shape."

He let his gaze trail over her hiking boots, past the jeans on her legs and long-sleeved T-shirt. His eyes nar-

rowed and filled with naked intensity. "Your shape looks pretty good to me."

Oh, my... Her heartbeat went all weird and thumpy. "Thanks, but I wasn't looking for a compliment, just explaining that I'm happy I made it and proud, too. You know?"

"Yeah."

"I'm more relaxed than I've been in a long time." If the paparazzi could follow her here, then more power to them. She took another sip of wine. "The campsite is cozy. Food was delicious."

"Always is in the fresh air."

"It's so clean and pure. Beautiful here." She dragged in a deep breath, then wiggled to get comfortable. "Although I can't say this log is especially comfy."

"Lean forward." When she obeyed, he put his arm behind her as a cushion, then pulled her against him.

"Much better. Thanks." She automatically curled into him as if she'd been doing it for years, and that was a different kind of danger from navigating the great outdoors. But at this particular moment she was too comfortable and content to worry about danger.

She leaned her head against his shoulder and stared at the sky. The beauty was breathtaking. "I don't think I've ever seen so many stars in my life."

He looked down at her and their mouths were only inches apart. When he spoke his voice was a little deeper, a lot huskier. "That's probably because there's too much nuisance light in L.A. or New York."

"But not here," she said reverently.

"No, not here." He gently put his fingers on her chin and held it at just the right angle for their mouths to meet. Searching her gaze he said, "I'd really like to kiss you."

Me, too, she wanted to say but barely managed to hold back the words. "That isn't part of the bargain."

"It should be." There was a hint of irritated frustration in his voice.

"Why?"

He thought for a moment. "Couples kiss openly all the time."

"PDA."

"Excuse me?"

"Public display of affection," she explained.

"Right."

"The thing is, we did that and ended up on the cover of a nationally syndicated magazine." Funny, she thought, right here and now with a sky full of glitter and the scent of pine surrounding her, the bad stuff just didn't seem to matter as much.

"To convince the skeptics, we need to do it again and make it look good, like it happens all the time in private."

She blinked up at him. "You're saying that we have to practice kissing?"

He nodded. "What do you think?"

That this is trouble, she thought. Trouble she could enthusiastically get behind. "I think if you think practicing is a good idea, then it's probably okay."

"That's not exactly wholehearted agreement." He glanced up at the sky. "Can you think of a better place?"

It was the most romantic spot she'd ever been in her entire life. "No," she whispered. "This is perfect."

"Okay then. Practice makes perfect, too." He shifted his shoulders toward her, getting ready to move in. "This first one we'll need around town. The playful peck on the cheek."

"You name kisses?"

"Don't you?"

It had been so long she couldn't remember. "Not really."

He brushed his thumb over her chin. "Now stop talking and concentrate."

"Okay." She realized she'd spoken and said, "Sorry." She shrugged.

"Here goes." He dipped his head and gave her a quick kiss just in front of her ear.

She felt his breath stir her hair and that raised tingles on her arms. "M-my family does that, but it's an air kiss."

He nodded. "Next up is the haven't-seen-you-all-day. This will come in handy at the lodge if you happen to be at the registration desk when I get back from the clinic."

"Definitely important to practice that one," she agreed, anticipation trickling through her.

"I'm glad you comprehend the full magnitude of the situation." He started to lower his head, then stopped and said, "Keep in mind we'll be standing up for this one."

"Got it."

She closed her eyes and lifted her chin just as his mouth met hers, lips slightly apart. Before she was ready to let go, he pulled back.

His chest was rising and falling quickly. "That was pretty good."

"Thanks." She stared into his eyes and asked breathlessly, "What else have you got?"

He touched his mouth to her cheek and nibbled his way to her neck. "I call that the wait-until-I-get-you-alone."

She didn't have to wait; they were alone.

"Very nice." She swallowed hard. "That's an impressive repertoire. I think that covers just about everything we should need—"

"There's one more we might have to pull off."

She settled her palm on his chest and felt his heart pounding. "Does it have a name?"

"I call it get-a-room."

"Oh, my—"

He called it right, she thought when he touched his mouth to hers. At the same time he pulled her tightly against him and wrapped her in his arms. Heat devoured her when he traced the seam of her lips with his tongue. She opened for him and he willingly took what she offered.

He stroked her and she let him, loving the feeling of being held and stroked. But it was more than that. It was the fact that *this* man was doing the holding making all the difference. She wanted this; she wanted him.

"Oh, Ben, this is so—"

"If you say it's not right, then I'm doing something wrong."

"No. Everything is perfect. Get-a-room delivers in a big way, and—"

He pulled back to look at her and seemed to know what she was thinking. "We don't have a room, but the tent is handy."

It had been so long for her and he felt so good that she just couldn't find the will to say this wasn't a good idea. At this moment it seemed like the best idea she'd ever heard.

"I'll race you."

Ben surged to his feet and pulled her up with him. He tugged her to the dome tent at the edge of the clearing, then led her inside and zipped the entrance closed after them. Cam dropped to the sleeping bag and pulled off her hiking boots. He did the same.

The sound of their rapid breathing filled the tiny space as they yanked at buttons, shirts and jeans. Clothes were gone in what was possibly a land speed record and she was naked in the sleeping bag with an equally naked Ben.

He settled his hand on her breast and brushed his thumb across the peak. The sensation started a throbbing between

her legs and she moaned with need. She put her hand on his chest, letting the dusting of hair tickle her palm, and her touch made him groan.

He kissed her over and over until she could hardly draw enough air into her lungs. When he pulled back she nearly whimpered with disappointment.

"What do you call that one?" she asked, cupping his lean cheek in her palm.

"The I-need-you-now." Just enough glow from the fire penetrated the tent to see the primal intensity in his eyes.

She nodded wordlessly and tried to pull him down.

"Hold that thought." He fumbled through the tangle of clothes beside them and finally found his jeans. After pulling something from his wallet, he was back. "Condom."

Cam didn't ask why he'd brought it; she was only grateful that he was prepared. When he'd put it on, he settled on top of her and she wrapped her legs around his waist as he entered her.

He was still for a moment, letting her get used to the feel of him. Then he started to move and in seconds she caught his rhythm, as if this weren't their first time together. He stroked her over and over, then slid an arm beneath her and rolled until she was straddling him.

"What do you call that move?" she asked, gently biting his earlobe.

He sucked in a breath and said, "I've got you right where I want you." His voice was a sexy growl that scraped over her bare skin.

Then he cupped her breasts in his hands and groaned as she arched her hips and lifted them up and down. He reached between their bodies and rubbed his thumb over the bundle of nerve endings between her thighs. Instantly pleasure exploded through her and she collapsed on top of

him. He held her until the shudders subsided, then gently rolled her to her back.

He moved inside her once, twice. The third time he groaned and his body went still as he found his release. Cam held him the same way he'd held her. She held him until he relaxed in her arms. It seemed as if they stayed that way for hours but probably was only minutes.

Ben lifted his weight onto his elbows and said, "We better put clothes on. It's going to get cold."

It wasn't the mountain air, but his words and tone that chilled Cam. Holy cow, she thought, sex wasn't even on the list of rules they'd discussed. But now that they'd done the deed, talking was probably mandatory.

When she was dressed and in her sleeping bag, she glanced at Ben. Their shoulders almost touched, but his face was in shadow and she couldn't see his expression.

"Are you awake?" she asked.

"Yeah." His tone somehow said that sleep was the last thing on his mind.

"So that probably wasn't the wisest thing we could have done."

"Fun though," he said.

She smiled in the dark. "It was fun. But this doesn't change anything."

"I know." There was a restless rustling as he shifted in the sleeping bag. "I'm not looking for a relationship."

"Right," she agreed.

"And you're not staying in Blackwater Lake, no matter what happens to the lodge."

"Right again. If it turns around financially, I'm gone. If not—same thing."

"So we're on the same page. Good, that's settled. We should probably get some sleep." He rolled onto his side, away from her. "'Night, Cam."

"Good night."

But there was nothing good about this night, and things *had* changed, no matter what he said. After what they'd done, the reasons for the bargain were less about practicality and logic. Just like that, there was an unforeseen personal investment, at least on her part. Suddenly the "no one gets hurt" clause of the agreement turned into gray area and she had to find a way to shift it back to black and white.

Chapter Nine

Bright and early Monday morning Cam walked out of her suite and came face-to-face with Ben, who was just coming out of his. She hadn't seen him since returning to town exhausted yesterday afternoon. They'd both worked very hard to pretend sex hadn't happened.

"Good morning."

"Hi," she said, brightly, still working to forget.

He fell into step beside her on the way to the elevator at the end of the hall. "Apparently a weekend in the mountains agrees with you."

"Oh? How can you tell?"

"Because you're looking particularly lovely this morning. And relaxed."

That just meant she was a good actress. "Thanks."

If he wasn't simply being charming, that was just proof of how good cosmetics could be. She wanted to say that he was looking particularly good, too, but she preferred the

sexy, scruffy, hair sticking up first thing in the morning look. And she'd never have experienced it if they hadn't gone camping. Though their rooms were side by side, there seemed to be an invisible line neither of them was willing to cross here in the civilized world.

A lot of things had changed because she'd gone away with him. For the first time since he'd invaded her serenity spot here in the civilized world she didn't know what to say to him. Finally she came up with, "I miss trout for breakfast."

He grinned. "That's the nicest thing you've ever said to me."

"I was talking about fish. That has nothing to do with you."

"Sure it does." At the end of the corridor he pressed the elevator's down button. "I caught it, cleaned it, cooked it. I feel a deep, personal satisfaction at having introduced you to the great outdoors."

He'd introduced her to more than that, but it was best not to go there. "I'll admit to doubts about hiking into the mountains."

"Doubts? You were looking for an exit strategy until we set up camp."

"You're not going to let up, are you?"

"That's not my current plan, no."

"Okay. I was wrong." Best to keep things light, she decided. "There, I said it."

"You're a big person," he said, looking down at her.

Two dings behind them indicated the elevator had arrived and when the doors opened they got in.

"What's on your agenda for today?" she asked, moving away from him. As much as she liked breathing in the scent of his skin, it was best to keep her distance.

"Patient appointments this morning, then a trek to the hospital for a hip replacement."

"That's close to a hundred miles away, isn't it?"

He nodded. "Plans are moving forward for the Mercy Medical Clinic expansion and part of that is an outpatient surgery center. That will make a huge difference to people here in town."

"And to you."

"Yup." They arrived on the first floor. "What's up for you today?"

"Battle damage assessment."

"Excuse me?" He took her elbow as they rounded the corner to the lodge lobby.

"That article wasn't especially flattering to me and I've been unavailable for the last couple of days since it hit."

"You're welcome for that." He wore a smug expression, but on him it looked good. Better than good.

"Your humility brings a tear to my eye." She shook her head. "Anyway, I need to evaluate the fallout and hope that it hasn't set me back in my quest to win the hearts and minds of the lodge staff."

"I think you'll be pleasantly surprised." He stopped by the corner of the registration desk. "People in Blackwater Lake can be stubborn, but if they decide you're a friend, you'll be one forever. They're incredibly loyal. Don't forget you started to break down the walls and show them the real Camille Halliday, not the one created by the media to sell newspapers and magazines."

"I'm not sure that will be enough." She glanced over to where M.J. talked to the night manager to coordinate any unresolved issues at the change of shift. "It could be back to them calling me Ms. Halliday, or better yet, the rich witch."

"Then maybe it's time for a couple refresher course."

He moved closer and his eyes went dark, the way they had by the campfire just before he took her into the tent. "I call this one the it-will-have-to-hold-you-until-later kiss."

Cam's heart started thumping wildly as he cupped her cheek in his hand, then lowered his mouth to hers. It wasn't a playful peck on the cheek, just a quick touch that left her wanting so much more.

He stared into her eyes and gently brushed his thumb over her jaw. "Have a good day."

This was a really good start. Dangerous, but good. "You, too. Drive carefully."

"Will do." He moved toward the front door and waved at M.J. before walking out.

Cam watched through the floor-to-ceiling windows until he disappeared. Then she took a deep breath and braced for a bad day. After pasting a big, everything's peachy smile on her face, she rounded the high registration desk.

"Hi, M.J."

The blonde looked up from the computer monitor, then pushed her square black glasses more firmly up on her nose. "Hi, Cam. How was your weekend? Did you and Ben have a good time?"

She wasn't getting any unpleasant vibes, at least not yet. "It was my first time. Camping," she added. To distinguish the outdoor experience from her first time with Ben, which had been pretty awesome. "As you can see I survived."

"When they do Survivor: Blackwater Lake, the celebrity season, you'll have to try out." Her smile said she didn't mean that in a bad way. "Seriously, I'd expect nothing less of Ben McKnight. There was no doubt that he'd take good care of you."

"He certainly did." And then some. A blush crept up her neck and she hoped her face didn't look as red from

the outside as it felt on the inside. "The mountains are so beautiful. I can't even put it into words. Everything took my breath away."

That was the honest truth in every single aspect.

M.J. smiled. "I'm glad."

"The next time a guest asks me what to do while they're here, I can recommend hiking and camping without hesitation." The other woman looked at her like a proud mother, as if Cam had somehow passed a test. "How was everything here at the lodge while I was gone?"

"No more scum-sucking journalists asking questions, I can tell you that."

"Good to know."

"Otherwise, it was busy. Really busy." She clicked her mouse and pulled up a computer screen. "Remember how sparse the reservations looked the last time you checked?"

"Unfortunately, yes." Cam scrolled through, studying the information. "Is this a mistake?"

"No. The phone's been practically ringing off the hook. The summer is filling up nicely." What looked like teasing stole into M.J.'s blue eyes.

Cam was afraid to trust both the woman's expression and the explosion of business. "This is on the level?"

"I think it's a direct result of the public finally discovering the whereabouts of the notorious Halliday heiress and her hunky boyfriend. Because curious people want to know."

This *was* teasing. A normal give-and-take between friends. And Cam liked it a lot. "You know, I still hate that story, but if it helped put Blackwater Lake Lodge on the map, then I'll gladly take one for the team."

"I didn't believe any of that stuff written about you. The jerk put the worst possible spin on it."

"Thanks for saying so." Cam meant that from the bottom of her heart.

"It's just wrong for someone to invade your privacy like that and imply what he did in that article. Anyone can see by the way you look at Ben McKnight that you've got genuine feelings for the man." She sighed. "Just the way he kisses you goodbye…"

"Oh?"

"Who's kissing?" Jenny the hostile waitress from Fireside walked up and rested her forearms on the high desk in front of them. "Hi, M.J. Hey, Cam."

"Good morning." Her good feeling disappeared and she tensed for the worst. It was best to ignore the kissing question. "What's up?"

"Amanda sent me to ask if you're still having lunch with her today. She said to tell you before you asked that she's too busy cooking to call or come herself."

"That sounds like her." Cam laughed. "Yes, I'm planning on it."

"Good." Jenny hesitated for a second, then said, "She also wants to hear all about your weekend with Dr. McKnight." She shrugged. "And she's not the only one. I'm curious, too. So shoot me. Did you have fun?"

"I had a great time. I'm no longer a wilderness virgin." The two women laughed as she'd hoped. "And the scenery is spectacular."

"A boyfriend like Dr. M doesn't hurt either." Jenny was just stating a fact and seemed genuinely interested.

"That man can definitely hold his own with Mother Nature and enhance any setting." Again that was the truth.

"Amen. Glad you had a good weekend. I have to get back before I get in trouble with the boss." Jenny winked. "I'll let Amanda know about lunch."

"Thanks."

Cam was truly amazed, and the feeling continued for the rest of the day. Dustin from the concierge desk strolled over to find out if she'd had a good time. Then someone from housekeeping stopped by to see how the weekend had gone. She felt as if they'd accepted her, as if she was one of their own.

The good news was that so far they all seemed to be talking to her. The bad was that they really believed she and Ben were a romantic couple. More astonishing was that the staff seemed to be in favor of the relationship, which made Cam feel like a fraud for deceiving everyone.

But worst of all, she couldn't stop thinking about her hunky wilderness guide. Cam wished she could tell Amanda everything and talk this through, but that was impossible. If she let the truth slip to anyone at the lodge, everything could blow up in her face.

Her only other real friend was Ben, and she couldn't discuss him with him? The bargain seemed to be working, but sometimes it was inconvenient when a plan came together.

Ben was glad he hadn't scheduled appointments until later in the morning and had taken his time getting to the clinic. It had been a late night at the hospital when the patient had a complication from surgery. She came through fine, but then there was the long drive home. He'd hung around the lodge longer because of that; at least that's what he'd told himself.

But if he was being completely honest, it was more about hoping to catch a glimpse of Cam. He hadn't. Now he wasn't sure if his bad mood was a reflection of that or simply fatigue. If he had to guess, it would be the former. Yesterday, kissing her goodbye before heading off to work had been the best part of his day.

Camping with her had been such a good time, and not

only because of the sex—although he couldn't deny that was a highlight. But seeing through her eyes the beauty of the mountains, streams and big blue sky he loved and had missed so much had been satisfying in a way he'd never experienced before. She could have been a whining, complaining diva, but that wasn't how it went down. The awe she'd felt was as clear as the blue of her eyes and she'd been a terrific sport.

Seeing her in the morning had been pretty amazing, too. All that tousled blond hair, messed up because he'd run his fingers through it the night before, was flat-out the sexiest thing he'd ever experienced. Even now the memory shot pure lust straight to his groin. Really inconvenient, since he'd just pulled into the clinic parking lot.

His office was on the second floor of the Victorian mansion donated to the town and turned into a medical facility. The first floor had exam rooms and reception and waiting areas. There was a lab for simple tests, nothing sophisticated since there wasn't the equipment or personnel for that. Anything complex went to the hospital. His footsteps sounded on the wooden floor after he walked in the back door and down the hall to the stairway.

After climbing it, he passed the first door, where Adam Stone's office was located. The other doctor was there talking to their nurse, Ginny Irwin.

"So—Bermuda, Tahiti or Fiji?"

Ben stopped and poked his head in. "Are those the only countries in the world without an extradition treaty with the United States? Is there something you want to share?"

Adam grinned. "Very funny. In case you were wondering, we had some patients cancel this morning, so I'm taking a minute to look through these travel brochures." He pointed to the oblong pamphlets spread out across his desk. "Those are the three places I've narrowed down for

a honeymoon destination after I marry the love of my life."
A satisfied expression settled in his brown eyes. "Jill's
going to be one knockout of a June bride."

It was obvious that the man was actually looking for-
ward to committing. Ben could see happiness written all
over his face. But tying the knot didn't guarantee a happy-
ever-after. His parents were proof of that. When the love
of your life dies in childbirth leaving you with three small
children and a business to run in order to support the fam-
ily, it's not especially idyllic. And his father had never got-
ten over the loss of his wife.

Ben pushed the dark thoughts away. "So, I take it that
Jill wants to go somewhere with a beach?"

"I plan to surprise her."

"She hasn't had a lot of good surprises in her life."
Ginny looked at Adam with an expression telling him that
this honeymoon better be a good one. "If you can pull this
off, you're a better man than I thought."

"Wow, that gave me a warm fuzzy. Feel the love." Adam
glanced down at the ads for the beaches. "I just want it to
be perfect for her. And I want to see my bride in a bikini
for a week. I don't think that's too much to ask."

"And there it is." Ben leaned a shoulder against the
doorjamb. "Ulterior motive."

"Do you blame me?"

"Absolutely not." He remembered the erotic sight of
Cam's naked body silhouetted inside the tent by the fire
just outside. Every single cell in his body ached to see her
that way again.

"Before Jill's mom died, I promised her I'd look out for
her daughter and grandson. She was my best friend since
grade school," the nurse explained to Ben, then leaned
over to study the brochures. She picked up the one from
Tahiti. "So keep this in mind about your bikini-wearing

bride. That girl's never been farther from home than Helena." She looked at Adam. "For the greenhorn who needs a geography lesson, that's the capital of Montana."

Ben reminded himself not to get on this woman's bad side. "I think I know where you're going with this."

Ginny grinned. "Take her to whichever one of these places is the farthest from Blackwater Lake. She'd be happy if you pitched a tent in the backyard so long as you're there with her."

"And she's with me. God, I love that woman," Adam said cheerfully.

"Good enough." Ginny patted his shoulder. "Then my work here is done."

"Speaking of work," Ben said, "I'll just go stash my briefcase and get downstairs—"

"Not so fast, buster. The patients can wait a few more minutes." Ginny put her hands on her hips and drilled him with a look. "You were in and out of here so fast yesterday we barely saw you. Let alone get a chance to grill you about your weekend. What happened with Miss Halliday hotel heiress?"

"We hiked up to that stream a couple miles above the lake." He shrugged, hoping to leave it right there. "So, it's time to get to work—"

"And you spent the night?" Ginny asked, not in the least sidetracked or discouraged.

"Yes."

Ben glanced at the other doctor, shooting him a help-a-brother-out look. Adam Stone might be a hyper-observant family practice doctor, but he was a crappy wingman. The grin on his face said he was enjoying this and had no intention of intervening on a brother's behalf.

"How did she handle that? It's hard to picture Miss Four-inch Heels and Short Skirts getting her hands dirty."

"She was a real trouper. Pulled her weight and didn't complain. She actually seemed to take to the whole outdoor experience." Including the kiss practicing and everything that came after. Don't think about it now, he cautioned himself. "She even tried fishing but swore if a miracle happened and she caught anything she'd throw it back. No one was going to accuse her of finding and filleting Nemo."

Ginny smiled. "Sounds like she's got a good sense of humor."

"That she does," he agreed, remembering her insisting on having wine in the wilderness. "I have to admit that I wasn't sure what to expect." He smiled as her words went through his mind. "To quote her: It wasn't hideous."

"So, her not liking that sort of thing would be a deal-breaker for you?" Ginny asked. "If she didn't take to the outdoors you'd be outta there?"

Ben couldn't tell her he had no "there" to be out of. The lying to everyone part of this bargain hadn't really become real until he'd started. With his family and everyone else. He'd been on the receiving end of being strung along and didn't like it. He wasn't that kind of person. In the end, he just told the truth without answering the question asked.

"Spending time in the outdoors is very important to me."

"Not hideous," Adam mused. "I'm hoping for a more enthusiastic reaction when I take Jill to Tahiti."

Ginny clapped her hands together. "And we have a winner."

"Yes." Adam gave her a warning look. "Keep it to yourself."

"I won't breathe a word." She looked at her watch. "The patients will be here for their appointments now. I'll get them in the exam rooms for you. We've got a full day, Doctors."

"Thanks, Ginny. Don't know what we'd do without you," Adam said.

"It's my job." The tone was matter-of-fact, but there was a smile on her face when she walked out the door.

"I guess we better get down there, too," Ben said.

"Just a second." Adam stood and walked around the desk. He was wearing the usual green scrubs and white lab coat. "Can we talk?"

"Sure." But Ben knew those words were never good. "Is something wrong?"

"No." The other man looked thoughtful. "Just something I thought you should know."

"Okay. What's up?"

"I guess you're aware of that article that came out in *The Rumor Report*."

"Yeah. Cam was really upset about it."

Adam nodded. "I can imagine. It was pretty unflattering to her."

"You read it?"

"Someone left it in the waiting room. You were on the cover. Kissing a woman." He shrugged. "I was curious."

"It's not true." Ben folded his arms over his chest.

"So, you're not going out with Camille Halliday?"

Not the way everyone thought, but he couldn't say that. "Yes, we're going out. What I meant was the unflattering stuff that was printed about her. It was blown out of proportion and laid out in a way that would make her look bad. Their goal isn't to tell the truth."

Adam studied him. "You look like you want to punch someone."

"I'm a supportive boyfriend." If you took the "boy" part out that statement was true. He was her friend. "So are we done here? Is that it?"

"Actually, no. I haven't gotten to that part yet."

"Okay. What?"

"Almost every patient I've seen in the last two days has asked about you and Ms. Halliday."

"In what way?"

"They're speculating that you're after her money—"

That had been implied in the article and he had to admit it ticked him off. "I don't need hers. I've got plenty of my own."

"I'm just saying. Don't kill the messenger." Adam held up his hands in a simmer-down gesture. "The other theory is that she's paying you to rehabilitate her bad-girl image."

"No to that, too. Trust me on this. No money is being exchanged."

"I wouldn't care if there was," Adam said. "It makes no difference to me. You're a good doctor and we work well together. I just wanted you to know that the patients you see are probably going to ask."

"I appreciate the warning." And he really did.

Ben wished he could tell his friend the truth, that what he had with Cam was a deal to keep the clinic from becoming a circus because of him. But living with this bargain was different from what he'd expected. People in town obviously had questions about him and Cam. They would be shocked to find out that he had some of his own about the two of them but had no answers. All he knew was that he liked her. Liked her a lot.

Everything was supposed to be casual, but he hadn't taken sex into account. Actually, he'd thought about it almost from the first time he'd seen Cam in the moonlight, but he hadn't thought to include rules about it in the bargain negotiations.

This whole deal had been about getting what each of them wanted. A win/win where no one gets hurt. From where he was standing, it didn't feel like anyone was winning.

Chapter Ten

"Welcome to the first annual Blackwater Lake Lodge employee appreciation dinner."

Cam stood at the head table during the applause that followed her opening remarks and looked around the small conference room. There were about twenty people in attendance, a better turnout than she'd expected.

Actually, since her disastrous track record after arriving, she'd tried to set a low bar for expectations, because the disappointment was easier to bear.

"Did everyone enjoy dinner?" she asked and barely got the words out before the eruption of applause, whistles and woo-hoos. "I'm glad. I'll be sure to pass that on to the chef. And, by the way, everyone who volunteered to serve your coworkers tonight will receive dinner on the house at Fireside. Just a special thanks for your loyalty and spirit of cooperation."

She waited while there was more clapping and a few

whistles. When it died down she continued. "I'll keep this short. I don't want anyone getting indigestion." There was a laugh as she'd hoped. "It's my goal to make the lodge successful and I can't do that alone. Reservations are increasing—"

"Thanks to you getting your name in the paper." The comment came from one of the guys in the back.

"I'm happy to do my part." Cam didn't mind the good-natured teasing. Now that she knew it *was* good-natured. More than one person in Blackwater Lake had told her they'd gotten a glimpse into her world from that tabloid story and seen the ugly side of fame, and she had their sympathy. It was new and different and wonderful. The comment just now had no animosity behind it. "And I just want to thank every one of you for your hard work every day. Without you, there wouldn't be a Blackwater Lake Lodge. Lately I have reason to be cautiously optimistic about the future of this property. If everyone continues pulling together, jobs will be preserved and we may be able to do more hiring soon."

Someone, again probably the guy in the back, started chanting, "Hall-i-day!"

Everyone in the room picked up on it and for a few moments Cam couldn't say anything. And not just because it was too noisy. There was a lump in her throat. She'd never felt accepted anywhere the way she did now. This group had given her a chance, thanks to Ben, but she wanted to believe that she'd won them over because of her fair management style and willingness to work harder than anyone.

Except somewhere along the way she'd started to care about these people, and if the enthusiastic clapping and chanting was any indication, the feeling was mutual. In that moment she realized the effort and hard work she'd put in wasn't just about her career anymore.

"Thanks, everyone." She held up her hands for quiet. "That means more to me than I can put into words. Now I just have one more thing to say. Dessert."

And the crowd went wild as servers brought out the seven-layer chocolate cake.

"How do you think it went?" She sat down and whispered to M.J. on her right.

"Really well. Everyone likes to be appreciated for their efforts and you did that."

"It was short and sweet." Jenny was on her left. She took a bite of her cake. "Speaking of sweet, I never get tired of this."

"It is pretty wonderful," Cam agreed.

"Speaking of wonderful..." M.J. looked around. "Where's Ben tonight?"

That was a good question, but Cam couldn't very well say that she had no legitimate right to have an answer. "He understands that tonight isn't about significant others or a plus-one."

"Somehow he seems like so much more than a plus-one." Jenny sighed dramatically. "Can I be honest with you, boss?"

Cam studied the pretty, heart-shaped face with the dark hair pulled back into a ponytail. There was no hostility in her brown eyes now, just new frankness and authenticity. That was to be encouraged.

And a little levity couldn't hurt. "Should I be afraid?"

Jenny laughed. "A couple months ago maybe, but not now."

"Okay, then. I much prefer candor."

"I'm pretty envious of you. Being with Dr. McKnight. I tried really hard to get him to notice me when he moved back here. And I'm not the only one. Patty and Crystal

did, too." She glanced at the two women who were seated to her left.

"I completely understand," Cam told her with absolute sincerity. "And the truth is, I can hardly believe this relationship myself."

"All the single women in town are envious of you. At first no one could understand what he saw in you," Jenny shared. "No offense."

"None taken."

"It's just that he's a great guy and we all had you pegged as a stuck-up, rich, self-centered heiress."

"Don't sugarcoat it, Jen. Tell me how you really feel."

The waitress laughed. "The thing is, you're not at all what we thought. In fact, the unofficial word-of-mouth poll is that the two of you make a great couple. So it's all good."

"That's nice to hear." And the guilt just kept on coming.

"I'm actually glad to see him with someone," M.J. said.

That made Cam curious, and a lot of questions popped into her mind. But it was important to set just the right tone, keep this casual. Too much prying would show insecurity and weakness and make them wonder why she didn't know. Not enough could imply she didn't care and that wasn't the vibe she wanted to project.

"Why are you glad?" she finally asked M.J. Jenny was talking to Crystal and Patty on her other side.

"I guess because Ben came back to Blackwater Lake still single and not in a relationship."

His status hadn't changed, although no one knew, but that still didn't answer Cam's question. "I'm not sure what you mean."

"Me either, to be honest. It's just that I was surprised to find out he'd never been married." She shrugged. "It crossed my mind that what Judy did might have turned him against commitment."

"He's too well-adjusted for that. He's sexy, funny, flirty and gorgeous. And he's a doctor."

"I know. It seems silly to even say it. I'm sure he has his reasons for waiting and that's fine. As long as it's not Judy who's keeping him from being happy."

"I don't think he gives her much thought," Cam said. And she truly believed that. Still, he was the kind of man that most women—not her, but the average female—would give almost anything to be with. "I know he's not gay."

M.J. grinned. "And just how would you know that?"

"I asked. He told me."

"And you believe him?"

"Yes." That and he'd made pretty amazing love to her in the mountains. Memories of that had heat creeping up her neck and into her cheeks. "Any theories about why he's not married?"

M.J. shrugged. "Since we agree he's emotionally stable, one would have to assume he's been busy. After medical school he started a practice in Las Vegas. That probably took a lot of time and dedication. The opposite sex can be a distraction when one is trying to focus on a career."

No kidding. But this conversation was hitting far too close to things she didn't want to get into. Too many questions could imply that she wasn't talking to her boyfriend, which was true. Time to change the subject. "So, how are the kids?"

"Great." A soft expression slid into M.J.'s eyes. "They're looking forward to the end of the school year."

A strategic question here and there had the other woman talking about all the activities available to children during the summer months in Montana. Cam put on an interested face and she truly was. But there was a part of her mind occupied with questions about Ben. Questions she hadn't thought about until M.J. said it out loud.

Why had he never been married? And was their fake romance really about what he'd claimed or something more?

"There's someone here to see you."

M.J. stood in Cam's office doorway smiling a sappy smile. The one every woman wore when she thought romance had come calling.

"Ben's out there, isn't he?"

"Yes—"

"I'm actually in here," he said, moving around M.J.

"I'll just leave you two alone." She walked out and closed the door.

Cam almost told her to leave the thing open. It wasn't like they were going to have sex. Their suites were side by side upstairs and neither had trespassed on the other's territory, although she'd been sorely tempted. But she was waiting for him.

"What are you doing here?" She looked at her watch, which said it was after noon. "No wonder I'm hungry."

"That's why I'm here. To take you out and feed you."

"I have a lot of work. My plan was to grab something quick at my desk and—"

"No."

She looked up and met his gaze. "Excuse me?"

"You're not going to eat at your desk, and I don't care if it's a seven-course meal that takes hours." He came around the desk and gently tugged her to her feet. "I'm taking you away from all this."

"But—"

He touched a finger to her lips, putting a stop to the protest. Her mouth tingled from his touch and she wished he'd kissed her instead. That would have worked really well for her.

"No excuses," he said. "Come with me."

"Where?"

"You'll see."

"Don't you have patients?"

"Not for a couple of hours. There's time." He smiled mysteriously.

"Can I have a hint where we're going?" Passing the registration desk, she waved goodbye to M.J. The sappy smile just got sappier.

His SUV was parked near the front of the lodge and he opened the passenger door for her. She got in and fastened her seat belt, which suddenly seemed an apt metaphor for her life. After he got in the driver's seat, it occurred to her that was another appropriate metaphor for them. He always seemed to be plotting the course. Of course it was working for her professionally. And yes, darn it, she was more personally involved than she'd expected.

"So," he said, "you want a hint about where we're going."

"That would be nice, yes."

"Okay. It's not in town."

"I don't understand." She looked at the smug expression on his face. "We're always in town. That's the point. So everyone can see us together. To keep up the charade."

"M.J. saw us. She'll spread the word that we're inseparable."

For now. But they'd be separating soon. If the upward trend continued, she'd be lobbying her father for a more high-profile position at a Halliday Hospitality Inc. property in a city far away from Blackwater Lake. The thought made her stomach feel empty and that had nothing to do with being hungry. She would miss Ben and that wasn't supposed to happen.

He drove out of town as promised and headed north on Lake View Drive. Trees lined both sides of the road

and the sky overhead was big and blue. Big sky country. Words couldn't describe how beautiful this place was. It was something a person had to experience firsthand. Oddly enough, she could feel the tension easing out of her.

"Okay. We're out of town. I need another hint. Is it bigger than a breadbox?"

"Yes. And it has great views." He glanced over, mischief in his eyes.

"Just so you know, I'm not dressed for camping and hiking."

He laughed. "Me either."

The mountain-man look on their weekend trip had been rugged and appealing, but she kind of liked him in the long-sleeved white cotton shirt and khaki pants he was wearing now. In fact, he didn't seem to have an unappealing look. She liked him in anything. Or nothing.

"Are you okay?"

"Dandy." She looked out the window so he couldn't see the heat in her cheeks.

He made a right turn onto a road that went uphill. At the top there was a lot littered with construction materials and in the center there was the shell of a structure going up.

"We're there." He put the car in Park and turned off the ignition.

"Is this your house?" she asked.

"Yes." He reached into the backseat. "I brought water and sandwiches from the diner."

"Good. Because I'm too hungry to wait for you to catch, clean and cook a fish." She opened her door and slid down. "It's like a picnic."

"Watch your step," he warned. "The ground is uneven and there's trash around."

And fresh air. "The breeze up here is wonderful."

He took her elbow in his free hand and guided her over

the uneven ground to where the solid foundation stood and the scent of sawdust tickled her nose. The framing was complete with wooden stairs up to the second floor, but no solid walls separated out the rooms. There was a lot of space.

Ben pretended to open the front door and let her precede him. "This is the entryway and leads all the way to the family room. To the left there will be a formal dining room and the living room is on the right."

"Formal dining?"

He shrugged. "Family dinner on Sunday night."

She walked to the back of the house and looked around. "Is this going to be all windows?"

"Yeah."

"Good. It would be a crime to block a view this spectacular."

"I couldn't agree more." Hands on hips, he stared at the view of the mountains, which was breathtaking. Then he pointed to a spot in the kitchen. "The sink is going there. You can see the lake while doing dishes."

She knew he meant that as a generic "you," not as in *she* would be around to see the lake or do dishes. On the cement floor there was writing that looked like measurements. "Is this going to be an island?"

"Yes. Big enough to land a jet and space for lots of cupboards underneath." He pointed to the corner. "Over there is a large, walk-in pantry. Beside it will be two built-in ovens and a microwave. A cooktop just there and room for a Sub-Zero refrigerator."

"Nice. Really nice. Can I see the upstairs?"

He grinned at her enthusiasm. "Follow me."

She held on to the wooden railing and at the top of the stairs he led her through what would be the double-door entry to the huge master suite, with a large dressing area

with his and hers closets. He took her through four more bedrooms, two baths and a big game room.

"How many square feet is this going to be?" she asked.

"Five thousand—give or take."

"Wow." She wandered back to the master bedroom with him behind her.

"Right there," he said indicating a corner, "there's going to be a fireplace."

"Nice." What she wanted to say was *almost as romantic as the stars in the mountains,* but she stopped herself just in time.

He pointed up. "I'm putting in skylights to bring in light for a dreary winter day."

"This is going to be wonderful," she said, filled with a longing she didn't understand. "Who's the builder?"

"My brother. This is the first of a development of custom homes in this area. I bought the lot from him. I'm the guinea pig, I guess. It will be sort of a model for buyers looking in this neighborhood."

"Willing to spend the big bucks," she guessed.

"Alex is looking at a tidy profit margin." He walked over to the wooden window seat, took a napkin out of the bag and brushed it off. "Your table."

"Thanks." She sat and took the club sandwich he held out.

Ben sat next to her with his own. "Bon appétit."

They ate in silence for a few minutes and the breeze drifting around them carried the fragrance of pine and spring wildflowers.

"This is a beautiful spot. And that doesn't even do it justice." She looked at him. "There are a lot of bedrooms in this house. You must be planning to have kids to fill them up."

"I hadn't really thought about it. It's big and that's good for resale."

"So you didn't factor in a wife and children when you had the plans drawn up?"

He shrugged. "Maybe someday."

She studied him, looking for signs of—something. She didn't see shadows or sadness in his expression. "Are you dragging your feet on marriage for any particular reason?"

"Are you psychoanalyzing me?" He chewed a bite of sandwich and there was nothing but amusement in his eyes.

"You can call it that if you want. Or it could come under the heading of making conversation. But pretty much I'm just being nosy."

He laughed. "I don't think I'm a marrying kind of guy—"

She wanted to leave it hanging there, but just couldn't. "Are you avoiding a commitment because of Judy?"

"What do you know about her?" *Now* he looked annoyed.

"She was your high school girlfriend. You gave up a prestigious college in the east to go to school close by because you didn't want to leave her. After graduation you proposed so you could take your wife to med school, but she wasn't ready to leave. You were willing to do the long-distance relationship thing and she agreed. Six months after you left she married a ski bum and moved to New York." She looked at him and shrugged. "People talk."

"Remind me to have a word with M.J." He scowled.

"Did I get it right?"

"Pretty much."

"Does it still bother you?" She watched his expression carefully.

"I hadn't thought about her for years. Not until we ran into her on the street."

The night he'd kissed her. Studying him, she saw no evidence in his expression that he still had feelings for the woman. "Have you had a significant relationship since?"

"I'm feeling a cross-examination vibe," he said, eyes narrowing.

"This is a great house. It would be a wonderful place to raise a family. We're putting on a show for Blackwater Lake, but I feel as if we've gotten to be friends." And lovers, even if it was only one time. Intensity shadowed his eyes and she'd bet he was remembering that night in the tent, too. "I'm trying to figure out why you're building a family house without thinking about a family to fill it."

He shrugged. "I dated in Las Vegas. But I was pretty busy growing my medical practice. There wasn't a lot of time to build a relationship. Women tend to lose interest if they get bumped for a medical emergency too many times." He finished his sandwich and wadded up the paper.

That confirmed what M.J. suspected. "So after Judy you didn't meet anyone who made you want to take a chance on marriage?"

"No. What about you? Anyone special?"

"I thought so once or twice, but they had another agenda. Now it's all about my career."

That was his way of changing the subject, because she'd already told him why she had good reasons not to trust. Once a Halliday, always a Halliday. Her last name would always be well-known and she'd never know whether a man wanted her or the recognition that went with her. But building a career was something she could trust.

"So, I'm curious. Why did you bring me here?" Certainly not for her approval. And he didn't seem like the kind of man who was a show-off.

"This is sort of taking our relationship to the next level."

"I don't understand," she said. "We don't have a relationship."

"Really? You said we were friends."

"Well, yes. But that's a one-level sort of thing. How is this taking it up?"

"My brother, Alex, was wondering if you'd seen this place yet."

"Ah. It would be a logical next step if we were actually dating." She should have known. It was all part of the act.

"Right. So, if you happen to see him, or any other members of my family, you don't have to pretend."

Like she was pretending to care about him. Except it was feeling less and less like pretending.

She'd never met a man who had the capacity to care as much as Ben did. She liked him a lot. She found herself wanting what they had to be more. And now she'd seen where he planned to live. It was a wonderful place to raise a family and the idea of that started a yearning deep inside her for the family she'd always wanted and stopped believing she'd ever have.

She couldn't help thinking what a waste it was that a family wasn't in his plans. That was silly, really, because it wasn't her plan either. But this bargain had become way more complicated than she'd expected and she was beginning to regret making it.

The only thing she regretted more was that she wouldn't be around to see Ben's house finished.

Chapter Eleven

Ben was beginning to regret the bargain he'd made with Cam Halliday.

After seeing his last patient of the day at the clinic, he drove back out to his house under construction. He walked through the opening where the front door would eventually be and swore he could still smell the fragrance of her perfume. In the big open room where the cement foundation was marked off for the kitchen island and cupboards, he could still see her looking out at the mountains, fascinated by the majestic sight. She'd picked up on the fact that it would be criminal to put in any walls and obstruct that view.

He climbed up the crude staircase and remembered the sensuous sway of her hips as she'd moved to the second floor. It had taken every ounce of his willpower to keep from scooping her into his arms and sweeping her the rest of the way up. Unfortunately that romantic ges-

ture would have been wasted since there was no big fluffy bed to put her on.

Then again, maybe that wasn't such a bad thing. It was the only reason he hadn't kissed the daylights out of her before loving the daylights out of her. He'd badly wanted to.

He wanted her so much it hurt.

In the master bedroom he stared at the window seat where they'd sat and the empty bag from lunch. It wasn't littering. Not really. This was his house. Eventually he would move in here. Alone.

Ben remembered Cam's words and the wistful look on her face when she'd said this would be a good place to raise a family. He could picture her here, putting her touch on everything, infusing her classiness into the decorating, adding a lot of color to the landscaping. And that gave him a bad feeling.

Inserting her personality into his life wasn't supposed to be part of this bargain.

It was so quiet out here he heard the sound of a car coming up the hill, then pull onto his lot. In one of the unfinished front bedrooms he looked out the window and saw his brother's black truck. Alex was just getting out.

"Thank God." He needed a distraction. Anything to keep him from thinking about Cam.

Ben jogged downstairs to the kitchen. His brother was carefully looking over the framing and whatever else a building contractor inspected. Alex was really good at what he did. He'd started McKnight Construction in California, then opened a branch here in Blackwater Lake when he brought his pregnant wife here to live. But she'd had secrets and Alex's family had unraveled. Ben wasn't sure his brother would ever get over that.

"Hi," he said.

Alex dragged his gaze away from the heavy-duty metal

floor brackets that held the weight-bearing beams in place. "Hey, little brother. What do you think of the place so far?"

"I think that everything you talked me into is perfect. So far."

"Good." He settled his hands on lean hips. "Like what?"

"The walk-in pantry." Cam's eyes had glowed with approval.

"What else?"

"The window seat in the master bedroom." Ben could still see her brushing her hand over it as if she was deciding on fabric for the cushion. With an effort he pulled his thoughts back to the here and now.

It was amazing how Alex managed to look confident and professional in jeans, boots, T-shirt and baseball hat sporting the McKnight Construction logo. But he carried it off beautifully. "And?"

"What?"

"Isn't there something else I was right about?"

His brother had suggested the corner fireplace in the master bedroom. Ben had pictured himself in a big, fluffy, king-size bed with a fire going and Cam in his arms after making love. It was romantic crap with zero chance of happening.

"I'm not feeding your Montana-size ego anymore."

Alex's eyes narrowed on him. "Bad day at the clinic?"

"No." Work wasn't the problem. Lunch had unsettled him.

"Has Cam seen the house?"

"Why would you ask that?" Ben demanded.

"Gosh, I don't know. Maybe because the two of you are always together." Alex shrugged. "Just seems to me you'd want her opinion on this place."

"I'm building it for me."

Could have been the words or the tone, but something

about that statement had his brother's eyes narrowing. "Is everything all right with the two of you?"

"Of course." Ben's voice was sharper and more defensive than he'd intended.

"That doesn't sound good at all." Alex moved closer, studying him. "Want to talk about it?"

"There's nothing to say."

"You're not a very good liar, little brother."

"What makes you think I'm not telling the truth? That there's nothing wrong?"

"Because you look like someone cut the ears off your favorite stethoscope. What's her name?"

"What makes you think it's a her?"

"Come on, Ben. Tell me what's going on."

"I could. But then I'd have to kill you." He was going for humor, but his brother's expression didn't lighten up.

"Seriously?" Alex shook his head. "This is me. No way I'm going down."

Ben figured he was probably right about that. The guy worked with his hands, swung tools, carried heavy building materials and was in really good shape. Ben ran and lifted weights, but that wouldn't tip the scales in his favor during a physical confrontation with his older brother.

"I was kidding. Just drop it, okay?"

Alex shook his head. "Not when you look like that. Spill it, bro."

Ben wondered when he'd become so easy to read. He really needed to talk to someone, because this bargain was dishonest and so not like him. Realistically, he didn't have much to lose if word got out about it. Cam would be leaving soon and he didn't have a plan B for when she was gone. So what if he confided in Alex, who then spilled the beans? It would be a relief to tell the truth. Maybe when

word spread, and it would, women would get the message that he wanted to be left alone.

He took a deep breath, then said, "Cam and I aren't really dating."

Alex stared at him for several moments. "That's funny, because the two of you have been spotted all over town together. And there was that backpacking trip. Your rooms at the lodge are right next door to each other, which makes things pretty convenient."

More like pretty tempting. Ben spent a lot of sleepless nights thinking about her on the other side of the wall. There was nothing convenient about it.

"All the dinners and hanging out? It's not real."

"It looked real. And what about that camping trip three or four weeks ago? Did you, or did you not, take her into the mountains?" Alex asked.

"I did. Just to further the pretense." Sex hadn't been a part of the charade. It had been real, and awesome. Unfortunately, having her had twisted everything up. "This whole dating thing is staged."

"Doesn't look that way. People all over town have betting pools going."

"Betting on what?" Ben demanded.

"When you're going to pop the question. Wedding dates. All kinds of stuff."

"People all over town need to get a life," Ben said. "I'm telling you it's all an act."

"I can't speak for the lady because I don't know her that well. But you're not that good an actor, bro. No offense."

"Cam and I made a bargain. My idea." He didn't want anyone to get the wrong impression about Cam. She wasn't dishonest, just the opposite. And funny, sweet, vulnerable, beautiful. Damn it. Even in his own head he was sticking

up for her. "I talked her into pretending to be my girlfriend so everyone would think I was off the dating market."

"The brilliance of that bachelor strategy makes me proud to be your brother." Alex shook his head with amazement. "But how did you get her to go along with it?"

"She was having trouble with the staff at the lodge. I gave her practical advice on how to handle different situations. Because I know most of the key players." He shrugged. "Women left me alone at the clinic. And everything at the lodge is running more efficiently."

"I see." His brother walked over to the doorway and leaned a shoulder against the exposed wood. "So you don't have romantic feelings for her?"

"No." Unless that included sleeping with her that one time. He wasn't sure where romantic feelings fit into wanting to sleep with her again. And just plain wanting to be with her.

"You're just friends," Alex persisted.

"Yeah." Ben knew this man. These weren't just idle questions. Something was on his mind and it wasn't good. "You could say that. Why?"

"Just wondering. I guess you wouldn't mind if I asked her out, then."

An image of Cam with his brother flashed through Ben's mind and white-hot anger roared in his head. No way, he thought. He didn't care if Alex could take him.

He moved a step closer and his hands curled into fists. "Don't go there, Alex. You stay away from her. I'm warning you—"

"Gotcha." The other man grinned. "You're too easy."

It took a couple seconds for anger to fade and reality to sink in. He'd been had, set up. Alex was right. He was easy. "I should pop you one for that."

"Gotta watch those surgeon's hands. Besides, you could

make more work for yourself. On the off chance you did me some damage, you'd just have to patch me up. I'm sorry about that." His brother didn't look sorry at all. "I thought you were feeling more than friendly toward the pretty lady and you just proved my point. I did it because someone had to make you see the truth."

Ben stared at his brother as thoughts raced through his mind, his conversation with Cam earlier. She'd asked about Judy, whether or not he was avoiding commitment because of her, and he hadn't lied. He'd been the one to leave and Judy had refused to go with him. Obviously she hadn't loved him, so he'd dodged a bullet. Eventually he'd realized that a long-distance relationship probably wouldn't have worked either.

His feelings for Cam were threatening to spill over the friendship limitation he'd put on them. And *she* was leaving. He'd suggested this bargain, but she'd agreed because she wanted to go somewhere else. He'd made a deliberate career choice to come back. And no one was supposed to get hurt.

Things were not going as originally planned.

Now Alex had just punked him by bluffing about asking Cam out. He'd done it to make a point. Ben asked, "What truth are you trying to make me see?"

"You've got to nip those feelings in the bud, Bud." Alex nodded emphatically. "If you don't, you're going to be in a lot of trouble."

Ben blew out a long breath. "Tell me something I don't know."

"I really feel awful," Cam said into the phone. Normally she was at work by now, but she was moving slowly. She leaned against the counter in her small kitchen. "I just wanted you to know that I'm going to be a little late today."

"What's wrong?" M.J. asked.

"Same as the last couple days. I'm nauseous and tired. I'll work here in my suite until I can shake it off. Then I'll come down to the office in a while."

"Cam, I'm coming up there," M.J. said.

"That's so nice of you, but really not necessary." She walked out into the living room because the smell of freshly brewed coffee turned her stomach. "It will pass soon."

"That's what you said yesterday. And the day before that. And the day before that."

"I'm okay. Room service is bringing ginger ale and crackers."

"Oh, my—"

Cam couldn't see M.J.'s face, but the tone of voice didn't sound good. "What's wrong?"

"I'll be right there. Glen's going to man the desk for me. Sit tight." There was a click on the line indicating she'd hung up.

Cam sat on the overstuffed sofa and leaned back, closing her eyes. If she could stay like this and not move, everything would be just fine. It was when she sat up or walked around that her stomach turned on her.

She thought about mentioning it to Ben but decided against that. She hadn't seen him for a few days, since he'd taken her to the construction site for his house. On the drive back to Blackwater Lake he'd given off a weird vibe. Probably she shouldn't have asked about Judy, but she couldn't help herself. It would be too sad if that's what was keeping him from being happy. He'd denied it and she believed him, but there was something standing in his way.

Her life hadn't been anywhere close to normal, but even she wondered about building a house big enough for a family when he didn't seem to want one. He might have

thought her questions were a hint, that she was trying to change the rules of their agreement on him. She wouldn't do that, but it had gotten her thinking.

There was a knock on her door, which was either room service or M.J. She could take on one or the other but not both at the same time. She managed to stand, walk to the door and open it, all the while keeping her rebellious stomach under control.

Peg Simmons wheeled in the room service cart. She was in her fifties and had more energy than a lot of people twenty years younger. Silver was liberally streaked in her short, dark hair and her brown eyes were warm. And concerned.

"Here you go, Cam." She looked uneasy. "You might want to try and get in some protein. I can go back downstairs and have them fix you an egg and toast—"

"No." She pressed a hand to her stomach. Just the thought of it was unpleasant. "Thanks, but this will be fine—"

M.J. appeared in the doorway. "How's our girl?"

If Cam had felt better the words would have produced a warm glow, but the nausea had put that reflex out of commission along with the rest of her.

She looked from one woman to the other, so grateful that they were on her side now. "I'll be fine," she told them.

"She's not eating," Peg said to the other woman. "Ginger ale and crackers isn't a well-balanced breakfast and this is the fourth morning in a row you've ordered this."

"Have you talked to Ben about not feeling well?" M.J. asked. There was edginess on her face, but something else, too, as she exchanged a look with Peg. It was as if the two of them knew a secret that she didn't have a clue about.

"As you both are aware, Ben is an orthopedic specialist. Nausea isn't in his field of expertise."

"Then maybe you should see Adam Stone. He's a *family* practice doctor." Peg nodded emphatically.

"I don't think it's necessary—"

"Peg is right." M.J. exchanged another knowing glance with the other woman. "Just get a checkup. You've been under a lot of stress lately."

"That's true." She chewed on the inside of her cheek. "Maybe this is female-related. My periods aren't regular but I'm a little late—"

Oh, dear God. She was late! She could be…

No way. That wasn't possible. She looked at the two women as panic scratched inside her. "I can't be pregnant."

Peg breathed a sigh of relief. "Oh, thank God. I didn't think you knew."

"You did?" Cam blinked at her.

"I suspected. Nausea and fatigue are classic symptoms, right, M.J.?"

"Hit me hard, both times. Ben will be so pleased. He's really great with kids." M.J.'s smile was happy and excited in that way women get when a female friend is doing the most womanly thing a woman can do.

"It's not true—I can't be pregnant," she said again.

"So you didn't have sex with your boyfriend the doctor?" Peg's look was skeptical.

Cam wasn't thinking rationally enough to lie. "We used protection."

"Sweetie, if you're not on the pill…" Peg's voice trailed off and let the truth hang there.

"I'm not."

Cam hadn't trusted any man enough to let him that close so there was no reason to take an oral contraceptive. She hadn't expected that to change in Blackwater Lake. She hadn't planned to have sex. She hadn't planned on meeting a guy like Ben McKnight.

"Only abstinence is a hundred percent effective," Peg informed her. "And when a couple gets…" She hesitated, searching for the most delicate word. "Athletic, condoms can be tricky. That's why my two oldest kids have a brother six years younger."

Cam waited for her cheeks to get warm at the frank talk. She didn't remember having a discussion this personal with her own mother, but somehow didn't mind it now, with these two women. They were her friends.

"I'm going to take a wild guess here that you haven't said anything about this to Ben." M.J. took her arm and led her to the sofa.

Cam couldn't sit. "No."

Peg took the soft drink can and a glass of ice from the room service cart and poured the carbonated liquid. She handed it to Cam. "It'll be okay, honey. He's a good man."

There would be no argument from her about that. But what a mess. And maybe it wasn't true. She put her drink on the coffee table and looked at them. "Before I tell him, I think it's important to know for sure."

"Pregnancy test," M.J. said, nodding.

"If I go get one at the drugstore it will be all over town." At least here in Blackwater Lake people's behavior was predictable. Her whole life paparazzi had stalked her every move and she never knew when, where or what she'd done that would result in a horrible, incriminating picture on the cover of a magazine. She met M.J.'s gaze. "Can you get one for me?"

"Of course. There will be talk about me, but I can take the heat." Her smile was reassuring. "I'll go on my lunch hour."

"I'll make it up to you—"

"No need. It's what friends do."

"Thank you—" Her voice caught and she pressed her fingers to her lips.

"Getting emotional is another sign," Peg said helpfully.

Cam hugged the older woman, then M.J. "Thank you for being here. Both of you."

"This is just the way folks in Blackwater Lake roll," Peg said with a shrug. She pushed her room service cart to the door and M.J. opened it.

Just after the two women left the suite, the phone on the desk rang. After picking it up she said, "Camille Halliday."

"Hi, Cam. It's Glen at the front desk."

"Hey," she said, trying to sound cool and collected, as if her whole life wasn't coming apart at the seams. "What's up?"

"Your parents are here."

Her heart stopped, then started to pound. "What?"

"Dean and Margaret Halliday just checked in with me here at the desk. You look a lot like your mom," he said cheerfully.

The assumption was that she'd be glad to see them. And she was. But the timing of this surprise visit couldn't be worse.

"Where are they now?" she asked.

"They said to tell you they'll be waiting in your office."

"Understood." Her hand was shaking when she hung up the phone. "I'll be down soon."

Waiting in the office was Halliday Hospitality code for *get your tush down here as soon as possible.* That didn't give her much time to transform herself from looking like something the cat yakked up to the business professional she wanted her father to believe she was.

The thought of facing Dean Halliday Senior made her stomach drop. With the exception of a roller-coaster ride,

she couldn't think of any other occasion when that was a good thing. She'd just realized that she might be pregnant.

All things considered, throwing up seemed like the sensible thing to do.

Chapter Twelve

"Mother. Dad." Cam walked into her office with a bright, phony smile plastered on her face for the parents who were seated in front of her desk. "This is really a surprise."

"I was anxious to see you." Margaret Halliday lifted her cheek for the traditional air kiss. She was blonde, blue-eyed, petite and perfect. Probably there was a resemblance until you got to the perfect part. "You look tired, Camille."

She glanced down at her designer suit and expensive heels, regretting the fact that she'd put herself together in a hurry. She also regretted that there wasn't enough concealer on the planet to hide the dark circles under her eyes. So much for plan A.

"It's been a busy few months. I'm fine." And possibly pregnant, she thought. But that wasn't something she would share until absolutely necessary. "How are you?"

"I'll be better when you give me a report on this property."

Dean Halliday Senior was a handsome man in his late fifties. His hair was dark with the exception of silver at his temples. Stray gray wouldn't dare crop up on his head to make him look anything but distinguished. If Hollywood was casting someone to play the president in a movie, Dean Halliday could be on the short list.

Cam leaned down to kiss his cheek and imagined that it was a lot like touching her lips to one of the Mount Rushmore commanders-in-chief. In all fairness, maybe her attitude toward her parents needed an adjustment. At least they were here. Then she half sat on the corner of her desk and met her father's gaze, bracing for the grilling she knew was coming.

"Things are going really well, Dad. This property could be something very special. A place to get away from it all. *Really* away, if you know what I mean."

"I do." Margaret crossed one slender leg over the other, rustling the silk of her black designer slacks. "The only airport is nearly a hundred miles away."

"Once you get here, the trip is worth it." Cam looked from one to the other. "Towering mountains. Lakes and streams so crystal clear you can see the bottom. Fresh air—"

"You sound like a travel brochure," her father said.

"If only a tri-fold glossy paper with words and pictures could adequately convey the splendor." She straightened away from the desk. "Let me show you. I'll give you a tour of the lodge."

"Lead the way." Her father stood and buttoned his dark suit jacket.

"Follow me." Cam walked out of her office and around to the lobby side of the registration desk, then looked at

the blonde wearing square black glasses behind it. "M.J., these are my parents, Dean and Margaret Halliday. This is Mary Jane Baxter, one of the best customer service representatives I've ever worked with."

"It's a pleasure to meet you both." M.J. smiled, but the expression in her eyes was questioning. Did the folks know yet about the suspected pregnancy?

Cam gave a slight shake of her head, then smoothed her hair. "The staff here at Blackwater Lake Lodge is excellent. If you need anything, just let us know and—"

"How are reservations?" her father asked. "Is there an improvement?"

"Up sixty percent from this time last year," Cam said. "We're completely full for the summer and already starting to take reservations for the fall and holidays. There are even a couple of small regional conferences scheduled."

"Hmm." Her father nodded, but there was no way to tell what he was thinking. Turning away, he inspected the furniture grouping in the lobby by the stone-front fireplace. "Rustic."

His tone wasn't necessarily critical or condescending, but Cam found herself wanting to defend the lodge. "This room reflects the mountain milieu. People from New York or Los Angeles don't want the chrome, crystal and marble they see there. Here in Blackwater Lake the wood and stone brings the outdoor magnificence inside."

"Hmm." He nodded. "Let's see the rest."

"Okay. Let's go to the dining room. Amanda will want to say hello."

She led the way to Fireside and through the dining room, which was currently dark and empty of people since it didn't open until five in the evening. All the tables had linens and silverware rolled in cloth napkins. The fireplace was cold now but in a few hours flames would be

dancing cheerfully. Through the double doors in the back of the room was the kitchen and that's where they found Amanda Carson.

She was about Cam's height, a beautiful brown-eyed brunette. At work she wore her long hair up in a twist and had on a white chef's coat with a single row of buttons up the front.

"I smell something burning." She sniffed and instantly the sous chef and food preparers were scrambling to find and fix the problem. "That's not the kind of smell that comes out of my kitchen."

Cam's high heels clicked on the tile floor as she walked over to where her friend stood by the long, stainless-steel work area. "Hi, Amanda."

"Cam." The chef turned and smiled. Then she spotted the elder Hallidays and moved to give each of them a hug. "I didn't know you guys were coming."

"That's because we didn't tell anyone. If you really want to know how a place is running, drop in. Advance warning gives people a chance to sweep everything they don't want you to see under the rug." Dean gave her a fond look. "How are you, Amanda?"

"Doing all right here in Mayberry." It's what she'd called the place when Cam first approached her with the deal to parlay six months into a career- and reputation-building job in the city of her choice. "Blackwater Lake is kind of growing on me."

Cam knew what she meant. The people were salt of the earth and the scenery had sort of gotten into her soul. "Tales of her culinary expertise are really bringing customers into the lodge."

"How many people could there possibly be?" Margaret asked. "This is the wilderness. Awfully far from the

airport, as I was telling Camille. It took the driver forever to get here."

"It's quiet, for sure, but there's something to be said for that." Amanda warmed to her subject. "The most excitement this town has seen was when that guy checked into the hotel pretending to be—"

"Do you have the profit numbers for the restaurant?" Cam interrupted. She knew where her friend was headed with that and it wouldn't go over well with her parents. She was still trying to live down the days when she was the tabloids' favorite target. The Hallidays would probably never forgive her for that.

"I can show you the spreadsheets." The chef pointed to her glassed-in office in the corner of the kitchen. "Or you can take my word that revenue is way up from this time last year. Your daughter has really turned this place around. The staff adores her."

"It's not a popularity contest," her father said. "Sometimes you have to irritate people to run a business."

"That's the thing," Amanda said. "Cam is great at running the business and doesn't irritate anyone."

Except maybe Ben. If the pregnancy test said what she thought it was going to say, he was going to be plenty irritated. No strings attached in this bargain, he'd said. A baby was kind of a big string.

"Cam?"

"Hmm?" She looked at her friend. "I'm sorry, my mind was wandering. Did you say something?"

"Yes. You look tired."

"That's what I told her," Margaret said.

A gleam stole into Amanda's dark eyes. "Is that dashing doctor keeping you up too late at night?"

"Would that be the doctor you were kissing in the pic-

ture on the front of that horrific newspaper?" her mother asked.

Cam's chest felt tight. "I was hoping you hadn't seen that."

"Yes, indeed we did." Dean fixed his blue eyes on her and there was no warmth in them. "How did that happen?"

"I have no idea." She shrugged. "Somehow I was tracked here and the guy checked into the lodge under false pretenses to spy on me. Nothing in that article was the truth."

"What about the man you were kissing?" Margaret asked.

That kiss hadn't been for real, either. Cam hadn't felt this uncomfortable, awkward and guilty since her arrest as a teenager. "That's Ben McKnight. He's a doctor."

"Hometown hero," Amanda added. "Good-looking and smart. He likes my seven-layer chocolate cake."

"Anyone who doesn't like it would be too dense to find their way out of a plastic bag, let alone complete medical school," Dean pointed out.

Cam was pleased that the president and CEO of Halliday Hospitality, Incorporated, liked her friend's cooking, but how she wished her father had a compliment for his own daughter. She knew she'd been a pain in the neck to them for a lot of years after her brother died. She knew she'd never be as good as Dean Junior, or be able to run the business as well as he would have. But she was trying to be a Halliday her father could be proud of. Didn't that count for something?

Her best was better because of Ben, and speaking of the good doctor, she needed to change the subject before Dean and Margaret could ask more questions and trip her up, make her slip and spill the beans about their phony relationship.

"Okay, I have a lot more to show you. We'll see you later for dinner, Amanda."

"You're going to love it," she said to the elder Hallidays. "I recommend the trout. It's going to be awesome."

"You're ever the humble cook," Cam teased.

Amanda grinned. "False humility is a waste of time."

"Well said," Dean commented.

"We look forward to it, dear," her mother added.

Cam showed them every square inch of Blackwater Lake Lodge, from the large suites to the pool and extensive grounds. She saved the second-story deck that overlooked the grass, shrubs, flowers and trees for last. It was nearly noon, but the Adirondack chairs were in the shade and she urged them to sit and soak in the fresh air and view. She was surprised when they actually took her suggestion.

"I love it up here," she told them, leaving out the part where she'd used it to find her serenity when exasperated with staff who didn't take her seriously. She sat on the ottoman by her mother's chair. This was also where she'd found Ben, where he'd proposed the dating bargain. Where she'd accepted, desperate to find a way to be successful and prove to her father that she could be. All she wanted was to make him proud.

She didn't think her getting pregnant was going to achieve that objective.

"This is a very beautiful spot," her mother said.

"It is," her husband agreed. "You've done a good job with this place, Camille."

She wanted to shake her head and make sure her hearing wasn't playing tricks on her. Had the daunting Dean Halliday just given her a compliment? "We have a way to go, but things are looking up. No more hemorrhaging money. Waste has been cut and the budget trimmed in a way guests won't notice. I've hired a trustworthy accoun-

tant, who assures me that if things continue as they are, next year we'll be in good shape."

Her father nodded. "The staff looks efficient and it would show in more than the books if that wasn't the case. The grounds and public areas are well-maintained. It's a property that Halliday Hospitality can be proud of."

He'd all but said he was proud of *her*. She wanted to grin from ear to ear and maybe do a little happy dance, but that wasn't what Hallidays did. The thought of dancing made her a little nauseous and all the joy imploded.

"So tell us more about the doctor you're seeing," her mother said. "I didn't read the dreadful article. I do hope there won't be any more of that."

"I'm sure it won't happen again," she assured them.

"We're going to hold you to that." Dean put his feet up on the wooden ottoman. "Now, how did you meet Dr. McKnight?"

And so the third degree began. "We met here. He's staying at the lodge while having a house built in an exclusive luxury development that overlooks Blackwater Lake. His medical specialty is orthopedics. He grew up here in town and came back because he loves it so much."

Everything she'd said was the truth. Her parents had never been overly into her feelings, so maybe facts were enough, because defining her feelings for Ben was difficult. She was grateful for his help. She liked being with him and missed him when they weren't together. He was funny and sexy and made her heart beat faster whenever she saw him. Just thinking about him quickened her pulse. She'd never felt this way about any man. Ever.

"I imagine he'll be pretty busy during ski season." Dean looked at his wife, who nodded. "We'd like to meet him."

Her stomach dropped and when it bounced back up

there was a huge knot in it. "How long are you going to be here?"

"A night. Maybe two," he said.

"I'll notify housekeeping. There's an unoccupied suite."

"We took care of that. Our luggage has already been delivered there," her father said.

"It was a noble attempt to change the subject, though." Strangely enough, there was a twinkle in her mother's eyes. "You're not going to get out of introducing us to your doctor. We promise to be on our best behavior, right, dear?"

"No. I intend to have a word with the man who is interested in my daughter and find out *why* he's interested."

Of course her father thought it was about money, because no man could possibly be interested in her for any other reason. Of course there was a reason, but they'd never guess it. In all fairness, they had as much reason to distrust her suitors as she did. But her deal with Ben was new and different. When she'd agreed, it never occurred to her that they would have to pretend in front of *his* family, which had been hard enough. Now they'd have to do it for *hers*.

"So, will we see him for dinner?" Her mother crossed one leg over the other.

"Yes."

She'd played the part for the McKnights, and now it was his turn. It was incredibly important to keep up the pretense with her parents, especially after hearing that she was doing a good job. Now wasn't the time for how screwed up her personal life was to come out.

There was reason to believe she was pregnant by a man who was building a big house for resale, not a family. And she had taken his help and advice in order to get the career she wanted in a place that was far away from Black-

water Lake. If that wasn't messed up, she didn't know the meaning of the words.

"I'll let Ben know to meet us for dinner here at the lodge. Seven o'clock?"

"Perfect," her mother answered.

She'd do her best to keep her parents from finding out this situation was anything but perfect.

"Do you like that label, Mother?"

Cam sat on the love seat across from her parents in their suite. She'd put her own wineglass down on the coffee table and hoped now wouldn't be the time they actually noticed her. No way she wanted to explain that she wasn't drinking alcohol because she might be pregnant.

Margaret took another sip of the red. "It's quite good, Camille. A wonderful choice."

Her father was having something stronger from the suite's full bar. "This is an excellent Scotch."

"I'm glad." She smiled. "And since there was no advance warning of your visit, you know we didn't get it in just for you. No special treatment. Every guest is treated in the same special way."

"The Halliday Hospitality mission statement." He nodded approvingly. "I propose a toast."

What? she thought. No. Not that. But both of them held out their glasses, so she picked hers up. "What are we drinking to?"

"The hotel business in general, Blackwater Lake in particular. To better times ahead."

Her mother and father clinked glasses, then held theirs out to her. Her crystal wineglass tinkled when she touched theirs, but she only put it to her lips without drinking. She could fake this. It occurred to her that she was getting pretty good at faking life in general. Look at her and

Ben. They'd successfully fooled everyone into believing they were in love.

Being spotted together had required an investment of time in each other's company. She'd begun to look forward to seeing him after a stressful day at work. He actually listened to her troubles, which was better than talking to herself in the serenity place. She enjoyed his sense of humor, his smart and practical approach to problems.

If she were being completely honest, she grew breathless and weak-kneed at the sight of him and ached for him to hold her. Kiss her. Since making love to her in the mountains, he'd only touched her because they were pretending to be in love.

But for Cam it was feeling less and less like a pretense, more and more like...

"Are you all right, Camille?" There was concern in her mother's voice.

"Yes. Why?" *Please don't ask why the level of my wine hasn't gone down.*

"You had the strangest expression on your face. Are you not feeling well?"

"I'm fine," she lied. She should be getting used to it, but deceit didn't come easily to her and never would. "My mind was just wandering. I'm sorry. I was thinking about Ben."

"So, the two of you are getting serious?" There was wariness on her father's face. "I wasn't aware that something like this was part of your career trajectory."

How to answer? Cam wondered. Things were getting serious, but not in the way he was talking about. "I'm enjoying Ben's company. The reality is that I never expected to meet someone like him here in Blackwater Lake, Montana. In fact, nothing about this place is the way I thought it would be. I even went camping."

"With Ben?" her mother asked.

"A Halliday in the wide-open spaces," her father mused. "Not in a hotel."

"I know, right? That's the first time in my life that I didn't have four solid walls around me and a bathroom." But she'd been with Ben and that was enough.

Margaret glanced at the delicate, diamond-trimmed Rolex on her wrist. "Is he as handsome as the photograph on the front page of that horrible newspaper?"

"Better." Cam smiled, picturing his boyish good looks and sigh-worthy grin. "It doesn't do him justice. Pretty soon you can judge for yourself."

"Then I'm even more anxious to meet him. And it's just about time to go downstairs. I think I'll take a few moments to freshen up." She stood and went into the other room.

Moments later there was a knock on the door and her father asked, "Did you order room service?"

"No. Maybe Mother did."

"She would have said something to me."

"I'll see what's going on." She was closest to the door and went to open it.

Mary Jane stood in the hall, twisting her fingers together. "Thank God it's you," she whispered. "Your father scares the crap out of me."

"Join the club. What's up?"

"I need to warn you—"

"About?" Dean Halliday was right behind her. "Ms. Baxter, for many years I have frightened employees and I'm very good at it."

"Yes, sir." Blue eyes behind the black-framed glasses grew wide.

"Now, what is the problem?"

"Mr. Halliday—" M.J. glanced first at him, then Cam.

"There are a bunch of reporters and photographers in the lobby."

"What in the world—"

"They've been badgering the hotel staff, attempting to get quotes. As far as I can tell they're trying to support a story in which Cam—" She hesitated. "I mean Ms. Halliday—that she's in trouble again." Her voice hardened when she met the gaze of the CEO of Halliday Hospitality, Inc. "With her parents."

No. No. No, Cam thought. *Not this. Not now. Think. Problem solve.* What would Ben do?

She glanced up at her father. "We don't have to go down to the restaurant for dinner. I'll order something from room service and—"

"Absolutely not." He shook his head. "Thank you, Ms. Baxter. You did the right thing."

"You're welcome."

"And for the record?" he said. "You have nothing to be afraid of on my account."

"Yes, sir. Thank you." She smiled at him, then looked at Cam. "Call me if there's anything I can do."

"I will. Thanks. I owe you."

She closed the door. "Dad, really, I'll call Ben. He can come up the back way and meet us here."

Dean shook his head again. "Hallidays don't sneak around. We face things head-on. We don't avoid even sleazy reporters who are looking to write a sordid story about my family in order to sell newspapers."

"Okay." She decided to share Ben's wisdom after the last paparazzi ambush. "Publicity is good. Even the bad stuff. It's important to get our name out there."

"Not in those sordid papers. Not when the name is Halliday."

"Curiosity can boost reservations." It was worth one more try.

Her father looked grim. "Let's get this ordeal over with. I'll fill your mother in."

Cam watched his back as he left the room and realized that it was a terrible thing when a person lost hope. She'd been so close to getting what she wanted, so close to an assignment in Los Angeles, New York or Phoenix. Now the same seedy reporters who had ruined her life before were sabotaging the career she was moving heaven and earth to resurrect.

And then there was Ben.

He was the one she was most worried about now. This wasn't what he'd signed up for when they made their bargain. She should be glad they weren't a real couple, because it was becoming more apparent that it would really hurt when he dumped her for being constantly pursued by the press. No guy who wasn't in it to get his name in the paper could put up with this.

Now he had to meet her parents with the press photographing everything. At least she could control who else was around when she broke the news to him that he was going to be a father.

Chapter Thirteen

There was something wrong with Cam.

Ben had heard it in her voice when she'd called about having dinner with her parents. He didn't know if it was about them being here or another issue with the press.

He was sitting by the fireplace waiting for the Hallidays in the lodge lobby and it would have been hard to miss the reporters and photographers milling around and grilling the employees for dirt on the family. One of them had said to a colleague that he'd been staking out Cam's parents, just waiting for them to meet her for a face-to-face about the doctor she'd been slumming with in Blackwater Lake, Montana.

Ben had to smile at the reporter's irony. He had a heck of a nerve talking about slumming considering how the guy made his living.

Although Ben had to admit that he was a little nervous about meeting Cam's parents. Considering that their rela-

tionship was based on a mutually beneficial bargain, he shouldn't give a rat's behind what her parents thought of him. But he did care.

So far the press hadn't noticed him, but one of the reporters drew his attention. The jerk was badgering M.J. at the registration desk. She was doing her best to ignore the questions fired at her, but apparently she'd lost patience.

She raised her voice and said, "I have only one comment. Camille Halliday is a terrific boss. She's the best one I've ever had and everyone here at Blackwater Lake Lodge feels the same way."

The boss in question was just coming around the corner with a nice-looking older couple. The energy level in the lobby had been hovering in the lower register and shot through the roof when the power family was spotted. Dean and Margaret Halliday were elegant and composed as cameras started flashing and reporters hit them with a barrage of questions.

"Is Cam in a jam again? I can see the headline." The jerk held out a digital recorder.

"What do you think about her and the doctor?" another one asked.

"Is it true she's pregnant?"

"Are you here to break them up?" This guy shoved a microphone at the older man. "Care to comment?"

Ben looked at Cam's face and again knew there was something wrong. He saw shadows in her eyes and a vulnerability that made him want to protect her, to wrap his arms around her and shield her from all this craziness. She'd been putting up with it her whole life and he wondered how she'd managed to stay so sweet and strong.

He stood and pushed his way to her side through the crush of people badgering her. Standing between her and the horde who wanted a piece of her, he forced a smile.

"I'll hold one if you want to kick him."

That got a small smile. "As appealing as that would be, I'd probably just hurt myself. Besides, the assault and battery charges would just be a win for them. And it wouldn't do your career as an orthopedic specialist any good either."

"I'm getting you out of here."

He put his arm around her shoulders and led her out of the lobby. She'd told him dinner would be at Fireside and he led the way. The noise was close behind them a minute later when they arrived at the restaurant doorway.

"Do you want me to call lodge security?" he asked her.

"It's already done."

He nodded. "I went to high school with local law enforcement. Sheriff Marshall probably owes me a favor."

There was humor in her eyes. "Really? Sheriff Marshall?"

"It's catchy," he said with a shrug.

She could smile under this kind of pressure and that took guts. Ben admired the hell out of her.

The hostess was at the podium and immediately said, "Your table is ready. Please follow me."

Dean Halliday said to her, "If anyone intrudes on our privacy, I want you to call the local authorities."

"Yes, sir."

Ben and Cam looked at each other and said at the same time, "Sheriff Marshall."

When they started laughing, her father lobbed a censoring look in her direction. Ben could imagine Cam as a little girl on the receiving end of that disapproving expression for even a small infraction like fidgeting at dinner. But the rigid upbringing hadn't managed to squeeze the spirit out of her. Thank God.

They were seated in a far corner of the sparsely filled dining room, far from prying eyes. Ben held out a chair for

Cam that would put her back to the rest of the room. Even if a nosy reporter managed to get in, she wouldn't have to see and no unflattering photos could be snapped. Her father and mother were barely seated when the waiter arrived.

"Good evening, Mr. and Mrs. Halliday, Ms. Halliday. Dr. McKnight." He looked at everyone. "Welcome to Fireside. What can I get you to drink?"

"A bottle of Jordan Pinot Noir, please, David," Cam said.

"That's an excellent choice," her mother agreed.

"I'd like something stronger," her father ordered. "Scotch."

"The best," Cam added, to the waiter.

"I'd like a beer. Whatever you have on tap is fine," Ben said.

"I'll bring that out right away. Would you like menus now or after drinks?" David was in his thirties, nice-looking and clearly knew how to provide exceptional service.

"After drinks," Cam said and her parents nodded.

Ben had a feeling she had talked to the staff here ahead of time to make sure there were no slipups in service with her parents. Probably even before she knew the press would descend like locusts.

"Well, that was unpleasant." Dean looked at his daughter. "One can never live down the past, it seems."

Ben was watching Cam's face, knew the exact moment when the barb pierced her and burrowed in. Anger instantly ignited inside him and he couldn't let the comment go unchallenged.

"We haven't been formally introduced, Mr. and Mrs. Halliday. I'm Ben McKnight." He held his hand out across the table and one after the other they each took it. "The thing is, that unpleasantness happened because the two of

you showed up here." He held up a hand to forestall her father's protest. "Not saying it's your fault, but the Halliday name brings them out no matter who's attached to it. I heard one of those reporters say he'd staked you out, just waiting for you to show up here in Montana."

The older man's eyes narrowed. "Be that as it may, Doctor, if my daughter had kept a low profile in her younger years, no one would care about the comings and goings of her parents."

"Dad, let's not do this now—"

Ben put his hand over hers and squeezed reassuringly. "The thing is that if presidents and movie stars can live down outrageous behavior and rehabilitate their images, a hardworking young woman like your daughter should get a pass on being a kid. Shouldn't there be a statute of limitations on immaturity?"

Dean opened his mouth, but the waiter arrived with their drinks and set the beer and Scotch in front of the men. Then he proceeded to open the wine deftly and pour a small amount for Cam to taste and approve.

She sniffed, then barely touched the glass to her lips. "Excellent."

"I'm glad to hear it." David filled crystal wineglasses for the ladies, then said, "I'll bring menus as soon as you're ready."

When the four of them were alone her father said, "So, tell me, Doctor, what's a guy like you doing in a small town like Blackwater Lake?"

"I grew up here."

"And what? You were homesick?"

Cam looked like she wanted the earth to swallow her whole. "Dad, please—"

"It's a fair question." Ben smiled at her, then met the other man's gaze. "This town has the very best of what the

United States of America is all about. The people take care of each other. You couldn't find a more picturesque place. The mountains offer outdoor opportunities—hiking, skiing, snowboarding. Then there's the lake for fishing and water sports."

"A great vacation spot. But for a career in the medical field, wouldn't your prospects be better in New York, Los Angeles or any other big city?"

Ben understood that this wasn't about his career as much as it was about whether or not he was after Cam's money. It wasn't bragging to let the man know he was just fine in that regard.

"I actually built a medical practice in Las Vegas and sold it for, let's just say, upwards of seven figures. Prudent investments have paid off and I don't have to work at all for the rest of my life."

"But you do. Here," Margaret Halliday interjected.

Cam's mother said "here" as if Blackwater Lake were the swamp planet where Luke Skywalker crash-landed in the second *Star Wars* movie. They would never understand, but he had to say it anyway.

"I love being a doctor and I'm good at what I do. This town and these people are a big part of the reason I've been successful in life. I wanted to give back to the community, but, believe me, I get more than I give. If the tourism industry is going to grow in this town, medical care needs to keep up."

"True enough. Cam tells us you're living at the lodge," her mother continued. The nesting questions.

"I also said you're building a big, beautiful house in an exclusive community on the lake." Cam was defending him, which wasn't necessarily part of their deal.

When Ben had proposed it, he'd never expected or intended for her to invest so much personally. He knew she

was going to hear from her family later about what a low bar she'd set and didn't mind for himself. He had no emotional investment in these people, but she cared very much what they thought. He wanted to tell her parents that there was no danger of him becoming part of the family, but that wouldn't help right now. Soon she'd be gone and in her world he'd be nothing more than a blip on the relationship radar.

Oddly enough, he wanted to be more than that to her.

After dinner the Hallidays said good-night and excused themselves from the table, pleading weariness from traveling and an eventful day. Obviously that was a jab at the paparazzi and proved that they couldn't resist one more dig at the prodigal daughter. Cam should have looked relieved when they were alone in the restaurant, but strangely enough she seemed more tense.

"I know what you're thinking," he said.

She seemed momentarily alarmed. "Oh?"

"You want to kick something, and I know just the spot."

"My serenity place." She nodded. "It's been neglected lately because thanks to you, things have been going well." She sighed. "Until today."

"It happens." He held out his hand. "Let's go."

Without a word she put her fingers in his palm, then set her cloth napkin on the table. They stood and walked out of the restaurant and turned right to the exit door on the first floor. The stairway to the upper deck was right there and they took it up.

Cam settled her forearms on the redwood railing and breathed deeply. "This fresh air is just what the doctor ordered."

"Take several deep breaths and call me in the morning." *Or right now,* he thought.

Just like the first time he'd seen her in this very spot he wanted to hold her, kiss her. Now he knew how soft her skin felt, how sweet she tasted, and *perfect* didn't do her justice. Making love with her seemed like a lifetime ago and right this second he couldn't recall why having her again was such a bad idea.

When she looked up at him there was gratitude in her eyes. "Thanks for defending me tonight at dinner."

"No problem. Speaking of dinner, I noticed that you didn't drink your wine." He rested his arms on the railing and stood as close to her as he dared. Their shoulders brushed and they could almost feel the heat of the sparks flickering and flashing, then flying into the night.

She tensed and said, "I needed to keep a clear head. I'm sorry my parents were so hard on you."

"I can take it."

"You shouldn't have to. Why now?" She shook her head. "I can't believe they picked tonight to be involved parents."

"Don't worry about it. Not on my account."

But she kept going as if she hadn't heard. "Although when I think about it, the timing in every other part of my life has been a disaster, so why not this, too?"

"What disaster?" He looked down and saw a troubled look in her eyes. Then he remembered the troubled tone in her voice earlier. "What's wrong?"

She shook her head, a nonanswer. "Between my parents and the paparazzi, you must be relieved that we have a bargain and not a real relationship. The Halliday heiress and her baggage are more challenge than any man should have to take on."

It was a statement, not a question, and he didn't answer. He had a feeling that there was a lot more going on with her that she wasn't telling him. He should ask, but he wasn't sure he wanted to know.

When she'd called earlier, he'd been aware that there was something wrong without even seeing her face. He knew her well enough to tell by the tone of her voice. Knowing a woman that well could change a man forever, and Ben wasn't sure he wanted to change.

She looked up. "I think I'll say good-night. I have some things to do."

"Okay. Sleep well."

He wasn't going to.

Cam looked at the stick from the pregnancy test M.J. had brought her. It said "pregnant."

"There must be some mistake," she whispered to herself. "A false positive. It could happen."

But in her heart she knew there was no mistake, unless she counted the one where she'd slept with a man who only wanted a pretend relationship. The nausea, fatigue and her highly evolved emotional state were all signs pointing to the fact that she was going to have a baby.

Ben's baby.

She'd just left him a little while ago after standing on the deck under the stars. More than anything she wanted to throw herself into his arms and have him assure her that everything was going to be all right. But she'd sensed a distance in him. She wasn't even sure how she knew that, but he'd definitely closed himself off.

None of that changed the fact that she was having a baby. It was surreal and she couldn't wrap her head around what was happening to her.

The doorbell in her suite rang and she jumped at the unexpected sound. Ben. Part of her desperately wanted to see him. Part of her didn't. She hoped it was him come to insist she tell him what was really wrong. Then she forced herself to get real. She hadn't let herself hope for anything

good since that awful day when she'd heard that her brother had been in a car accident. She'd prayed and hoped with everything she had that he would be all right, but it hadn't been enough. Dean Junior had died in spite of her hope.

She heard the doorbell again and sighed. Whoever stood there wasn't going away. If it was Ben, this was as good a time as any to give him the big news.

But when she opened the door her father stood there. "Dad. I wasn't expecting you."

"Am I interrupting?" He looked around as if there would be someone else there.

Probably anticipating Ben, since the man lived right next door. Ironically, he'd never come into her place. Neutral ground camping in the mountains was where common sense had gone out the window—and the tent didn't even have windows.

Cam looked down at her socks, sweatpants and matching zip-up cardigan. "I'm alone. Is Mom okay?"

"Fine. She's asleep. May I come in?"

"Sure. Of course. Sorry." Apparently being pregnant affected a woman's manners and basic brain function. She stepped back and pulled the door wider. "Come in."

"Thanks."

"Would you like a drink?" She looked longingly at Ben's door before closing her own. "I don't have anything here, but I can call downstairs if you—"

He held up a hand. "No. I'm fine."

"Okay." She indicated the conversation area in her suite living room. "Have a seat. It's kind of late, so I'm a little curious why you're here."

He nodded, then sat on one of the small sofas. "There's something I'd like to talk to you about."

"I'll take care of whatever it is. If there's a problem that you noticed here at the lodge, just let me know and

consider it done. I have a terrific staff and we can make things happen—"

"It's not about trouble," he interrupted. "I just wanted to talk to you."

"About what?"

"I saw your employees in action with those sleazy reporters earlier. Will you give me your secret to securing loyalty like that?"

Ben. He was her secret and her strength. He'd been her conduit, the bridge to winning the hearts and minds of the workers. "The people here in Blackwater Lake are, quite simply, awesome."

"I actually want to talk about one person in particular, but there's something I need to say first." He leaned back into the cushiness of the love seat and crossed one leg over the other. It wasn't the body language of a father getting ready to grill her about the man in her life. "Your mother and I are heading back to Los Angeles in the morning."

Cam sat down across from him. "But I thought you'd be here for another day."

"I changed my mind. It didn't take as long as I'd figured to see everything I needed to see."

Was that a good thing or bad? "The lodge has turned the corner, Dad. It has the potential to be a very successful property for Halliday Hospitality, Inc. Think Vail. Aspen. Park City, Utah. The town council is investing in infrastructure so that more people will come, tourists and permanent residents both. In fact, that's why Mercy Medical Clinic wanted Ben. And they're expanding the existing clinic to provide more services. Eventually there will be a hospital here. The demographic is going to need Ben's particular skills set for the master plan—"

"Whoa." Her father laughed and shook his head. "You

had me at 'the lodge turned a corner.' I can see that from the financial reports. I'm not here to close it down."

"Good. A lot of people would lose their jobs if you did that." She was relieved to hear that was off the table. Also even more curious. "Then what did you want to talk about?"

"You've done everything you promised when you convinced me to give you a chance to prove yourself. I wanted to personally deliver the news that you're being promoted."

"I am?" Another surreal moment. She couldn't quite believe that at least one part of her life had gone according to plan.

"You can have your pick of any Halliday Hospitality property to manage." He grinned. "So, what's it going to be? Los Angeles? New York? San Francisco? Scottsdale, Arizona?"

"I don't want to push anyone out or cause someone to lose their job."

"Don't worry about that. We'll juggle assignments. No one will be out in the cold or demoted. But you've got my attention. You've earned this, Camille."

She nodded, thinking back to employee hostility and no respect when she'd arrived here at Blackwater Lake Lodge. The collective attitude of the staff and townspeople began to change when she started "seeing" Ben. And seeing him had not been a hardship—just the opposite. It had been far too easy to get used to having him in her life. She could get used to it. But now…

It was time for her to move on, just as she'd planned. She'd earned a promotion.

"Camille?" Her father looked puzzled.

"Hmm?"

"Are you all right?"

Define all right, she wanted to say. Professionally all was good. Personally? Not so much.

"Yes, I'm fine," she lied.

Dean leaned forward, forearms on knees, blue eyes intent on her. "Then why don't you look happier about this news?"

That was a very good question, because this certainly wasn't the way she'd expected to feel if this moment ever arrived, and she'd had her doubts in the beginning. When she'd talked her way into getting a chance, and that chance meant exile in Blackwater Lake, Montana, she hadn't expected to fall in love. Or get pregnant.

"I'm just really surprised by this," she finally said.

"You shouldn't be. Hard work should be rewarded. And at Halliday we do that."

"I never wanted any special treatment."

"And you didn't get any."

So spoke her boss. "Good, then."

Her father watched her for several moments, then frowned. "What is the nature of your relationship with Dr. McKnight?"

There was a loaded question if she'd ever heard one. She and Ben didn't have a relationship. All they had was a deal. Then they had sex. Now she was pregnant. All of the above would be tricky to explain in a way he would understand.

Finally she said, "Why do you ask?"

"Because I'm your father."

"Since when?"

Cam wasn't sure why she'd said that or why she wasn't horrified that she had. Maybe the baby made her do it. Whatever the reason she'd surprised her father. The expression on his face was one she'd never seen before, which

meant Dean Halliday Senior wasn't accustomed to being caught off guard.

"What does that mean?" he asked.

"Tonight Ben stood up for me." And she loved him for that. There, she'd actually formed her feelings into that thought. She loved Ben. "He protected and defended me."

"From what?"

"You," she went on quickly, before rational thought stepped in to make her stop. "The press being here wasn't my fault any more than it was when they stalked me as a teenager. That was all about being the daughter of Dean Halliday, being from a wealthy hotel family." He opened his mouth and she raised her hand to let him know she wasn't finished. "I take responsibility for my bad choices in friends and the things I did. But I'd just lost my brother—"

Sadness and a grief that would never go away darkened his eyes. "I lost my only son."

She refused to back down. "When he died not only did I lose my protector, the guy who ran interference for me, I lost my father, too. You went from parent to boss, training me to be a stand-in for Dean Junior. My only qualification was being the oldest surviving Halliday heir."

"Camille, you don't know—"

"I'm not blaming you, just explaining things from my perspective. I have no idea what it feels like to lose a child." God willing she never would. "It's got to be the worst thing that can happen and I understand that you went through an awful time. But I did, too. I was sinking fast and no one noticed, no one reached out a hand." Not until she got to Blackwater Lake and met Ben. "It's okay, Dad. I finally grew up. And it just has to be said. I'll never be as good as Dean Junior would have been, but I promise to do my best not to let you down ever again."

His head was bowed, elbows resting on his knees with

fingers linked between the wide V of his legs, as if he was praying. "I appreciate that."

"Good."

He sighed and stood up. "So, you'll think about where you'd like to be transferred?"

"Yes." Then she remembered. "And wherever that is, I'm taking Amanda with me. I made her a deal."

He nodded. "A Halliday's word is more than a promise."

"All right. When do you need my decision?"

"As soon as possible." He suddenly looked tired, and a little older than when he'd walked in. "We need time to reassign personnel."

"Okay." They stared at each other for several moments without speaking, because apparently there was nothing more to say if it wasn't about business. "Will I see you and Mother in the morning to say goodbye?"

"An early breakfast?"

"Just let me know what time. I'll be there."

"Very well. Good night, Camille."

"'Night, Dad."

Without another word he left. Cam wasn't sure whether or not she felt better because of unburdening herself. She was only sad that she and her father could never have had this conversation when she needed it most. He would have told her that Hallidays don't make excuses, because they don't make mistakes.

Eventually she would have to confess to them that she'd messed up again and was pregnant. But first she had to break the news to Ben.

Chapter Fourteen

The next evening Cam called Los Angeles to make sure her parents had made it home safely. Her father informed her that the executive manager of the Halliday Hospitality Inn, Scottsdale, Arizona, was retiring and she could have the job if she wanted it. She agreed to think things over and let him know in twenty-four hours. He'd given no hint that there were any hard feelings about what she'd said to him regarding her childhood. Then again, her father was like Teflon. Things were thrown at him, but nothing stuck. Just as well.

But before she could give him an answer about the new job and relocation, she had to tell Ben about the baby. Staring at the single wall that separated their suites, she decided that putting it off any longer was just cowardly. Hallidays weren't gutless.

She was casually dressed in jeans, a T-shirt with the Blackwater Lake Lodge logo on it and sneakers. Briefly

she considered putting on a power outfit, then decided against it. She was in this predicament because she'd taken her clothes *off* and no ensemble would make a difference when telling a man who'd successfully avoided commitment that he was going to be a father.

She did, however, check her hair and put on fresh lipstick. In this situation, a girl needed all the confidence she could get. With head held high and shoulders back she left her room and turned right, then knocked on his door.

A few moments later Ben opened it, saw who was there, and a slow grin turned up the corners of his mouth. The warmth moved to his eyes and for just a second there was a flicker of what looked a lot like lust.

He leaned one broad shoulder against the doorjamb in just about the sexiest pose ever. "Hi."

"Hi."

Cam's heart hammered in her chest, partly because of what she had to say, but mostly it was simply her uncontrollable reaction to this man. She lifted her hand in a small wave, then stuck her fingers in her jeans pockets. Apparently her tongue was stuck, too, because she couldn't think what to say next.

"I'm glad you finally came over."

"Oh?" She'd been tempted many times and wondered if the word *finally* meant he had been, too. But his glad reaction wouldn't last very long when she told him. "Why are you glad?"

"Word around the lodge is that your parents are gone and I was wondering how everything is." The pose got even sexier when he folded his arms over his chest. "I was going to call if you hadn't stopped by."

That was something positive, wasn't it? At least he was thinking about her. And he'd stood up to her father last night. No one had ever done that for her, not even the older

brother she'd idolized. In spite of her effort to suppress it, she knew hope was hovering.

"Can I come in?" Just about twenty-four hours ago her father had asked her the same thing and she'd wanted to say no. If Ben felt that way...

"Of course." He straightened out of the lazy pose and stepped back from the door to open it wider. "Do you want a beer or glass of wine?"

Her stomach dropped. Last night, out on the deck, he'd commented on the fact that she hadn't had any of her wine at dinner. Now she was here to tell him the real reason. She toyed with the idea of mentioning that he might want a drink before hearing the news, but decided not to. Looking on the bright side, it was possible the information that he was going to be a father might not produce a response that required alcohol.

"No, thanks," she said.

He closed the door and walked over to her. She was standing by the back of the love seat. His suite was a duplicate of hers, the mirror image. As he looked down, Ben curled his fingers into his palms, as if he was fighting the urge to touch her, pull her into his arms. At least she hoped... There was that word again.

The expression in his eyes grew more intense as he stared at her. "Sit. Stay awhile."

"Maybe I will." She'd really like to if this conversation went well.

"Did your folks give you a hard time about last night?" He seemed genuinely concerned. "I didn't mean to cause trouble. But none of what happened was your fault."

"I know. Dad didn't mention it again."

"Good." There was a question in his eyes. "So. I'm curious. To what do I owe the honor of a visit from senior management here at Blackwater Lake Lodge?"

"Well." She blew out a breath. "I have news. And some other news."

"Okay." He settled his hands on lean hips. "Why don't you start with the news first."

"My father is extremely pleased with my work here at the lodge."

"That's good." But the easygoing manner disappeared. "Right?"

She nodded. "He's offered me the top management position at Halliday Hospitality Inn, Scottsdale, Arizona."

"Congratulations." His voice was oddly flat. "Desert. That's different."

And he seemed indifferent to the information that she would be leaving Montana. Cam waited for more, a reaction indicating he cared even a little. It didn't happen. She supposed him asking her not to go had been a stupid fantasy, but it had been there in spite of her warning to herself.

Even so, she had no right to be disappointed. He was sticking to the letter of the agreement. He'd helped her get what she wanted and it wasn't his fault she wanted him now.

"What's the other news?" he finally asked.

It was best to say straight out what she had to say. There were no words that could possibly soften the blow. "I'm pregnant."

He looked at her for several moments, then actually laughed. This wasn't anywhere near the expected response. "You're kidding, right? It was a test. To make sure I was listening?"

She blinked back tears and double-damned the out-of-control hormones that were making her react in this hyperemotional way. When she could speak without a sob sneaking out, she answered.

"No, it's not a joke. I'm going to have a baby. Your baby." Her chin inched up slightly.

He stared at her as if waiting for her to say "gotcha." "I don't understand. How could this have happened?"

"Maybe it's time for a refresher physiology course, one that highlights bodily functions, Doctor. It's called—"

"I know what happened. I was there. We used protection."

"Yes, we did."

She remembered being really grateful that he'd had some, for all the good it had done. She'd known the risk and in the heat of wanting him so badly, she'd been willing to take that chance. She was also a victim of that natural human malady known as the it-won't-happen-to-me syndrome. Now she was just a terrible warning.

"If you recall—" She put as much primness as possible into her voice. "It was very—athletic—when we, you know—"

"Slept together," he finished.

"Yes." Although if they'd actually slept, they wouldn't be in this mess. She wanted to look anywhere except at the grim expression on his face but wouldn't let her gaze wander. "I'm told that under those circumstances condoms can be ineffective."

And that was when she realized her second fantasy of the evening had bitten the dust along with the one where he asked her not to leave. It had crossed her mind that there could be the cliché hug and twirl of happiness when he scooped her up in his arms because he was happy about becoming a father. But there wasn't so much of that reaction, either. There wasn't a speck of joy on his face, just dark looks and frowning.

"Are you sure about this?" he asked.

"I took a pregnancy test. Still have the stick if you want

to see it." She pointed at the wall separating their suites. "I can bring it over."

"Not necessary."

She knew he wanted to ask if the baby was his, but to his credit he held the words back. "Just so you know, I haven't been with anyone else."

"It never crossed my mind." Again to his credit, he sounded sincere.

She nodded. "Thanks for that."

He dragged his fingers through his hair and seemed on the verge of saying something. *Ask me to stay,* she wanted to beg him.

But that wasn't what came out of his mouth. "This is a lot to process."

Oddly enough, those were the words that broke her heart. His voice wasn't unkind and certainly what he said was true. But she'd wanted so much to hear something different.

"I know what you mean. I'm still trying to—process. But we can work something out. Visitation," she said lamely.

"Yeah." He dragged his fingers through his hair.

They stared at each other for several moments, both in shock for different reasons. Finally she realized there was nothing left to say. "I need to go."

"Right. Okay." He went to the door and opened it. "I'll call you. We'll talk."

She nodded, then walked out without another word. There was no way to speak without bursting into tears and she didn't want pity.

She wanted the fairy tale. She wanted him to love her.

Moments later, when the tears started rolling down her cheeks, she was in her own suite where no one could see her break down. Up-and-coming hotel entrepreneur heir-

esses didn't do this sort of thing in public. Ben hadn't intentionally lied when he'd said the bargain would keep either of them from getting hurt, but that didn't help when the pain overwhelmed her.

In her rebellious stage people had always wanted something from her. She'd thought knowing up front what Ben wanted would insulate her from feeling used. It wasn't fair, and certainly wasn't what had happened, but that didn't make losing the man she loved hurt any less.

When she stopped crying, she'd call her father and tell him Scottsdale near Phoenix was where she wanted to go. She couldn't think of a place that was more different from Blackwater Lake, and maybe a change of scenery would help her forget Ben McKnight.

"What's the holdup with this house, Alex?" Ben stood in his newly wallboarded family room and glared at his brother while their father looked on. Cam had left without a goodbye two weeks ago and every day that went by without her in it shortened his temper. She was going to have a baby. *His* baby. The news had blown his mind.

"There's no delay," Alex answered. "It's all part of the building process."

"You could have built a whole block in the time you've spent on this thing."

Brown eyes a lot like his own stared back at him, but Alex's were brimming with amusement. "Who are you and what have you done with my laid-back little brother? You remember him, right? Doctor. Easygoing. Great sense of humor. The guy who said, 'Take your time. Get everything right.'"

"Now I just want it done."

When Ben had brought Cam here the framing was complete but you could see into everything downstairs, in-

cluding the garage. Now the wallboard was up, closing things off. Much like himself, he thought. And that made him angry.

The last time he'd seen her standing in his hotel room doorway, lust had hit him like a speeding train. He wanted her in his arms, in his bed, but there was more to it and he didn't think about that. She'd dropped her bombshell, then kept to their bargain and left for a better job. Just as promised, she'd packed up and brushed the mud of Montana from her pumps. And she'd done it without saying goodbye.

Ben dragged his fingers through his hair. "What's the delay?"

"There are building codes." The exaggerated patience in his brother's voice grated on already frayed nerves. "Inspectors need to examine everything to make sure it's built to those codes. After the job is done on each phase, we can't move on to the next until the city inspector signs off on the work. We have to wait."

"So can we buy this guy a drink or something and persuade him to make this place a priority?"

"Are you talking bribe?" One of Alex's dark eyebrows rose questioningly. "Because I'm pretty sure there are laws against that sort of thing."

"Might be worth breaking the law to move this project forward at maybe a pace just a tad faster than a snail's."

Tom McKnight had simply been observing the back and forth between his sons. Until now. "What's your hurry, Ben?"

His hurry was that he wanted out of Blackwater Lake Lodge. He swore his room still held the scent of Cam's skin, but that was impossible because she'd only ever been in it once. Every night of looking at the wall that had separated his room from hers made him sorry for all the missed

opportunities. He regretted not going next door and kissing the living daylights out of her when he could have.

The memories were driving him crazy.

"This is about Alex dragging his feet," he said.

Tom shook his head. "Your brother is the best builder around. His reputation in California and Montana is above reproach."

"Thanks, Dad." Alex gave him a "so there" look.

The older man continued, "And you're not acting like yourself, son."

"Who am I acting like?"

"Me." His father's pale blue eyes filled with sadness. "After your mom died."

Ben couldn't believe he'd heard right and glanced at his brother. The shocked expression on Alex's face said he'd heard the same thing.

"I don't understand, Dad."

"Let me spell it out. You're acting like a damn jackass because Camille Halliday is gone." Tom's voice went hard. "The difference between you and me is that you're in a position to do something about her."

"Maybe he shouldn't." Alex was dead serious now.

"Of course he should."

His older brother faced off with their father. "In my opinion Ben dodged a bullet when she left Blackwater Lake."

"She never promised to stay," Ben defended. "It was always her plan to prove herself here then move on to a higher-profile property."

There was no reason for his father to know about the bargain. Obviously he'd pulled off making him believe he cared about her, but somewhere in the pretending he'd begun to actually *care*.

"Women are trouble," Alex continued. "Thank your

lucky stars she's outta here before doing real damage to your impressionable young heart."

Too late, Ben thought. She'd made an impression on his heart that would never go away. He was in love with her. He hadn't seen it coming, hadn't been looking for this to happen, but every night the truth hit him like cold water in the face. She was gone. The worst part was that he missed talking to her. He needed to hold her. Touch her.

"You know, big brother, just because you had a bad experience doesn't mean every woman can't be trusted."

"From what I've seen, your track record with women isn't great." Alex's mouth pulled tight. "Judy dumped you for a ski bum and went back east. Cam headed west. That only leaves ladies from north and south to put you in your place."

"Judy was wrong for him. And Cam isn't like the woman you brought here, Alex." It took some of the sting out of Tom's words when he put his hand on his oldest son's shoulder.

Oddly enough Ben's anger was anesthetized by his brother's bitterness. He'd been deceived and dumped by a woman who took away everything he'd ever wanted, everything he loved. Ben understood where he was coming from, but their father was right. Cam wasn't like that woman. She was straightforward and honest. She'd told him about the baby and he didn't say the right thing, hadn't stepped up. Being in a state of shock was no excuse. Then she'd left without a word. He'd called her, but she was dodging him.

Ben knew he'd go crazy if he didn't talk about it. He looked first at his brother, then his father. "Cam is pregnant with my baby."

"Are you sure it's yours?" Alex's eyes turned dark

and hard. Obviously he was remembering how he'd been lied to.

"I'm sure."

"Damn it, Ben—" His father wasn't in the habit of swearing, so when he did, the McKnight kids listened up. "That's even more reason not to do what I did."

"I'm not sure what you mean, Dad."

"When your mom died after giving birth to Sydney, I was angrier than I'd ever been. Mad at her."

"Why?" Alex stared at him.

"She left me with three small kids to raise all on my own. I didn't know how. She was your mom and I couldn't do it the way she did. I couldn't do it without her."

"At the risk of sounding conceited," Alex said, "you did a great job. The three of us turned out pretty good."

Tom's expression was full of regret when he looked at his oldest son. "You raised your brother and sister when you were just a boy yourself. Because you're like your mother." He sighed. "I couldn't get over her and I didn't want to try. I'm sorry I wasn't there. I'm a one-woman man and Linda was the only woman for me. And take it from me, Alex, that woman you brought here to Blackwater Lake wasn't the one."

"Doesn't matter." Alex shook his head, clearly not open to trying again any more than his father was.

"As for you," Tom said to Ben, "I don't want you to shut down like I did. You're different with Camille. Your spirit is lighter. You were happy—"

"Please don't say she completes me." Ben was going for humor but sounded kind of desperate. Because the truth was that Cam did complete him.

His dad's eyes twinkled. "When a man's been completed, he can see when it's happening to someone else. Especially when that someone is his son."

"Cam is something special," he agreed.

"So what are you going to do about that?"

"Give her time," he said.

"How long has she been gone?"

"Two weeks." It felt like two years.

"Have you talked to her?"

"I've called and left messages because she doesn't pick up. She calls back and leaves voice mail that she's fine." He shook his head. "But—"

"Yeah, but. So you haven't *talked* to her. It's been long enough." Tom's voice was firm. "Don't be stupid, Ben."

"Don't sugarcoat it, Dad. Tell him how you really feel." Alex grinned. "As fun as it is watching you call my little brother names, I've got to go. Work to do."

"What could possibly be more important than my house?" Ben demanded.

"Mercy Medical Clinic. We're finalizing all the details to start the expansion. I have a meeting with the architect. Suellen Hart. From Texas."

"A belle from the Lone Star state." *Payback time, bro,* he thought. "All big hair, sexy Southern drawl and attitude."

"Bite me." Alex scowled, then turned his back and walked away. "I'm so out of here."

Ben watched until his brother's truck peeled out of the lot, the big tires spinning and spraying dirt. He stopped laughing when he saw the determined look on his father's face. "What?"

"I'm serious, son. Camille is good people. Not only that, she's carrying your child. What are you going to do about her?"

He definitely could have handled the situation better when she'd told him about the baby, but the more he thought about it, the more he knew biding just a little time

was the right thing. Somehow he had to find the words to explain to his father.

"I know waiting isn't a proactive strategy, but in this case it's the best way. Dad, her family gave her the lodge because to them it was a losing proposition anyway. She was set up for failure."

"They didn't trust her?"

Ben nodded. "She had a rough childhood and made some bad decisions, but she matured and changed. To her the lodge was a way up the success ladder, a way to prove to her family she's not that screwed-up kid anymore. The job in Arizona was her goal all along."

"Goals change. She got the job." His father frowned. "She didn't need to take it."

"Yeah, she did. That's what I'm trying to explain. She needed to know that she could follow her dream if that's what she wanted. She needed to know she was worthy. I had to let her go."

"Is this like that bird analogy? If you let it go and it comes back of its own free will—"

"Yeah. If she does that, then I know I'm her first choice."

"If she doesn't?"

"Then I'd have made her miserable by standing in the way of her trying." Ben blew out a long breath. "I love her too much to do that."

His father nodded. "Have you thought about the baby?"

"Of course. Whatever happens, my child will know me and I'll be a part of his life. Even if I have to leave Blackwater Lake and practice medicine in Scottsdale."

Tom nodded. "Okay, son. That's good enough for me. I trust your judgment."

Ben really hoped that trust was justified. When he'd first discussed the bargain with Cam, she'd wondered what would happen when she left, how he would keep the

women away. He'd said he would pretend a broken heart, then come up with plan B.

He'd never dreamed his heart was in real danger, or that Cam *was* his plan B.

Chapter Fifteen

Cam looked around her new office at the Halliday Hospitality Inn. It was decorated with enlarged photos of the Grand Canyon and beautiful rock formations. The colors were Southwest-inspired—brick red, gold, beige. One wall was windows and gave her a view of Camelback Mountain and the clear blue Arizona sky. She even had a conversation area with a leather couch and chair separated by a coffee table for more informal meetings. It was big, beautiful and her heart ached because it wasn't Blackwater Lake.

There were no trees, towering mountains or grass. That wasn't entirely true, but most of the landscaping was done with rock. Very creative designs, but still hard stone. Never in her life had it occurred to her that she'd look at a pile of rocks and think landscaping. But Scottsdale was in the desert and one couldn't afford to waste water.

"Oh, who am I kidding?" She looked at her cell phone resting on the desk. It was her only connection to Ben. It

was where all his texts and messages were stored, where she could hear his voice. "I wouldn't care if peanut shells were used in my yard if Ben wanted me."

A knock sounded on her office door just before it opened. Her father stood there. "Got a minute?"

"Dad. This is unexpected." She stood and moved from behind her desk. "Are you checking up on me? Have I screwed up already?"

"I just want to see if you're settling in all right." Something that looked like regret flashed in his eyes. "And I'm here because I can be. You're only a hop, skip and jump from L.A. now."

As opposed to Blackwater Lake, which wasn't easy to get to. It wasn't an easy place to forget, either.

"Is Mother with you?"

"Yes. The spa at this property is one of her favorites. She's getting some kind of facial, or massage, that involves eggplant and arugula."

She laughed. "It's probably seaweed and cucumber."

"Whatever." He waved his hand dismissively. "I heard her say something about vegetables and tuned out the rest. Don't tell her I said that."

"Mum with Mom. Got it." She tilted her head and stared at him. Who was this funny, playful man and what had he done with her father? He looked the same in his pin-striped navy suit, powder-blue shirt and coordinating tie, but this was a side of him that she didn't know.

"I didn't tune out the part where she wanted me to tell you to clear your schedule for this evening. There's a place we'd like to take you to dinner."

"There's nothing to clear because I don't have any plans." That sounded just too pathetic, but was also the truth.

"That's not good. You need a social life. All work and no play..." He shrugged. "You get my drift."

"I do." M.J. had said the same thing. "But I'm really busy right now. Still doing my homework on this property and getting up to speed. There's a lot to learn, especially before beginning construction on the new tower."

Her father sat on the couch and she settled beside him. "How are things here?" he asked.

"Not bad. Even in this slow economy we have the capital to add rooms." She crossed one leg over the other. "We get a lot of businesspeople and families on vacation. I'm going to check into the marketing campaign to see what we can do about getting more people in the door."

"You should call those friends of yours from the tabloids." He actually winked.

Now she was really weirded out. The same man who'd held her responsible for being stalked by reporters could actually make a joke about it? The world had gone mad, or maybe it was just her.

This was about business. "The employees are on their best behavior, but that's to be expected with a new sheriff in town."

Cam remembered joking with Ben about Blackwater Lake's Sheriff Marshall and then gave herself a mental shake. It was another reminder that she hadn't found the saying "out of sight, out of mind" to be true. She hadn't seen Ben for a few weeks and couldn't stop thinking about him. And the baby.

"So the place is running like a well-oiled machine?"

"Pretty much." If you didn't count the little problem she'd brought with her. Settling her hand protectively over her still-flat abdomen, she gave her father the best carefree smile she could manage.

He looked around the room. "How do you like your office?"

"It's really big." And very far removed from the registration desk. No M.J. right outside her door. Although she had a very efficient assistant, it just wasn't the same.

Dean Halliday nodded his approval. "You're doing a great job, Camille."

And that was another thing. No one here called her "Cam." It was either the full first name or "Ms. Halliday." Maybe it was too soon and she was too impatient, but she missed the personal connection.

"Thanks, Dad."

"I'm really proud of you."

"Probably surprised, too, considering that I didn't set a very high bar in my formative years."

"That's in the past. You've put it behind you and worked incredibly hard. I'm very proud of the woman you've become."

This level of praise was unprecedented and unexpected. When he found out about the baby he'd want those words back. "I appreciate you saying that."

"You've blossomed into an astute businesswoman. If your brother had lived, I don't believe he could have done better. It's important that you know I have every confidence in you to take over for me when I step down."

Cam stared at her father, trying to absorb what he'd said. This was something she'd never thought to hear and, to her horror, she burst into tears and buried her face in her hands.

"What's wrong?" He sounded bewildered and patted her shoulder.

She was just as surprised and wanted the earth to swallow her whole. "S-some b-businesswoman."

"I meant what I said. Never expected tears and I'm get-

ting the feeling they're not happy ones. So let me say this. You don't have to take over for me if you don't want to."

She dropped her hands and stared at him. This time she asked the question out loud. "Who are you and what have you done with my father?"

"I deserve that." He sighed. "After what you said in Blackwater Lake, I've done a lot of soul-searching. Your mother, too."

"You told Mom?"

"Yes. And you're right. We just weren't there for you after your brother died. Stupid, really. We lost one child and instead of focusing on our two surviving girls, it's like we lost them, too." Sadness made the lines by his nose and mouth deeper. "We were devastated and immersed ourselves in work. And I put too much pressure on you. When life is out of control, you control what you can."

"I'm sorry, Dad, about what I put you and Mom through."

"In hindsight I believe you were trying to get our attention. Your mom and I were just too emotionally drained to understand the behavior. I'm the one who's sorry."

"It's okay." She twisted her fingers together.

"It's not." He shook his head. "But I'll do better. And I want you to know I'm incredibly proud of you, Cammie."

The childhood nickname started the tears all over again, and this time her father pulled her into his arms.

"Tell me what's wrong, sweetheart."

"You might want to take back what you just said about being proud. I've messed up again, Dad."

"It can't be that bad."

"It is. I'm pregnant." She lifted her head and met his gaze. "The baby is Ben's, in case you were wondering."

"I wasn't." He tightened his arm around her. "I'm at a loss here. If this were business, I'd know what to do, what

to say. But this is you and I've already made so many mistakes."

"You don't have to do or say anything."

"Yes, I do. I'm your father, but this is new territory. Should I ask what his intentions are? Beat him up? Throw vegetables at him?"

"It's my problem." She brushed moisture from her cheeks.

"You're my daughter and that makes it mine." He thought for a moment. "Does Ben know?"

"I told him before I left town."

"And he still let you go?"

"He was in shock."

"I know how he feels, but that's no excuse."

"He's called, but I've been avoiding talking to him."

"You have to sooner or later," he said.

"I know." So much for Halliday backbone.

Her father blew out a breath. "Do you like it here in Scottsdale?"

"Yes," she said automatically.

"Be honest. You can tell me the truth."

"Okay. I miss Blackwater Lake. I miss the town, the wilderness, the people." It was a place where someone noticed you were pregnant and bought you a test to find out for sure.

"I miss Ben."

"Do you love him?"

"Yes." She felt the tears welling again. "I guess I hoped he'd come after me."

"Okay, then. *This* I can help you with."

"What?"

"Don't be a doormat," he said. "Go after what you want."

"I don't think he wants me. Or the baby."

"Did he say that?"

"No." Not exactly, but the house he was building wasn't for a family. "But I didn't give him much chance to say anything." She met his gaze. "The thing is, at first we were just pretending to be a couple."

"What?" He stared at her. "Why?"

"Women were coming on to him. Faking sprained ankles to get his attention. It was disruptive to his medical practice and he felt the need to do something. He figured if word got out that he was dating someone, they'd leave him alone. In return, he helped me connect with the people. He grew up there. He knows the quirks, the personalities, and gave me practical, commonsense advice. More than anything I wanted to be successful there so I could prove to you I could do it. Then I'd get my dream job. So we made a bargain."

Her father thought this over, then nodded. "You wanted it badly enough to make a deal. I think I see what's going on here. Why he didn't come after you."

"Care to share?"

"Unlike me, Dr. McKnight is *not* putting pressure on you. He's giving you space. You have to let him know it's not what you want."

"But what if he doesn't want me? What if he doesn't want the baby?"

"Then he's not the man I think he is and I'll throw more than vegetables at him." His expression was hard. "But I'd bet everything I own that he cares about you very much. Don't forget, I saw him in action." He smiled. "I know it's hard, but you have to try. You might get everything or nothing, but whatever happens, you're not alone."

"Really?"

"You've got your family and we'll be there for you and

the baby." He grinned suddenly. "I'm going to be a grand-father."

"Yeah. How do you think Mom will feel about being a grandmother?"

"Over the moon. She loves babies and she loves you."

"You're going to make me cry again."

"Heaven forbid." His smile turned tender. "But I've got one more thing to say. And this is something I learned the hard way. Life is too short not to grab happiness with both hands. Ben loves you and you'd be a fool to let him get away."

"Don't sugarcoat it, Dad. Tell me how you really feel."

"Damn right." He nodded emphatically. "I haven't al-ways been a good parent, but I'm not in the habit of fa-thering fools."

"Good to know. And speaking of how you really feel…" She met his gaze. "No matter what happens, I won't be taking over for you."

"It's okay." He kissed her forehead. "I had a feeling. Then I had a long talk with your sister and she'd really like a shot at it."

"Good. Leighton will do a terrific job. Thanks for un-derstanding, Dad."

"Don't mention it. Just take care of my grandchild and go talk to that doctor."

That was her plan.

Cam drove through downtown Blackwater Lake and couldn't look at everything hard enough. Tanya's Trea-sures. The Grizzly Bear Diner. Al's Dry Cleaning. Even the hardware store was a sight for sore eyes. Finally Black-water Lake Lodge came into view, with the unbelievably beautiful mountains in the distance. She felt a swelling sensation inside and figured that was just her heart and

soul filling up again. After her time away, she'd been several quarts low on scenic beauty and fresh air.

And Ben.

She kept one hand on the wheel and settled the other over her belly. "We're going to see your daddy soon, little one. Hopefully he'll be happy to see us."

It had been a month and he'd continued to text and leave voice mails that had a steadily increasing note of frustration. Once she'd caught him just as he was going into surgery and couldn't talk, but the short back-and-forth made her heart ache.

Except for her parents, no one knew she was coming home to Montana because she wanted to surprise Ben. She turned right into the Mercy Medical Clinic parking lot and noticed piles of lumber and other supplies that indicated construction on the expansion was imminent. Ben would be happy about that.

She pulled her sporty little Mercedes to a stop beside his SUV. Never before had she felt such a rush of anticipation at the sight of a car. After shutting hers off, she grabbed her purse and the small covered dish beside her, then stepped out. Summer was coming and the air was warm and sweet with the scent of pine. A feeling of contentment joined scenic beauty and fresh air in her heart and soul.

Her goal was to top it all off with a healthy dose of love.

Clinic hours were over and since his was the only other vehicle in the lot, it looked like Ben was alone. Walking past his car, Cam glanced into the back and saw his backpack, obviously full. It was the one he'd brought when they camped out. Was he going into the mountains? With another woman? Judy?

Cam's chest squeezed tight as her conviction slipped. What if she was too late? Then she remembered her fa-

ther's words about fools. If the window of opportunity was that small, she never had a chance in the first place.

Practicing the walk she'd planned to use, she moved to the front door and tried the knob. It was locked, so she rang the bell. She didn't know if he was angry enough to leave *her* out here, but he'd never abandon a patient. Finally the door was opened and he stood there looking too wonderful for words.

"Cam—"

"Hi, Ben."

Surprise was evident in his expression as he studied her from head to toe like he couldn't look hard enough. Then his gaze settled on what she was holding. "What's in the dish?"

"A casserole. Tuna. Cheese. Noodles. A little of this and that."

"Sounds yummy."

"So is it okay if I bring it inside?"

"If you want to." He pulled the door wide and let her pass in front of him.

"Where should I put it?"

"There's a break room in the back. It's past the reception desk. At the waiting area turn right. Go all the way down the hall. Last room on the left before the back door."

Cam had never been this nervous when she was pretending to be his main squeeze. Now she had a lot to lose. She'd missed his smile and the masculine scent of his skin. Her heart was beating so hard it was about to jump out of her chest and her legs were shaking. She wasn't sure she could pull off what she wanted to, but she would give it her best shot.

She moved in front of him and poured on an exaggerated, uneven walk down the long hall, trying to remember

how it had felt after she'd kicked the railing on the second floor deck of the lodge.

She turned into the room with a table in the middle and a refrigerator. Holding out the dish she asked, "Where do you want this?"

"In the freezer." There was amusement in his eyes.

She opened the top door and saw quite a few other dishes there. "Wow."

"I'm a popular guy."

"I guess so."

He took the covered dish from her and set it inside, then closed the door and looked down at her. "Are things going well in Scottsdale?"

"Why do you ask?"

"I was sort of hoping you were having problems with the staff and came back for your serenity place."

"Arizona was fine." Her chest was so tight she could hardly talk. "The employees are extraordinarily nice and cooperative."

"Oh." He sounded disappointed.

"Why?"

"Because you're limping."

She searched his eyes for a clue that he cared for her, that she wasn't just a woman he needed a pretend girlfriend to avoid.

"You noticed that. I heard a rumor that there's a very good orthopedic doctor here who can fix what's wrong with me."

"As it happens, I am a really good doctor. Top of my class in med school and a real hotshot during internship and residency." He stared at her. "All that expertise tells me that there's nothing wrong with your leg. In fact you've got great legs and you're using them to get my attention."

"Is it working?"

"Pretty much." His eyes darkened. "Which makes me wonder why you brought food."

"You of all people should know that saying about the way to a man's heart being through his stomach—"

"Not true."

That gave her pause. Maybe she'd been wrong to hope. Maybe the calls and messages while she was away were only because of the baby. Maybe her father was right and she'd need to rely on her family's support after all.

"I noticed the full backpack in your car," she said. "Are you going somewhere?"

"To Scottsdale."

She could hardly believe it. "Really?"

He nodded. "It's been long enough. I gave you space, but I couldn't stand it anymore. I had to see you."

"Really?" Happiness flooded her.

"Yes. And if I couldn't persuade you to come back here, I was fully prepared to move to Arizona and practice medicine there."

"You would give up Blackwater Lake for—" She hesitated, wanting to say for her, but couldn't. "For the baby?"

"I want the baby very much," he said, his voice deep with emotion. "Never, ever doubt that. But I was coming after you."

"I see." She tried to be cool, but the corners of her mouth curved up. "You do realize that I was throwing myself at you just now with the limp and the casserole."

"I got it." He grinned, looking very pleased with himself.

"So I guess I gave up all the power in the relationship."

He took her purse and set it on the table, then pulled her into his arms. "You didn't give up anything because you always had the power and always will. I'm officially giving you notice that I'd like to change the terms of our bargain."

She snuggled into the warmth of him. Scottsdale had been lonely and cold, which was hard to do at this time of year in the desert Southwest. "Okay. I'm willing to negotiate."

"I'd like to propose something more permanent than our previous bargain."

"Oh?"

"Instead of dating, I'd like you to be my wife. My bachelor days are over. All the fun times filled with creative casseroles and phony limps just don't have the appeal they used to."

"I'm very glad to hear that."

"Good, because I'm not pretending. I love you. I think you should marry me and help me fill that big house with a family. Lots of kids and laughter. Make memories with me, Camille Halliday."

"That's the best offer I've ever had." Her eyes filled with tears of happiness. "And that means I'll get to stay in Blackwater Lake, which I've come to love very much."

"What about me?"

Her eyes locked with his and she willed him to see into her soul. "I love you with all my heart. Anywhere you are is home to me."

"Thank God." He pulled her tight against him and let out a long breath that sounded a lot like relief. "I was such an idiot."

"Is that so? What about top of your class in med school?"

"There I was the man. This condition called love is where I exhibited symptoms of stupid. I was so sure that dating you and having a beginning and end all planned out would control pesky emotions."

"You're not the only one. I thought knowing what you wanted up front would protect me." She pulled back a little. "Love is the last thing I expected or wanted."

"And now?"

"I wouldn't have it any other way."

Love and longing slid into his eyes. He lowered his head and whispered against her lips, "This is what I call the will-you-marry-me kiss."

His mouth settled on hers, warm and sweet in the best kiss she'd ever had. It promised love, happiness and the family she'd always longed for.

She smiled. "I would love to marry you."

And she wasn't pretending. The doctor's dating bargain was the best deal she'd ever made.

* * * * *

afterglow BOOKS

Introducing our newest series, Afterglow.

From showing up to glowing up, Afterglow characters are on the path to leading their best lives and finding romance along the way – with a dash of sizzling spice!

Follow characters from all walks of life as they chase their dreams and find that true love is only the beginning...

OUT NOW

millsandboon.co.uk

OUT NOW!

Available at
millsandboon.co.uk

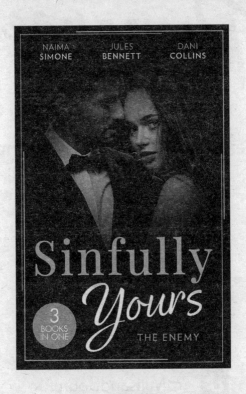

LET'S TALK

Romance

For exclusive extracts, competitions and special offers, find us online:

- **f** MillsandBoon
- **X** @MillsandBoon
- **◉** @MillsandBoonUK
- **♪** @MillsandBoonUK

Get in touch on 01413 063 232

MILLS & BOON

THE HEART OF ROMANCE

A ROMANCE FOR EVERY READER

MODERN

Prepare to be swept off your feet by sophisticated, sexy and seductive heroes, in some of the world's most glamourous and romantic locations, where power and passion collide.

HISTORICAL

Escape with historical heroes from time gone by. Whether your passion is for wicked Regency Rakes, muscled Vikings or rugged Highlanders, awaken the romance of the past.

MEDICAL

Set your pulse racing with dedicated, delectable doctors in the high-pressure world of medicine, where emotions run high and passion, comfort and love are the best medicine.

True Love

Celebrate true love with tender stories of heartfelt romance, from the rush of falling in love to the joy a new baby can bring, and a focus on the emotional heart of a relationship.

HEROES

The excitement of a gripping thriller, with intense romance at its heart. Resourceful, true-to-life women and strong, fearless men face danger and desire - a killer combination!

From showing up to glowing up, these characters are on the path to leading their best lives and finding romance along the way – with plenty of sizzling spice!

To see which titles are coming soon, please visit

millsandboon.co.uk/nextmonth